WOLF

SWAT: SPECIAL WOLF ALPHA TEAM

UNLEASHED

PAIGE TYLER

sourcebooks
casablanca

Published by Sourcebooks Casablanca, an imprint of Sourcebooks, Inc.
P.O. Box 4410, Naperville, Illinois 60567-4410
(630) 961-3900
Fax: (630) 961-2168
www.sourcebooks.com

Printed and bound in Canada.
MBP 10 9 8 7 6 5 4 3 2 1

With special thanks to my extremely patient and under-standing husband, without whose help and support, I couldn't have pursued my dream job of becoming a writer. You're my sounding board, my idea man, my critique partner, and the absolute best research assistant any girl could ask for!

Thank you.

Prologue

Rochester, New York, July 2012

"LAKE-3, THIS IS DISPATCH. PROCEED TO THE TWO-HUNDRED block of Burley Road and investigate reports of a noise disturbance in the area. Possible fireworks. Do you copy?"

At the sound of his patrol cruiser's call sign, Officer Alex Trevino snatched the radio mic off the hook on the dash, trying to visualize the area dispatch had described. Rochester wasn't exactly New York City, but it was still damn big, and since he'd only been patrolling there for a few months, he needed to look at the map on his screen every once in a while to figure out where the hell he was supposed to go.

"Roger that, dispatch," he said, finally figuring out that the road was near the river. "Proceeding to the two-hundred block of Burley. ETA ten minutes."

He spun his car in a U-turn and headed north, flipping on the flashing lights. It was probably just a couple of kids popping off some leftover fireworks from the Fourth of July. That end of Burley was close to the woods and the Genesee River Trail, and teens frequently went there at night to drink and make out. He wouldn't be surprised to find a few of them fooling around with cherry bombs and bottle rockets.

It was nearly one a.m., so it took him even less time to get to the address dispatch had given him than he estimated. It was one of the reasons he liked working the night shift. During the day, it could take a cop fifteen or twenty minutes to get across the Lake Area patrol district, with lights flashing and sirens blaring. He'd made it in five.

Alex slowed as he drove toward the end of Burley Road. He rolled down his window but didn't hear anything. He was just passing a two-story colonial on the right when an older man wearing pajamas, a robe, and slippers hurried out and waved him down. Alex pulled up to the curb and got out of his cruiser.

"You got here fast." The man gave him an appraising look, taking in Alex's crisp blue uniform and shiny badge. "I was sleeping when I heard the noise, so I'm not even sure exactly which direction it came from, but it sounded like gunshots. Could have been firecrackers, I guess. Figured I should call the cops just to be on the safe side."

"You did the right thing," Alex said. He thumbed the mic on the radio clipped on his shoulder, letting dispatch know he was on the scene, then slowly walked along the road, eyeing each house as he went. Nothing seemed off. Maybe he should check out the trail, see if there was anything suspicious in the woods.

He turned to head that way when he heard a noise coming from a house on the other side of the street. It almost sounded like a bottle rocket but not quite. He walked back over to the older man.

"Do you know who lives in that house?" Alex asked.

"Archie and Carole Barrett and their fourteen-year-old daughter, Jessica. My grandson took her to the middle-school dance back in the spring." He frowned, his eyes filling with concern. "I hope they're okay."

The man started across the road, but Alex quickly

held out his arm, barring his way. "Please go back inside your house, sir, while I check it out."

He crossed the street and strode over the freshly mowed lawn, praying the neighbor didn't do anything stupid—like try to follow. Climbing the two steps to the front porch, he knocked on the door.

"Rochester Police. Anyone home?"

No answer. He gave it a few seconds and rapped on the wood again, harder this time. Still nothing.

He peeked in the long rectangular window to one side of the door, but the house was too dark to see anything. Hoping the picture window on the other side might offer a better view since there was a streetlamp nearby, he stepped into the flower bed and took a look but didn't see anything to alarm him.

Alex scowled. While his eyes and ears told him the sound he'd heard had simply been some kids goofing off in the woods behind the house, he knew that sometimes you couldn't believe everything you saw or heard. Sometimes you had to go with what your gut was telling you instead.

Not counting his time in the police academy, Alex had been on the street as a patrol officer for barely more than a year, but his time in the Marine Corps made him trust his instincts more than most new cops. He'd spent the past four years in the 1st Recon Battalion, deploying three times to Iraq and once to Afghanistan. He'd learned that when your gut talked, you listened. And right now, it was shouting that something was wrong inside that home.

He circled around to the back of the house, past the colorful swing set that looked like it hadn't been used in a while and the covered pool, until he came to the sliding glass door. The house blocked any light coming from the street, so he couldn't see a damn thing inside it from here, either.

Cursing under his breath, he turned to go around to the front so he could bang on the door again, when he caught sight of a metal dog bowl half filled with water on the concrete patio. He glanced around, frowning at the chewed-up rawhide bone and a few other dog toys. If the Barretts had a dog, why hadn't the animal barked when Alex knocked on the door? There wasn't a dog on the planet who'd accept a stranger stomping around his territory.

Alex reached for the handle of the sliding glass door before his head even figured out what he was doing. His stomach plummeted when it slid open. Most people didn't leave their doors unlocked, regardless of how nice the neighborhood was.

He rested his hand on his weapon as he entered the house, wanting to be ready if he needed to use it. "Mr. and Mrs. Barrett, this is Officer Trevino of the Rochester Police Department. I heard a noise coming from in here. Are you all right?"

Silence.

Alex opened his mouth to call out again when he heard a soft, high-pitched sound that made the hair stand up on the back of his neck.

What the hell?

He drew his Glock and ran across the dark living room in the direction of the noise, reaching up to thumb the mic on his radio as he circled around a coffee table.

"Dispatch, this is Lake-3," he said softly. "Possible home invasion in progress. Requesting backup."

Alex finished rattling off the address on the way up

the steps, almost tripping over the man lying on the floor at the top. Dressed in a pair of sweatpants and a T-shirt, he stared at Alex unseeingly. Despite the single bullet to the chest, Alex dropped to one knee and pressed his fingers to the side of the man's neck to confirm what he already suspected. The man was dead, but hadn't been that way for long.

There wasn't anything he could do for Mr. Barrett, but he might still be able to save the man's wife and daughter. There was a good possibility that whoever had murdered Mr. Barrett was up here somewhere. Alex would bet a month's pay the intruder had Mrs. Bennett and Jessica with them.

Ignoring the dispatcher on the radio asking for details, Alex cautiously moved down the hallway. All the instruction in the police academy, not to mention four years of room-to-room clearance training he'd gotten in the Corps, took over as he left the first victim behind and continued along the dark hallway looking for the women and praying he'd find them alive. He cleared the bathroom first, then the laundry room, before coming to the master bedroom and the body of a middle-aged woman lying half off the bed, her throat slit. Dark red blood stained the pillow and sheets, spilling onto the carpeted floor.

Shit.

Alex swallowed hard. He'd seen wounds like this enough times in Iraq and Afghanistan to know there wasn't any hope she was still alive.

Turning on his heel, he strode for the last room at the end of the hall. The door, adorned with a poster of some boy band hunk that Alex couldn't have identified even in good light, was closed. There was part of Alex that didn't want to open it.

He'd seen enough death when he was in the Corps. It was one of the biggest reasons he'd gotten out and become a cop. He'd hoped that as a police officer, he could actually save lives instead of seeing carnage every day.

That wasn't working out so far tonight.

His heart in his throat, Alex turned the knob. He'd seen more than his fair share of man's inhumanity to man, but even he wasn't quite ready for what he found when he opened the door.

The bedroom was bathed in the glow of an active computer monitor sitting on the desk by the far wall. Jessica was tied to a chair a few feet away, her eyes wide and filled with tears above the duct tape covering her mouth, her curly red hair tousled all over the place.

But all the tape in the world couldn't keep the girl quiet, not with the man standing behind her holding a long kitchen knife to her throat. Smirking, he pressed the blade more tightly against her skin. In his twenties, with short blond hair, he seemed so relaxed he might as well have been standing in line at Starbucks.

Alex lined up the three glowing dots on the Glock's sights with the man's head at the same time as he scanned the small room. The asshole in front of him was the obvious threat, but being in Force Recon had taught him that the most dangerous threat was frequently the one you didn't see until it was too late. But there wasn't much else to see, not unless you counted the closed closet door and boy band posters lining the walls.

That was when he caught sight of the big dog lying on the floor at the foot of the bed, blood matting the animal's fur and staining the carpet, his side heaving as he labored to breathe.

Shit.

Alex's gaze snapped back to the man behind Jessica, his finger tightening on the trigger. One little pull and the .45 caliber bullet would cleanly blow off the man's head from this distance.

"Drop the knife and step away from the girl."

He didn't intend to give the asshole a lot of time to decide how this was going to go. The guy had already demonstrated he was more than willing to kill. If he refused to step away from the girl, Alex would have no problem putting him down.

The jackass only smiled broader and dug the blade into Jessica's neck even more. She screamed louder under the tape covering her mouth.

Fuck this. He didn't have time to talk this guy down.

Alex had just started squeezing the trigger when he realized that Jessica wasn't looking at him or even up at the sicko holding the knife to her throat. She was staring at something over Alex's left shoulder. Suddenly, the panic in her eyes sent a completely different message than the one he'd received earlier.

Gut clenching, Alex spun around just as a big blond man with a beard burst out of the closet and started shooting.

The first bullet hit Alex in the center of the chest and knocked him backward, driving the air out of his lungs and hurting like hell. He would be dead if it weren't for the bulletpoof vest he was wearing.

He was still getting his feet back under him when the second and third shot hit him in the side, just under his left arm. He knew he was screwed the second the bullets tore through him. Lightweight covert Kevlar vests like the one he wore under his duty uniform weren't meant to protect every inch of your torso, just as much as was practical. The sides were one of their weak areas.

Alex fell back hard, the intense pain in his chest telling him the shots had hit something that was vitally important to his continued existence. Ignoring the long-term implications of that, he brought his right hand around until his Glock was pointing at the gunman. He squeezed off two shots and was rewarded with the image of both rounds drilling the sneaky fucker right through the center of the chest.

Suddenly, breathing seemed more painful than it was worth. Alex's whole chest felt like it was on fire. He wanted to say the hell with it. He'd fought hard and taken out a lot of bad guys in his time—including the son of a bitch hiding in the closet—and he liked to think all that had earned him a pain-free express checkout. But he couldn't leave yet. Jessica was still in trouble with a psychopath holding a knife to her throat. There was more to do before he was finished.

Gritting his teeth, he rolled onto his left side, dragging his right arm off the floor and straining with every muscle in his body to get his gun pointed in the general direction of the guy with the knife. Only, the asshole wasn't standing behind the girl anymore. He was right there in Alex's face, kicking his Glock out of his hand and sending it bouncing across the carpet.

Alex braced himself, expecting the guy to plunge the knife into him, but instead, the bastard kicked him in the ribs, head, face, stomach, and anywhere else he could reach.

Pain exploded through Alex's body. He got his right arm up—his left wouldn't even function now—and tried to defend himself, but it was useless. He was losing buckets of blood by the second. Sooner or later, the guy would get tired of what he was doing and skewer him with that damn knife.

Just then, a snarl broke through the wave of darkness washing over him. Alex opened his eyes to see a big, furry shape lunge at the guy. The dog, covered in his own blood and so weak he'd barely been able to breathe moments ago, had somehow found the strength to clamp his teeth down on the man's arm.

The asshole shouted in pain and turned his attention on the dog, lifting the knife to stab the animal.

Jessica screamed behind the tape, probably begging the dog to run and save himself. But that wasn't the way this dog was going to go out. Alex decided it wasn't the way he was going out, either.

The gun was too far across the room to reach, but he still had one weapon left—his feet. He lashed out with his right leg, catching the psychopath in the side of the knee with his heavy patrol shoes. The kick didn't have a lot of force behind it, but then again, knees weren't built to bend sideways, so it didn't take a lot. The man's leg buckled, and he went down hard, the dog still on him.

Climbing on top of the guy, Alex grabbed his knife hand, wrenching it away from the dog. The man struggled to get free of both him and the dog, and it was all Alex could do to keep his bloody hands wrapped around the asshole's wrist.

He had to hurry up and finish this—before the guy finished him.

Growling as loudly as the dog helping him, he yanked the knife out of the killer's hands, even though it sliced his fingers to the bone to do it. The man balled his free hand into a fist and punched Alex solidly in the jaw.

Ignoring the pain, Alex took a deep breath and twisted the knife around to get it lined up with the psychopath's chest. Then he collapsed on the hilt, driving the blade deep. The guy jerked once, then went still.

Alex's vision went black as the adrenaline rush disappeared, and he closed his eyes, unable to muster the energy to do anything else.

Something wet and warm lapped his face, and he opened his eyes just as a smooth, slimy tongue hit his cheek. He groaned and halfheartedly shoved the animal away. But the beast refused to stop, instead licking even more insistently. It was like he was trying to keep Alex from giving up. This dog was too frigging much.

Alex pushed himself off the dead guy and flopped onto his back, so weak he could barely move. The dog lay on the floor beside him, gazing at him with pain and sadness in his eyes. The animal's breathing was so labored that Alex wasn't sure how the dog had been able to attack the killer as fiercely as he had.

Wincing, Alex spared a quick glance down at his side, then looked away just as fast. Shit, there was a lot of blood down there. He didn't know a person could lose so much and still be conscious. Then again, he'd always been a little slow picking up the obvious.

He dimly heard the sound of sirens in the distance, but something told him they weren't going to make it in time for him. His gaze went to the girl still tied to the chair. Her parents were dead, and now she was going to watch him—and her dog—die too.

Not having anything better to do with the short time he had left, Alex jerked the knife out of the dead man's chest, then crawled over to the girl on his hands and knees so he could slice the rope holding one of her hands to the chair. He got through one and was halfway through the bindings around her other hand when the lights suddenly went out. He didn't even realize he was falling until he felt his head thump against the carpet hard enough to make him see stars.

He opened his eyes for a second and saw the big, furry dog staring at him with an expression that seemed to imply he thought Alex was a complete wimp.

"Sorry, dude," he whispered as he closed his eyes again. "Guess I'm just not as tough as you."

Chapter 1

Dallas, Texas, Present Day

"IF WE DON'T GET ANYTHING IN THE NEXT FIFTEEN MINUTES, I'm calling it a night," Sergeant Rodriguez said, his voice as rough as sandpaper in Alex's earpiece. "We knew it was a long shot that our dealers would come back to this same location anyway."

Thank God, Alex thought. He and his spotter, fellow werewolf and SWAT officer Remy Boudreaux, had been lying motionless on this rooftop for most of the night, and he for one was more than ready to be done with this op. It was a bust—again. If they wrapped this up quickly, he might be able to grab a few hours of sleep on one of the cots at the SWAT compound before taking Tuffie to her appointment at the vet in the morning.

Of course, not catching the bad guys tonight meant they'd be back on some other roof tomorrow night providing oversight for this snipe hunt.

"I don't know how narcotics puts up with this crap," Remy said from his position a couple of feet farther along the roofline. He sounded just as frustrated as Alex felt. "Another night, another frigging waste of time."

Alex silently agreed. He and Remy, along with Max Lowry and Jayden Brooks, had been working with Sergeant José Rodriguez of the Dallas Police narcotics division on this task force gig every night for nearly three weeks now. The duty schedule wasn't Rodriguez's fault. If you wanted to catch people selling designer drugs, you had to do it on their schedule — which seemed to be directly associated with those hours when the rest of the world was tucked in bed all happy and oblivious.

"How the hell can it be so hard to find the dirtbags selling this new drug?" Remy asked in his distinctive Cajun drawl. "This stuff is killing people who use it. You'd think there'd be a line a mile long willing to give up these dealers."

"No kidding," Alex said. "But something tells me the people who use this crap are more afraid of losing access to their supply than they are of dying from an overdose."

That was why they were out here trying to catch the guys selling the drug that had killed eight people in the past month and put more than twenty others in the hospital. Because no one would talk.

Alex leaned over the edge of the roof to scan the group of people gathered down on the corner. There was a good chance that some of them were simply hanging out, but at this time of the night — in an area well known as one of the city's go-to locations for drug deals — there was an equally good chance that a few of them were looking to buy some of those drugs. That was why the narcotics division had one of their undercover officers buried in the middle of the group, risking his life to get any information he could on the people responsible for putting fireball on the street.

Users supposedly called the stuff fireball because it burned through you like fire, making you feel an incredible rush of heat and energy, only to leave you drained and wrung out when you came down from the high. No one in the Dallas PD had even known there was a new drug on the streets until the bodies started showing up at the hospital—and in the morgue. At first, everyone thought it was simply a strong batch of heroin or some of that nasty krokodil crap coming out of Eastern Europe. But they'd quickly figured out it wasn't either of those things when a derivative of fentanyl, a type of synthetic opiate, showed up in the toxicology reports. Fentanyl was one hundred times more powerful than heroin and would have been bad enough by itself, but whoever was making fireball was cutting in other drugs like codeine, caffeine, and ecstasy, along with a whole bunch of crud that had chemical names Alex couldn't even pronounce. In addition to creating an intense and long-lasting high, fireball was so addictive that people were out looking for more mere hours after almost dying from an overdose.

Alex couldn't understand why someone would put crap like that into their bodies, but within weeks, fireball had spread to the club scene and college campuses. If the cops didn't get it off the street ASAP, it would only be a matter of time before the stuff started showing up in the local high schools.

Luckily, SWAT had a good working relationship with the DPD narcotics division. Mostly because Mike Taylor, one of their squad leaders, had spent a good portion of his career working undercover for them. So when Rodriguez had come looking for help, Gage Dixon, the SWAT commander and alpha of their pack of werewolves, had quickly agreed. Mike's relationship with the narcotics division wasn't the only reason Gage had been so willing to loan out Alex and teammates. The way Gage saw it, SWAT was partially responsible for this latest drug epidemic.

Over the past year, the Dallas SWAT team had taken

out some major crime figures. Gage had killed Walter Hardy, destroying a syndicate that controlled most of the crime in the southwestern United States; Alex's squad leader, Xander Riggs, had taken down a major bank robbery ring; Eric Becker had single-handedly wiped out the Albanian mobsters who'd moved in to take over; and Landry Cooper had ended up putting a family full of arms dealers in prison.

All of that was great, but by taking out those big fish, the local ocean had become swarmed with dozens of little fish all trying to get their piece of the pie. With so many small fish running around doing business on their own, it was damn near impossible to keep an eye on them all. That was why the task force hadn't been able to find the people distributing this new drug yet. There were just too many new players in town.

"Five minutes and we're finally out of here," Remy muttered, glancing at his watch.

Alex lifted a brow. "What? You have a date or something?"

Remy flashed him a grin, his hazel eyes twinkling. "I wouldn't call it a date. More like a booty call."

"At three o'clock in the morning? Who the hell would be awake now and looking to hook up?"

"That would be Vivian." Remy's smile broadened. "She's *always* ready for a hookup."

Alex dug through his memory, trying to figure out if he'd ever met Vivian. After mentally scrolling through the Rolodex of Remy's girlfriends, he gave up. The man had a lot of women in his life. Alex didn't know if it was Remy's accent or what, but it seemed like every time he turned around, women were throwing their panties at the guy left and right.

It wasn't that Alex was a monk or anything—not by a long shot. He enjoyed the company of a beautiful woman as much as the next man, but he needed something beyond the physical to hold his attention.

"Is she the tall one with long, dark hair?" he finally asked.

"Nah. That's Leslie." Remy shook his head. "Vivian's the fiery redhead who drives the Ferrari."

Alex opened his mouth to ask why the hell a woman who could afford a Ferrari would hang out with a SWAT cop whose paycheck probably couldn't even cover the detailing on a ride like that, when a dark blue Toyota came down the street. It slowed to a crawl as it passed the small group gathered at the corner, then pulled into a parking lot a few hundred feet away. Not much chance they were stopping for gas or munchies, since the old Gas-n-Go that used to be there had gone out of business a long time ago.

The people on the corner stood up a little straighter, practically bouncing on their toes as three men climbed out of the Toyota and surveyed the area. Well, if that didn't scream they were up to something shady, Alex didn't know what did.

He leaned over his rifle, using the low-light scope to see details that even his werewolf enhanced vision couldn't pick up from this distance. Apparently, the men must have thought the coast was clear, because one of them ducked into the back of the car and came out with a handful of small plastic bags that he casually shoved into the pocket of his jacket.

"We're hot," Alex said into his mic. "The big guy with the mountain-man beard just tucked several baggies inside his right pocket."

The other cops listening in immediately started talking among themselves, their voices a jumble over the radio.

"Relax and maintain position," Rodriguez said softly, as if he were worried the dealers would hear his rough voice. "The guys are going to take a little time to feel out their customers first and make sure there's nothing fishy going on. We wait until my undercover guy confirms they're dealing fireball, then move in when he gives the signal. And remember, don't blow his cover. We arrest him along with the rest of them and make sure he spends a night or two in lockup like everyone else."

"Talk about a crappy job," Remy muttered. "I wonder if he gets overtime for that."

Alex turned off his mic. "I doubt it. Mike said that having narcotic cops spend time in jail is good for their street cred—or at least the street cred of their under-cover identity."

Remy made a face. "That's a pretty harsh price to pay for a little street cred. Remind me never to request a transfer into narcotics."

Alex didn't argue with that as he peered down his scope so he could keep an eye on the three dealers—and Rodriguez's UC officer. Everyone in the group down on the corner was talking like they were all old friends. Unfortunately, no one seemed to want to bring up the reason they were standing on a dark street corner at oh dark thirty in the morning—drugs.

"Dammit, why don't they just get on with it?" Remy growled. "Everyone knows they're down there to buy drugs. Just do it already."

Alex chuckled. "Maybe you should send Vivian a text and tell her that you probably won't be able to make it."

"No way," Remy said. "You don't just pass up a chance to spend quality time with a woman like Vivian. She's special."

Alex was pretty confident Remy wasn't implying Vivian might be *The One* for him, that mythical one-in-a-billion soul mate that apparently existed for every werewolf out there. It was funny really. Considering Remy constantly had women in and out of his bed, Alex always thought he'd be the first werewolf to find his perfect soul mate. Instead, Gage, Xander, Becker, and Cooper had stumbled across the women they were meant to be with for the rest of their lives.

He would have pointed that out to Remy, but a soft voice coming through the UC cop's wire caught his attention.

"You got anything special with you tonight?" the woman asked, her hesitant voice barely audible above the chatter of the other people in the group.

"That depends on how special you want," the bearded guy with the baggies in his pocket said. "You looking for something in particular?"

Alex moved his rifle until he had his scope trained on the woman talking. Even in the dark, he could see that she was small, thin, and frail looking. She boldly stuck out her chin and met the man's gaze.

"I'm looking for fireball. You got any?"

Everyone suddenly went quiet.

The big man smiled behind his beard. "Yeah, I got some. How much you looking to buy, sweet thing?"

She might have been the only one who asked, but everyone dug out their money along with her, clearly wanting to buy some too.

Over the radio, Rodriguez gave the call for the other

cops to move in. Alex and Remy stayed where they were. Their job was to cover the UC cop's back and make sure the dealers didn't do anything stupid when the cavalry charged, like try to take out him and the rest of the junkies.

At the far end of the street, the distinct sound of a gunshot echoed in the night. The people on the corner jumped, turning to look that way.

"Shit," Alex growled even as Rodriguez shouted for everyone to move in ASAP.

Lights flashed and sirens blared, but it was too late. The junkies and dealers on the corner scattered in every direction at the same time. One of the dealers headed for the car, jumping in and squealing out of the parking lot, leaving his buddies behind.

Alex swiveled his rifle to take out the tires and saw three cops already moving to intercept the vehicle. For a normal human, chasing a speeding car would be a waste of time, but two of those cops were Brooks and Max. Getting away from two werewolves wasn't going to be easy. Although, he wasn't sure what his pack mates were going to do about the female narcotics cop behind them. It wasn't like they could shift in front of her.

As much as Alex wanted to hang around and see how the chase turned out, he didn't have time. The other two dealers had given up going after their friend and instead turned and ran right toward the alley between the two-story building he and Remy were on and the one beside it. Alex jumped up and ran for the back side of the building, slinging his rifle over his shoulder as he went. Shooting the fleeing men wasn't an option, so that meant getting off the roof and chasing them down on foot.

"I have a beautiful redhead waiting for me in her

bed, and these assholes are going to make us chase them?" Remy growled when he caught up to Alex. "They'd better not resist, or I won't be accountable for what happens."

Alex didn't answer as they both leapt off the building. The concrete of the alley rushed up to meet him in a hurry, and the impact made his teeth clack together, not to mention sent a brief stab of pain surging up both legs and through his spine into the base of his skull. Werewolves could absorb a lot of punishment, but jumping off a building still hurt like hell—werewolf or not. He and Remy were up and sprinting after the dealers without pausing to catch their breath, though.

Up ahead, Alex saw one of the dealers turn back and nearly crap himself at the sight of him and Remy running down the alley behind them when there'd been no one there mere moments before. The bad guys put on more speed as they cut across a dark, overgrown area, probably figuring they could easily outrun a couple of cops loaded down with weapons, tactical vests, and all the other crap they carried. Even with all their gear, Alex and Remy easily closed the distance between them and the men they were chasing.

There were almost certainly other police officers behind them, maybe even patrol cars racing to head them off, but this part of West Dallas was filled with abandoned lots, old buildings, and lightly wooded areas. With all the twists and turns they were making, he and Remy would outdistance anyone trailing behind them. They were on their own.

He and Remy had just jumped over the remnants of a building foundation when the two dealers must have realized what they were doing wasn't working and that they needed a new plan. Without a word to each other, the two assholes split up, one heading away down the sidewalk, the other moving deeper into the shadows of another overgrown lot.

"Watch yourself," Remy warned as he peeled off after the guy heading down the sidewalk, leaving Alex to chase down the big guy with the beard who'd been carrying the drugs.

The thrill of the chase took hold of him, and Alex let out a growl as he ran through the hip-deep grass. He felt his canines extend a little, quickly followed by his claws. He fought for control, trying to get the fangs and claws to retract, but he was crappy at staying under control in tense situations like this. He wasn't the only werewolf in the Pack who had that problem, wolfing out frequently in the heat of a SWAT mission, but while he appreciated the extra speed and strength that came with a partial shift, letting a suspect see him with canines hanging two inches over his lower lip wasn't exactly a good way to keep the existence of werewolves a secret.

Alex couldn't focus on both the dealer and his out-of-control fangs at the same time, so he stopped thinking about the latter. They would take care of themselves when he calmed down, and catching this guy with a pocket full of fireball would definitely help him do that.

For a big guy, the dealer was damn slippery. He did anything and everything to throw Alex off his trail, but none of it worked. Finally, in desperation, he made a sudden left turn and came to a stop. Tossing the baggies of drugs as far away as he could, he picked up a two-by-four from the ground and grinned.

"You fucked up chasing after me, pig. You outran your backup."

The words probably would have sounded more menacing if the dealer weren't gasping for breath. Alex wanted to point out that he was carrying a rifle, a pistol, and a Taser—any of which trumped the piece of wood in the guy's hands—but that would probably just be a waste of time. Something told him the man wasn't too bright.

The dealer rushed him with a roar, swinging the piece of wood like it was a baseball bat. Alex caught the two-by-four in his hand and gave it a sharp twist, ripping it away from the guy and tossing it aside. The move fired up his inner werewolf a little more, and he felt his fangs and claws extend even farther. All at once, the whole area around him brightened, a clear sign his eyes had shifted as well.

"What the hell?" The dealer stared at Alex's eyes like they were glowing, which they likely were.

While Alex's eyes might have freaked out the dealer, it wasn't enough to keep the guy from taking another swing at Alex, this time with his fist.

Alex stepped sideways, avoiding the blow and fighting the urge to pound the jackass into the ground like a tent stake. He couldn't let himself get any more out of control. But he could sure as hell go far enough that this guy would probably need intensive therapy for the rest of his life.

"I'd stop fighting if I were you," Alex suggested as he fought to shift back. "Before you embarrass yourself."

The big man didn't seem interested in taking that advice and only lowered his head and charged Alex like a damn bull. Alex sidestepped him, slamming his forearm into the man's back as the guy barreled past. The blow drove the dealer to the ground, shoving his face into the dirt with a thud. Alex didn't wait for him to get up. Instead, he bent over and cuffed him before the guy got his wits back together. Then he dragged the man to his feet and walked straight over to pick up the plastic bags he'd tossed.

"That's not mine!" the bearded man claimed, struggling against Alex's grip.

Alex snorted. "Right. Then I'm sure your fingerprints won't be all over the bags."

The dealer didn't say anything as Alex led him back to the intersection where the chase had started. Either the man was thinking about whether he really had left fingerprints on the baggies, or he was stewing over the fact that he was screwed.

Alex got back just as Remy arrived, the other dealer slung over his shoulder in a fireman's carry. The man was out cold, a nasty bruise already developing across the side of his face.

"What the hell happened to him?" Alex asked as two uniformed officers came over to relieve them of their suspects and the drugs.

"He ran into a tree," Remy said.

Alex arched a brow. He couldn't help but remember what his pack mate had said about not being responsible if the man resisted.

"What? I'm serious." Remy gave him an indignant look. "He was so worried about me chasing him that he wasn't watching where he was going. He smacked into a tree like some cartoon character, I swear. It was pure Wile E. Coyote stuff."

Some werewolves in the Pack had the ability to sense when someone was lying to them—Alex wasn't one of them. But he got the feeling Remy was telling the truth. The story was too crazy not to be true.

As they walked back toward the corner where the drug deal had been going down, he caught sight of Brooks and Max across the street, along with Vaughn, the female narcotics officer. As he and Remy approached, he couldn't help but notice that Vaughn was staring at Brooks like he had horns sprouting from his head and a rainbow flying out his butt.

She opened her mouth to say something to Brooks, but then closed it again. After a moment, she shook her head and walked away, looking back over her shoulder at Brooks every other step. The attractive dark-skinned cop was eyeballing him so much she almost smacked into a parked patrol car.

"What the heck was that about?" Alex asked Max as Brooks hurried to catch up with her.

Max shrugged, his blue eyes following their pack mate. "Brooks tackled a car again. He hit that little Toyota so hard that both wheels came up off the street, and Vaughn saw it. I guess she's trying hard as hell to convince herself that her eyes must have been playing tricks on her."

Alex knew he shouldn't be surprised. In a pack of really big alpha werewolves, Brooks was frigging huge. And with his football background, he had a bad habit of tackling anything that either tried to stand in his way or get away from him—including cars. He'd pay the price for it later in the form of bruises over half his body and broken bones that would take hours to heal. That had never stopped him before though and probably wouldn't any time soon.

Then again, maybe he'd just been showing off for that narcotics cop. Vaughn was definitely cute, and Brooks was attracted to her. Alex had seen him putting the moves on the woman several times over the past couple of weeks.

"Maybe we should get him a tackling dummy for the compound," Max suggested. "You know, so he can work out his aggression issues."

"Or get him paired up with *The One* for him as fast as possible," Remy suggested. "It's bound to mellow him out. If we can find somebody big enough and rough enough to match him."

Alex was thinking maybe Vaughn could be that match. Working narcotics, she certainly wasn't a push-over. Beside him, Remy's phone vibrated.

"That Vivian telling you to hurry up?" Alex asked.

Remy scowled as he read her text. "It's Vivian telling me not to bother coming over. She found someone else to keep her bed warm for what's left of the night."

Max winced. "Dude, that's harsh."

"It's just as well," Alex said. "She would have been pissed when you told her you couldn't make it because you're going to be filling out paperwork for the next couple of hours."

"I am?" Remy asked, clearly confused.

"Hell, yeah. And you'd better dot your i's and cross your t's, because something tells me Detective Coletti in IA is going to be looking at that report real hard." Alex grinned. "I hope that charming accent of yours works on guys as well as it does on women, because I think he's going to have a real hard time believing that drug dealer ran into a tree."

Remy groaned and shoved his phone in his pocket.

Alex watched as the uniformed officers provid-ing backup finished getting all the suspects safely tucked away in the back of police cruisers, including

the undercover cop and the slim, frail-looking woman.
Both of them looked equally despondent. Alex couldn't
blame them. One was heading to jail to gain street cred,
and the other was going because she was addicted to a
nasty drug that was slowly killing her.

At least in the case of the cop, spending a night or two
in jail might be worth it if it ended up getting fireball—
and whoever was making it—off the street.

―――ⵠ―――

Alex stifled a yawn as he stared at the TV mounted on
the far wall of the waiting area in the veterinary clinic.
He'd gotten thirty minutes of sleep this morning and
was frigging exhausted. Several of the other guys in the
Pack had offered to take Tuffie to her appointment so
he could head home and crash, but he hadn't taken any
of them up on it. Taking Tuffie for her checkups wasn't
something he'd ever let anyone else do for him. So he'd
showered off, changed into one of the fresh uniforms he
kept in his locker at the SWAT compound, and headed
out with the team's mascot and community pet in tow.

He glanced at Tuffie sitting on the floor beside his
chair and couldn't help but smile. The girl was an absolute doll, even after the horrendous life she'd had. It was
obvious from all the scars on her body that the pit bull
mix had spent a portion of it in a dogfighting ring—
something that pissed him off every time he thought
about it. Thankfully, she'd been rescued by the owner
of a local junkyard who'd given her a new life and
taken good care of her. Unfortunately, that life had been
cut short when the psycho ex-boyfriend of the Pack's
newest member, Khaki Blake, had shot Tuffie and killed
her owner. Alex had stabilized her as well as he could,

along with Trey Duncan, the team's other medic, but the injuries had been severe, and she'd been in surgery for a long time. It was a miracle she'd survived at all.

So while it could sometimes be tricky getting her to the clinic for all her appointments, Alex made it a priority. Tuffie was a survivor. If she could find it in her to keep smiling and wagging her tail after everything she'd been through, he could certainly rearrange his schedule a little to get her there.

He was still sitting there watching the news an hour later when a dark-haired vet tech came out to apologize for the wait, saying they were down to one doctor and that everything was backed up.

"I can reschedule Tuffie for another day, if you want?" she offered.

Alex shook his head. "It's okay. We'll wait."

He leaned his head back against the wall and closed his eyes, promising himself he'd just rest them for a second, when he heard the front door open. He opened his eyes to see a female DPD uniformed officer come in cradling a tiny malnourished-looking beagle mix in her arms. She checked in with the front desk, then took a seat next to Alex. The fragile-looking puppy curled into a ball and immediately fell asleep in the cop's lap.

Tuffie opened her eyes and gave the puppy a once-over, then went back to sleep.

"Who's this little guy?" Alex asked.

The officer—her name tag read Bell—smiled down at the tiny puppy, then explained that she worked in the department's new Animal Cruelty Squad. "We mostly investigate rooster and dogfighting operations because of their frequent connection to gang activity and the drug trade, but we also respond to emergency calls when

Animal Services is overwhelmed. We found this little guy trapped in an abandoned warehouse. We would never have found him if some homeless people hadn't heard him whining and reported it."

Alex gently ran his fingers over the puppy's soft fur, careful not to wake him up. He'd heard a little about the new ACS, but hadn't met any of the cops assigned to it yet. Too many times, city animal control officers were asked to deal with situations that should have been handled by armed law enforcement personnel. The squad was organized under the Field Services Division, along with other special services like K-9 and SWAT, and from what Alex had heard, they'd already started making a difference. If he weren't in SWAT, he would have transferred to ACS in a heartbeat.

Officer Bell glanced at Tuffie. "I'd heard that SWAT had taken in an abused pit fighter. Is this her?"

Alex started to answer when the local channel interrupted the program on the TV with breaking news. Judging from all the cameras and media types visible on the scene, something big was going on. He realized what it was the moment a woman stepped up to the podium in front of the crowd and earnestly begged anyone out there watching who might have information concerning the whereabouts of her missing daughter to call the DPD Missing Persons Squad.

Admittedly, Alex had been buried in the drug task force stuff, but he vaguely remembered seeing a department alert on the girl. Abigail Elliott, a junior at Regional Texas College, had been missing for four days. As far as he knew, missing persons hadn't come up with anything to even substantiate whether her disappearance involved foul play, much less found a lead that might bring her home. Her family was obviously hoping a public plea would generate something the police could use.

When the girl's mother finished speaking, a distinguished-looking man with salt-and-pepper hair and dressed in an impeccable suit stepped up and begged people to take a moment out of their busy lives and call the police if they saw anything suspicious. Alex couldn't remember the man's name, but he recognized a powerful speaker when he saw one. The impassioned words might just make a difference for this girl.

"Poor woman," Officer Bell said quietly. "I can't imagine what she's going through. If Councilman McDonald wasn't a friend of the Elliotts, the news probably wouldn't even waste the time putting her on camera."

Councilman McDonald. Now that Alex had a name to put with the face, it was easier to remember where he'd seen the guy. He didn't know much about the man personally, but he knew McDonald was a big supporter of the Dallas Police Department and had been instrumental in getting the current chief of police, Randy Curtis, appointed to his position. He seemed sincere in his efforts to help Ms. Elliott, which was kind of surprising. In Alex's experience, there were few politicians who did anything that wasn't directly related to getting votes in the next election.

McDonald was just answering questions from reporters when the vet tech walked over. "Dr. Barton will be able to see you and Tuffie now."

Alex frowned as he stood up. "Dr. Barton? Where's Doc Jones? He's been taking care of Tuffie from day one."

The vet tech gave him an apologetic smile. "Like I said, we're down to one vet today—Dr. Barton. If you want to see Dr. Jones, you'll need to make another appointment."

Alex hesitated. Jones had done all of Tuffie's surgeries, and Alex trusted the guy to take care of her. He wasn't sure what he thought about someone who didn't have previous experience with Tuffie's injuries checking her out. But with the task force workload, Alex also didn't have a clue what his schedule was going to look like.

"No, we'll see Dr. Barton."

The vet tech nodded. "She's waiting for you in exam room four," she said, then hurried over to talk to a woman who'd just walked in with an angry, hissing cat that didn't want anything to do with being in a room full of dogs.

"Don't worry," Officer Bell said. "Dr. Barton knows her stuff. I think you'll be impressed."

Alex nodded his thanks, then led Tuffie into the exam room.

Dr. Barton was bent over rummaging through a bottom drawer of the built-ins on the far wall. Even though Alex did his best not to stare, it was impossible not to notice that she had an incredibly spectacular ass. He'd always been a leg man, but one look at her derrière and he suddenly decided he'd been missing out. Then she stood up, turned around, and flipped her long, wavy blond hair over her shoulder, and he realized that the rest of her was equally stunning. While her baggy white lab coat hid a lot, he could still tell that she had an athletic build and some really nice curves. It was her face that made his heart beat faster, though. She had the most captivating pair of blue eyes he'd ever seen and full red lips just begging to be kissed. From this moment forward, whenever he pictured an angel, he would think of the beautiful Dr. Barton.

Alex smiled, and when she smiled back, he heard her heart thudding a little quicker. But then she looked down at Tuffie, and her entire expression changed. Hurrying over, she dropped down to one knee beside Tuffie, gently examining her ears and face.

She gave Alex an angry glare. "Please tell me you arrested the people who put this beautiful girl in a dog-fighting ring. Even better—tell me you shot them."

If Alex had thought her heart was beating fast before, it was nothing compared to the way it was thumping now. Clearly, Dr. Barton was very passionate about protecting dogs. In his book, that made her even more beautiful than she already was.

"I wish I could, but unfortunately, we never found the people who did it," Alex said. "We rescued Tuffie when her owner was killed. He died trying to protect her from a psychopath armed with a rifle."

Dr. Barton's gaze went back to Tuffie, her expression turning from anger to sadness as she ran her fingers down the fresh scars along the dog's chest and side. "Looks like she got shot anyway."

"Yeah. It's a miracle she lived long enough for my teammate and me to get her here in time for Doc Jones to save her. Thank God for sirens. I think we ran every red light in town."

The veterinarian straightened, gracing him with another dazzling grin, and Alex felt his knees go a little loose. Damn, what a smile.

"I knew there was something I liked about you the second you walked in."

Alex felt his face flush. "It wasn't a big deal. I'm

a cop. Saving people—and dogs—comes with the job description."

He cringed the moment the words left his mouth. Had he really just said something that lame?

Thankfully, the beautiful Dr. Barton didn't seem to notice the cheesy line. Or if she had, she was too polite to laugh at him.

"And is bringing Tuffie to her appointments also in your job description?" she asked, her eyes twinkling.

Was her heart beating even faster than before? Unless it was his own heart pounding in his ears. That was a definite possibility. Because it seemed like he had a real thing for Dr. Barton.

He smiled. "It is if the rest of the SWAT team and I adopted her and gave her a new home."

Alex knew it was a shameless grab to get further into the doctor's good graces, but he couldn't seem to stop himself.

"Not only did you save her life, but you adopted her too? I think Tuffie hit the lottery with you, Officer…?"

"Trevino," he said, filling in the blank and offering his hand. "But please, call me Alex."

She took his hand and gave it a shake. "Nice to meet you, Alex. I'm Lacey Barton."

Her hand was small in comparison to his, her skin soft and warm, and Alex found himself holding on a bit longer than was customary. Lacey didn't seem to mind. In fact, she appeared just as reluctant to let go as he did.

She pushed her hair behind her ear and cleared her throat. "I guess we ought to get on with Tuffie's checkup. So you can get back to saving the world and everything."

"Yeah, of course."

Reaching down, Alex gently picked up Tuffie and set her on the stainless steel exam table.

"Nice muscle tone," Lacey murmured.

Alex felt the compliment go right to his head. "Thanks."

"Actually, I was talking about Tuffie," Lacey said as she tenderly ran her hands over the dog's shoulders.

"Oh."

She looked up at him from beneath her lashes. "But yours is pretty good too."

Alex chuckled. Damn, this woman was good. He had her by a foot in height and more than a hundred pounds in weight, yet she was playing him like a fiddle, and he didn't mind one bit. He couldn't remember ever having such an immediate and intense reaction to any woman he'd ever met. Suddenly, he wanted to know everything there was to know about her—and then some.

Lacey was more than accommodating, telling him about how she'd recently gotten a job here after working several years at a place on the west side of Dallas closer to Arlington.

"I loved it there, but this place is closer to my apartment," she told him as she continued to examine Tuffie. "I've cut my commute time by about an hour and a half each way, so it's like getting a whole extra day off to do stuff I want to do instead of sitting in traffic."

"And what do you like to do with all this extra time?" he asked.

Lacey leaned over to read something in Tuffie's medical records. Alex tensed, worried she'd found something wrong, but after a moment, she merely nodded to herself, then went back to checking Tuffie.

"I do a lot of volunteer work at one of the nearby

animal shelters," she said. "I'm also on call to help out both Animal Services and the DPD Animal Cruelty Squad when they run into injured dogs."

Whoa. A woman who spent her days taking care of dogs for a living, then did it during her spare time for free? That was definitely a woman Alex could appreciate.

"It's pretty amazing that you give so much of your time to animal causes," he said. "Getting called out at all hours of the day and night must be tough on your boyfriend, though."

Lacey urged Tuffie over on her back, pressing carefully along one of the long scars that ran all the way from the base of her rib cage to the middle of her cute pink tummy.

"I don't have a boyfriend right now," she said, the corners of her mouth turning up. "My life is a little too busy for that at the moment."

Bingo! Alex had already noticed she wasn't wearing a ring. Now he knew she wasn't seeing anyone. Could this get any better?

Lacey finished her inspection of Tuffie's surgical scars, then rolled her back over and gave her an affectionate pat on the head.

"Everything looks great," she announced.

Alex grinned. "Excellent." He picked up Tuffie and set her on the floor. "I know you spend a lot of your off time volunteering, but I'd really love to take you out to dinner sometime."

Lacey picked up Tuffie's chart and made some notes as she walked around to his side of the exam table. Alex took a deep breath, taking in her scent. His nose wasn't usually the best, but damn, she smelled good.

"I'd really love to, but I can't." She smiled up at him.

"Like I said, my life is way too hectic right now. Thanks for asking, though."

A sinking feeling like he'd never felt before settled in the pit of Alex's stomach. Shit, it felt like he'd been punched in the gut. He cleared his throat, muttering something about it being no big deal, then quickly left the room with Tuffie. He did everything he could not to let anything show on his face, but on the inside, he was disappointed as hell. He was so bummed he barely remembered paying the receptionist, but since no one stopped him when he left, he supposed he must have.

Alex paused when he got to his pickup, still trying to figure out what the hell had just happened. He looked down at Tuffie, but she seemed just as confused as he was. He'd never considered himself a smooth talker like Remy or some of the other guys in the Pack, but when he asked a woman out, he never got turned down. At least not since he'd gone through his change more than three years ago.

"Did I miss something?" he asked Tuffie. "She was flirting with me in there, wasn't she?"

The pit bull mix didn't say anything one way or the other, but the expression on her face seemed to indicate she agreed with him. Lacey Barton had been feeling him. The chemistry he'd been picking up on hadn't been a figment of his imagination. None of that mattered though, because she'd shot him down without a moment's hesitation. And damn, it stung like a son of a bitch.

Tuffie gave his hand a lick as he helped her into the backseat of his truck's extended cab. "Thanks, girl, I appreciate it. Don't worry about it. Dr. Barton's probably a closet cat person."

As he closed the door and climbed in the front, Tuffie's brows rose, as if to say she seriously doubted it but that he could go ahead and believe it if it made him feel better.

Chapter 2

LACEY WAS WIPING DOWN THE EXAM TABLE WHEN SHE FELT eyes on her. She looked up to see Wendy Bell standing in the doorway. Since it was the middle of the day, Lacey would have known this was a work-related visit even if her dark-haired friend hadn't been wearing her DPD uniform.

"I didn't know you were here," Lacey said. "Did you bring in another emergency?"

Wendy shook her head, her ponytail swinging back and forth. "Not really an emergency. I brought in a dehydrated rescue, but one of the vet techs put him on an IV a while ago. The little guy is going to be fine."

Lacey breathed a sigh of relief. Even before Wendy had been assigned to the relatively new Animal Cruelty Squad, she'd brought in strays and the occasional injured dog or cat. Now that she was with ACS, there tended to be less of the former and more of the latter, with the injuries being much worse. In her line of work, Wendy had to deal with a lot of nasty people who treated animals like they were nothing but disposable forms of entertainment. It was nice to hear that this time the situation hadn't involved some poor, horribly abused animal.

"You should have stuck your head in." Lacey tossed the disposable towel in the trash. "I was just giving a checkup to the cutest pit bull mix one of your DPD coworkers brought in—a guy from SWAT named Alex Trevino."

"Oh, I stuck my head in," Wendy said. "Just in time to hear you blow the guy off when he asked you out. Why would you turn down a hunk like that?"

Lacey laughed. Wendy was always on her about her love life—or lack thereof. "If you think he's so cute, why don't you go out with him?"

"Are you kidding me? I'd be all over that if I got the chance." Wendy leaned against the doorjamb and folded her arms. "But that's never going to happen. Alex Trevino only had eyes for you."

Lacey fought the urge to roll her eyes. "That's crazy! We just met. I won't deny that he's certainly cute, but if he was as into me as you seem to think, it's probably because he's like that with all the women he meets, just like every other guy out there."

Wendy frowned. "You are way too young to be so cynical."

"I'm not cynical. Just realistic."

Her friend probably would have argued the point, but one of the vet techs stuck her head in the door. "Lacey we have an emergency coming in—a dog ate a pair of panty hose. I'm getting the OR prepped for you."

"I'll be right there," Lacey told the vet tech, then turned to Wendy. "It looks like this discussion of my love life is going to have to wait until later."

And while she wished it wasn't because a dog had eaten a pair of panty hose, she was glad she didn't have to listen to Wendy nag her about her lack of male companionship.

~~~

Kelsey was on the couch doing homework when Lacey walked into the two-bedroom apartment they shared.

While the TV was on, the sound was so low you could barely hear it. Not that her sister was paying attention anyway. She was too focused on whatever was on her laptop. Around her, books and papers covered nearly every square inch of available space on both the couch and coffee table. Poor Kelsey looked like she was about to be eaten by the huge piles stacked around her. Lacey knew her sister had loaded up on extra courses this semester so she could finish her degree program at Regional Texas College early, but this was insane.

Before Lacey could say anything, a black lab mix trotted out from the back of the apartment and did excited laps around her feet.

"Hey, Leonardo! What have you been up to today?"

She laughed, petting him as he got busy checking out all the other scents she always came home covered in. He must have found one particularly interesting, because he spent a long time sniffing her right hand with blatant curiosity. When he was finally done, he gave her hand a lick, then headed into the kitchen to get some water. Over on the couch, her sister looked up from what she was doing.

"Hey, you're home." Kelsey set her laptop aside and waded out of the paperwork maze. "How long have you been standing there?"

"I just came in," Lacey said, dropping her purse and tote bag in the entryway so she could give Kelsey a hug.

A few inches shorter than Lacey, Kelsey had shoulder-length blond hair and a sprinkle of freckles across her nose. Even though Kelsey was twenty now and a sophomore in college, Lacey still thought of her as her baby sister. That was probably because Lacey had practically raised Kelsey since she was twelve, when their dad had bailed on them and their mom had stopped caring about anyone and anything.

"Did you eat anything yet?" Lacey asked.

"No. There's still half a pizza in the fridge from the other night, though. I was waiting for you to get home before I heated it up."

Lacey doubted that. Her sister tended to get lost in her schoolwork—which Lacey supposed was a good thing—but she sometimes worried that if she didn't check on Kelsey now and then, her sister wouldn't eat at all. Lacey started to head into the kitchen to wash up and make a salad to go with the pizza only to stop when she caught sight of the television.

She blinked. "Since when do you watch the news?"

Kelsey looked up as she scooped dry dog food into Leo's bowl. "I got a text from one of my friends telling me to turn it on. They're talking about that missing girl who goes to RTC—Abigail Elliott. It has everyone on campus scared to death."

Lacey didn't blame them. Just thinking about the missing girl—and the fact that nobody knew what had happened to her—had Lacey freaked out too. And thankful as heck it wasn't Kelsey.

As they ate, Lacey asked Kelsey how her nursing classes were going, but her sister was more interested in hearing about whether anything interesting had happened at the veterinary clinic. Lacey considered telling her about the dog with the appetite for panty hose but decided that was not exactly something that should be shared at the dinner table.

"A cop asked me out on a date," she said instead.

Kelsey choked on her diet soda, which led to a coughing fit that made Lacey wonder why she'd even brought up the SWAT cop in the first place. Yeah, Alex Trevino had been cute. Okay, more than cute. Actually, he was possibly the most attractive man she'd ever met. He had to be at least six foot four, and that tight T-shirt he had on showed off the kind of muscles that you usually only expected to see on a marble statue carved by one of the great masters in Italy.

Then there was his face. That strong jaw covered with the barest hint of scruff and those high cheekbones to go along with a pair of beautiful brown eyes and sensual mouth—they all fit together perfectly. The more she thought of him, the more she realized that attractive wasn't the right word, either. He was gorgeous.

In her experience, guys who were that good-looking were usually full of themselves, but Alex seemed like he was a pretty humble and down-to-earth person. And the way he cared about Tuffie made him seem like an absolute dream.

Lacey caught herself before she let out a loud, heartfelt sigh. Good Lord, she needed to get ahold of herself. She wasn't the kind of woman who went gaga over a guy, yet she'd practically swooned over Alex the moment he'd walked in.

On the other side of the table, Kelsey got her coughing fit under control, then took another sip of soda to clear her throat.

"You okay?" Lacey asked.

Her sister waved her hand. "Forget about that. You're going out on a date?"

Lacey scowled. "You don't have to sound so shocked. It's not like I don't go out."

Kelsey leaned back and gave her a look that said someone was full of crap—and it wasn't her. "Sure you do. I think the last time was when I was a junior in high school."

Lacey opened her mouth to deny it, but then realized she couldn't, because her sister was right. Crap, had it really been that long since she'd gone out?

"So, where are you going on your date?" Kelsey asked excitedly.

"Whoa! I never said I was going on a date with the guy." Lacey picked up her slice of pizza. "You asked me if anything interesting had happened today, and I said a cop asked me out."

Kelsey looked confused. "Why aren't you going out with him? Was he an asshole or something?"

"No! He was really nice."

"Then what's the big deal?"

Lacey shrugged and took a bite of pizza, chewing slowly. "I just started this new job. I need to focus on work right now."

Kelsey snorted. "Seriously? You're too busy making a good impression at the new office to go out on even one date?"

Lacey tried not to let her sister's words get to her. She loved Kelsey to no end, but the girl had a seriously naïve outlook on life. That was Lacey's fault, of course. She'd done her best to shelter Kelsey from all the crap that had happened after their dad had left. Looking back now, she realized she hadn't done Kelsey any favors. By shielding her sister from the harsh realities of life, Kelsey had grown up thinking there was no reason you couldn't have your cake and eat it too.

"Life is all about priorities, Kelsey, and right now, my priority is you and my new job. There'll be time for guys later."

Kelsey made a face and chomped down on her pizza. Not that Kelsey needed to say anything to make her position clear. There wasn't anything Lacey could say to change her sister's mind, so she didn't bother to try. She was just glad that Kelsey still lived at home, was too young to drink, and was more focused on college than on boys. As naive as her sister could sometimes be, it terrified Lacey to think what Kelsey might get into if she lived on campus with all the alcohol, guys, and parties. Lacey wouldn't even be able to sleep at night.

As the silence stretched out between them over the dinner table, Lacey wished again that she hadn't mentioned Alex. Meeting him had been nothing more than a chance encounter. Tuffie wasn't her regular patient, so it wasn't like she was ever going to see the man again.

She wasn't sure why that bummed her out so much.

—⁓—

Alex leaned against the wall outside the training classroom at the SWAT compound along with Max, Brooks, and two other members of the team, Hale Delaney and Zane Kendrick, when Remy jogged down the hallway. His hair was a mess, and he was tucking in his T-shirt as he ran.

"Am I late? Did Khaki start the training session yet?" Remy asked as he slid to a stop beside them.

"You're good. Training is running late." Alex jerked his head toward the door. "Khaki's over in the admin building with Everly and Jayna, helping them figure out the seating arrangement for the engagement party."

Remy frowned. "Cooper and Everly are going to have a seating chart for an engagement party. Seriously?"

Alex nodded as Remy combed his dark blond hair

back with his fingers. He and the team's armorer, Trevor McCall, tended to keep their hair a little longer than most of the other guys on the team, insisting women liked to run their fingers through it.

"I'm not even going to bother asking if you overslept or got stuck in traffic," Brooks said in his deep voice. "She smells familiar. Who is she?"

Remy grinned as he got his hair under control. "Vivian O'Neil. She felt bad about not waiting for me to get finished with that drug surveillance thing and made it up to me last night."

Alex shook his head. His nose told him that Remy had been with a woman last night, but unlike Brooks, she hadn't smelled familiar to him at all. That was likely why Gage and Xander had wanted him to take part in another one of Khaki's scent memorization exercises. She'd been putting a lot of effort into helping them identify different scents as well as hold on to those scents for long periods of time. Khaki's amazing nose was a new asset to the team, and Gage wanted her to try to help develop the same ability in the rest of them. Alex wasn't holding out much luck. His nose was okay but certainly nothing to write home about. And while Khaki's training was helping, he doubted it would ever really get his sense of smell to significantly improve.

But Gage had decided this training was a priority, so they were doing it. And with their drug task force duties on temporary hold at the moment, now was a good time for it.

The tests conducted on the drugs taken off the dealers they'd caught the other night had confirmed the stuff was definitely fireball. Even better, after serving warrants on the three dealers' residences, narcotics had recovered more than two hundred bags of the nasty stuff. Rodriguez was hoping they'd not only gotten the dangerous drug off the streets but had also arrested the people responsible for making it. Until the lawyers sorted this out though, they weren't going to know for sure.

Beside Alex, Remy glanced at his watch. "Any idea why it's taking Everly so long to come up with a simple seating chart? I mean, it's just a party, right?"

"Yeah, but I heard Everly say that she wants her family spread out among the tables so they're not all sitting around talking among themselves in French the whole night," Max said.

"That might be difficult, considering Everly's dad and brothers hate werewolves," Brooks pointed out. "Or at least they did up until a couple months ago."

Remy considered that. "I guess it's more complicated than I thought. But that's pretty much our extended werewolf pack in a nutshell—complicated."

Alex snorted. That was one hell of an understatement. It was kind of crazy really. For a long time, the SWAT team had been a pack of alpha males, working hard, playing harder, sweating and bleeding for each other and the city of Dallas. There'd been the occasional girlfriend among the guys, but for reasons they'd only recently started to understand, none of those relationships had ever worked out.

Everything had changed a year ago when Gage had met Mackenzie Stone, a reporter who'd been close to exposing their werewolf secret to the world until she and Gage realized they were each other's soul mates.

Up until then, few members of the Pack had even heard of the fairy-tale concept of *The One*, yet here was their alpha falling hard for a woman within a week of meeting her. Having a human know their secret had taken a little while to get used to, but it had turned out okay. Mac was seriously cool, and no one could begrudge Gage the happiness he'd found.

About the time everyone had gotten comfortable with the idea of having Mac around, Khaki Blake had joined the team and thrown them all for another loop. The new SWAT officer was also an alpha like the rest of them and as completely capable of kicking ass as any guy on the team. Alex and his teammates had been so psyched to find out female werewolves existed that they'd completely missed the part where Xander fell for Khaki.

A little while after that, their world had been flipped upside down again after Becker met Jayna Winston in the middle of a werewolf-on-werewolf firefight in a warehouse as she'd been pointing an automatic weapon at him and robbing the place. Considering that she and the rest of her pack of beta werewolves had been working as enforcers for the Albanian mob at the time, there should have been zero chance of a romance between her and Becker, but once a werewolf met *The One* for him, logic and reason got tossed out the window.

Maybe all those months of turmoil and insanity had taught Alex and the other guys on the team something, because when Cooper and Everly's romance had blown up in the Pack's face thanks to a frigging suicide bomber, it barely raised any eyebrows.

"Is it me, or does this whole marriage train seem to be moving fast?" Max asked.

Alex snorted. "You can say that again."

All the werewolves in the Pack lucky enough to meet their soul mates had fallen fast, but none of them had moved to get married as quickly as Cooper and Everly. Gage and Mac had been together for ten months before tying the knot. Xander and Khaki weren't even talking about it yet. Though to be honest, that could have been because they knew there was no way the DPD would let them stay on the SWAT team together if they found out they were in a relationship. And while Becker had moved in with Jayna and her beta pack within a couple of weeks of getting together, they didn't seem interested in rushing anything.

But Cooper and Everly's wedding plans were moving at warp speed. They'd met in June and were getting married in September—a month from now. Not that Alex didn't think it was real between Cooper and Everly. It was just scary how fast it was going. He and the other guys had been in the SWAT pack for years, and none of them had even sniffed *The One*. Now women were falling into their laps faster than a werewolf could catch them.

"Speaking of moving fast," Remy said, glancing at him. "What's going on with Lacey? She still playing hard to get?"

Alex bit back a growl. He knew he was going to regret telling Remy about Lacey. As the rest of the guys all turned to regard him with intense interest, he wished now that he'd kept his mouth shut. He'd only mentioned her to Remy because he thought the team's in-house Romeo might have a few thoughts on how to get the attractive vet to go out with him. Obviously, that had been a bad idea.

"Who's Lacey?" Max asked, his blue eyes curious.

Damn. This was exactly why he hadn't wanted to mention Lacey to anyone. Now his pack mates were going to jump to the conclusion that he met *The One*, and that wasn't even close to the truth.

Despite the fact that she turned him down, putting Lacey out of his mind hadn't been as easy as he thought. Against his better judgment, he'd stopped by the clinic several times over the past few days on the off chance she'd changed her mind about going out with him. She hadn't. He was pretty sure that meant Lacey wasn't *The One* for him. He might be ready to give up on her, but he was running out of lame excuses to stop in and see her. He could only buy Tuffie so much in the way of food, dental treats, and chew toys. Lacey was going to think he was a stalker.

"Lacey is the new vet at the animal clinic," he finally said. "I met her when I took Tuffie in the other day. I asked her out. She turned me down. It wasn't a big deal."

Alex expected the guys to say something sarcastic, maybe point out that Lacey's lack of interest in him was likely just a sign of her good taste. But instead, they shook their heads and acknowledged how much that must suck. Too bad. He could use a little ribbing to get his mind off Lacey.

"Did you try the flowers like I suggested?" Remy asked. "Women love them. There's, like, a direct connection between their noses and their hearts."

Alex almost winced. He'd tried flowers, but Lacey hadn't seemed very impressed. In fact, when he stopped to see her the next day, the flowers had been sitting on the receptionist's desk. Lacey hadn't even bothered to take them home.

He gave Remy a wry smile. "Something tells me that Lacey isn't the kind of woman who likes flowers."

Remy opened his mouth to say something but closed it again as Khaki came running down the hall. Tall and athletic, she wore the same SWAT uniform they did and had her long dark hair pulled back in a bun.

"Sorry I'm late," she said. "Everly was having a crisis she needed help with."

Brooks frowned. "Everything okay with the engagement party?"

"I think so." Khaki glanced over her shoulder at them as she opened the door to the training room and led the way inside. "Just make sure all the guys know whom they can talk openly to and whom they can't. Even though her father and brothers know about werewolves, the rest of her family doesn't. Everly doesn't want one of us slipping up and exposing the existence of werewolves to one of her brothers' wives—or their kids. She doesn't want any of them freaking out during the party."

"Much better to wait until the wedding for the rest of her family to find out that she's marrying a werewolf," Alex said sarcastically as he followed the other guys in.

"Today's exercise is simple," Khaki said after they had all assembled inside. "Yesterday, I gave you a few minutes to smell a piece of cloth that I'd sprayed with a particular cologne. The day before, I did the same thing with another scrap of fabric covered with a different fragrance." She gestured to the cardboard boxes on the table along the far wall. "Each of those holds a single piece of cloth. Two are ones you already smelled. The other three are decoys sprayed with a similar but different cologne. All you have to do is tell me which two are the right ones and which cloth came from which day. There's no time limit, so just relax and let yourself get lost in the scents."

Alex got a sinking feeling in the pit of his stomach. Until they'd started this training with Khaki, he'd always thought his nose was as good as any other werewolf in the Pack. He could pick up on all the usual scents they ran into on a frequent basic in their line of work, like gunpowder, explosives, drugs, or alcohol. He could tell the difference between two people's scents and easily identify if they belonged to a man, a woman, or a werewolf. He could even pick up on subtle smells, like the one a woman gave off when she was aroused. But Trey knew exactly who was at the gate of the compound before Alex even realized anyone was there. Brooks recognized the scent of each woman Remy hung out with. And Max could pick up the scent of a girl he'd danced with the night before, even when she was all the way across a crowded bar. Alex's nose wasn't good enough to do any of that stuff.

Khaki walked along the table, taking the lid off each box. "The scents you memorized the past two days are in your heads. You just have to figure out where you put them."

Alex wasn't sure he could discern one cologne from another, much less remember which piece of cloth he'd smelled before. But he leaned over the first box and took a deep breath anyway. He immediately picked up the strong smell of a man's masculine cologne. Unfortunately, when he sniffed the second box, it smelled the same as the first one. Worse, he couldn't say whether he'd smelled either fragrance before.

He moved to the next box, trading places with the other guys as they each took their turn, but he didn't recognize the scent coming from there, either. Shit, he was never going to be able to get this. He glanced over at Max and saw him grinning. Clearly, his pack mate wasn't having any problem. Alex had always been a competitive guy, and it irritated the hell out of him that his teammates could do this and he couldn't. There wasn't anything he couldn't do physically as a werewolf, and when it came to tactical techniques like shooting, climbing, rappelling, hand-to-hand, you name it, he could it and do it well. But for some reason, this scent stuff seemed to be beyond him, and the harder he pushed, the worse his nose functioned.

If that weren't bad enough, his claws and fangs slipped out. He tried to get the damn things to retract, but they refused to behave. *Shit.*

"You know, letting your inner wolf out isn't necessarily a bad thing," Khaki said from beside him. "I've discovered lately that the further I push my shift, the better my nose works."

He glanced at her. "Really?"

She smiled. "Yeah. Give it a shot."

Why the hell not? It couldn't hurt. Ignoring his protruding fangs and claws, he leaned over the last box in the row and took a good sniff. The scent seemed richer and deeper than it had been.

"Damn, it really does work better," he muttered.

He probably shouldn't have been surprised. His pack mates who had a better handle on their werewolf abilities—definitely did better at this scent training stuff. The fact that Khaki, who seemed to be gaining control over her inner wolf ten times faster than anyone else in the Pack ever had, also had the best nose on the team probably wasn't a coincidence. Alex wouldn't be shocked if she learned how to shift into a real wolf soon.

"Can you push your shift a little more?" Khaki asked softly. "Let go and see how much it helps."

Alex tried to follow her advice but immediately ran up against another obstacle. While he could definitely pick up scents better, he wasn't in any more control of his inner wolf than he was of his nose. His ability to shift had always been limited to the basics. With the exception of those rare moments when he was really fired up, claws and fangs were as far as his shift went.

He growled and pushed harder, breaking a sweat as he tried to make his fangs extend further. They slid out another half inch before he ended up slamming into the same damn brick wall that always kept him from truly connecting with his werewolf nature. And while he had an inkling about which pieces of cloth were the ones Khaki had shown them earlier, it wasn't much more than a guess.

"I think this is one of the scents you had us smell the other day," he said, pointing at the third box.

"Excellent," Khaki said. "How about the other one?"

Alex tried again, but he'd already lost control over his inner wolf. Just like that, his claws and fangs disappeared—and so did his improved sense of smell.

He shook his head. "Nothing. It's gone."

Khaki thumped him on the arm. "Don't worry about it. You did really well, and you're getting better. Your nose will improve as you gain more control over your inner wolf. By the time you're capable of a full shift, your nose will be as good as mine."

Alex doubted that was ever going to happen, but he didn't correct her. He looked around the room and saw that everyone but Hale had already left. Well, at least there was one werewolf in the Pack whose nose was worse than his. Hale had a good excuse for having a crappy sniffer, though. His nose had been smashed in by some asshole when he was a teenager, and it hadn't worked right even before he'd gone through his change.

Alex snorted. Great. He'd beaten a werewolf with a broken sniffer. He should be so proud.

He would have been even more disgusted with himself if it wasn't for the fact that he couldn't imagine ever needing a werewolf super smeller. If they needed someone with a great nose, they had Khaki or one of the guys. Because if anyone ever had to depend on his nose to save them, they were screwed.

Chapter 3

"SOMEONE DRIVING BY HEARD THE SOUNDS OF DOGS fighting in there last night around one in the morning." The uniformed officer motioned toward the big junk-yard several yards from where Lacey was standing with Wendy and the rest of the ACS team. "They said there were a bunch of cars parked up and down the street and a lot of people laughing and shouting. The county sent a patrol car out a couple of hours later, but the place had been locked up by then."

Lacey cursed silently. She knew what all that meant—a dogfighting event. This place was well outside the more populated parts of the city, so they probably thought no one would be around to hear anything. If that person with a conscience who happened to drive by at just the right time hadn't called the police, no one would have been the wiser. As hard as Wendy and the other members of her squad worked, there was only so much they could do. Dallas had a long history of dogfighting, and it only seemed to be getting worse. The number of dead and injured dogs they'd found lately made her sick to the stomach even thinking about it.

Wendy left the patrolman to keep an eye on Lacey while she and the other officer from the Animal Cruelty Squad served the warrant that would get them into the huge, sprawling complex of old cars, racks of repair parts, and do-it-yourself garage facilities.

Lacey clutched the shoulder strap of her big first-aid

bag and fought to control the butterflies filling her stomach. She'd been going out with Wendy and the other cops from ACS for a while now, but that still didn't mean she was used to these situations. There was a good chance she was going to see some broken and abused dogs in there, and that was something she would never get used to.

She used to wait back at the vet clinic while Wendy went out on these calls. Wendy would find the injured animals and get them transported to the clinic as fast as she could, but after four horribly injured dogs had died en route, Lacey decided that had to change. There was simply no way she was going to sit around and hope that the dogs survived long enough to reach her. She needed to be there when the animals were found.

Wendy hadn't been very supportive of the idea at first, but once she realized it was actually a benefit having someone who knew dogs so well on the team—and that Lacey was smart enough to stay out of harm's way while the police were doing their thing—she'd finally relented.

"I'm just the caretaker here, Officer," the old man who answered the door said after Wendy showed him the warrant. "I ain't the owner and have no authority to let you in here. The owner wouldn't like it much."

"It doesn't matter what the owner likes or doesn't like," Wendy said firmly. "This piece of paper means we get to go in there and search the property for signs of dogfighting. You can either let us in or wait all cool and cozy in the back of a patrol car while we let ourselves in."

The crotchety old man squinted at Wendy from behind his glasses and grumbled something under his

breath but let them in. The minute they were inside, he
pulled out his old-style flip phone and started punching
buttons. Lacey didn't doubt that the man was calling
the owner.

A few minutes later, Wendy came back outside, her
face grim.

"It's bad, but I don't think the dogs are here anymore," she said.

Lacey's heart sank. If there weren't any dogs around,
it likely meant that all of the animals had already been
disposed of.

Wendy led her into the junkyard, then took a cir-
cuitous route toward the back, which opened up to an
obvious fighting pit—a chain-link fence set up in a
circle fifteen feet across with a single makeshift gate
to let animals and handlers into the ring. Lacey didn't
have to look hard to see the splatters of blood everywhere or chunks of flesh. The ground all around the
pit had been trampled flat. A lot of people had been
standing around watching.

"I told you there weren't any dogs here," the caretaker said from behind them. "You can all just shove
off now."

Wendy pointed at the dark reddish-brown stains on
the ground inside the fence. "Where'd all the blood
come from then?"

"What blood?" The old man squinted, trying to see.
"Oh, that. It was probably just some of the boys goofin'
off and gettin' into a fight."

Wendy walked over to pick up a bloody bit of fluff
lying on the ground just inside the gate of the fenced-in
circle, then held it up. "So I guess those boys have fur?"

The old man started stammering and trying to talk

his way out of the lie, but Lacey ignored him. Right now, she was more interested in the clear trail of blood leading away from the pit. She followed it, knowing it would probably stop wherever the dogs' bodies had been loaded into a vehicle, but she had to know for sure.

The old man moved faster than Lacey would ever have imagined, jumping in front of her and cutting her off. "You cops can't just go wanderin' around wherever you want. I know my rights!"

"I'm not a cop," Lacey told him.

At times like these, it was probably a good thing she didn't own a gun. Lacey shoved past the man without waiting for Wendy or any of the other officers to intercede. She didn't need their help to deal with a piece of crud like this. She despised people who abused animals, and the anger she felt made her fearless.

She followed the trail of blood until it stopped cold at the edge of a gravel road that circled around the property. Behind her, Wendy was arguing with the old man, but Lacey tuned them out, more interested in the separate trail of blood heading off to the left. She broke into a run, ignoring the caretaker shouting at her to stop and Wendy urging her to slow down.

Lacey was moving so fast she almost missed the sudden right turn the trail made. She quickly doubled back and saw that the blood disappeared under the back end of a Honda Accord. She held up her hand, motioning everyone else back, then dropped to her knees and leaned forward to get a look under the car. Her heart broke at the sight of the three pit bulls she found there, bloody and savaged beyond belief. Only one of the dogs was even conscious, and he growled at her in a menacing tone.

"Easy there, big boy," she whispered. "I'm here to help you guys, I promise."

She slipped her first-aid kit off her shoulder, then dropped flat on her belly, wiggling forward to get herself under the back of the car. The dog growled again, but it was halfhearted, like he didn't have the energy to even put up a good front.

Lacey ignored Wendy and the other cops as they told her not to go under the car, that it was too dangerous and they would get the dogs out another way. But these guys didn't have time for another way, and they sure as hell couldn't survive being dragged out with a dog catcher's noose.

She stopped short of the conscious dog, assessing not only his damage, but the injuries of the other two animals. Tears stung her eyes. Their ears were tattered, their faces and necks torn and lacerated, and their chests and shoulders matted with thick, clotted blood. But at least they were alive. All three of them needed urgent care though, and likely hours of surgery. How they'd been able to drag themselves this far was anyone's guess. If she was going to help any of them, she had to deal with the conscious guy first.

"You did a good job hiding out under this car, but I'm here now, and you need to let me help you," she told him.

She moved closer to the dog inch by inch, speaking in a calm but assertive voice that she hoped the pit bull would take as authoritative and alpha-like. It took five minutes to get close enough to touch the dog, and by then, the poor guy had dropped his chin to the dirt in exhaustion. She gently ran her hand along his back.

"Come on, baby. Let's get you out of here."

Lacey worried the dog wouldn't want to leave his friends, but he was too tired to resist her prodding hands. Or maybe he actually trusted her. Either way, he let her nudge him out from under the car, where two of Wendy's coworkers met them with glove-covered hands. Both officers were good with dogs, having a gentle, calming energy about them that kept the pit bull from getting upset as they moved him away from the car.

Another cop handed her a length of plywood, which she used like a makeshift litter, gently moving the dogs on it one at a time, then sliding them out. In full light, all three dogs looked even worse than she'd thought. How the heck had they made it through the night?

She looked up to see Wendy and another cop leading the old man away in cuffs. The caretaker complained the whole way, alternating between stating that he had no idea where those dogs had come from and declaring that he didn't see what the big deal was.

"They're just dogs," he grumbled.

Lacey focused her attention on the injured animals, knowing that if she didn't, she'd give in to the urge to throw herself at the wasted piece of humanity and rip him to pieces. The other officers left her alone as she worked to get the three dogs stabilized for the trip to the clinic. They usually did that—one, because they knew there wasn't a lot they could do to help, and two, because they knew she hated to let anyone see her cry. She always cried when she worked on abused animals.

As she set up IV lines and treated the worst of the lacerations with trauma foam, she mentally tallied the extent of the dogs' injuries. They were looking at a lot of surgeries and care. The owner of the clinic where she

worked provided everything she needed for the surgeries at cost—that had been part of the agreement when
she'd taken the job—but she'd also cover some of the
cost of caring for the animals herself. Wendy and her
ACS team would come up with donations to cover the
rest. While there were too many people in the world who
were horrible to animals, there were also just as many
who were amazingly generous.

For reasons she couldn't really understand, Lacey
found herself thinking about Alex as she treated the
injured dogs. The big cop had stopped by the clinic
every day since their first meeting under the guise of
buying food, treats, and toys for that adorable pit bull
mix of his, but it was obvious he'd come to see her—
and ask her out. She was flattered. The guy was sinfully
gorgeous, with an unbelievable body and a voice that
made it hard not to stare at his mouth every time he
uttered a single word. It didn't hurt that he had an adorable Northeastern accent, either. She'd be a big, fat liar
if she said she didn't enjoy talking to him. But she had
no intention of going out with him—be it for dinner,
lunch, or coffee—and she'd turned him down politely
each time he'd asked.

Unfortunately, Alex was making it darn hard to
resist. He was always so relaxed and casual, and when
he smiled at her, she couldn't help smiling back, even
as she hated herself for sending mixed signals. And then
the other day, he'd shown up with flowers. She didn't
think guys even did stuff like that anymore. While the
bouquet was beautiful, she hadn't kept them. The way
she saw it, if she wasn't going to entertain his repeated
offers for a date, it didn't seem right to keep the flowers,
no matter how sweet the gesture happened to be.

Wendy thought she was insane, of course. "He's gorgeous, charming, muscular, and has all his teeth, not to mention a job. You obviously like him, so why the hell won't you give him the time of day?"

Lacey wished she could explain it to her friend, but it was too complicated to get into. The truth was, while there was a part of her that desperately wanted to give in and go out with Alex, she knew it would only lead to trouble. She had no doubt that if they went on a date, she'd have a wonderful time. She was also just as sure that if they ended up in bed together, she'd enjoy the hell out of it.

The problem was that Alex didn't strike her as the kind of guy looking for a quick roll in the hay. They'd go out, have fun, maybe end up in bed at some point— then he'd want to keep seeing her. She supposed there were a lot of women who would love to have a relationship with someone like Alex, but she wasn't one of them. She'd never been in anything even remotely resembling a long-term relationship with a guy, and she didn't imagine she ever would.

She couldn't go out with Alex because she feared the date would go so well he'd want another one.

God, that made her sound crazy. Maybe she was. But if so, she had her reasons. After all the deadbeats her mom had gone out with after her dad left, she didn't have a high opinion of men in general. In her experience, they didn't stick around.

Lacey was still musing over those thoughts as she finished getting all three dogs ready for transport. They were weak, but the IVs had already worked miracles on them. She was just getting ready to transfer them to her SUV when she looked up and saw Wendy heading in her direction. Behind her, there were two men who couldn't have stuck out more in a junkyard if they tried. Both wore suits and ties, though the clothing worn by the older, more frail-looking of the two was obviously much more expensive than that sported by the younger, powerfully built guy with him.

"This is Mr. Bensen, the owner," Wendy said, her voice tight as she motioned to the older man. "And this is his chief of security, Mr. Pendergraff. They were of the opinion that we must have been mistaken about someone running a dogfight on this property. They were quite surprised that we found injured dogs, and insisted on seeing them."

Bensen had an unhealthy, yellow-brown cast to his complexion that screamed medical issues in Lacey's mind, but she forgot about it as the man gave the injured dogs a disdainful look. It was like he was offended the animals had the audacity to bleed on his property. The dismissive expression on his face was enough to make her hate the man. He'd known about the dogfighting all right. His only surprise was that his people had failed to clean up properly.

She turned her attention to the other man—Pendergraff—and had to stop herself from taking a step back. The man had pale skin, platinum-white hair, and cornflower-blue eyes with dark pupils. As a medical professional, Lacey knew she shouldn't let the man's genetic condition affect her, but he was scary-looking as hell. It wasn't just the man's albino condition that freaked her out, either. It was the ragged scars across the left side of the man's face and his dead, emotionless stare. He regarded the dogs as if they were discarded junk like the rest of the stuff in this place. She could definitely see a man like him running a dogfight.

"How do you know these animals were hurt in a dog-fighting event?" Bensen asked caustically. "Maybe they slipped through the fence and got in a fight with each other. They're dogs. That's what they do."

Lacey advanced on the old man so fast that his albino security guard took a step forward to intercept her.

"That's not what they do," she ground out. "It's what sick, depraved people make them do. They put them in chains, then choke and goad them until they're half-mad from pain and fear. Then they put them in a small pit with another dog. They attack each other because they think they're about to die."

Bensen raised a brow. "You certainly don't have to get so excited about it. Or look at me like I'm the culprit. I run over a dozen different business endeavors in this city and don't have the time or the inclination to keep an eye on every one of them. If someone here was responsible for staging a dogfight, you can arrest them."

"We will," Wendy assured him. "We took your caretaker in for questioning, but I'd be interested in knowing where you were last night."

Bensen laughed as if that were the silliest question anyone had asked him. "Not here, I can assure you. I was at a party with several investors. The mayor was there as well. I can give you his number if you need to verify where I was."

"That might just be necessary," Wendy said. "But before we do that, I'd appreciate if you and Mr. Pendergraff could come down to the station to fill out a statement and get this all straightened out."

Pendergraff didn't blink. Bensen, on the other hand, looked like he'd just sucked a lemon.

"I have an hour or two to spare, but then I need to

be on my way," he said. "Unless you actually intend to
arrest me for this?"

Wendy didn't answer but merely pointed the men
toward the exit. "I'll call you later to find out how the
dogs are doing," she said to Lacey.

"What about Bensen? You know he's fully aware that
someone was holding a dogfight on his property."

Wendy sighed. "Yeah, you and I know it, but I doubt
I'll get a chance to prove it, not with Bensen's money
and connections. The DA isn't a big fan of prosecuting
these kind of cases to begin with, and he's definitely
against it if the defendant doesn't fit his idea of the typical person who runs a dogfighting ring. I'll be lucky if
Bensen spends an hour at the station."

Lacey felt her hackles rise. People like Bensen
thought they could get away with anything. "But you'll
still investigate him, right?"

Wendy shrugged. "I'll do what I can. We don't have
the budget or manpower to conduct any real investiga-
tions. Plus, the DA will scream bloody murder if he hears
we're looking at an upstanding citizen like Bensen."

Lacey seethed at the unfairness of it all as she helped
the ACS officers carefully move the dogs to her SUV.
She wished there was something she could do to help
Wendy catch this asshole. But all she could do was care
for the dogs he'd almost killed.

Alex slammed on the SUV's brakes and slid the SWAT
vehicle to a halt in front of the big five-story building on the RTC campus. A moment later, Max and
Brooks arrived in a second SUV, parking beside him
and Remy. This part of the campus was almost eerily

quiet. Then again, you'd expect that after a school had been put into lockdown.

Brooks got out and strode over to meet the elderly campus security guard and a DPD patrol officer heading in their direction. Typically, Mike or Xander would be heading up the response team, but since Brooks had already been running the crew as part of the drug task force, Gage had put the Pack's big senior corporal in charge.

"What do we have?" Brooks asked as Alex, Remy, and Max pulled weapons, tactical vests, and radio gear out of the SUVs.

"The assailant was seen going into the science building about ten minutes ago," the uniformed officer said. "He was half naked, staggering around, bleeding, and swinging a big knife at anyone who got near him. He cut several people, but we have no confirmed fatalities. My partner and I cleared out a few stray students running around, then locked down the campus, including three classes in there." He jerked his thumb at the science building. "One is on the second floor, and two are on the fourth. All the rooms have heavy metal doors, and we thought it safer to leave the students in there rather than risk bringing them out when we didn't have a good location on the assailant."

"Good call," Brooks said. "If all he has is a knife, he'll never get through those doors. Do you have a perimeter set up around the building?"

The DPD officer nodded. "There are three exits, and we have officers on all of them."

"Any chance the guy slipped out before the perimeter went up?" Brooks asked.

"Don't think so," the cop said. "A lot of people saw

him go in, and no one saw him come out. Unfortunately, no one knows where he came from."

Alex loaded his M4 carbine, checking to make sure the safety was on, then slung it over his back. Taking the radio headset Max held out, he slipped the bud in his ear. By the time he and the other guys were ready, Brooks was on the line and calling out orders.

"Alex and Max, you two head into the building and get me a situation report. Remy, you figure out where the hell this guy came from. I want to make sure all that blood he had on him was his own."

The uniformed officer gave Brooks a dubious look. "You're going to clear a building that size with just two of your guys? Want a couple of us to go in with you?"

Brooks shook his head. "I appreciate the offer, but if that guy is bleeding as much as you say, it won't be very hard to track him down in there. Plus, we really need you to keep the perimeter clear of people."

But it would be difficult to do with regular cops along for the ride, Alex thought. He was heading for the front door of the science building with Max when the campus security guard spoke.

"What about your other guy?" he asked Brooks. "You think he can figure out where this crazy guy came from by himself?"

As Max pulled open the main doors of the building and led the way in, Alex glanced over his shoulder to see Brooks grin. "Officer Boudreaux was raised in the swamps of Louisiana. If it walks, crawls, or slithers, he can track it."

Alex's mouth twitched. Understatement there. When it came to finding someone, Remy was the best. The big front doors clanged closed behind him and Max before

Alex could hear any more, but no doubt the cop and
security guard thought Brooks was insane.

As the quiet of the building surrounded them, Alex
and Max drew their pistols and moved toward the big
central staircase that dominated the entryway of the science building. Max's nose was better than his for sure,
but in this case, it didn't matter. The distinct metallic
scent of blood was something that any werewolf could
pick up, no matter how crappy their sniffer was.

There were dark red droplets about every three feet
along the floor, with a few smears here and there along
the walls, as if the man had put his hands out occasionally for balance.

"We have a track," Alex said softly into his mic.
"Heading toward the second floor."

"Roger that," Brooks said. "Witnesses only saw a
knife, but I still want you two to be careful in there."

"Copy that," Alex answered.

He and Max climbed the stairs, covering each other
as they moved higher. Like Brooks said, no one had seen
a gun on this guy, but that didn't mean he didn't have
one. If the guy was so inclined, a stairwell like this was
the perfect place to ambush some cops. But the blood
droplets—and the man's scent that accompanied them—
kept leading straight up the stairs without any indication
that the guy had even hesitated at the second- or third-
floor landing.

"Where the hell was this guy going?" Max whispered.

Alex shrugged. "I guess we'll find out soon enough."

When the trail led straight past the fourth floor, then
the fifth, Alex wondered if maybe he and Max had
missed something, but then he saw the bloody smear on
the railing leading up to the roof.

"The guy's on the roof," Alex said into the mic. "Looks like he headed straight there the moment he entered the building. Anyone have a visual on him from down there?"

"Negative," Brooks's voice came back a moment later.

The door to the roof was wide open, blood smeared all over the inside of it. A quick peek outside revealed a gravel-covered roof and a knee-high wall that was probably there to keep people from accidently falling off the five-story building. No sign of the guy, though. Maybe he'd passed out. If all the blood they saw was his, that was a distinct possibility.

He and Max stepped onto the roof and cautiously made their way around the side of the stairway enclosure, only to stop in their tracks. The man was standing on the far side of the roof. White with dark, shaggy hair and a light scruff along his jaw, he couldn't have been any more than twenty-five. He was wearing a pair of plaid golf shorts and nothing else, and he was bleeding from dozens of cuts along his chest, stomach, arms, and legs.

As Alex watched, the man stabbed the tip of his long kitchen knife into the muscle of his upper forearm, slowly cutting upward until he'd opened a serious gash two inches long. Then he poked his fingers into the wound and dug around like he was looking for something.

Max stepped back a few feet, whispering into his mic as Alex slowly walked toward the man. The crunch of his boots on the gravel distracted the man from what he was doing, and he jerked his head up to stare at Alex with unfocused eyes. Muttering something unintelligible, he lunged with the knife, slashing it back and forth through the air. Clearly, he didn't want Alex coming any closer.

Alex released his M4, letting it hang from the strap as he held up his hands. "It's okay, buddy. I'm not here to hurt you. I just want to help. Can you put down the knife?"

The man cocked his head to one side, reminding Alex of a confused animal. Alex wasn't sure if he was on drugs or had mental issues, but he was leaning toward the former.

"Drop the knife, guy. We can deal with this."

Alex tried to make his voice as soft and soothing as he could, and for a moment, it seemed to work. The man's eyes cleared a little, and his arm started coming down. But then his gaze darted to the air over Alex's head, and a look of pure terror came into his eyes. He viciously sliced at the air in front of him with the knife, then flailed at himself, uncaring that he was gashing his arm.

Shit, if Alex didn't do something soon, this guy was going to slash his own throat.

The moment Alex lunged, the man threw the knife at him. Alex ducked under the spinning blade, closing the distance between them. Eyes wide, the guy turned and ran toward the edge of the roof.

Double shit. The kid was going to throw himself off the building.

Alex surged forward as hard as he could, almost losing his footing on the loose gravel of the rooftop. Behind him, he heard Max racing after them, but his teammate was too far away. If he didn't stop the kid from jumping, the guy was dead.

Growling, Alex pushed harder, feeling his fangs and claws coming out as his body shifted automatically in

response to the urgency of the situation. Letting the terrified kid see him like this was obviously a bad idea, but
it wasn't like there was anything he could do about it, so
he simply gave in to his inner wolf and accepted all the
help he could get.

The kid went over the knee-high wall at the edge
of the roof, his arms flailing and his hands slapping at
things only he could see. He didn't even seem to realize
he was about to fall to his death.

Alex leaped through the air, grabbing the guy's
bloody forearm before he completely disappeared from
view. The kid's momentum pulled Alex forward, and he
fell, slamming chest first into the low wall, his head and
shoulders hanging over the five-story drop. Alex barely
got a grip on the edge before he went completely over.
Below him, Brooks, the cops, and the older security
guard stared up as the insane scene played out. He only
prayed he was too far away for any of them to see his
fangs and claws.

Max grabbed Alex by the belt, keeping him from
being dragged over by the kid's weight. "I got you,"
he said. "Get a good grip on him, and I'll drag both of
you up."

The kid didn't make it easy on them. He flailed
around like mad, grunting and hollering, slapping and
clawing at Alex's hand like he was fighting to get away
from a monster. As much as Alex hated to do it, he dug
his claws into the man's wrist. It was either that or let
him fall. Whatever demons had sent him jumping off the
roof were apparently still there, and the kid was doing
anything he could to get away from them.

He was much stronger than any normal person had a
right to be, and it took Alex and Max working together

to keep him under control after they finally got him back on the roof.

"Drugs?" Max asked as they carried him down the steps.

Alex jerked his hand back to keep the kid from biting it. "Probably."

"You think it's fireball?"

Alex hoped not. He'd been so sure they'd gotten that crap off the street, but his instincts were telling him they hadn't. "Maybe."

That hope got dashed when they finally got downstairs and Brooks told them to hook up with Remy at a dorm on the far side of the campus after the paramedics sedated the kid and loaded him into an ambulance.

"I have to finish up with campus security and school officials, but you shouldn't have a problem finding Remy," Brooks added. "Just look for the dorm with the ambulances in front of it. You can't miss them."

Either the lockdown had been called off, or people were ignoring it. There had to be fifty students outside the dorm when Alex and Max got there. Luckily, DPD had arrived on the scene and were keeping everyone away from the entrance. He and Max found Remy in a room on the second floor, along with two paramedics who were strapping an unconscious red-haired girl to a gurney. They had already rigged her up to a mobile ECG monitor and put a breathing mask on her, but she didn't look good.

"I tracked the assailant here," Remy said. "The door was halfway open, and when I came in, I found her passed out on the bed. At first, I thought she was just sleeping—or drunk—until I heard how slowly her heart was beating. My guess is an overdose."

Alex and the other guys stepped aside as the grim-faced paramedics hurriedly pushed the gurney through the door and into the hallway. Now that the room wasn't as crowded, Alex could see the pile of empty beer bottles and stack of equally empty pizza boxes, along with drug paraphernalia.

Remy jerked his head at the stuff. "I found a couple baggies of fireball too."

Alex ground his jaw. *Shit.* Either they'd grabbed the wrong dealers, or there was a whole lot more of this drug on the street than they'd ever imagined. Both of those things scared the hell out of him and pissed him off at the same time.

Chapter 4

"DID YOU EVEN HEAR A WORD I JUST SAID?" REMY demanded.

Alex gave himself a mental shake. "What?"

Remy glanced at him from behind the wheel. Remy had offered to drive back from RTC, and Alex had gladly let him. He hadn't been in the mood to fight Dallas traffic after his run-in with the strung-out kid on the roof. One gut-wrenching battle per morning, thank you very much. But not driving had left him free to think, and while he'd certainly thought about fireball and what had happened at the college, he also found himself daydreaming about a particular beautiful veterinarian.

"You still thinking about Lacey?" Remy laughed as he stopped the SUV at an intersection. "From the look on your face, I'll take that as a yes."

Alex frowned. "How'd you know?"

Remy shrugged as he took off again. "You get this thoughtful smile on your face every time you talk about her. Since you had the same look on your face just now, it wasn't hard to figure out what was going on in that thick skull of yours."

Alex thought about that. He didn't smile very often, mostly because he was a serious person at heart. But something about Lacey made him happy. Even if she wouldn't go out with him.

"You going to stop by and ask her out again?" Remy asked.

"I don't think so." Alex gazed out the side window, taking in the skyscrapers with their reflective windows as they passed. "It's kind of in that category of the definition of insanity. You know, doing the same thing over and over the same way, expecting a different result. At a certain point, I have to accept that Lacey doesn't want to have anything to do with me."

"Is that so shocking?" Remy snorted. "I'm your pack mate, and I barely want to have anything to do with you."

Alex pulled a face. "Very funny."

"I wasn't trying to be funny. I completely understand why being ignored by a woman is bothering you." He shook his head. "No, wait. I really don't."

"Thanks for that," Alex said drily.

"Anytime," Remy said. "Look, I hate to point out the obvious, but there are a lot of other women out there besides Lacey. It makes me wonder what the big deal is about her. Did you ever think that maybe there's something going on here beyond simple sexual attraction?"

Alex considered that. Since Remy had brought it up, there was no use denying his thoughts had been heading in that direction too. "You think she might be *The One* for me?"

Remy snorted. "*The One*? God, no. I wasn't thinking that at all. I was simply speculating that there had to be some deeper meaning to the fact that you—a werewolf—are attracted to a vet who specializes in dogs. Maybe you're just looking to get fixed."

Alex growled. If Remy weren't driving, he would have leaned over and punched him.

His friend chuckled. "Sorry, guy, I'm just messing with you. Seriously, you really think you've met *The One* for you?"

Alex shifted in his seat. Damn, he hated talking about personal crap like this. "I don't frigging know. All I know is that I'm really attracted to her, and I can tell she's attracted to me too. I mean, pheromones don't lie, right? There's some serious arousal going on when we flirt, but when I bring up the subject of us going out, she slams a door in my face. It'd be depressing if it wasn't so confusing."

Remy didn't say anything—which Alex supposed was better than his wiseass comments.

"Maybe it's Lacey, not you," he finally said.

Alex frowned. "What the hell does that mean?"

"That maybe she has a thing about not dating cops," Remy explained. "Would that be so shocking? There are lots of women out there who avoid relationships with cops because they know how tough it can be."

Huh. Alex hadn't really thought about that, but it made sense. He knew a lot of guys in the DPD who had watched relationships fall apart because of the job. "Okay, let's say you're right. What about the attraction I'm picking up on? Doesn't that count for something?"

"Something tells me that Lacey thinks with her head, not her heart. And certainly not with her hormones."

Alex clenched his jaw. "So, what, I should just give up on her?"

It was crazy. He and Lacey hadn't even gone on a date, and already, the thought of not seeing her made his chest ache.

"I didn't say that," Remy told him. "But maybe you need to stop with the direct approach and instead come at her from a different angle."

Now he was really confused. "Like what?"

He didn't remember Gage, Xander, Becker, or

Cooper having to work this hard to get the attention of the women they thought were *The One* for them—not that he was sure Lacey was *The One* for him yet.

"Start by finding out what kind of stuff she's into. Get into her world that way, and see if it helps." Remy gave him a sidelong glance. "One thing for damn sure, stop being so obvious about how interested you are. Not only does that give her all the power in the situation, it's also a sure way to blow any chance you have with her. You need to play it cool and let her think that you've lost interest in her."

That seemed counterintuitive to Alex. Then again, Remy didn't have trouble getting women to go out with him, so maybe he knew more about the subject.

"That works for you?" Alex asked. "Playing it cool when a woman isn't interested in you, I mean."

Remy shrugged. "Hell if I know. I've never met a woman who wasn't interested in me. I'm just making up this crap in the hope that it helps you."

Wonderful. "And if it doesn't? Then what?"

Remy glanced at him as he pulled the SUV into the parking lot of the SWAT compound. "Then you'll just have to accept the fact that Lacey has extremely good taste and is way out of your league."

Now that they were safely parked, Alex gave in to his earlier urge and thumped his friend in the shoulder hard enough to make something crack. "Thanks."

Remy shrugged it off with a laugh. "That's what pack mates are for."

—∿∿—

The barking in the no-kill animal shelter's kennel was so loud, Lacey could barely hear herself think. But that was okay. She loved volunteering here on the weekends anyway. This place brought in tons of strays and abandoned dogs, and a lot of local veterinarians and techs helped them out by providing routine checkups as part of their in-processing. Unfortunately, the noise tended to get some dogs so spun up, they became difficult to control, which made giving them a physical dang near impossible.

Like the hundred-and-fifty-pound Great Dane who was acting like he'd drunk a gallon of espresso. The big guy was spinning in circles so fast, he was about to screw himself into the floor—or choke himself on his own leash.

"Sheesh, chill out, Scooby-Doo, before you hurt yourself," she told him.

But Scooby—or at least the dog she'd been calling Scooby for the last ten minutes—seemed to have no desire to chill out. If anything, he was getting more excited by the second. At this pace, the pooch was going to create his own weather pattern soon.

Lacey was about to give up and head to the front office for some help when suddenly, the big crazy dog sat down as if his butt was on fire. He remained perfectly still, gazing at her with big amber-colored eyes. She was still trying to figure out what the hell was up with Scooby—and whether his sudden change in personality might be a bad thing—when she realized that the entire kennel had fallen silent. Every single dog had stopped barking and was now staring at her.

She'd been around dogs for most of her life, and she'd never seen a large group of them act like this. It was strange. No, check that. It was flat-out eerie.

Thinking it might be a good idea to leave, she started

backing away, but then stopped as she realized the dogs weren't actually looking at her. They were gazing at something over her right shoulder.

She spun around, nearly jumping out of her shoes when she caught sight of Alex Trevino standing behind her—all six-foot-four muscled inches of him. Her heart beat faster. She tried to convince herself it was because he'd startled her, but she knew that was a lie. Her pulse was racing because he looked so damn hot in his jeans and snug-fitting T-shirt. Even better than in his SWAT uniform—if that was possible.

He gave her a lopsided grin. "Sorry. I didn't mean to scare you. The people up front thought you might need some help with the dogs."

Lacey shook her head, for some silly reason not wanting him to know he'd spooked her—or made her heart go all pitter-patter. "No, you didn't startle me. The dogs were just acting weird. I thought there was something wrong."

"Nothing wrong," he said. "Just me."

She looked around to see that the all the dogs—including Scooby-Doo—were still looking adoringly at Alex. She turned back to him. "I've never see an entire kennel behave like this around anyone. Does this happen to you often?"

Alex's grin broadened, and for a moment, all she could do was stare at his mouth. Damn, he had a really nice smile. She gave herself a mental shake and forced herself to focus on what he was saying.

"I guess they just like me. But that might wear off, so let's get this big dog checked out before he decides to lose it again."

Lacey opened her mouth to say she could handle

Scooby on her own, but the big SWAT cop had already knelt down beside the dog. Well, at least the Great Dane appeared to be content to sit there calmly for now. She might as well make use of the dog's good behavior while it lasted. Grabbing her clipboard and stethoscope from her bag, she got to work.

Alex didn't just have a way with calming down dogs, he had a way with them period. Scooby did anything Alex wanted him to do, including lying down and rolling onto his back so Lacey could palpate his stomach. The funny thing was, Alex barely had to say or do anything. The dog just seemed to know what Alex wanted him to do.

"Dogs seem to like you," she pointed out.

He flashed her another grin that inspired some nice tingles here, there, and everywhere. "Maybe they're onto something."

Lacey braced herself, assuming Alex would almost certainly ask her out again after a line like that, but instead, he went back to holding Scooby still for the next part of the examination.

Huh. Well, if he wanted to play the strong, silent type, she was fine with that. She really didn't feel like fending off any more advances anyway, she told herself as she turned her full attention to Scooby and his chart.

That plan lasted for a little while. Until she noticed how incredibly nice Alex smelled, and that the stubble along his jaw looked so soft and touchable that it was all she could do to not reach out and run her fingertips over his strong chin. Her gaze moved lower, focusing on the way his thigh muscles bulged in his jeans as he crouched beside her. The mere thought of the word *bulge* had her eyes wandering somewhere they really shouldn't be going.

Okay, enough of that. She needed a distraction STAT!

"How did you know I was volunteering here today?" she asked. "Unless you expect me to believe this is just coincidence?"

His dark eyes met hers. "I ran into your friend Wendy, and she mentioned that you like to spend your free time here."

"And why would Wendy tell you that?" she asked, even though she already had a pretty good idea.

"I don't know. I guess she thought you might enjoy some company while you worked. She was the one who suggested I come and help."

Lacey would have pointed out that her best friend was a conniving weasel, but Alex had already gotten to his feet and was leading Scooby back to his kennel. While he did that, she got the next dog out. The little Boston terrier was like putty in Alex's hands. She leaned contently against his big, muscular leg as he kneeled on the floor, a happy smile pasted on her furry lips the whole time they examined her.

As she worked, Lacey kept expecting Alex to try to charm her like he had the previous times they'd met, but he didn't. Instead, he was completely focused on wordlessly transcribing her findings and comments into each dog's record and handing her equipment as she requested it. Lacey smiled as they slipped into a smooth routine. They worked well together. So well, in fact, that it took her a while to realize that he never asked her what any of the medical terms she called out meant or how to spell them. On top of that, he handed her certain pieces of med gear before she even asked.

"If I didn't know better, I'd think you had a medical background," she remarked.

"I'm a licensed paramedic in the state of Texas and have some Marine Corps Combat Lifesaver training."

"Oh," she murmured, embarrassed to admit that his answer surprised her.

For some reason, she'd assumed a big guy like him would have more knowledge of guns and violence than about medicine. She blushed as she realized how shallow that was.

She waited for him to explain how a DPD officer in SWAT had come to possess—and maintain—the state's highest level of EMS certification, but Alex didn't say a word. Instead, he went back to helping her with the labradoodle they were examining, moving not just with efficiency, but with a level of gentleness that she would have never expected from a man his size.

They worked in comfortable relative silence for the next three hours. After checking out nearly twenty dogs, including a few with minor injuries that needed tending, Lacey decided to call it a day. With Alex's help, she'd seen more pooches in a single day than she would have normally seen in a week. And to tell the truth, she was beat.

She was also curious as hell. Working this close to him had been more fun than she would ever have thought possible, and she found herself wanting to ask him a hundred different questions. Where had he developed this knack for handling dogs? How could he be SWAT and a paramedic? Had he been in the Marines long, and how had he gotten from there to the Dallas police department?

Those weren't things she could ask as they stood in the middle of an animal shelter, though. Questions like that demanded a good meal and a glass or two of wine. But that would mean going out on a date.

The funny thing was, after today, she was finding it hard to remember why she'd been so obstinately set against going out with him. He seemed like a genuinely amazing guy. How bad would it be to go on one, teensy-weensy date? Only an idiot would keep standing on silly principle at this point.

"Okay," she said as they left the shelter and stepped out into the late-day heat. "You win. We can go out to dinner sometime."

He looked at her with what she was sure was faux surprise. "Win? Do you think that the only reason I came out here on a Saturday was to get you to go on a date with me?"

She lifted a brow.

His mouth curved. "Maybe you're right. But I don't want you to go out with me because you feel you owe me something. I want you to do it because you think it would be fun and because you're interested in me. If that's not the case, just say so, and we can save each other any embarrassment later."

Lacey mentally cringed. Crap, that sounded like something she would say. But he'd hit the nail right on the head—and called her out at the same time.

"I am interested in you," she said. "But to be honest, I'm not looking for a relationship right now. I can't make any promises that this date will lead anywhere, not even a second date."

Alex regarded her in silence for so long that she suddenly wondered if she should have tempered her words a bit. She hadn't needed to be so blunt about the whole thing. She wouldn't be surprised if he bailed. Who wanted to go out with someone who essentially just declared that the date was going to suck before they even went on it?

She opened her mouth to apologize, but before she could get the words out, Alex spoke.

"Fair enough. I'll pick you up tomorrow night around seven. It's just dinner—no expectations beyond that."

Lacey sighed with relief, glad that he hadn't been offended. They exchanged numbers, and she gave him her address, then watched him get into his blue pickup truck. She smiled as she climbed in her SUV, actually looking forward to not only seeing Alex again, but going on a date. She hadn't felt this kind of excitement about seeing a guy in a long time, if ever.

But the moment Alex pulled out of the parking lot and disappeared from view, it was like a glamour was lifted from her eyes, and tension gripped her. What he'd said about this simply being a dinner date with no expectations had sounded very mature, but something told her even a single date with Alex would lead to more. Her stomach clenched. She really hoped she'd done the right thing. Her life was going so smoothly right then, and getting tangled up with a man—even one as amazing as Alex—was a complication she didn't need.

⁓⁓⁓

Lacey sat in her car a few blocks down from Bensen's junkyard, tucked behind the side of a big brick building so no one would see her. She wasn't sure what the hell she was doing there. If she was smart, she'd be at home in bed, getting her beauty sleep so she'd look gorgeous for her date with Alex tomorrow night. Instead, she was parked outside the fanciest junkyard she'd ever seen, trying hard to peer through the darkness and steady rain as she attempted to work up the courage to climb the fence and sneak inside.

This wasn't the small junkyard they'd rescued the dogs from the other day. This place out on Interstate 20 just past Lawson was the heart of Bensen's car-part empire. It was as much of a do-it-yourself car-repair depot as a junkyard, but this late at night, it was closed. She'd seen Bensen and his albino security chief walking around the place about an hour ago, so she knew they were still there.

While they probably weren't planning to run a dog-fighting event on this particular property anytime soon, she'd come hoping to see something—anything—she could give Wendy to help put some heat on this guy. She would have hired a PI if she had the money, but she didn't. If she wanted to find something, she'd have to do the digging herself.

After leaving the shelter, Lacey had gone to the vet clinic to check on the three pit bulls they'd rescued from the junkyard. They'd survived their first round of surgeries but were still fighting for their lives and definitely looking at a long, difficult, uphill battle. Every time she thought about them, she wanted to hit something or someone. Preferably Bensen and his security goon Pendergraff. According to Wendy, the brass wasn't interested in going after a man like Bensen for dogfighting without any slam-dunk evidence. Instead, the caretaker at the junkyard would be issued a citation, and the case would be closed.

"Not if I have anything to say about it," she muttered to herself.

She wasn't leaving until she had something on Bensen.

Of course, this had seemed like a good plan on the way over. But now, as she sat there in the darkness, it didn't seem like such a great idea. The place was dark and creepy looking, with all the abandoned cars and racks upon racks of extra parts, and the rain only made it worse. It also didn't help that the facility looked damn near impossible to get into, with its single entry gate and ten-foot-high fence.

Lacey was ready to admit she'd made a mistake coming when a car pulled up to the closed gates of the place and honked its horn. Silence reigned for a few long moments, but the car didn't move or sound its horn again. The man behind the wheel sat there unmoving as well, eyes fixed on the building. A minute later, Pendergraff stepped outside and walked toward the gate, his hair practically glowing phosphorescent in the darkness.

The driver got out of his car as Pendergraff opened the gate. From where she was parked, Lacey couldn't see the newcomer's face or hear anything they were saying, but if she had to describe the meeting in a single word, it would be suspicious. The way both men looked around like they thought someone was watching them screamed out loud and clear that they were up to no good.

After a few minutes of conversation, the man opened the back door of the car, then reached inside and dragged out a good-sized cardboard box, handing it to Pendergraff.

Lacey sat up a little straighter, staring hard through the rain and trying to see what might be in that box. Dogs for fighting were normally transported in cages, but the box was certainly big enough to hold a dog. She couldn't tell how heavy the box was, though. Was it sturdy enough to carry a dog? The albino didn't seem to be straining under the weight, but then again, he was a big man.

The two men talked some more, then the mysterious

stranger got back in his car and drove away. Pendergraff stood there for a moment in the rain, his pale eyes surveying the area as if he were worried someone had witnessed the exchange. When the man's eyes swept over Lacey's hiding place, she couldn't help but scrunch down in her seat a little—even if there was no way the albino could possibly see her. Still, she sighed with relief when Pendergraff finally walked back into the building.

Lacey was out of the car and running for the fence before she realized what she was doing. She had to get in there and see what was inside that box. If it were a fighting dog, Wendy might be able to use that knowledge as probable cause for a search warrant or something.

She was soaking wet before she reached the chain-link fence surrounding the place. It didn't help that she was forced to follow the fence along the road, trying to find a place she'd be able to climb. Preferably a section that wasn't rusty as hell.

The climb over the fence demonstrated that she was still as uncoordinated and unathletic as she'd been in high school. She'd been a klutz as long as she could remember and was lucky she didn't fall off and kill herself.

When she finally dropped down on the other side of the fence, she ran through the maze that was the junkyard as fast as she could, eager to reach the main building where Pendergraff had taken the box in time to see what it contained. She made it there and saw that the big garage door on the side of the building was up, revealing a well-lit interior. She pushed her long, wet hair back and pressed close to the building, taking a quick peek inside. Pendergraff and Bensen were standing over the open cardboard box, talking.

Blinking water from her eyes, she moved a little

farther to the left, trying to see what they were looking at—without them seeing her—and ended up behind a rack of mufflers that were dirty, rusty, and twisted into all kind of shapes. She was careful to stay well away from them. All she needed was to knock one down and bring Pendergraff running.

"Is this the best our supplier could do?" Bensen asked sharply.

Pendergraff nodded. "For the moment."

Lacey stood up on tiptoes, trying to see what the two men were looking at. Was it a dog? That didn't make sense. The animal would have been out of the box in a flash now that it was open. Unless the poor creature was drugged.

She glanced at the rack of mufflers, tempted to climb it so she could see into the box. But that was insane. She'd end up slipping on the wet metal, and they'd hear her for sure.

"It's not good enough," Bensen snapped. "I want more, and I want it now."

The albino didn't even blink. "There's a lot of heat on us and our supplier. It might be best to back off and wait until things calm down a little."

Bensen's face turned red under his sickly yellow complexion. "I don't have time to wait, and you know it. Contact our supplier and tell him that if this is the best he can give me, I'm going to feed his ass to the dogs!"

Turning, Bensen stormed off. Well, as much as a man that old and infirm could storm off. Pendergraff watched him go, then looked back at the box for a moment before walking away.

Lacey's heart beat a little faster. This might be her only chance to get in there and snap a picture of what was in that box. It might be a sedated fighting dog or it might not, but it was sure as hell something shady.

She cautiously came out from behind the rack of mufflers, then hurried over to the building. That was when her plan fell apart, thanks to her lack of coordination and general klutzy nature. She didn't even see the piece of gravel she kicked until it was already sailing through the air. For a split second, she thought it might fall harmlessly to the ground, but instead, it hit a corner of the parts rack, clanking like a little baby bell.

Lacey spun around and ran the other direction, knowing without looking that Pendergraff had heard that noise—there was no way he could have missed it. She weaved in and out of the rows of parts, finally darting behind an enormous metal storage box and ducking down.

Thank God she did, because a few seconds later, Pendergraff ran by, a pistol in his hand. But instead of continuing on his way, he stopped half a dozen feet away. Lacey held her breath, sure her heart was going to explode in her chest.

Pendergraff swept his disturbing eyes back and forth across the area, but after several long, tense moments, he turned and headed back the direction he'd come from.

Lacey breathed a sigh of relief. Should she hide here for a little while longer, then go back to see if she could get a peek at what was in the box, or escape while she had the chance? She desperately wanted to go back and see what was in the box, but the thought of getting caught by Pendergraff—and what the man would do to her—had her up and running for the perimeter fence.

She was shaking so badly that it took her three tries to

get over the damn thing, but she finally managed, mostly because she pictured the pale-eyed albino right behind her, ready to kill her in some unspeakable manner if she fell back onto his boss's property.

Once in her car, Lacey sat there, breathing deeply and berating herself for being an idiot, all while trying her best to stop trembling. By the time she started the SUV and pulled onto the road, her head was functioning clearly again. What had she stumbled onto back there?

Bensen and Pendergraff sure as hell hadn't been talking about car parts. But it didn't sound like they were talking about dogfighting, either.

As she merged onto the highway, she thought about calling Wendy and telling her what she'd seen, but then decided that was a bad idea. In reality, she hadn't seen anything incriminating. However, she would definitely incriminate herself if she admitted to climbing that fence and trespassing on Bensen's property. She knew Wendy wouldn't arrest her, but her friend would sure as hell be furious, and Lacey wasn't in any mood to get yelled at tonight. All she wanted was a warm bath and pleasant dreams about her date with Alex tomorrow night. Then she'd figure out a way to tie Bensen to dogfighting.

Chapter 5

Alex stood in the hallway outside Lacey's apartment, staring at the door and taking deep breaths. He hadn't been this nervous since he took Teri Sue Whitman to the junior prom. He needed to calm the hell down. That was easier said than done, of course. Regardless of what he'd said yesterday about there being no expectation for this date, he still wanted it to go well. Actually, he wanted it to go better than that. He wanted it to be amazing.

That wasn't likely to happen if he couldn't get his head screwed on right. He had to stop thinking about this as a date with a woman who might be his one-in-a-billion soul mate and focus on having a normal, old-fashioned, good time. If he didn't, he was going to blow this for sure.

Up until a few hours ago, he hadn't even thought about tonight's date with Lacey. That was because he'd been preoccupied with what had happened at Texas Regional College the other day. Both the kid with the knife and the girl from the dorm were still in critical condition. While he was facing serious neurological damage, she might never come out of her coma.

At least the lab results had come back on the drugs they'd recovered from the dorm room. As expected, it had been fireball, though it appeared that now the hallucinogenic component of the mix was amped up to some degree. Considering how the kid on the roof had behaved, that wasn't a surprise.

As much as Alex wished he could do something about it, he and his teammates were SWAT, not narcotics. They kicked in doors; they didn't investigate. Rodriguez and the other cops on the task force would be the ones to track down whoever was selling this crap. Once they found out who it was, they'd call in SWAT. It was their job to be ready when narcotics called.

Deciding that standing out in the hallway was only going to make him more nervous, Alex took another deep breath, then knocked on the door. He heard the sound of whispered voices inside, followed by a soft laugh and the sound of high heels clacking on a hardwood floor. When the door opened, all he could do was stare.

Lacey's long blond hair was done up fancier than he was used to seeing it, hanging in sexy waves around her face. Her makeup was a bit smokier and sultry than usual too, and she was wearing a little black dress, which shimmered in the light when she moved. Besides showing off her spectacular cleavage, the dress stopped a few inches above the knee, displaying enough leg to make his pants suddenly feel a bit too tight.

It wasn't until Lacey arched one of her perfect brows that Alex realized he'd been staring a little too long.

"Are you going to come inside or just stand out there gawking all night?" she asked with a smile.

He chuckled and stepped into the foyer. "Can't I do both?"

Alex let his gaze wander casually up and down her body. Damn, she looked good in that LBD.

Lacey must have known the effect she was having on him, because she blushed. He was so caught up in the intrigued expression in her blue eyes that he barely noticed the black lab mix standing in the living room studying him with blatant curiosity. The guy probably had a little beagle or dachshund in the bloodline somewhere, because he was definitely a lot smaller than a full-breed lab.

Alex moved closer and crouched down but didn't say anything, instead letting the dog decide if he was in the mood for a formal meet-and-greet. The dog turned his head, regarding Alex with a confused look. Alex had dealt with enough animals to know that his werewolf scent baffled the heck out of them. Lacey's dog was probably thinking that Alex looked like a human but didn't smell like one. After a few seconds, the dog must have decided he was worth checking out, because he padded over and took a few extra sniffs, then licked Alex's hand.

"This is Leonardo," Lacey said, crouching down beside him. The move made her dress slide up a few inches higher, revealing even more leg.

"After the artist?"

Alex was surprised. Lacey struck him as more traditional when it came to dog names. He'd expected something more along the lines of Spot or Fido.

"No," she said. "After the turtle."

She had a turtle named Leonardo too? That made absolutely no sense, and all he could do was stare at her blankly.

"The Ninja Turtle," she clarified.

That still didn't help. Alex opened his mouth to admit total ignorance and ask if he could phone a friend or something when he heard footsteps. He looked up to see a younger version of Lacey standing there, her blond hair pulled up in a ponytail, her blue eyes unabashedly checking him out. He'd been so distracted by Lacey, he hadn't even picked up on the girl's scent.

"You didn't mention Alex was so hot," she said. "He's smoking!"

Lacey straightened, a wry look on her face. "This is my sister, Kelsey. Due to a horrible misfortune of genetics, she was born without the normal filter between her brain and her mouth. She says the first thing that pops into her head, even when she shouldn't."

Kelsey grinned. "Just saying what I know my big sis is thinking."

Lacey rolled her eyes but laughed. Alex let out a chuckle of his own as he stood up.

"So, where are you two crazy kids heading off to tonight?" Kelsey asked.

Lacey glanced at him. "That's a good question."

He considered keeping their destination a secret just to tease her, but something told him that Lacey wasn't the kind of woman to play those types of games. "I got us a reservation at a nice Italian place over on Oak Lawn Avenue. If that's okay?"

Lacey's eyes sparkled. "Italian works for me."

"Me too," Kelsey chimed in. "Bring Leo and me a doggie bag."

Lacey promised they would just as a bell chimed, sending Kelsey scrambling into the kitchen. She came back out a moment later, her brow creased in a frown as she furiously typed something on her cell phone.

"Everything okay?" Lacey asked.

Kelsey finished the text she was working on, then shoved the phone in the back pocket of her shorts with a sigh. "It's my friend Sara. She's missing, and we're all freaking out. We've been checking in with each other all day, hoping somebody hears something."

Lacey looked at Alex in alarm. It didn't take a genius

to know what she was thinking. The local news channels had the Abigail Elliott story on 24–7, especially since Councilman McDonald had just announced a sizable reward for information on the location of the missing girl. It was natural for Lacey to assume the worst.

"What exactly do you mean when you say your friend is missing?" Alex asked Kelsey. "Has her family contacted the police yet?"

"Sara doesn't have any family. She grew up in the foster system." Kelsey played with the end of her ponytail. "Maybe *missing* is the wrong word. All we know for sure is that she sent an email to the registrar's office on Friday telling them that she was dropping all her classes and taking a break from school and that she plans to come back next semester."

Beside him, Lacey relaxed visibly. Alex felt the tension leave his shoulders too. There was a big difference between missing and bailing on school for a while.

Lacey walked over and gave Kelsey a hug. "I know you're worried, honey, but it sounds like Sara is just stressed out and decided to take a little break. It's not that uncommon in college; you know that."

Kelsey didn't look convinced. "Sara is an English lit major with a solid 4.0 GPA. My other friends and I are like her family. If she was so stressed out, why wouldn't she have told one of us? She didn't even clean out her dorm room when she left. Now she's not updating her status on Facebook or returning any of our calls or texts."

"She will," Lacey promised. "Just give her a little time to get herself together."

Lacey brushed back a stray strand of hair that had come loose from her sister's ponytail before hugging

Kelsey again. After a moment, Kelsey pulled back and gave a Lacey a small smile.

"Enough about my friends and me. You guys need to leave if you're going to make your reservation." When Lacey looked like she wanted to argue, her sister spun her around and shoved her at the door. "Go. I'm leaving in a little while anyway. I'm sure you're right about Sara just needing a break, but my friends and I are heading out to a few of our usual hangouts to see if anyone else has heard from her."

Lacey gave in with a laugh, grabbing her purse off the couch. "Okay, okay. Just don't stay out too late. You have class tomorrow."

"I won't," Kelsey promised. "I don't have any classes until the afternoon, so some of my friends and I are going to hit the campus quad and soak up some sun while we check out hot guys. Sara was going to join us, but I guess that's not going to happen now." Kelsey threw Alex a look, then winked at Lacey. "Maybe you should play hooky and bring Alex with you. I'm sure my girlfriends would appreciate the view. Hell, some of my guy friends would too."

Lacey's face turned red, but Alex laughed it off as he opened the door for her. Kelsey definitely knew how to push her sister's buttons.

~~~

Even though it was Sunday night, the restaurant was crowded. The aroma coming from the huge open kitchen probably had a lot to do with that, Lacey supposed. The smell of food was enough to make her drool. Then again, maybe Alex was the one making her do that. He certainly looked good enough to eat.

When she'd opened her apartment door an hour ago and seen him standing there in a suit with that perfect amount of scruff still covering his jawline, she'd just about gasped out loud. Did he clean up nice or what? She wasn't the only woman who thought so, either. Most of the female patrons had almost snapped their necks as the hostess led them to their table.

Even though she'd never admit it out loud to anyone, the best part was that Alex hadn't looked at a single one of those women the whole time. Heck, he'd barely looked at their waitress as they ordered drinks and appetizers. Instead, he'd gazed warmly into Lacey's eyes as they sat there across from each other.

"Do you mind if I ask you something personal?" he said after the waitress had brought the bottle of wine they'd ordered.

Lacey tensed, unable to help it. She'd never been a big fan of getting too personal with any guy, especially one she'd just met. She forced herself to relax. If Alex asked her anything she wasn't comfortable talking about, she had the feeling he wouldn't get upset if she told him just that.

She nodded. "Sure. Within reason, I guess."

He smiled. "I couldn't help noticing how close you and Kelsey are. Something tells me that you've been looking out for your sister for a long time. How old were you when your parents disappeared from of the picture?"

The question was so unexpected—and perceptive—that Lacey was speechless. Alex must have taken her silence to mean she was upset, because he held up his hand.

"You don't have to answer that," he said. "I apologize if I touched on a sensitive subject."

Lacey shook her head. "No, it's okay. It's not something I talk about very often, but it's not some big secret."

The fact that she'd just said those words was as shocking as Alex's question. She never talked about this part of her past with guys—or anyone, really. Other than Wendy, no one else knew about any of it. But something about Alex made her want to share stuff she normally didn't.

"Our dad bailed when I was twelve," she said quietly. "Kelsey was only five, so she doesn't really remember him. Mom didn't handle his leaving very well, and I ended up being the one who had to take care of my sister. It wasn't a big deal really. I just made sure she got to school, ate her veggies, did her homework—stuff like that."

Across from her, Alex sipped his wine. Lacey mimicked him without thinking. The Cabernet was dark with just the hint of blackberry, dry but still easy to drink.

"It sounds like a big deal to me." He set down his glass. "What about your mom? Is she around these days?"

Lacey debated telling Alex the truth but decided against it. He might be easy to talk to, but telling him exactly why their mom wasn't around anymore was a surefire way to ruin the night's mood.

"No. She left right after I graduated high school," Lacey said simply, leaving out the details—and the unpleasant parts. "Kelsey and I moved in with an aunt who lived in Weatherford, just a few miles from where we grew up. She was involved with the rodeo circuit though, so we rarely saw her either."

"Wow. It sounds like you and Kelsey were dealt a pretty crappy hand. It's impressive that you were able to make it through all that and still go to college to become a vet."

Lacey snorted. "You want impressive, you should see my student loan balances. I'll be paying for those until I'm forty, if I'm lucky."

"That doesn't diminish the fact that you got yourself and your sister out of a really bad situation," Alex insisted. "You have a good job and a nice place to live. And let me guess, you're paying her way through school so she won't be strapped with the same student loans you're stuck with, right?"

She *was* paying for her sister's education. Why wouldn't she? Kelsey meant the world to her. But the way Alex said it—not to mention the look of admiration on his face—made Lacey's face heat. Dang, he actually had her blushing.

She grabbed her wine and took a quick sip, hoping the dim lighting and flickering candles on the table hid her reaction, but when she glanced up from under her lashes, Alex was smiling at her. Yeah, he'd seen.

"Enough about me and my student loans," she said. "I'm just a simple Texas girl. How about you? From that slight accent of yours, I'm guessing you didn't grow up around here."

He gave her a confused look. "Accent? What accent?"

The way he deliberately put extra emphasis on the w-h-a part of the sentence made her laugh.

"That one!" she said, pointing at him across the table. "Where'd you grow up? Somewhere in the Northeast, right?"

He grinned, and Lacey felt a little tremor roll through her. Okay, *that* was different. Getting turned on by a guy's smile was definitely a first. But dang, that grin of his could make a girl's knees weak.

"Rochester, New York," he said, dropping back into

that sexy voice of his, the one that had barely a hint of inflection that she'd first picked up on. "It's upstate, so we don't have the usual heavy accent that everyone seems to associate with New Yorkers. I'm surprised you even noticed it."

"Oh, I noticed." She smiled. "It's slight, but it's there. Especially compared to the Texas twang I'm used to hearing around here. So, what's the story? How'd an upstate New York kid end up in Dallas?"

He waited as the waitress placed their first course on the table. The woman had said the entrées were big, so Alex had agreed to share the deep-fried ravioli appetizer with her. She hadn't wanted to pass up a chance to try the crunchy pasta treat, especially since the waitress had said they were amazing.

It turned out that the woman was right. The cheese-filled goodies were delicious. Lacey didn't realize just how much she was enjoying them until she looked up and saw Alex regarding her with an amused look on his face. She quickly lifted her hand to cover her mouth, sure she'd dribbled marinara sauce down her chin. It certainly wouldn't be the first time. But she didn't feel anything.

"What?" she asked.

"You were moaning," he said.

She blinked. "I wasn't moaning. I was just making appreciative sounds because the ravioli tastes so good."

His mouth twitched. "I see. And aren't appreciative sounds just another word for moaning?"

Lacey considered arguing the point, but then dropped her face into her hands. "I can't believe I did that. Kelsey teases me about doing it at home, but I never realized I did it in public. I'm so sorry."

"Don't be," he said softly. "You have a nice moan. Feel free to do it as often as you like."

Lacey dropped her hands to see Alex looking at her with a glint in his dark eyes. The way the candlelight was reflecting off them, it almost seemed like they were glowing. It was enough to send a little shiver through her and quickly had her forgetting why she'd been so embarrassed a moment ago.

They stared at each other for what might have been five minutes or five seconds. Either way, Lacey felt heat coalesce between her legs. She squeezed her thighs together under the table.

"Weren't we talking about how you ended up in Dallas?" she asked.

She needed to get her mind on something other than the suddenly rising temperature in the restaurant.

"Were we?" His mouth edged up. "I thought we were talking about you moaning."

"Yes, I'm sure that's what we were talking about before the waitress brought our appetizer," she reminded him. "You mentioned you were from Rochester."

For a moment, he looked as if he'd rather not change the subject, but then he broke eye contact and concentrated on using his fork to cut into his ravioli. "I grew up in Rochester, but then I left after graduating from high school to serve four years in the Marine Corps."

She sipped her wine, forcing herself to pay close attention to his story. It was either that or think about exactly what Alex had meant when he said she had a nice moan.

"After I got out, I went back home to Rochester and became a police officer," he continued. "A couple of years later, I ran into Sergeant Gage Dixon—the commander of the Dallas SWAT team. He offered me a job, and I took it. That was over four years ago, and I never looked back."

Leave it to a guy to distill such an amazing amount of life down to a few sentences. Considering the fact that she'd never gotten the chance to leave Texas, she needed more details.

"Wait a minute." She gestured with her fork. "Go back to the first part. What did you do in the Marines? Did you get to go anywhere overseas?"

He took another bite of ravioli before answering. "I was a sniper in the 1st Recon Battalion. And yes, I got to see the world. Not exactly the parts I would have preferred to see—mostly Iraq and Afghanistan. But I guess if I wanted to see vacation destinations, I should have gone to work for a cruise line."

She didn't know what a Recon Battalion was, but she understood the sniper part. That seemed like a difficult job.

"Did you ever have to…?" Lacey hesitated, abruptly realizing it probably wasn't something she had a right to even bring up.

"Did I ever have to shoot anyone?" he finished softly, then nodded. "Yeah, I did. I try not to spend too much time thinking about the people who were in my scope, though. I prefer to focus on the people I saved by pulling that trigger. My fellow marines, soldiers, coalition forces, civilians who were just trying to get on with their lives—they lived because of the things I did."

The words brought tears to her eyes, and she blinked them back. In a few simple sentences, Alex had admitted to taking on a responsibility that few people in the world would ever be asked to bear. Yet he'd seemed

more impressed with her getting through college and
taking care of her sister. He probably didn't even see
the disparity.

She cleared her throat. "Since you went back to
Rochester, I'm assuming you have family there. Why'd
you leave?"

He shrugged, pushing his empty appetizer plate
away. That was when she realized he'd eaten the three
big raviolis she'd left for him while she'd barely put a
dent in the one she had.

"I'm not really close with my family," he said. "I
needed a change, and Dallas was it."

Okay, that was a non-answer if she'd ever heard one.
And she had, because she used them herself anytime
people asked her about subjects she didn't want to get
into. Something serious had definitely happened in
Rochester to get him to move halfway across the country. But Lacey didn't push. She knew what it was like to
carry a lot of baggage.

The waitress appeared with heaping plates of spaghetti and meatballs then, and as they started in on their
entrees, Lacey asked Alex what he'd been doing since
moving to Dallas. While she knew he was a SWAT
cop, truthfully, she didn't know what that entailed. Alex
didn't seem to mind talking about the subject, though
she noticed he talked more about his teammates than
about himself. No big shock there.

"So you're a sniper and a paramedic in SWAT?" she
asked. "Don't take this the wrong way, but isn't that a
little strange?"

He casually shrugged as he twirled spaghetti around
his fork. She couldn't eat pasta that way. It would end
up all over her lap.

"Not really," he said. "When I was deployed, being able to help a marine who'd been shot or injured by an IED—improvised explosive device—was a crucial skill. That's why I went through combat lifesaver training. It's like being an EMT on the battlefield. When I joined SWAT, I was amazed at how many times I was the first person on the scene after someone had been injured. It just wasn't in me to stand there and do nothing, but my combat lifesaving training wasn't enough. I was just going to get my EMT basic certification, but my boss encouraged me to get my paramedic license. There are two of us on the team now, one on each squad."

When he put it that way, it made sense.

Alex continued to entertain her with stories of the kind of work he did with SWAT, focusing more on the fun things he and his team did, not as much on the scary stuff that she doubted she wanted to know about anyway. It quickly became apparent that Alex loved his job as well as the other members of the team.

"They're my family," he said simply.

They were halfway through their meal when Alex turned the conversation back to her. They talked mostly about how much she loved animals, especially dogs, and why she became a veterinarian. She told him the stories of playing vet with all the neighborhood dogs when she was a kid, both of them laughing as she described how she'd wrapped all of them up like little mummies only to have to chase them around to get the bandages off once they got tired of the game. She admitted that she dreamed about running her own clinic one day.

"If I were rich, that's what I'd do with my money," she admitted. "I'd open up a no-kill shelter for dogs. I'd save them all if I could."

The next thing Lacey knew, she was describing her dream shelter with a huge place for the dogs to run and play, dozens of treatment rooms, and hundreds of kennels. Alex never laughed at her crazy dream. In fact, he helped her plan it out while they ate. Clearly, he loved dogs as much as she did.

As she nibbled on a piece of garlic bread, she marveled at how good he was at getting her to open up. If she wasn't careful, she'd be telling him all kinds of secrets. Like that insanity from last night when she'd climbed a ten-foot-tall fence because she thought she could help the police catch a man involved in dogfighting. That probably wouldn't be a good subject to bring up, especially to a cop.

"Hey, you don't have a problem with your date trespassing, breaking and entering, and stalking, right? No? Cool, because that's what I do on my day off."

Nah, that wouldn't go over well. Maybe she should stick to talking about how much she loved animals.

The SWAT team's dog, Tuffie, came up in conversation a little while after that. She almost cried when Alex told her how he and the other paramedic on the SWAT team had saved Tuffie's life.

"You actually stopped working on one of your teammates to help Tuffie?" she asked in awe. "That's amazing. I can't imagine he was too thrilled with that, though."

"Xander?" Alex chuckled. "He barely got scratched. I think he was just trying to show off for the female SWAT officer on our team."

Lacey laughed. She was having such a good time with Alex that she barely paid any attention to her dinner. She didn't care. She hadn't had this much fun just sitting around talking to a guy ever. Which was why she was bummed when Alex glanced at his watch.

She checked her own and discovered it was after ten already. "Do you have to work tonight?"

He shook his head. "No. It's just that I set up something special for us to do around eleven."

"Something special?" Her interest was piqued. "Like what?"

He grinned. "If I told you, it wouldn't be special."

Lacey looked at her plate of spaghetti, then back at Alex. She'd been having an amazing time with him, but if he'd set up something special, she hated the idea of not getting to do it. That didn't seem right. Besides, she was curious.

"I'll get this put in that doggie bag we promised Kelsey," she told him. "I'm full anyway."

"You sure?"

Lacey caught the waitress's eye as the woman finished up at another table, then motioned down at her plate. "Definitely. I can't wait."

"Good." He pulled out his wallet. "You're okay doing a little walking in high heels, right?"

Okay, now she was even more intrigued. What the heck did he have planned?

Alex wouldn't tell her though, no matter how much she begged. Lacey was confused when they turned into the deserted parking lot of the Dallas Zoo twenty minutes later.

"What are we doing here?" she asked. "They're closed at this time of night."

Alex pulled into a space and shut off the engine. "Yeah, they are. But it just so happens that I know the carnivore keeper here. She agreed to slip us in to spend a little time with one of their special guests."

"What kind of animal?" she asked. "Lion? Tiger?"

His mouth twitched. "You'll just have to wait and see. But I will tell you that it's not one of the animals they normally have here on exhibit."

Lacey ran through all the animals they had at the zoo, trying to figure out what it could be. She was so excited to find out, she almost ran toward the entrance, then she realized she had no idea where they were going, especially when they passed the front entrance and started around the side of the place.

Alex pulled out his phone and dialed a number. "We're here, Hannah. Meet you at the gate."

A few minutes later, they were met at a wood gate by a petite redhead wearing khaki shorts and a Dallas Zoo polo shirt. Alex introduced her as Hannah Wells, the person in charge of taking care of the zoo's carnivores.

"Take your time," Hannah told them before walking off and leaving them alone.

"She's just going to let us wander around?" Lacey whispered as the woman disappeared around a corner.

"Pretty much," Alex said as he led her along the path in the same direction Hannah had gone, albeit at a much slower pace. "You don't have to whisper, you know. The animals don't care that we're here."

Even though the zoo wasn't open, there were still enough lights on to see the pathway. Not that it seemed like Alex needed lights to see. He walked with smooth, confident steps like he had the pathways and sidewalks memorized. Or could see in the dark. Lacey couldn't say the same about herself. Beside her, Alex immediately slowed his pace, reaching his hand out for her to hold. She took a grip on his big hand without thinking, letting him guide and steady her in the darkness.

"You okay in those heels?" he asked.

"Fine."

She squeezed his hand tighter anyway. That's when she realized that she hadn't ever held a guy's hand on a date. Alex's hand was strong and warm and felt good wrapped around hers. She had to admit she enjoyed it.

They meandered slowly through the zoo, listening to the sounds of the animals. It seemed so different than any other time she'd been here. More muted but wilder at the same time. The grunts and coughs of the big cats were especially disconcerting, probably because she could hear them but not see them.

As they walked past the African savanna area, Lacey was disappointed when the impalas and zebras—the ones she could see, at least—immediately took off running at their approach.

"What scared them?" she asked.

"Maybe they just aren't used to having visitors at night," Alex said.

At least the elephants didn't run. In fact, they did the opposite. Two of the larger ones came closer and put themselves between Lacey and Alex and the rest of their little herd, like they didn't want them getting a look at the others. Not that Lacey could see much to begin with. But it seemed like strangely protective behavior.

Still, even if they couldn't get a good look at the animals, it was fun to stroll through the zoo with Alex. She pulled his arm close, leaning into him more.

"So, how do you know Hannah?" she asked softly.

Lacey winced the moment the words were out of her mouth. *Crap, had that come out sounding as jealous as it seemed?* She hoped not. She had absolutely no reason to be jealous. She couldn't be anyway. This was a first date, after all. *But Hannah is young and kind of cute.* She groaned inwardly. *Stop being silly.*

Luckily, Alex didn't seem to notice the mental anxiety she was going through. "I met her a couple years ago when we raided a ranch outside the city that was involved in the illegal animal trade. She helped relocate some of the big cats we recovered. I've stopped by to help her out at the zoo a few times since then, and she said if I ever needed a favor, I should just call. So, I called."

Lacey decided that sounded innocent enough, then chided herself for being so juvenile. It was none of her business, even if Alex and Hannah had dated at some point.

What the heck? Why was she even thinking stuff like that?

Fortunately, a distraction in the form of a big building in their path appeared at that moment.

"This is the zoo's treatment center," Alex explained. "It's where they bring animals when they're injured or when they're passing through on their way somewhere else, which is what's going on in this case."

Lacey's excitement level began to ratchet up again. At least it kept her from thinking about Alex and anyone he might have dated in the past.

Stop that!

The interior of the building was a lot like the vet clinic where she worked, only much larger. There were about a dozen cubicle office spaces, then a separate section with lots of treatment and surgical rooms.

At the far end of the building, they found Hannah standing outside a holding pen area. In one of the pens, Lacey spotted a dark gray wolf, bigger than any dog she had ever seen. Of course, some of that had to do with the incredibly thick coat of fur covering him. Regardless, he was huge.

"This is Ralph," Hannah said with a smile. "He's a North American gray wolf, sometimes called a timber wolf. He's a recent arrival from Canada as part of a breeding study trying to increase gene diversity in the U.S. captive population."

All Lacey could do was stare. The wolf stared right back at them through the bars of the enclosure gate. Since she loved dogs, she obviously loved wolves too. But she'd never seen one this close before, not even in a normal zoo environment. Now she was only four feet away.

"Are they always this big?" Lacey asked.

Hannah shook her head. "Gray wolves normally get up to about a hundred and seventy pounds, but Ralph is two hundred, so he's bigger than average. It's part of the reason he's in the breeding program."

"You want to go in and see him up close?" Alex asked.

Lacey whipped her head around to look at him. "We can do that? Is he tame?"

Hannah's lips curved. "Ralph is a wolf. He's not domesticated and will never be tame, but he is used to people. Still, I'd normally never let anyone go in there with him." She jerked her thumb at Alex. "He and Ralph are bros, though. I think they were related in a previous life or something. Ralph gets along with Alex better than I get along with my sister. As long as Alex is with you, it's cool."

Even though Lacey was sure the woman knew what she was talking about, she was still nervous. The wolf was huge—and looking at them like he was wondering if Lacey's head would fit in his mouth. Lacey was pretty sure it would.

Alex took her hand again, and Lacey jumped a little at the spark of contact that passed between them. Then a feeling of calm confidence settled over her, and she nodded at him. "Let's do it."

Reaching out with his free hand, Alex opened the door of the enclosure and led her inside. Ralph seemed to grow in size the closer she got to him, but the wolf never did anything except stare at her. That was disconcerting enough.

They stopped a foot away from the wolf, whose head was easily level with Lacey's belly button. Ralph regarded them calmly, then suddenly lunged forward, lifting up on his hind feet.

Lacey opened her mouth to scream bloody murder, but before she could get out a squeak, Alex laughed and caught the wolf in a bear hug.

She gaped as Ralph licked Alex's face, the wolf chuffing like an idiot. She'd known Alex liked dogs, but he was standing there in an expensive suit letting a big wolf practically slobber all over him. Ralph's canines had to be almost two inches long. And they were right there in Alex's face. But he didn't even seem to care.

"Oh my God," she whispered, barely believing what she was seeing.

"Yeah, I told you," Hannah said from behind her. "These two are bros."

The next thirty minutes were the most amazing of Lacey's life as she knelt there on the floor beside Ralph and got a chance to pet an animal she'd never imagined she would ever get close to. Ralph's fur was so thick and soft that just caressing it made her laugh. And his amber eyes were so trusting, they brought tears to her own. When Hannah told them it was time for Ralph to go to bed, Lacey didn't want to leave. She wanted to stay here and pet this incredible animal forever. But Alex said the guy had a big day tomorrow.

"He gets to meet his new girlfriend down at the Austin Zoo. We want him feeling fresh and looking his best."

Lacey laughed. "Well, I can certainly understand that. A guy needs his beauty rest if he's going to impress the ladies."

They left a little while later, after Lacey made sure to thank Hannah profusely for the opportunity. She was so giddy that she practically ran back to Alex's truck, dragging him all the way.

"That was so amazing!" she said, unable to control the laughter bubbling up inside her. She felt like a kid at Christmas who'd gotten the exact present she'd been waiting for the whole year but didn't know she wanted. And Alex had given it to her. She was still bouncing as he helped her into the passenger seat and walked around to his side. When he climbed in beside her, she couldn't stop herself from leaning over to kiss him on the cheek.

"Thank you for a perfect date," she said softly.

He grinned as he started the truck. "You're welcome. Dinner and a trip to the zoo for a kiss from you? Seems like a fair trade to me."

Lacey laughed. Alex was the kind of guy she'd happily give a whole lot more to than a peck on the cheek for a date like this one. Then again, the date wasn't over yet.

———

"You want to come in?" she asked as she unlocked the door to her apartment.

"I'd love to," Alex said. "If you're sure it won't wake Kelsey up."

Lacey laughed. "Kelsey could sleep through a cattle stampede. Don't worry about her."

Leonardo was waiting for them in the foyer. He ignored her and Alex, wagging his tail and eyeballing the doggie bag she held with interest.

"Forget it, Leo," she whispered. "Too many carbs for you."

He backed off but gave her a look that seemed to say, *If there are too many carbs in there for me, why were you eating it then?*

Even though Kelsey was a heavy sleeper, Lacey still pulled off her heels so they wouldn't make too much noise. But the moment she saw the empty countertop in the kitchen, she knew Kelsey wasn't home yet. Her sister always left her purse on the counter when she came in. Lacey dug through her own purse for her phone and saw that there was a text from Kelsey.

"Everything okay?" Alex asked.

She dropped her phone back in her bag. "Uh-huh. Kelsey said she got tired after running around all over the place looking for Sara, so she decided to stay at a girlfriend's place instead of taking a chance she'd nod off behind the wheel."

"You're not worried that she's out partying with her friends?"

Lacey shook her head. "I know how this is going to sound, but Kelsey's not like that. We have a good relationship and talk about that stuff. She knows I wouldn't care if she were out partying with friends—unless she was drinking, of course. We always tell each other where we are and when we'll be home."

Alex nodded but didn't say anything. She saw the skepticism in his eyes, though. He probably couldn't imagine a twenty-year-old not going out to party, but Kelsey had always been focused and dependable like that.

She smiled. "Since we have the place to ourselves, you want something to drink?"

"No, thanks. I'm not really thirsty."

Something in the way Alex looked at her as he said the words made her skin tingle. His chocolate-brown eyes swirled with heat, and she caught her breath. In her super high heels, he'd still been quite a bit taller than she was. With her heels off, he towered over her.

Lacey tried to think of something witty to say, but for some reason, her mind seemed to have completely shut down. Stringing together more than a word or two—much less something clever—was impossible. Luckily, when Alex reached out to take her hand and tug her closer, her instincts took over for her misfiring head, and her hands lifted to grasp his shoulders.

A moment later, Alex lowered his head to kiss her. Her lips parted in anticipation, and she melted against him as his warm mouth covered hers. She moaned loudly as his tongue found hers. At least this time, she had good cause for making noises like that. Alex tasted scrumptious.

She slipped one hand up to his short, dark hair, tucking her fingers in deep and yanking him closer, urging him to kiss her harder. But he refused, instead continuing his slow, careful, teasing exploration. Every once in a while, he pulled away to trace his lips along her jawline and make her whole body shiver, but mostly he teased her with his delectable kisses.

She slipped her tongue into his mouth to play with

his, trembling as hers glided across sharp teeth. She was going to have to be careful kissing him—a girl could cut herself on those babies.

Lacey rarely took part in casual flings. In fact, she hadn't done it since early on in college. She had to admit, she was definitely thinking about it now. The truth was, with just a few kisses, Alex had her more excited than she could ever remember being. She couldn't imagine what it would be like if they were naked and rolling around in each other's arms. She might just spontaneously combust.

And with her sister out, there would never be a better time.

She leaned into Alex, pressing her breasts against the hard, muscular planes of his chest as she felt something firm and insistent poking her in the stomach. Nice to know she wasn't the only one aroused.

She was sliding her hand down his chest to see just how aroused Alex really was when he broke their kiss with a soft growl and took a step back.

"It's getting late, and I'm sure you have to get up early tomorrow for work." His eyes smoldered so much, they nearly glowed from the heat. "I should be going."

Lacey thought for sure he had to be kidding, but when she slipped her hand down to one of his belt loops to tug him close again, he held firm. He tipped his head down for another quick kiss, then just as her fingers and knees went weak, he broke away and started for the door.

She blinked. "That's it? You're just going to get me all hot and bothered, then leave?"

Alex turned to face her, his mouth curving into a sexy smile as he continued backing toward the door. "We could always pick this up where we left off, but only if you were willing to go out on a second date. I wouldn't want you thinking I was trying to force you into a relationship or anything."

He was using her own words against her, dang him. She'd told him she wasn't looking for a relationship and that a second date probably wasn't in the cards. He'd taken her on the best first date of her life, then gotten her as turned on as a lightbulb just to make sure she'd definitely be coming back for more. He was so bad.

Lacey returned his smile. "You're resorting to sexual arousal to blackmail me into another date?"

He stopped as he reached the door. "A desperate man does what he has to."

She lifted a brow. "I make you that desperate?"

"I guess it will take another date—or two—for you to find that out."

That dangerous smile of his flashed across his face again before he turned and walked out.

She followed after him, catching a glimpse of his powerful form just before the door closed behind him. She looked out the peephole, hoping he'd glance back. He didn't.

Sighing, she flipped the lock, then leaned back against the door. Her whole body was tingling like she'd had an allover body massage, and the pulse between her legs told her she was more aroused than she'd ever been in her life. All from a kiss.

From where he was seated on the couch, Leo lifted his head and looked at her.

"Leo, I think your human is in deep trouble," she said.

Chapter 6

"THEY MAKE A GOOD COUPLE, DON'T THEY?" REMY SAID from beside Alex. "I've always thought that Brooks would fit best with a rough-and-tumble type of woman, and a veteran narcotics cop like Vaughn definitely fills the bill. I can see her holding him at gunpoint, demanding he get naked."

On the other side of the narcotics briefing room, Brooks turned and flashed them a grin, clearly hearing what Remy had just said. That, of course, had been Remy's intention all along.

Alex and Remy, along with Max and Brooks, had been called over to the narcotics division office for a task force briefing. Brooks had made a beeline for Vaughn the moment they walked in, and if the big smile on her face was any indication, the woman must have decided she had a thing for big, muscular men who tackled cars for fun.

"You think she's *The One* for him?" Alex asked, trying to picture the huge dark-skinned alpha werewolf with the attractive but rough-around-the-edges narcotics officer.

Remy shrugged. "Maybe, but if not, there's nothing wrong with her being *The-One-for-Right-Now*. Enough about Brooks and who he might end up with. How'd the date with Lacey go last night? Everything you hoped and expected?"

Alex had to work really hard to keep the goofy-ass

grin off his face. As far as he was concerned, last night's date had gone perfect…awesome…amazing…pick the adjective. He was trying not to get too carried away by refusing to allow himself to think that she might be… well, someone special. But he could honestly say that he'd never met anyone like Lacey Barton. She was about as perfect as he could imagine a woman being.

He'd been so buzzed after their date that the idea of sleeping had seemed ludicrous. Instead, he'd simply lain in bed and replayed every minute of the evening. He was tempted to explain away his sleeplessness with his crazy work schedule, but he knew that wasn't true. It was Lacey. She had his head spinning. And it wasn't just the kissing at the end of the date, though that had been pretty frigging amazing. No, it was the way he felt when he was with her, like he was alive for the first time. It was scary how fantastic the feeling was.

"I'm guessing by the way your heart rate just sky-rocketed that last night went very well," Remy surmised.

Alex grinned. "Yeah, it did. We had a really great time."

His friend regarded him thoughtfully. "Then why am I sensing a *but* coming?"

"No buts," Alex said. "It's just that I think I'm going to have to take it slow with her. She seems hesitant about jumping into anything. I'm just guessing, but I think some stuff in her past has soured her on relationships."

"You don't think it's anything that would keep the two of you from getting together, do you?"

Alex shrugged. "I definitely hope not."

Remy shook his head. "I always thought the hard part of finding *The One* was *finding* her. I never considered that you might luck onto your one-in-a-billion soul mate and discover she's not interested in a relationship because some other guy was an asshole to her."

There wasn't much Alex could add to that. Not only was Remy right, but at that moment, Sergeant Rodriguez walked in. Giving everyone a nod, the wiry, dark-haired cop signaled to a fellow narcotics officer to turn off the lights, then picked up the remote on the podium and turned on the ceiling-mounted projector. A moment later, a photo of a man appeared on the screen.

Alex did a double take—along with everyone else in the room. The guy had skin so pale, it was almost ghostly, along with white-blond hair and eyes so blue, Alex was sure they had to be contacts. But the thing that was most unsettling about the man were his pupils. Surrounded by the lightness in the rest of the man's features, those small points of pitch black were freaky to look at. They made him seem like a demon from a sci-fi movie.

As if all that didn't make him look disturbing enough, scars from old claw marks tugged up one side of the man's upper lip, adding a touch of menace to his expression. If the four claw marks hadn't been so close together, Alex would have thought the man had tangled with a werewolf.

"When the assistant district attorney told the dealers we picked up the other night that she intended to connect them to the deaths related to fireball, one of them cracked and identified the person who'd provided them their drug stash," Rodriguez said. "He didn't know the man's name, but once he described the guy, we didn't have too much problem tracking him down, as you can imagine."

No kidding.

Rodriguez gestured to the screen. "This is Michael Pendergraff. He's prior military, was a cop in Washington DC for a while, then a private investigator. For the past five years, he's worked security for this man." Another picture took the place of the albino, this one of an older man with gray hair and weathered skin. "Alfred Bensen, as in Bensen Automotive. He started out about thirty years ago with a single junkyard down in Houston, but since then, his business has grown considerably. He now owns nearly twenty junkyards, multiple car dealerships, and even runs a few manufacturing companies that make small parts for new cars."

"And we think this is the guy making fireball?" Vaughn asked. "Or are we thinking it's just Pendergraff?"

Rodriguez shrugged. "The truth is, we don't know. There's nothing in Pendergraff's background to indicate that he possesses the chemical expertise to make the drug himself. And while there do seem to be a few curious growth spurts in Bensen's business endeavors in the last few years, there's nothing to pin him to the drug."

"Other than our dealer saying he got his stash from Bensen's private bodyguard," Alex pointed out.

"Pretty much," Rodriguez said. "While we might be able to get a search warrant for Pendergraff's residence, we really doubt he's cooking up these new heroin blends in his kitchen. Everyone at the DEA assures us that this crap is coming out of a high-tech lab facility."

"So, what's the plan?" Remy asked.

Rodriguez moved to the next slide. This one had names, addresses, and times. Everyone in the room groaned, including Alex.

"That's right, people." Rodriguez pinned them all with a look. "Around-the-clock surveillance at six of

Bensen's junkyards that the DPD Criminal Intel Unit
thinks are the ones most likely to be involved in the
drug-making and distribution activities. DEA has agreed
to step in and help us cover the overtime, so no bitching.
The sooner we get some actionable evidence proving
Bensen is involved in either the making or distribution
of fireball, the sooner we can get back to normal life."

Even with the promise of overtime pay, there was
still a lot of complaining…and not just from the narcotics folks. After weeks of hiding on rooftops and behind
Dumpsters looking for drug dealers, none of Alex's
SWAT teammates were thrilled at the idea of spending
a few more weeks sitting in surveillance vans staring
at junkyards. They preferred operations that involved
more action.

As Alex looked over the schedule projected up on the
screen, he was thrilled to see that most of his evenings
were free, including Wednesday. That's when Cooper
and Everly were having their engagement party, and
he'd been thinking about asking Lacey to go with him—
assuming she'd actually want to go out with him again.

"It's beautiful," Lacey said, admiring the diamond
engagement ring on Everly's hand. "You must be so
excited about the wedding."

The ring really was gorgeous, and Landry Cooper,
the SWAT officer who'd put it on her finger, was definitely a hunk. Lacey didn't doubt that Everly was giddy
at the prospect of marrying the man. Lacey was also
pretty sure the woman was insane. How else would you
describe a woman who was getting married to a man
she'd only known for two months?

Not that Lacey had a lot of room to judge, considering how fast she'd jumped at the chance to go out with Alex again when he asked if she'd like to go to an engagement party for one of his coworkers. But jumping at a chance for a second date with a guy—no matter how undignified that jump might be—was completely different from leaping into marriage with a man you barely knew.

Lacey and Alex had been hanging out in the big party tent set up at the SWAT compound for the last two hours, talking to the newly engaged couple and with Alex's other friends and coworkers. While Lacey already felt a growing kinship with several of the women at the party, she especially hit it off with Everly, even if she found it hard to believe that any rational woman would throw herself into marriage so quickly.

"All I can tell you is that when it's right, it's right," Everly told her when Lacey had subtly asked why they were moving so quickly with the wedding. "Once you find the person you're meant to spend the rest of your life with, doing anything other than being with them feels like you're wasting time."

Lacey just nodded as Everly and Cooper continued to make the rounds. That sounded a lot like something she'd expect her naive twenty-year-old sister to say. Coming from a woman Everly's age was a little crazy.

"You ready for another burger?" Gage asked, stopping by their table with an enormous tray of food from the grill. Tall with dark hair and brown eyes, the SWAT commander was older than Alex and almost as handsome. "Maybe some ribs?"

Lacey smiled. "No, thanks. I'm stuffed."

Gage pointed at one of the smaller burgers on the tray—at least compared to the others. "You sure? How about this one?" His mouth quirked. "It's tiny, like Alex's brain."

She laughed, unable to help herself. She was tempted—the guys made amazing burgers—but she really was full. It was cool that the senior people on the SWAT team—Gage, Xander, and Mike—were running the grills and serving the food. Alex hadn't been kidding when he said the SWAT team was like one big family, right down to the ribbing and insults. It was also pretty awesome that their definition of the word *family* included significant others and friends. The group of people filling the party tent tonight was broad and diverse, and they all made her feel welcome.

"I'm so glad you asked me to come to the party," Lacey said softly to Alex after his boss had moved to the next table. "I'm having fun."

While she'd agreed to go out again with Alex, there'd been a part of her a little worried about showing up at an engagement party for a couple she'd never even met. What if they didn't feel like including a complete stranger in their special evening? But Alex had promised Everly and Cooper weren't like that, and she'd be more than welcome at the party. Then he'd gone one step further to make sure she'd be relaxed at the party, telling her she should bring Leo so her dog could hang out with Tuffie and run around the big, wide-open compound.

That had turned out to be a wonderful idea, except now Tuffie was leading Leo around from table to table, apparently teaching him how to beg for scraps. She could totally see him giving her that sad puppy face every time she and Kelsey ordered pizza from now on.

"I'm glad you agreed to come," Alex whispered in her ear.

As his warm breath brushed across the sensitive skin of her neck, her heart began to beat faster, and she bit her lip. It took everything she had to keep from leaning into his body. The desire to feel his lips on her neck was so intense, it was scary. What the heck was wrong with her? Since when did she go all X-rated over a man's warm breath on her neck?

Fortunately, Alex pulled back before she embarrassed herself. His face betrayed nothing as he turned to listen to something another SWAT cop named Remy was saying on the other side of the table, like he didn't notice the effect he had on her. But then a little smile flitted briefly across his lips, indicating he had a perfectly good idea what he was doing to her. Once again, she reminded herself that she needed to be careful around this guy. He was dangerous—to her self-control if nothing else.

"Are you coming to the wedding?"

Lacey glanced up to see Jayna Winston regarding her with interest. Like Everly, the blond woman was close to her age, and Lacey had immediately felt comfortable around her. Also like Everly, Jayna was a bit crazy. She was currently living with Becker—another of Alex's hunky coworkers—and five of their friends in a single loft apartment. It sounded more like a frat house to Lacey. Jayna was definitely a lot bolder than she could ever be, that was for sure.

Beside Lacey, Alex was looking at her out of the corner of his eye. Jayna's innocent-sounding question suddenly took on a lot more weight. How was Lacey supposed to answer a question like that? She and Alex had only known each other barely more than a week, and this was only their second date. She didn't even know if they'd still be dating by the time Everly and Cooper got married.

She had to say something, though.

"I'm not sure," she said to Jayna. "I mean, I just met Everly and Cooper tonight. I'm sure the wedding invitations have already been sent out, and I wouldn't want to cause a problem with seating charts, catering, and stuff."

She was silently congratulating herself on such a diplomatic answer until Remy laughed.

"Alex, I think Lacey is trying to hedge her bets in case you turn out to be a dud and she dumps you before Cooper and Everly get married."

Lacey's jaw dropped, but Alex just laughed.

"I told you she was smart," he said.

Jayna made a face. "Don't pay attention to those two. They're constantly nipping at each other. You don't have to decide about the wedding right away. It's going to be a really low-key affair, so there will be plenty of space for last-minute friends. If you haven't grown tired of Alex by then, you're more than welcome to come. In fact, you're still invited even if you've smartened up and figured out that he's a soup sandwich."

"Soup sandwich? Now who's nipping?" Remy drawled.

Lacey couldn't help but laugh. Alex's friends were amazing. She felt more at home with them than she did with people she'd known for years. Of course, she'd never go to Cooper and Everly's wedding if things didn't work out with Alex, but it was nice to feel welcome.

They spent the remainder of the night moving from table to table, meeting the rest of Alex's coworkers as well as the other people at the party. She tried hard to remember each of his teammate's names, but after a while, she gave up. There were way too many of them. She sure as heck noticed they were all dangerously good looking, not to mention muscular. While Alex was definitely the most handsome, his teammates were certainly nothing to sneeze at. It made her wonder what it was about SWAT that attracted so many hot guys. They were all so charming too. She couldn't remember ever having such a good time simply talking.

As the evening wore on—and Alex's glances became hungrier—Lacey found herself thinking more about the kisses at her place after their date on Sunday night. If she were lucky, Kelsey would be out with her friends when Alex took her home, and they could pick up where they'd left off after their first date.

When the party wound down a little after ten, she and Alex helped clean up in spite of Gage and his wife's complaints. The hardest part of the night turned out to be collecting Leo so they could head home. Her dog flat-out didn't want to leave Tuffie.

"I promise you and Tuffie can have lots of play dates," Alex said as he crouched down in front of Leo and affectionately ran his hand over the dog's head. "All you have to do is convince your mom to keep seeing me, and I'll hook you up."

Lacey folded her arms with a laugh. "Now you're trying to blackmail my dog into supporting your dastardly schemes?"

Alex flashed her a grin. "A desperate man does what he has to," he said, repeating the same line he'd dropped on her at the end of their date the other night.

She didn't believe it any more now than she had then.

—◌◌◌—

Kelsey wasn't out like Lacey had hoped. Instead, she was sitting on the floor in the living room with three of her girlfriends, buried in books and study notes. Crud, why did her sister have to be so responsible and focused on her schoolwork all the time? Leo immediately trotted over to see what they were up to but quickly walked off in disappointment when it became obvious that there was no food to be had.

Kelsey looked up with a smile. "Hey, you two! How was the party?"

"Great," Lacey said, but her sister already had her nose back in a book.

Apparently, her three friends weren't as committed to their studying. They were all staring at Alex like he was a naked rock star. Their mouths were even hanging open.

Lacey would have said something about at least trying to make it look like they weren't staring but didn't want to embarrass them. Instead, she took Alex's hand and led him into the kitchen. They might not have the apartment to themselves, but she didn't want the date to end just yet. If nothing else, they could hang out in the kitchen for a bit. It was either that or invite him into her bedroom— and she wasn't ready to send that kind of message.

She checked to make sure there was water in Leo's bowl, then glanced at Alex. "You want something to drink?"

She reached for the handle of the refrigerator just as Kelsey and her friends let out loud laughs followed by a round of girlish chatter. One look at Alex's face confirmed that he was thinking the same thing she was. This wasn't a very good environment if they wanted some quality time together.

"Maybe we should have stayed at the SWAT compound," she said wryly. "It would have been quieter at least."

"We don't have to stay here if you don't want to," he said. "I know a quiet place over on Abrams Parkway. In the middle of the week, they usually have jazz or blues performers playing. We can just sit and listen, even dance a little if you want."

Suddenly, the idea of having Alex's big, strong arms around her as they swayed to some smooth blues rhythms seemed very appealing. She hadn't been out dancing in so long, she wasn't sure if she remembered how, but with Alex, she was willing to learn all over again.

Lacey smiled, kind of surprised that she was doing something like this but exhilarated too. "Okay. Let's go."

Kelsey barely looked up when Lacey told her sister they were going out again. "Have fun, just not too much fun. I don't want to have to bail you out of jail."

"You never let me have any fun," Lacey said, a fake whine in her voice as Alex opened the door for her. "What good is dating a cop if I can't use his get-out-of-jail-free card now and then?"

Alex just chuckled.

—⁂—

"How'd you find this place?" Lacey asked.

Alex glanced around as he led her through the cozy club. There was a small stage positioned near the back of the place, a bar along the far wall, and lots of small tables and booths scattered about in between. The dance floor in front of the stage was only big enough to hold ten people, but that was okay. This place was mostly about listening to good music and having a quiet conversation with friends. It was the perfect place to bring Lacey.

"The daughter of the owner was held hostage by her

ex-boyfriend a few years ago," Alex explained as they slid into a secluded booth in the corner. "When we got her out safely, he invited us to come by for some drinks on the house. I liked the place, so I kept coming back."

She pursed her lips, eyeing him thoughtfully. "First a raid on an illegal animal operation that gets you backstage access to the Dallas Zoo, and now a hostage situation that ends with you getting free drinks at a jazz club. Does your entire social life revolve around people that you've helped?"

Alex laughed. "Pretty much."

A waitress came by to take their drink orders, then told them that the blues band would start their set soon.

"I'm going to run to the ladies' room," Lacey said after the woman left. "I'll be right back."

Giving him a quick kiss, she slid out of the booth, flashing him a smile over her shoulder as she left. Alex leaned back in the booth, resting his arms on either side of him, following the sexy sway of her hips underneath her silky skirt. While he was thrilled with how well the date was going, Lacey had him more than a little off balance. He knew she was interested in him—he could hear the rapid beating of her heart, see her breasts rise and fall as her breathing picked up, smell her arousal.

But there were times when he could feel her put up a wall as she actively fought to control her body's reactions. He had no idea why she'd do something like that. Worse, he wondered if she was doing it in response to something he'd done. He hated to think he was the reason she occasionally shut down on him.

He only hoped it wouldn't happen tonight.

The waitress showed up with their drinks just as an extremely familiar scent hit his nose. His head snapped around, tracking the scent he was so used to smelling every day. That's when he realized he wasn't picking up one werewolf but two—and one was a woman.

Alex locked in on the band onstage. The guy was whipcord lean and wore jeans and a T-shirt as well as a tweed fedora cocked a little sideways on his head. He had a couple of tats visible along his arms and across the top of each finger too. The woman was about the same age, dressed with a little bit more attention to style, but with a bit of boho rebel thrown in, and her sandy blond hair was pulled back in a ponytail.

There was a third man on the stage, setting up drums in the back, but Alex was only interested in the couple. They were the werewolves. Their size and demeanor suggested they were betas, but he wasn't necessarily sure of that. Jayna wasn't very big, yet she was an alpha, while her pack mate Moe—who was almost as big as Alex—was a beta. What kind of werewolves they were wasn't really important, though. The important part was that they were in town.

There might be a lot more werewolves in Dallas than there used to be, especially with Jayna and her beta pack, but Alex had never walked into a place and stumbled over any before. It wasn't like they could all ignore each other and act like none of this had happened, since they were staring straight at him.

There was no mistaking the fear in the woman's eyes or the concern in the guy's. They were terrified of him. Alex was going to have to make the first move. It was either that or sit there and stare at them until they panicked and ran.

Sliding out of the booth, Alex slowly walked over to the couple, keeping his hands in plain sight and trying to project a sense of calm. As he got closer to the stage, the man in the hat stepped forward, taking up a defensive position in front of the woman who Alex realized now must be his mate. The guy in the back kept working on his drums, completely oblivious to the drama at the front of the stage.

"We're not here to cause trouble," the woman said, ignoring the warning look her mate threw her way. "We just moved here with our kids because we thought it would be a safe place to live."

Alex frowned. He was a cop. If these two were in trouble, he would help them. It was as simple as that. "Safe from what?"

The man and woman exchanged looks, silent communication passing between them. Yeah, these two were definitely betas. Alex could tell by the way they moved closer to each other for support. If they'd been alphas, they would have moved further apart to make it easier to attack him from two sides.

"From the hunters," the guy said finally. "They've always been out there, but it seems like they're becoming more aggressive. A lot of people like us have been killed lately."

Alex's jaw dropped. He knew what hunters were—at least in the general sense. Cooper had mentioned that Everly's family had been involved with a werewolf hunter years ago over in France after a rogue werewolf had attacked and killed her mother. But he'd thought hunters were something that were limited to the Old World. The idea that there were people running around the United States killing werewolves was crazy—and disconcerting.

"So you came here looking for protection?" he prompted.

They both nodded.

"Every werewolf in the country has heard rumors about the huge pack of alpha werewolves all living together in Dallas." The man glanced at his mate. "Season thought that maybe the hunters would think twice before coming here and messing with us."

"We were hoping this is a place we could raise our kids without having to worry about them all the time," Season explained. "If it was just Allen and me, we would have gone on the run, but kids need a place to call home. They need friends and a good school. I swear we weren't trying to move in on your territory." She wet her lips nervously. "You are part of the alpha pack, right?"

Alex nodded.

"But if your pack doesn't want us here, we'll leave," Allen said quickly. "Like Season said, we're not looking for trouble."

Alex couldn't imagine being in the position these two betas found themselves in—terrified to come to Dallas and risk a pack of alphas attacking them, or staying away and risking the hunters finding them.

"There won't be any trouble," Alex assured them. "I'll have to let my alpha know, but I can promise you that he'll do everything he can to keep you and your family safe. He'll want to meet with you, though."

Allen and Season exchanged looks again, and Alex got the feeling that they were a little hesitant to deal with a werewolf someone his size answered to, but in the end, they exchanged phone numbers and gave up the location of the apartment complex where they were living.

"If you see anything suspicious, call," Alex told them.

When he got back to the table, Lacey was already seated, waiting for him.

"Sorry," he said as he slipped into the booth and sidled up close to her. "I didn't see you come back."

"No problem. I take it you know those two?"

"Not really. They just moved into the area, and when they found out I was a cop, they wanted to know if I thought Dallas was a safe place to raise their kids."

He figured that was a close enough synopsis of the conversation he'd just had—minus the whole were-wolf part.

She smiled. "That's sweet of you, going out of your way to help people you just met."

He chuckled and slipped his arm around her. "That's me—Officer Friendly."

It turned out that Season and Allen's band was good—really good. Soulful with a little bit of melan-choly and a whole lot of hope. Alex could almost close his eyes and picture the lives the two werewolves had led. The running, the worry, the hope that tomorrow would be better than today.

He and Lacey sat listening for a while before she wordlessly took his hand, pulling him out of the booth and onto the dance floor. This wasn't the kind of music that required elaborate dance steps. With the blues, you just got close, then let the rhythm move you. That was fine with Alex. He liked holding Lacey close.

Lacey rested her head on his shoulder, wrapping one arm around him possessively, holding his left hand with her right. Alex slipped his right hand down to her lower back, letting his fingers graze that perfect curve right at the top of her ass as he pulled her hips tighter against him.

The music all but faded into the background as Lacey's scent enveloped him. His cock hardened immediately at the feel of her firm breasts coming into contact with his chest. She wiggled her hips a little, grinding against him as she swayed to the music. His claws were behaving right now, thank God, but being this close to Lacey and smelling how aroused she was had him so turned on that it was taking everything he had to keep his canines from slipping out.

Lacey suddenly lifted her head off his shoulder to gaze up at him. One look at the sensuality in her eyes, and he was completely undone. His mouth was coming down on hers before he even realized what he was doing. Her lips eagerly parted for his questing tongue, the hunger in her kiss pushing him further toward the edge of his control.

Alex wasn't sure how long the kiss lasted—maybe a few minutes, maybe a few songs—but when they finally broke apart, he was absolutely sure he'd never experienced anything like it before. He couldn't believe how much he wanted to strip off Lacey's clothes and make love to her right there on the dance floor—or at the very least take her back to his place and hold her captive in his bed for days on end.

Yet as he gazed down at her, he remembered how many times she'd pulled away from him. How many times he'd felt that wall of hers go up and snuff out the most powerful emotion he'd ever experienced.

So he forced himself to slow down and take his time. This was way too important to rush. Lacey gave him a little frowny face when he gently urged her head back onto his shoulder, but she didn't complain. She didn't shut down on him, either. That had to be good, right?

On stage, Allen caught Alex's eye as he and Lacey went back to swaying to the music, giving him a knowing nod as he put a harmonica to his mouth and slipped into another soulful tune.

———ᨔᨔ———

Alex hated waking up Gage and Mac in the middle of the night, but he knew his boss would want to know about the betas moving into the area—and the hunters they were running from. It was something that might affect the Pack at some point, though Alex wasn't sure exactly how. Like Season and Allen had said, he couldn't imagine hunters showing up in Dallas, not when there was a pack of alpha SWAT cops waiting here for them.

When he pulled into the driveway of Gage and Mac's new two-story home, however, Armand Danu's minivan was there and the lights were on in the house. Alex frowned as he got out of his pickup. What the hell was Everly's oldest brother doing here at this hour?

Alex rang the doorbell, replaying the evening in his mind while he waited for his boss to answer.

He and Lacey had left the club around two o'clock, then gone back to her place. He'd kissed her at the door, mostly because he knew he'd never want to leave if he went inside. As it was, walking away from her had been about the hardest thing he'd ever done. Not only did Lacey have to get up early for work, but he still didn't want to rush into anything.

Even so, he couldn't help but think that their relationship had turned some kind of metaphorical corner.

The door opened, and Mac stood there, a smile on her face. Tall with long, dark hair and blue eyes, she was a journalist for the *Dallas Daily Star*. While her job should have put her and the SWAT commander at odds, instead, it had brought them together.

"Hey!" she said, opening the door wider. "Come in. Gage is in the office. Go on back."

Any other person probably would have asked him what he was doing there, but Gage's wife was so used to him and the other guys in the Pack coming over, she didn't even blink.

Gage was studying a big map of the United States attached to the far wall in his office, Armand on one side of him, Everly's father Florian Danu on the other. There were at least twenty colored pins tacked randomly about the map, with photographs of people positioned near each.

Alex's boss glanced his way, apparently not surprised to see him. Why should he be? Gage had smelled him the moment Mac had let him in. Hell, Gage had been a werewolf for so long, he'd probably recognized the sound of Alex's truck when he pulled into the driveway.

"What brings you by at this time of night?" Gage asked. "Please tell me you haven't done something that's going to end up with you in jail again."

Alex chuckled. He couldn't blame Gage for being worried. Two months ago, he and Brooks had been arrested for coming to Cooper's assistance after a little misunderstanding with the FBI.

"No, nothing like that."

He nodded to Everly's father and brother, then explained about the betas he met at the club downtown. Gage didn't seem surprised by any of it, not even when he mentioned the hunters. Come to think of it, neither did Florian or Armand.

Alex gestured to the map. "What's all this?"

Gage's mouth tightened. "You're looking at

werewolves who have been murdered by hunters across the United States in the past year."

Alex did a double take. There were a hell of a lot of people up there, including women and even some kids. Alex was pretty sure the kids hadn't been werewolves, which had to mean they were collateral damage.

Shit.

"How do you even know these people were werewolves?" Alex asked.

"I don't know, not with a hundred-percent certainty anyway," Gage said. "But after almost fifteen years of looking for werewolves to put on the SWAT team, I've gotten pretty good at recognizing the red flags after a person goes through their change. I could be wrong about some of them, but my gut tells me I'm not."

Alex knew from personal experience that Gage had ID'd him simply from reading about how he'd survived that shooting in Rochester. He supposed the bigger question was what had made Gage start looking for these particular people in the first place. It wasn't like most of them would ever have been SWAT candidates.

"And you just happened to stumble over these dead werewolves by accident?"

Alex didn't want Gage to think he was questioning the way he ran the Pack, but he had to know.

"No, I didn't just stumble over them." Gage glanced at Everly's father. "After meeting Florian, I realized there was a lot about hunters that I didn't know, so we started doing some digging."

"It was time consuming cross-referencing the list of unsolved murders in the United States with people we thought might be werewolves," Florian added in heavily accented English. "We've been working on it for weeks."

Alex looked at the photos pinned to the map again. The people were from every walk of life. They were young, old, male, female, black, white, Hispanic, Asian. Even after all the crazy stuff that had been going down lately, he'd never realized there were so many werewolves out there.

"Do you know who the hunters are?" he asked.

Gage shook his head. "No, but it seems like they're escalating the killings. If our assumptions are right, ten werewolves have been killed in the past few months alone."

"Which explains why those betas I met tonight were running scared." Alex's gums started to tingle at the urge to find these hunters and stop them. "Do you think these assholes would come here?"

"I don't think so," Gage said. "So far, they seem to be going after weaker beta packs and lone omegas. I don't see them coming after a large pack like ours. Then again, we don't even know who the hell these people are, whether there's more than one group of them. The most we can do right now is let the Pack know what's out there and keep an eye out for them. Then be ready if they try to make a move against us."

Chapter 7

"YOU DID WHAT?" WENDY PRACTICALLY SHOUTED. "TELL me you didn't do anything that stupid!"

Lacey winced as she looked at her friend's reflection in the bathroom mirror. Maybe she shouldn't have brought up the subject of breaking into Bensen's junkyard minutes before Alex was due to pick her up for their date.

Wendy had stopped by to chat as Lacey was getting ready to go to dinner and a movie with Alex. This was their third date—*and* it was on Friday night—so she was a little geeked. That was probably why she'd slipped up and told Wendy about her little adventure at Bensen's place. That and the fact that her friend had just told her the ACS crew hadn't been able to find enough on Bensen to even bother talking to their deputy chief, much less the assistant district attorney.

"I was just trying to help," Lacey pointed out as she tried to hold the curling iron at what she hoped was the right angle. She didn't use it very often, and the last thing she wanted was to burn herself with the dang thing. All she needed was to go out on a date with a scorch mark across her forehead.

Wendy pushed away from the doorjamb and walked over to stand beside Lacey. "How? By getting yourself killed? You're right, that would have been a big help. We could have arrested Bensen for murder then. No, wait. You were trespassing on private property in the middle of the night. Bensen could have had Pendergraff shoot you, and he'd be completely within his rights to do it."

"Dammit, Bensen is up to something in that junkyard," Lacey said firmly, jerking the curling iron away and giving up on the whole curly hair concept. Her hair was wavy, and that was as good as it was going to get. "I saw them standing over a big cardboard box, and with the way they were talking, I know they were doing something illegal."

Wendy looked like she wanted to yell at her again, but she stopped herself and took a deep breath, then gave Lacey a patient look and started again. "What did you see?"

Lacey hesitated as she dug through the makeup drawer, looking for her mascara. She liked to think that the poor state of her cosmetics was because Kelsey was always raiding her bathroom, but that wasn't it. She just hadn't bought much of the stuff in a while.

That wasn't the only thing keeping her from responding to Wendy's question. Honestly, she didn't know how to describe what she'd seen in that junkyard.

"I didn't really see anything," she admitted. "But Bensen was shouting at Pendergraff about getting on their supplier, threatening to feed the guy to the dogs if he couldn't do better."

Wendy frowned. "Lacey, they could have been talking about anything—rebuilt carburetors, for heaven's sake."

Lacey picked up the tube of mascara. She didn't know what the heck a carburetor looked like, but she knew that wasn't what Bensen had been so steamed about. "Wendy, you didn't see his face the way I did. He was furious at his supplier. I don't know what was in the box, but I know Bensen is a piece of crap who should be in prison."

Wendy sighed. "I know he's a piece of crap. But he's also a dangerous piece of crap. What would have happened if they'd caught you in there? What would happen to Kelsey if you were gone?"

Lacey felt herself pale. Kelsey was her life. The thought of her little sister without someone to take care of her tore Lacey's heart out. The hand holding the tube of mascara shook.

Wendy reached out and gently took the mascara from her. "Here, let me do that. You just stand there and look pretty, okay?"

Lacey stood still as Wendy applied mascara to her lashes. The truth was that Wendy did a better job than Lacey would have done herself anyway. She simply wasn't good at this kind of stuff.

"You know I love you like a sister, right?" Wendy asked as she finished one eye and started on the other. "You need to promise me that you'll stay away from Bensen and Pendergraff. Let me worry about them."

Lacey was about to agree when Kelsey poked her head in the bathroom door and interrupted her.

"Getting ready for the big night?" Kelsey grinned. "Should I wait up for you or just assume you won't be back until morning?"

Wendy laughed and tightened the top on the mascara. "Oh yeah, no way you're seeing your sister until tomorrow."

Lacey shook her head as she looked at her friend and sister in the mirror. These two were just plain bad. "Come on, you guys. It's just dinner and a movie."

"Really?" Kelsey gestured at Lacey. "Is that why you've been in here for an hour doing your hair and makeup?"

Lacey turned to face them, arms crossed over her

chest. "What's wrong with wanting to look nice for a date?"

"Nothing at all," Kelsey assured her. "But trust me, all this work won't mean much when you wake up tomorrow with morning-after bedhead."

Lacey gaped at her sister. "And what do you know about morning-after bedhead?"

Kelsey laughed. "I read about it in *Cosmo* once. Have fun on your date."

Giving her a wave, Kelsey turned and walked out.

Lacey looked at Wendy. "That's it, I'm calling up that convent we talked about."

Wendy laughed, turning Lacey back to the mirror and picking up her chubby cosmetic brush. "Lacey, she's not a kid. She's twenty."

"She's a kid to me and always will be."

Her friend shook her head as she dipped the brush in the powdered blush. "Well, Kelsey's right about one thing. You're not spending this much time fussing with your hair and makeup to go see a movie. You really like this guy, don't you?"

Lacey started to deny it, then decided not to bother. "Yeah, I guess I do."

Wendy lightly ran the brush over Lacey's cheeks. "You make it sound like that's a bad thing."

Lacey shrugged. "Maybe it is. I want this to work out with Alex—I really do. But I just can't help feeling like the other shoe is going to drop any minute now, and then I'm going to find out that Alex isn't anything like the man I thought he was."

Her friend placed the cosmetic brush in the drawer, a sad expression in her eyes. "Lacey, it doesn't have to be that way."

"Experience tells me otherwise, but you already know that."

Lacey tried to keep the bitterness out of her voice. She was excited about tonight, and she didn't want to ruin that by thinking too far ahead. Things were good right now. Why did it have to be about anything more than that?

Wendy regarded her for a moment, then reached out and hugged the stuffing out of her. "Just because your mom had shit luck with men doesn't mean you will. You're not like your mom, and Alex isn't like your dad—or any of the other guys who came after him."

Lacey hugged Wendy back, wishing her friend was right but unable to put much faith in the possibility. While Lacey was smart enough to know she was too young to be this cynical, she was also wise enough to know there wasn't much she could do about it. Life had made her this way.

She pushed away from her friend and pasted a smile on her face. "Enough. If you make me start crying and mess up my mascara, I'm going to whack you."

"Definitely can't have that." Wendy gave her a wan smile. "But seriously, I don't want to see you blow this thing with Alex because you're so busy looking for problems that aren't there."

"I won't. I promise. Come on. He's going to be here soon, and I don't want Kelsey getting to him without me in the room. She might ask him what his intentions are toward me."

This time, Wendy's grin was one of amusement. "It could be worse. She might ask if he plans on using protection."

Lacey blinked. "You don't think she'd really ask him something like that, do you?"

"Actually, yeah, I do."

Groaning, Lacey hurried out of the bathroom. Fortunately, she made it to the living room before the doorbell rang. Not that it mattered. Kelsey was too preoccupied with her cell phone to run for the door shouting about the importance of safe sex, so Lacey was able to answer it herself.

A smile spread across her face the moment she saw Alex standing there, all the silly stuff she and Wendy had been talking about in the bathroom fading away like a fuzzy dream.

"Hey there." She took in his tight T-shirt and jeans, deciding she liked him even more in casual clothes than she had in the suit he'd worn on the first date, especially when those casual clothes were formfitting and showed off all those perfect muscles. "Come on in. I just have to grab my purse." She motioned at Wendy as she walked over to the couch. "I'd introduce the two of you, but it's obvious you already know each other, since you conspired together to ambush me at the rescue shelter."

Her friend let out a short laugh. "Ambush? You make it sound like I did something horrible. If one of my friends sent a hunky single guy out to spend the day with me, I sure as heck wouldn't complain."

Lacey snorted. "You have friends? When did that happen?"

She was so busy grinning at her snappy comeback that it took her a moment to realize Kelsey still hadn't looked up from her phone, even though Lacey was sure that zinger at Wendy had been one of her better ones.

"Everything okay, Kelsey?"

Her sister frowned at her phone for a second, then

tossed it on the couch beside her. "Yeah. I just got a text from Sara."

"That's great!"

"I guess so," Kelsey said. "She said she met some guy and decided to go to Mexico with him."

"Mexico?"

Lacey couldn't keep the surprise out of her voice. This was Texas, so it wasn't like Mexico was on the other side of the world. But from the little she knew about Sara Collins, she didn't sound like the kind of girl who'd run off with a guy she just met.

Kelsey nodded. "Yup. She makes it sound like it's not a big deal. She said she'd see me in a few weeks."

Lacey reached down to give her sister's hand a squeeze. "The important thing is that Sara's okay. I'm sure she'll catch you up on everything when she gets back."

Kelsey considered that for a moment, then smiled. "You're right. Have a good time tonight." She winked. "And don't worry. I won't wait up."

⁓

Lacey assumed they were going to one of the bazillion restaurants in the Dallas/Fort Worth area, followed by a movie at one of the bazillion theaters. Instead, Alex drove to a quiet residential area and stopped in front of an apartment complex with assigned parking and lots of curb appeal.

"You don't mind dinner and a movie at my place, do you?" he asked as he pulled into his space.

"Not at all."

She'd been wondering what kind of place a SWAT cop who loved dogs called home. When he unlocked the door of his second-floor apartment a few minutes later, she was pleased to see that it was just as down-to-earth and warm as he was.

The living room opened to an eat-in kitchen. A small hallway led to the back of the apartment and what she assumed were bedrooms. She could tell by the fresh scent in the air and complete lack of dust around that he'd cleaned before bringing her over.

"Feel free to look around while I get dinner going." He flashed her a smile as he tossed his keys on the table in the entryway. "Be careful you don't get lost, though. The place is bigger than it looks."

Lacey's mouth curved as she followed him into the kitchen. "Sure. It's like a TARDIS apartment, right?" When he gave her a blank look, she laughed. "Not a big *Doctor Who* fan, huh?"

"Who?"

"Exactly."

Alex turned and frowned at her. "Are we having the same conversation? Because I'm officially lost."

Lacey giggled and quickly moved to put the small kitchen island between her and Alex, since it suddenly looked like he had the urge to spank her. Where had *that* thought come from?

"Doctor Who is a character on a TV show of the same name," she explained. "He travels through time and space in an old British police call box that's called the TARDIS. It's bigger on the inside than it is on the outside."

Alex stared at her for a moment before shaking his head. "That's just strange."

"No, Doctor Strange is completely different," she pointed out, proud that she could keep a straight face. "He uses magic."

Alex's mouth twitched, but he refused to bite this time. Instead, he turned to wash his hands. "You okay with veal scallopini?"

Lacey blinked as Alex pulled a frying pan from one cabinet and a baking sheet from another before preheating the oven. He moved with the sure, confident steps of a person who knew exactly what he was doing in the kitchen.

"Scallopini sounds great. Are you really going to cook me a homemade Italian dinner?"

He smiled at her as he took a loaf of some kind of baguette bread off the top of the fridge. "I'm Italian—at least on my father's side—and we're in my home, so yes, I'm making you a homemade Italian dinner."

She perched on one of the stools at the island, watching as he cut several slices off the loaf of bread, then cut those into cubes. Her jaw dropped when he sprayed them with olive oil, then tossed them in a bowl with garlic powder and Italian seasoning.

"You're making croutons?"

He chuckled. "That's the general idea. You don't like croutons?"

"I love them. I just usually buy the ones that come in the foil bag at the grocery store."

"Those are good too. I just figured I'd go all out for our first dinner in."

She sure as heck wasn't going to complain. "Can I help?"

He grinned. "I have this. I wouldn't mind you talking to me as I work, though. Or you can check out the place if you want."

Lacey would rather have helped, but as fast as he was moving around the kitchen, she didn't want to get in the way. He might run her over. Besides, she'd never had a guy cook for her before. Watching would be fun.

As he worked, he filled her in on what he was making—veal cutlets with a mushroom, white wine, and broth reduction over angel hair pasta, salad with home-made Italian dressing, and lightly seasoned garlic bread. The description alone was enough to impress her, not to mention make her mouth water. As she watched him sauté the mushrooms, she had to admit the whole thing was damn sexy. His big hands moved so surely and fast that she couldn't stop herself from imagining what they would feel like running all over her body.

Lacey bit her lip. If she didn't focus on something else, she was going to start drooling—and it wouldn't be over the veal cutlets.

She slid off the stool and wandered into the living room, admiring the big screen TV mounted on the wall. "Considering you've never heard of the Ninja Turtles or Doctor Who, I'm guessing you don't watch a lot of TV?"

Alex didn't look up from what he was doing. "Not really. When I do, I usually watch sports or movies. I mostly read."

Huh. Lacey didn't run into a lot of guys who liked to read. Another point in Alex's favor.

Interested to see what kind of books he liked, she found his home office down the hall, figuring that's where he'd probably keep them. She was right. There was a built-in bookcase along one wall. He had a lot of law enforcement books, which wasn't surprising considering his profession, but there were just as many law books and medical texts. Not just basic first-aid manuals, either. He had some serious human anatomy books on the shelves too.

His taste in fiction seemed to lean toward spy novels and action thrillers, but she also saw a few titles that looked suspiciously like they were firmly in the sci-fi/ fantasy genre. She hadn't pegged Alex for a paranormal type of guy.

Back in the hallway, she couldn't resist a quick peek into his bedroom. It was decidedly masculine, right down to the king-sized bed. Of course he'd have a king bed—he was huge. Still, that really was a lot of bed for one person.

Sighing, she walked into the living room and checked out the various framed photos on the wall. There were some of him with his fellow marines back when he was in the military. If the arid, desolate background in the pictures was any indication, they looked like they'd been taken during deployments.

All the more recent photos were of him with his SWAT teammates, either dressed in tactical gear, formal dress uniform as part of a ceremony of some kind, or hanging around the barbecue grills at the compound. He really looked happy with the guys, which only reinforced what he'd said about them being like his family.

She frowned as she realized something. She walked back into the office to check, then did the same in his bedroom. There wasn't a single picture that wasn't related to his time in the Marines or SWAT.

That was when she spotted an eight-by-ten frame on the table beside the couch. In the photo, a shy-looking girl of about eighteen smiled at the camera. At her feet sat a big, bushy golden retriever. But while the girl was smiling, it wasn't a happy smile. It was the kind of smile you put on because someone pointed a camera at you.

Lacey picked up the frame. Yeah, she knew all about that kind of smile. Anyone looking at a picture of her in her teenage years would have seen one very similar.

"Is this your sister?" she asked.

Alex looked up from the stove at the picture she was holding. Maybe she was just seeing things, but it seemed like, for a moment, his eyes filled with pain. But then he smiled.

"No," he said. "That's Jessica. She's a friend from back in Rochester. I like to think of her as the sister I never had, if that counts."

Something told her there was a story there, but Alex didn't seem inclined to talk about it, and Lacey didn't want to push. She carefully placed the picture frame back on the end table and rejoined him in the kitchen. Since it seemed like the dinner was almost ready, she offered to set the table.

"Okay, so no sisters other than Jessica. What about brothers?" She glanced at him over her shoulder as she carried the dishes and flatware over to the kitchen table. "If you don't mind my asking."

He bent down to take the croutons out of the oven before answering. Lacey's eyes widened. Wow, they looked better than anything she'd ever seen in a restaurant. She was no slouch in the kitchen, but she got the feeling that Alex was better.

"No, I don't mind. Since I'd like to think that we're going to keep seeing each other, I might as well tell you about my family, however dysfunctional they may be." He jerked his head at the stove. "Let me get everything out of the oven, then I'll give you the low-down on the Trevinos."

Lacey finished setting the table, then brought the salad and dressing over before going back to drain the pasta while Alex took the veal scallopini out of the oven where it'd been warming. Everything looked and smelled amazing, and she suddenly decided that maybe Wendy was onto something. A guy as great as Alex who was not only gorgeous, built like Adonis, loved dogs, and was easy to talk to, but could cook too? That just might be a man too good to pass up.

She served the salad and put the pasta on the plates while Alex took care of the scallopini and added freshly grated Romano cheese. Then he poured each of them white wine.

Lacey tried really hard not to moan after the first bite, but she was pretty sure she failed. It was absolutely delicious, not to mention so tender she didn't even have to use a knife. Oh yeah, Alex was definitely a keeper. The only thing that concerned her now was why a guy like this hadn't been snatched up already. He seemed as close to perfect as a man could get.

"So to answer your question, I don't have any brothers," Alex said as he twirled pasta around his fork. "I'm the only child to a mother and father who had a kid because that's what all their friends in Rochester were doing at the time. It's also likely that I was conceived as a way to save a marriage that was about to fall apart."

Lacey took a bite of her garlic bread. She had a good idea where this was going. She supposed she and Kelsey weren't the only ones who'd had a crappy home life.

"I guess it worked to some degree, since my parents

kept it together until I was about five years old, but in
the end, they got divorced anyway."

She didn't like the picture she had in her head of a
five-year-old Alex being told by his parents that they
were separating. That was one thing she and Kelsey had
never had to go through at least. "Who got custody?"

"It started out as joint custody." He paused to eat his
salad. "It didn't stay that way for long, though. I didn't
realize it at the time, but my parents were fiercely competitive people, and I was the prize each of them wanted
to win. I spent a good portion of my early years in court
as my mom and dad both fought to get full custody,
saying the nastiest crap about each other to do it. They
spent a decade fighting for custody, then ignored me
on those occasions when they actually had me around."

She reached across the table and took his hand. "I'm
sorry you had to go through that."

He squeezed her hand in return and shrugged. "I left
to join the Corps the day I turned eighteen and never
looked back. I haven't talked to either of my parents
since, and I don't plan to. It sucks, but I got over it."

Lacey doubted that. She knew firsthand that you
didn't just *get over* having crappy parents. Even though
she'd just met him, there were certain qualities about
Alex—the attention he put into being the best paramedic he could be, his willingness to throw himself into
danger to help complete strangers, the trust he had in
his SWAT teammates—that could all be traced back
to the things that had happened to him when he was
young. Considering how much her own family life had
affected her, it was almost funny the way they'd found
each other. Like fate had taken a hand in bringing two
screwed-up people together.

"How about you?" He picked up his wineglass. "You mentioned that your dad took off, then your mom left. Did you ever have an urge to find either of them and reconnect?"

Now she was sorry she hadn't been completely honest with him about her parents the first time they'd talked about it. The way she'd avoided the truth just made it harder to talk about now. She was tempted to fudge the details again and skip over the painful parts. But that didn't feel right, not after Alex had opened up about his background.

Lacey chased her food around on the plate for a while before finally answering. "I don't know where my dad is and don't care. As for my mom, I can't. She committed suicide."

Alex paused, his fork halfway to his mouth. He slowly lowered it to his plate. "I'm sorry. I didn't realize."

She nodded. The funny thing was, sharing that with Alex made it feel like a weight had suddenly been lifted from her shoulders. "It's okay. It's just not something I talk about very much." She made a face. "Okay, actually, I never talk about it. But it feels good to put it out there, if that makes any sense?"

"Yeah, it does. I've seen what it's like on someone who tries to carry a heavy burden around all by themselves—and how much better they feel when they finally get that weight off their chest." He regarded her sadly. "Did your dad leaving have anything to do with your mom's suicide?"

She swallowed hard. "Mom was insanely in love with my dad, even though he was nothing but a womanizing jerk. When he ran off and left us, she fell apart. It was like she didn't know who she was without him."

"That's when you started taking care of Kelsey, right?" he asked, spearing a piece of veal.

"Yeah. I had to. Mom simply couldn't." Lacey sipped her wine. "She spent weeks on end sitting on the couch in the living room, smoking cigarettes and waiting for Dad to come home. When she realized that wasn't going to happen, she started drinking and going out with a lot of guys—none of whom were worth a crap."

Lacey remembered that time in her life like it was yesterday. Remembered watching her mom throw herself at guys who she normally would never have otherwise looked twice at. Drunks, druggies, bums—anyone who would give her the time of day. It was like she was desperate for a guy to take care of her, and she didn't care who.

The muscle in Alex's jaw flexed. "None of them ever messed with you or Kelsey, did they?"

"No," she said quickly. "I made sure we left when Mom brought them around. And I would always leave Kelsey at a friend's house whenever I went home to see if they were gone." Tears burned her eyes, and she ducked her head to look down at her plate while she blinked them back so Alex wouldn't see. "That actually turned out to be a good thing, because if Kelsey had been with me when I went home to check, she would have seen Mom kill herself."

"Oh God." Alex drew in a sharp breath. "You were there when it happened?"

Lacey nodded, still not looking at him. Now that the story was coming out, she couldn't seem to stop. Maybe because Alex was so easy to talk to.

"We lived in a tiny fifth-floor apartment," she continued quietly. "I came home around midnight like I usually did when Mom had a guy over. I'd get her off the couch and into bed, then clean up the empty bottles, air out the cigarette smoke before I brought Kelsey home—stuff like that. But this time was different. When I came in, Mom was sober enough to be upright. She was standing by the sliding door to the little balcony."

Lacey paused, replaying the last time she'd seen her mother alive over and over in her head. Alex didn't rush her.

"When I walked in, she didn't say anything. She just looked at me like she'd been waiting for me to show up. I asked her if she was okay, but she ignored me." Lacey looked at him. "Then she walked out onto the balcony, and threw herself off."

"Damn." Alex reached out to take her hand, gently squeezing it like she'd done to his minutes before. The gesture was more comforting than she expected.

"I never told Kelsey what happened," she added. "She thinks Mom fell off the balcony by accident. The police knew, of course, but no one felt it necessary to tell a ten-year-old that kind of news."

She and Alex sat there for a long time, holding hands. He asked her about things that brought up feelings and doubts she purposely hadn't thought about for a long time. Like whether she hated her mom for killing herself, what she'd say to her dad if she ever saw him again, and most important, whether she ever blamed herself for what her mom had done.

Lacey told herself that Alex wasn't her shrink, he was a guy she was dating, but even though she tried to filter what she said, she found herself opening up and telling him everything. She hated looking weak and needy in front of him, like some damaged chick who couldn't afford therapy. By the time they finished dinner, however, she felt more relaxed and at peace with her past than she'd ever been in her life. Alex was better than any therapist, even if she could have afforded one. Ten years was a long time to keep things bottled up inside, she supposed.

"Sorry if the night took a depressing turn," he said as they loaded the dishwasher. "If you want to put the movie on hold until another night, I'm okay with that."

Lacey shook her head. "Definitely not. You promised me dinner and a movie. We're only halfway done."

He grinned. "All right. If you insist."

She smiled back. "I insist."

Grabbing a dish rag, she wiped down the table while he finished with the dishwasher. If she'd thought Alex was a keeper before, now she was convinced she needed to kidnap him and keep him locked in her apartment. He was simply too perfect to let get away.

Chapter 8

LACEY BROWSED THE SELECTION OF BLU-RAY DISCS THAT Alex had set out on the coffee table, trying to imagine him picking them out at a Redbox kiosk. Romantic comedies and chick flicks predominated. To say they seemed like movies a man like Alex wouldn't be caught dead watching, much less paying for, was an understatement.

She glanced at him. "You chose these yourself?"

"I admit, I had to get help, but yeah. I talked to Everly, Jayna, Mac, and Khaki for some suggestions."

"And they suggested these?"

He gave her a sheepish look. "Actually, they suggested I ask you what movie you wanted to watch. But that would have ruined the surprise, so I went with their best guesses as to what you might like. Anything here catch your fancy?"

She almost picked one at random just to be nice, but then decided against it. After this evening, she had the feeling she didn't have to play games with Alex.

It was her turn to look a little embarrassed. "Truthfully, I'm not much for rom-coms and chick flicks. Do you have any action or horror movies? They're more my thing."

Alex looked surprised but chuckled. "I guess I should have just asked you. I have a lot of those kind of movies."

He led her over to the big entertainment unit underneath the TV and pulled out the two top drawers. They were filled to the brim with DVDs and Blu-rays, and all of them were action movies, thrillers, and horror flicks. In fact, he had one whole drawer filled with werewolf movies.

She slanted him a look. "Have a thing for were-wolves, do we?"

"You noticed that, huh?" His mouth twitched. "I kind of collect them. For whatever reason, I find stories about werewolves intriguing."

Lacey ran her fingers over the spines, picking up a few and reading the blurbs on the back. In the end, she picked out one of the werewolf titles she recognized—*An American Werewolf in London*—without even checking to see what it was about.

She turned to Alex. "Is this one any good?"

"It's a classic," he said. "A little scary, though."

She handed it to him, deciding she liked the sound of that. Nothing better than cuddling on the couch with a hot guy and burying her face against his shoulder at all the scary parts.

Alex refilled their wine and grabbed a big bag of Hershey's Kisses from the kitchen, then turned down the lights and got the movie started before joining her on the couch.

"I've seen this movie about twenty times," he said as the first scene opened up with two guys walking across a fog-shrouded landscape. "If you have any questions—or just feel the need to blurt out a random meaningless observation about the feasibility of a werewolf running around the streets of London without being seen—feel free."

Lacey laughed and wiggled closer to Alex. She was glad he wasn't one of those guys who demanded total silence during a movie, because that wasn't the way she rolled.

Alex put his bare feet up on the coffee table, dropped a big pile of Hershey's Kisses on his T-shirt-covered abs, then wrapped his arm around her shoulders to pull her even closer. Now this was the way to watch a scary movie.

Lacey tried to pay attention to the film—at first anyway. The action started right from the beginning, and there were people screaming and blood flying within the first ten minutes. It also helped that the acting was way better than she'd expected for a monster movie. She could see why Alex liked this one.

But lying in the dark, with her body pressed close to Alex, eating chocolates off his rock-hard abs was a bit distracting. By the time the hero's dead friend showed up on screen attempting to convince the hero that he was a monster and should kill himself, Lacey was far more interested in tracing the lines of Alex's abs through his T-shirt than in watching the movie. It felt like he had a seriously nice six-pack under the thin material, and her imagination filled in all the details her curious fingers couldn't provide. Alex certainly didn't seem to mind her playful roaming. In fact, if the bulge growing in his jeans was any indication, he was definitely enjoying himself.

Lacey had never been very aggressive with guys, but there was something about Alex that made the idea of being shy around him seem silly. A moment later, she decided there wasn't any good reason to resist the temptation any longer. Knocking aside the remaining chocolates, she tugged the bottom of his shirt up until it came out of the waist of his jeans. That gave her a perfect view of all the lean muscles of his stomach, his yummy-looking belly button, and a faint, happy trail of hair that made her groan with delight. Yup, this was exactly the six-pack she'd been seeing in her mind.

Without a word, she traced her fingers over the hills and valleys of his abs, enjoying the way Alex's muscles flexed and twitched under her touch, especially when she ventured close to his belt. It almost felt like there were sparks dancing along her skin when she touched him.

She was having so much fun exploring, she didn't even realize Alex was watching her until his hand suddenly came down on her hers, stopping her cold. Had she been wrong about how much he'd liked her teasing?

She tipped her head back to look at him, but when she saw the fire in his eyes, she knew he hadn't stopped her because he didn't like what she was doing. No, definitely not that.

Gaze locked with hers, he got a firm grip on her hip and dragged her astride his lap like she was as light as a feather. The bulge in his jeans pressed nicely against the juncture of her thighs, and she wiggled so that he was hitting the perfect spot.

"What about the movie?" she teased.

"What about it?" he growled, his mouth possessing hers and taking her breath away.

One hand came up and tangled in her hair, holding her captive as his tongue slipped into her mouth. His other hand moved down to her ass, getting a firm grip and slowly rocking her back and forth on his hard-on. All Lacey could do was clutch his shoulders, twist her fingers into his T-shirt, and hold on as his taste flooded her mouth and made her dizzy. It was a tantalizing mix of wine, chocolate, and that magical something that Alex alone seemed to possess.

Arousal rushed through her body, tightening her nipples and engulfing her pussy with heat. She'd never been turned on so fast or so completely from a kiss. Then again, she'd never been kissed with a hunger so complete, it felt like she was being consumed.

Lacey wasn't sure who broke away first. All she knew was that she was trying to get Alex's T-shirt off at the same time he tugged hers up. She won—but only because he let her—and was rewarded with the sight of a truly magnificent chest, complete with broad muscles and a wolf head tattoo.

Her shirt came off next, flying across the room in a way that was far more arousing than she would ever have thought possible. When her bra hit the floor a moment later, she had the feeling the clasp on it wasn't going to work again. She'd never been one to enjoy rough play, so she was surprised at how turned on that forceful act made her. Maybe Alex was bringing out something in her that she'd never known was there.

Alex bent his head, closing his mouth on the tip of her breast, drawing the nipple into her mouth and nibbling on it in a way that drove her crazy. It wasn't just that warm, wet tongue of his—though that was really hot—that had her writhing on his lap. It was the way he occasionally nipped at her with those sharp teeth of his. No guy had ever done that to her before, and she liked it more than she ever would have imagined.

As he suckled, he moved his hands up to cup her breasts, holding them firmly so he could move from one to the other, teasing back and forth until she felt like she was on fire. She tangled her fingers in his hair, not trying to control his movements but instead urging him to keep going.

She was so caught up in what he was doing to her breasts that she barely noticed when he slipped one hand under her ass and effortlessly got to his feet. He didn't even stop nibbling on her breast as he walked down the hall toward his bedroom.

The doubts she'd shared with Wendy earlier, not to mention the even greater doubts she'd harbored in the corners of her own mind, didn't seem to matter now. Being with Alex like this felt completely right.

Halfway to the bedroom, however, reality intruded. "Wait. I need my purse!"

He lifted his head to look at her in confusion. "What?"

"I need my purse," she said softly. "I have condoms in it."

Sticking condoms in her purse had seemed like a smart thing to do. Even though she rarely needed them, she always kept some. Kind of like extra batteries for the flashlight.

He continued to stare at her for a moment, his eyes widening as realization dawned on him. Turning around, he carried her back into the living room. Holding on to her with one arm, he snagged her purse from the end of the couch with the other, then headed for the bedroom again.

Once there, Alex tossed her gently onto his great big bed. Lacey laughed as he yanked off her wedge sandals, sending one into the hallway and the other across the room. He hadn't turned on the bedroom lights when he'd carried her in, but the glow from the one in the hallway provided more than enough illumination for them to see, and the mood lighting provided a sexy ambience to the whole thing.

She worked quickly to get her belt unbuckled and jeans

unbuttoned, because Alex was pulling them off one way or the other. After he tossed them aside, he stepped back to take in her nearly naked body. The scrap of silky material that made up her panties was the only thing she still had on, and it was so small, it barely qualified as clothing. She made no move to take off the tiny piece of underwear. Alex was still half dressed, after all. Fair's fair.

The hunger in his dark eyes was palpable as he gazed down at her, and seeing that lust only made her body burn hotter with need. She had no desire to wait another second.

She looked around for her purse and saw it on the nightstand. She absently wondered when he'd put it there, then decided she didn't care. She eagerly reached for it, but Alex stopped her with a firm hand on her leg.

He smiled, a slight quirk of the lips that always seemed to have such a devastating effect on her. "I don't think you need that yet."

She opened her mouth to ask what that meant, only to gasp when he locked his hands around both ankles and dragged her a little closer to the edge of the bed, then spread her legs wide. Eyes fixed on hers, he leaned forward and pressed his mouth to her calf, slowly kissing his way up to her inner thigh.

Lacey abruptly realized why they didn't need a condom yet.

His mouth felt unbelievably good as he teased her with his tongue, not to mention those magical teeth of his. Every time he nipped her, he immediately followed it up with a warm lick of the tongue, making her groan.

When Alex reached the sensitive skin at the top of her thighs, along the edges of her panties, she expected him to stop and strip them off like he'd done to the rest of her clothes. But he didn't even slow down. Instead, he nibbled her pussy through the silky material of her panties.

"Oh God," she moaned, throwing back her head and bucking her hips up off the bed.

Alex responded by placing a big, strong hand on the inside of each thigh, spreading her wider and firmly pressing her down to the bed. Then he went right back to nibbling, driving her even more crazy, because she couldn't squirm away from his touch. He was too strong.

The silky barrier allowed him to do things with his mouth that would almost certainly be too much for her if she weren't wearing panties. But even with them, she knew she was going to come soon.

She buried her hands in his hair, silently urging him a little bit higher, right at that place she needed him to be. He resisted for a second with a growl, as if telling her that he'd get there when he was good and ready, but then he relented, moving his amazing mouth up to her clit.

She lasted thirty seconds, tops. Then she exploded.

Even Alex's strong hands couldn't keep her from writhing on the bed as she climaxed. She bucked and jerked, crying out as she came long and hard. The moment the climax started to trail off, Alex ripped off her panties, the torn scrap of fabric disappearing behind him. Then his mouth was back on her clit. His tongue had felt sublime before, but now it was indescribable. The previous orgasm, which had been slowly dissipating to nothing but a tremor, shot up to the top of the Richter scale again, making her scream even louder.

As Alex worked his magic down there, she was sure she would pass out and miss the tail end of her orgasm roller coaster ride, but he didn't let that happen. He was a master at drawing out every ounce of pleasure until she was one exhausted bundle of happiness.

When she finally opened her eyes, she found him grinning at her from between her thighs. "You back with the rest of us yet?"

She laughed and shook her head. "No. You've completely ruined me. I'll never be able to watch another werewolf movie again without thinking about what you just did to me."

"Ruined you, huh?" He released his hold on her legs and got to his feet. "That's too bad, considering we've just started."

The low, rumbling words coupled with the obvious heat in his eyes—not to mention the way he started undoing his belt—had her body vibrating with excitement all over again. That shouldn't have been possible. She'd just come so hard she should have been satisfied for a month of Sundays, but she got the feeling that as long as she was with Alex, she was going to have to get used to orgasming a lot more often than she had in the past.

It was something she thought she could handle.

Lacey pushed herself up on her elbows and watched with rapt attention as Alex dropped his jeans. It took him a bit to get his briefs down, since there seemed to be a whole lot of stuff in there trying to force its way out. When he was done, all she could do was lie there and stare. With the bedroom lights off, she couldn't see everything, but that was okay. She could see everything she needed to see.

I've just seen proof of heaven, because I'm looking at an angel.

Broad shoulders, muscular chest, ripped abs, long athletic legs, along with a hard, thick cock that looked as beautiful and perfect as the rest of him. Just the thought of what that shaft would feel like had Lacey's knees shaking. This was going to be so good.

"Now can I get that condom?" she asked.

He flashed her a grin. "Now you can get that condom."

Lacey didn't waste any time digging in her purse, then opening the packet and rolling it down his cock. Alex did look mildly disappointed when he realized she'd only brought three of them, however.

"That might get us through the night—maybe," he murmured softly.

Apparently, they wouldn't be doing any sleeping in this bed tonight. Fine with her.

When she was finished, Lacey started to slide back on the bed, more than ready for Alex to join her, but once again, he had other ideas. Cupping her butt, he dragged her forward until she was right on the edge. She'd never been a fan of caveman behavior in the bedroom, but she was quickly coming to the conclusion that in Alex's case, she was completely fine with it.

Eyes molten, Alex spread her legs wide again—he really liked doing that, didn't he?—then he moved close and settled his shaft against her pussy. He moved his hips a little, sliding his length back and forth along her clit, making her gasp and quiver over and over. She bit her lip. Any more teasing and she was going to explode.

Alex must have sensed her frustration, because he only teased her for a few more moments before he climbed on the bed and angled the tip of his erection down, wedging it firmly at the opening of her pussy.

Lacey lifted herself up higher on her elbows, wanting—*needing*—to watch as he entered her.

She wasn't disappointed by the view as he slowly

rocked back and forth, sliding into her one agonizing inch at a time. Her breath hitched, then all at once sped up, a tingling sensation beginning to build as Alex moved deeper and deeper into her. She was going to die from pleasure before he even got all the way in.

His hands glided down her thighs, gripping them possessively and holding on tightly as he plunged into her. As mesmerizing as that was, Lacey found her gaze drawn to his handsome face.

His eyes were filled with that same animalistic fire she'd seen before, but it was more primal now, and she lay there transfixed as the dim light in the room reflected off them, making them seem to glow from within. Damn, that was so sexy!

Lacey wasn't sure when his thrusts changed from rhythmic rocking to bed-shaking pounding, but at some point, she realized her head was thrown back and she was staring at the ceiling, her mouth open wide in a continuous moan.

She grasped her inner thighs, pushing them open even wider as Alex took her in a way she'd never been possessed. Sex with him was powerful, passionate, and primal, and she knew she'd never experience anything better than this.

Lacey held off, wanting to climax with him, only letting herself go when she heard him growl with pleasure. Not that she could have stopped herself if she wanted to. What he was doing to her felt too good. Knowing he was enjoying it just as much was the cherry on top.

The hoarse groan he let out as he came seemed to resonate with something deep inside her, forming a connection that seemed almost transcendent. Lacey opened her eyes just in time to see him bury his face in her neck.

He nibbled her skin, murmuring words she couldn't hear but easily understood.

Lacey wrapped her arms and legs around Alex, holding him inside her and letting the heat of his muscular body warm her very soul. She alternated between caressing his skin and running her hands through his hair, knowing something very special had just happened. She didn't know exactly what, but she was sure that after tonight, her life was going to be changed forever.

Chapter 9

ALEX YAWNED AS HE STEPPED OFF THE ELEVATOR AND walked down the hall to Lacey's apartment. He doubted he'd gotten more than an hour of sleep last night. He'd gotten up early that morning so he could take Lacey home, then pulled an eight-hour shift at one of Bensen's junkyards.

It hadn't helped any that surveillance had been dull. Even with all the patience he'd developed during his time in the Marines as a sniper, when it hadn't been unusual to lay unmoving for hours on end waiting for a target to appear, he still hated staring at camera monitors all day. It simply didn't feel like police work to him.

The worst part was that it seemed like they were wasting their time. Crews from the task force had been sitting on Bensen's various businesses for nearly a week and hadn't seen a damn thing. Alex had pulled surveillance shifts at three different places so far and was starting to think that maybe the dealer who'd ratted out Bensen had sold them a load of bull.

He was off duty for the next twenty-four hours though, and he intended to make the most of it—with Lacey.

Alex grinned as her delectable scent hit his nose. It wafted under the door of her apartment, filling the space around him like pure ambrosia, and he inhaled deeply. He might have been exhausted as hell all day, but last night made it all worth it.

While the sex had definitely been epic, it was the

time they'd spent talking afterward, sharing secrets that neither of them had ever shared with anyone. He felt closer to Lacey than he'd ever felt to anyone in his life, even his pack mates. He recognized the significance of that, even if he still refused to so much as say those two little words out loud to himself, for fear of jinxing everything.

A couple of days ago, he'd told Remy that Lacey seemed hesitant about jumping into a relationship. He'd assumed then it was because she was just getting over a bad breakup, but now he knew better. After everything she'd watched her mom go through with her dad and all the other men who'd followed, Lacey simply didn't trust men. He couldn't blame her. In her experience, guys stayed around long enough to get what they wanted and then bailed, leaving the woman behind to deal with the mess.

But after last night, Alex thought he might have convinced Lacey he wasn't going to be that guy, that she could trust him and that he'd be there as long as she wanted him. Somewhere between bringing her over to his place last night and waking up with her in his arms, they'd made a connection. When Lacey had kissed him this morning and said she couldn't wait to see him again, it seemed like she was feeling at least some of the same things he was. She'd definitely been thrilled when he'd called and told her he'd gotten them dinner reservations at Chambre Française.

He started to ring the doorbell, then stopped himself when he heard movement inside the apartment. He let his nose follow Lacey's scent as she moved around, amazed at how easy it was to track her. For a werewolf who had never trusted his nose before, that was pretty incredible.

It wasn't only Lacey's scent he was getting a clear read on, either. He could smell Kelsey's too. Even more surprising, he picked up a few other lingering female scents as well. He closed his eyes, frowning as he tried to remember where he recognized them from. His fangs and claws slid out a little as he sorted through the scents. That's when it hit him. The scents belonged to Kelsey's girlfriends, the ones she'd been studying with Wednesday night. He couldn't necessarily match each scent to a particular face, but hell, he was just impressed he could identify the scents at all. Maybe those lessons with Khaki were starting to pay off.

Or maybe having great sex just made a werewolf's nose work better.

Grinning, he made sure his fangs and claws were safely retracted, then rang the doorbell. Inside, he could hear the sound of bare feet slapping the floor just moments before Lacey yanked open the door, a big smile on her face. She was wearing a pair of skimpy boy shorts and a tight T-shirt that showed off her curves, not to mention her long legs. The scent of arousal pouring off her was almost enough to make his fangs—and everything else—pop out.

She leaned against the doorjamb, her gaze sweeping over him. "Do you have any idea how yummy you look in that suit?"

Alex returned the favor, his gaze lingering on her bare legs. "Do you have any idea how yummy you look wearing next to nothing?"

He opened his mouth to ask her if this was the way she always answered the door, but she stopped him before he could even get a word out, grabbing the lapels of his jacket and yanking him in for a hungry kiss. Inside his pants, his cock went rock hard, and he suppressed a low growl, fighting to keep his inner werewolf from making an appearance.

He wrapped an arm around her waist and pulled her closer, deepening the kiss as he dropped his other hand down to slowly massage her ass. It would be so easy to tear off her clothes and make love to her right there in the doorway. But that probably wouldn't be a good idea, at least not out here where anyone could get an eyeful.

Lacey didn't hide a groan of disappointment when he broke off the kiss and shooed her into the apartment.

Leo met him in the entryway for a sniff and a pet. The dog circled Alex a couple of times, eyeballing him with as much curiosity as he had the first time they met. Alex could only assume the poor guy was still weirded out by a two-legged thing that looked like a person but smelled like a wolf.

"Kelsey isn't home right now, if that's what you're worried about." Lacey glanced over her shoulder as she headed down the hallway toward her bedroom. "She's got finals coming up in a couple of weeks, so she's cramming at the library on campus. We have the apartment completely to ourselves."

Alex locked on her swaying bottom as she walked. Damn, what an ass. "And I'm guessing you already have something in mind for what we could do with this apartment since we have it all to ourselves?"

Lacey didn't say anything as she walked into her bedroom. But from the way her heart rate suddenly sped up, he had a pretty good idea what she had in mind. His assumption was confirmed a few seconds later when she came back out with a little foil package in her hand.

She held it up with a smile. "I'm sure we can think of something…if you're up for it."

He sauntered over to meet her. "Aren't you worried about being late for our reservation?"

She gave him a coy look. "Haven't you ever heard of a quickie?"

Alex didn't pause to think—he just pounced. Lacey had enough time to yank her T-shirt over her head before he was on her, his mouth coming down on hers, the force of his body pushing her back against the wall. She moaned, wrapping her arms around him and kissing him back.

Alex growled softly, praying his fangs wouldn't slip out. They'd done it a few times last night while he and Lacey had been making love, and he'd been forced to shove his face in her neck so she couldn't see anything. He seemed to be doing better at controlling them—at least right now—but his gums were already tingling.

He'd intended to tease her a little there in the hallway, then take things into her bedroom, but those thoughts disappeared the moment Lacey's scorching hot and nearly naked body pressed up against his fully clothed one. His erection right now was so hard it was almost painful. The only thing he could think about was getting that condom on as fast as possible so he could take her right there in the hallway.

Lacey seemed just as eager. She worked to loosen his belt and pants at the same time he shoved down her panties. He'd never felt anything like this before. The overwhelming need to be inside her was like the urge to breathe. It couldn't be ignored.

Lacey shoved his pants down just far enough to get his cock out and the condom on. Then she lifted one leg, wrapped it around his waist, and practically climbed onto him.

Alex tried to slow her down so he could tease her and make sure she was ready. But she was having none of that. She got the tip of his shaft lined up with her pussy, then shoved herself down on him.

The growl that tore from his lips probably would have scared Lacey if she hadn't moaned so loud herself. She locked eyes with him, lifted her other leg to encircle his waist, then clutched the back of his suit jacket with her fingers, urging him to move. He couldn't have resisted even if he'd wanted to. She was so hot, so ready, that all he could do was take her exactly the way she wanted him to—hard and fast.

He slipped his hands under her ass, gripping her tightly as he shoved her back against the wall and drove himself deep. She buried one hand in his hair, yanked his head against her neck, and moved her body along his in a way that demanded even more.

Alex nipped at her skin, knowing this wouldn't last long. But he was going to make the most of it. He drove himself into her over and over, loving her gasps of pleasure.

He knew her climax was approaching from the way her legs tightened around his waist, as well as the quickening of her heartbeat. He sped up and thrust harder, wanting to come with her.

He was so focused on their combined orgasms that he didn't hear the sound outside the apartment until the keys rattled in the door.

Lacey gasped again, but this time, it was in surprise as he pulled her away from the wall of the hallway and carried her three quick strides into her bedroom.

"Your sister's home," he rasped.

He caught the edge of the door with an elbow, twisting his body to slam it closed. In the same movement, he shoved her against the wall, plunging himself as deep as he could go. The force of his thrust thumped her ass against the drywall so hard, it shook the wall, but he didn't care. He was too close to care.

Lacey tightened her legs around him, throwing her head back against the wall and biting her lower lip as her climax began to crest.

"Lacey, is that you?" Kelsey's voice came hesitantly from just outside the bedroom door. "I thought I heard something. Are you okay?"

When the hell had Lacey's sister moved down the hall? Alex hadn't really been paying attention, but how had he missed that?

Lacey's eyes met his, panic showing clearly in their blue depths as he felt her orgasm start to slip away. "Yeah, it's me," she managed. "I'm just getting dressed for dinner."

Alex was impressed by her ability to string words together. Because he was thrusting into her the entire time she spoke, albeit slower and less forcefully, determined not to make any noise but refusing to let her climax slip away.

She moaned as he squeezed her ass and shoved his cock in as far as it would go, then held it there.

"Do you need help?" Kelsey's concerned voice came again as the doorknob started to turn. "You sound like you're having trouble in there."

Lacey's eyes widened. "No!" she said, a little too loudly. "I mean... No, I'm good. I'm just putting on my shoes, and the strap was too tight. I'll be out in a minute."

Her eyes went from panicked to unfocused as he

began to thrust again. She was close. Alex dropped his head and nibbled. He knew from last night that the move would push her over the edge. Lacey clearly had a thing for the feel of his teeth on her neck.

Outside, Kelsey started to walk away. But then Alex heard her stop. "Why are your clothes on the floor in the hallway?"

Lacey didn't answer. Alex lifted his head to see her head resting against the wall, her eyes practically rolling back into her head. She was right on the edge. There was no way in hell she could answer.

Alex had no idea what to say, but he opened his mouth anyway. It was better to let Kelsey know he was in here than to have her walk in and confirm the fact in an even worse way. But before he could get the words out, Lacey's hands gripped his shoulders through his suit jacket, and her eyes refocused.

"They must have fallen out of the laundry basket," she called. "I'll get them later."

That seemed to satisfy Kelsey, because Alex heard her footsteps receding from the door. That was all the info he needed. He buried his face in Lacey's neck again and thrust hard into her one more time.

Lacey started moaning as she came, but before the sound could bring her sister running again, she dropped her head and bit down on Alex's neck right above the collar of his shirt. Then she started to shake and spasm, squeezing him so tightly he could barely move.

But he didn't need to move, not now. He pulled her harder against him and exploded with her.

He'd never made love to a woman up against the wall like this, especially with her completely naked, wrapped around his fully clothed body. He'd also never had a woman bite him so hard on the neck that it was likely to leave a mark. With Lacey, it all worked—and it was amazing. He thrust over and over as they came together, sure Kelsey would hear but unable to care. This was simply too perfect to hold back.

When he finally came back down to earth, he found Lacey staring at him with a twinkle in her satiated eyes. "That was different."

Alex smiled, pulsing inside her. He was still hard. He could go again if she wanted to. "Different good or different bad?"

Her breath hitched at the movement, and she reached out to gently caress his face. "Different very good."

He started to move again, but she gave him a stern look. "Don't even think about it. I need to get ready for dinner, and you need to get out there and somehow convince my sister you were in here helping me get dressed."

"Do you think she's really going to believe that?" he asked as he slowly lowered her to the floor.

"She'd better," Lacey said. "Or I'm never going to be able to look at her again without blushing."

—✳—

"So, how did you end up getting us reservations for the fanciest French restaurant in the city?" Lacey asked as they drove. "Same-day reservations at that."

Not that she really cared how Alex had gotten them into the swanky place. She'd wanted to go there since she was old enough to know what French cuisine was. If he'd had to mug someone for the seats, she could probably live with that.

Alex checked the rearview mirror and changed lanes before answering. "Gage got the head chef's kid out of trouble with a gang situation a few years ago, and now there's a table available any time he asks. Gage doesn't go all that often, so he lets the rest of us use the table every now and then."

Lacey shook her head. Another case of people doing favors for the SWAT team. She should have known. But again, she wasn't going to complain. About pretty much anything.

She was still humming from that amazing sex they'd had less than an hour ago. She'd never done anything that remotely crazy before. Having sex up against a wall was completely insane, like something a couple of teenagers would do. But truthfully, she'd loved it. It was the most outrageous and spontaneous thing she'd ever done, and it had felt incredible. In fact, she was already thinking of what they could do for an encore once they got back to her place.

If Alex was willing to come back to her place.

"What's the plan after dinner?" she asked hesitantly.

For all she knew, Alex might not want to go back to her place, not with Kelsey there. Lacey didn't know much about guys, but she imagined that having a younger sister in the picture could complicate it for some of them.

Alex threw her a quick look before focusing on the road again. "I don't have another surveillance shift until late tomorrow night, so I was thinking that we could head back to your place and hang out. Maybe sleep in tomorrow, if that's okay with you?"

"You don't mind that Kelsey's around?" she asked carefully, studiously looking at the mile markers zipping past outside the truck.

"No," he said. "I was going to ask you the same question. Do you think Kelsey will have a problem if she sees me there in the morning?"

Lacey felt the tension drain out of her. What the heck had she been thinking? This wasn't some guy. This was Alex, the greatest man on the planet. Of course, his only concern had been how Kelsey would handle finding out about the two of them being together.

"Kelsey will be fine with it. In fact, she'll probably be thrilled that I'm finally spending time with someone."

Alex smiled. "Then it's a plan. Dinner and back to your place for the night."

Lacey definitely liked the sound of that. In fact, that was the type of plan she could see herself getting used to.

They were still fifteen minutes from the restaurant when Lacey's phone rang. A part of her wished she could ignore it, but she couldn't. It could be Kelsey. Or the vet clinic, Wendy's ACS squad, or the dispatchers from Animal Services.

It turned out to be the latter. They usually called if they had a severely injured animal that had been picked up by one of their officers. If they were calling on a Saturday night, it probably wasn't good.

"What's up, Rachel?" she asked, pulling a pad and pen out of her purse.

If this wasn't a call to ask her to come to the city's main shelter, Rachel would be giving her an address to some other location. If so, it meant the animal was in bad shape, and Lacey wanted to be ready.

"Lacey, thank God! I hate to call you on the weekend like this, but I didn't know what else to do."

"What's wrong?" Lacey asked.

She'd worked with Rachel Carr dozens of times before.

As a dispatcher, Rachel dealt with a lot of bad stuff. If she was unsure about what to do, Lacey was really worried.

"We got a call about forty-five minutes ago," Rachel explained. "The woman wouldn't leave her name, but said she heard a bunch of dogs whimpering in pain somewhere behind the abandoned warehouse off Ridgecrest, about a block from where it intersects Park Lane."

Lacey frowned. This wasn't the information Rachel and the other dispatchers usually provided in a situation like this. "Are the Animal Service officers there now? Do you need me to meet them?"

"That's the thing," Rachel said. "They reported that they couldn't find anything, but..."

The hair on the back of Lacey's neck stood up. This was getting weird. "But what, Rachel?"

"The woman on the phone sounded really, really sure about what she heard, and the officers I dispatched called back really, really fast—if you know what I mean. I was hoping you could go over and take a look around?"

Lacey knew exactly what Rachel meant.

"I wouldn't normally ask you to do something like this," Rachel said urgently. "I tried to get someone to cover my shift so I could look myself, but I couldn't find anyone. Can you go...please?"

If there was anyone who loved dogs as much as Lacey did, it was Rachel. If she thought there was something wrong, Lacey needed to check it out.

"What's the full address, Rachel?"

Lacey wrote it down, then hung up. She hated to ask Alex to postpone the reservation, since he'd gone to so much trouble making it. But...

"I know that place," Alex said, glancing at her. "It's not surprising those Animal Services officers didn't find anything—if they even got out of their vehicle. It's not the kind of place you want to go at night without a really good reason—and a weapon."

She blinked. "You heard all that?"

He nodded, swung the truck around, and started driving the other direction. Lacey could only shake her head as he called the restaurant to let them know they wouldn't be able to make it for at least an hour. Was this guy a catch or what?

They arrived at the address Rachel had given her twenty minutes later. Lacey was definitely glad Alex was with her. This particular stretch of Ridgecrest was beyond scary. She wasn't sure how anyone could have heard a dog whining out here. There was no one around that she could tell. There was nothing but abandoned and boarded-up buildings, lots of broken glass, and not a damn light anywhere.

Alex pulled into the parking lot of what looked like an old convenience store, then got out of the truck and walked around to her side. He pulled two flashlights out from behind the seat, handing one to her. She watched in amazement as he reached down and pulled a small handgun from a holster around his ankle. They'd just made love an hour ago, and she'd never even known he was wearing the thing. Then again, he'd been completely dressed at the time, so she supposed there was no way she would have known.

That said, the fact that he felt it necessary to pull it out now scared the crap out of her.

Lacey looked around, trying to imagine how they were going find anything out here. Not only was it pitch-black, but there were at least a dozen different old buildings an injured dog could have dragged himself off to—and that wasn't counting the random piles of rubble that stuck up out of the darkness here and there. Lacey stood still and tried to listen for anything that might help, like a dog's whimper or a growl, but there was nothing. If an injured dog was out here, she prayed he could make it until morning, because they weren't going to find anything stumbling around in the dark.

Alex, however, headed toward one of the collection of buildings, not even swinging his flashlight around as he strode through piles of junk that took her much longer to get around. Lacey was about to ask if he'd heard anything when he slowed as he approached a big pile of bricks and concrete rubble.

"Wait there," he said.

She waited—for about two seconds. Then she took off after him, wanting to see what was on the far side of the heap of rubble.

Lacey almost wished she hadn't. There, in the beam of both their flashlights, was a group of dogs piled on top of each other in a mound that could have been mistaken for garbage if it wasn't for all the fur and blood.

Heedless of the rough terrain and the high heels she wore, she ran forward with a cry and reached for the first dog—a pit bull without a doubt. Lacey knew the animal was dead the moment she touched it, if not from the stiffness in the dog's legs, then from the gaping wound in its throat.

She moved the dog gently aside, then reached for the next. Alex put away his gun and joined her. Together, they went through the pile one by one, looking to see if any of them were still alive. There were pit bulls, Rottweilers, and bulldogs along with smaller animals most likely used as bait to drive the fighting dogs into a frenzy. All of the animals were chewed up, though some seemed to have had their throats cut as well.

There were a lot of dogs, and it took a while to get to the bottom. By the time they did, tears were pouring down Lacey's face. None of the animals were alive. One or two of them must have been when the anonymous caller had heard whimpering, but they were all gone now.

"This is what happens to animals that don't win in the fighting pits," she shouted. She knew she was losing it. Her anger wasn't directed at Alex, but since he was the only one there, he would have to do. "Or the ones too injured to fight again. They just throw them away like garbage. I could kill people who do this!"

Lacey wasn't sure how long she ranted like that, screaming at the assholes who would do something like this to poor defenseless animals, but when she finally looked up, she realized that Alex wasn't paying attention to her. He was staring off into the darkness with an unfocused expression on his face. She was about to ask if something was wrong, but he was already walking away, farther into the darkness toward the nearest crumbling building. Lacy jumped up and followed.

"Is it another dog?" she whispered as Alex came to a stop in front of a shadow-shrouded mound on the ground.

His flashlight wasn't even on. She didn't know how he'd seen anything.

"No," he said simply.

Lacey swung her own flashlight down toward the shape—and almost got sick as she realized it was the body of a woman. She was half hidden under a piece of cardboard, so it was hard to tell in the dark, but she looked like she had curly red hair.

Without a word, Alex dropped to one knee beside the

woman, then moved the cardboard aside and checked for a pulse. Lacey already knew he wouldn't find one. The woman had been mutilated beyond belief.

She wasn't too proud to take Alex's hand as he led her back to his truck and helped her into the passenger seat. If he hadn't, she probably would have fallen down. As a vet, she'd seen a lot of stuff people shouldn't have to see, but she'd never seen anything like that.

"What happened to that girl?" she asked softly as he pulled out his cell. "Did the dogs get her?"

Alex shook his head. "No, those weren't bite wounds. She was definitely dumped at the same time as the dogs, though. Maybe she stumbled over the dogfighting ring and it got her killed."

Lacey didn't say anything as he punched some buttons on his phone and called the police, then gave his badge number to whoever answered. The memory of Pendergraff coming after her in Bensen's junkyard the other night filled her head, his disturbing eyes sweeping back and forth as he searched for her. If Pendergraff had found her, would she be lying over there behind that rubble, all torn and bloody?

A part of her felt a surge of fear at that thought. But the larger part was consumed with rage. She knew there was no reason to think this had anything to do with Bensen and Pendergraff, but her instincts were screaming that their filthy hands were all over this and it infuriated her. She was even more enraged that no one seemed able to do a damn thing about it.

Well, she was going to do something.

Chapter 10

"SO, IS CORPORAL BROOKS SEEING ANYONE SERIOUSLY?" Vaughn asked casually.

Well, as casually as a woman could ask a loaded question like that, Alex thought. He and Remy had been in the surveillance van with the narcotics officer for the past three hours, staring at the bank of monitors that lined the interior wall.

Remy threw Alex a quick glance and a smile. Alex immediately knew that glint in his teammate's eyes meant Remy was planning to tease the narcotics cop about something. Damn, that guy simply couldn't stop himself, could he?

"Unfortunately, Corporal Brooks doesn't have a lot of time for women," Remy said grimly. "Not with the two young children he's raising on his own."

Vaughn's eyes widened in shock, not to mention what looked a hell of a lot like panic.

"Remy's messing with you," Alex said, figuring he'd better step in before this got too out of hand. "Brooks doesn't have any kids, and he isn't seeing anyone at the moment."

Vaughn relaxed in her chair. "Thank God. I slipped the shift scheduler twenty bucks to put me on late-night surveillance with him later in the week—alone. I'd hate to think I wasted a Jackson for nothing."

Alex chuckled. They'd figured Brooks would need a woman who was bold and outgoing. That description seemed to fit Vaughn to a T. He only hoped his pack mate was able to handle her.

Remy looked like he was ready to complain about Alex putting a stop to his antics, but then he leaned forward and adjusted the controls on one of the monitors. "Pendergraff just showed up at the front gate. Maybe that means something interesting will happen tonight."

"For a change," Alex muttered.

This was the third different automotive location of Bensen's that he'd worked since this surveillance job had started. This one was not only the largest, but the one where Bensen spent most of his time, and Alex was hoping they might catch a break here. Having both Bensen and Pendergraff in the building at the same time had to improve the odds.

"You're recording, right?" he asked Remy.

His teammate nodded. They had half a dozen cameras set up around three sides of the junkyard, praying they might catch a glimpse of something that would tie Bensen to the manufacturing and distribution of fireball. But so far, other than recording the faces and license plates of a lot of visitors—most of whom had no connection to the illegal drug trade—they didn't have much to show for their efforts.

After ten minutes, Alex sat back in his chair. Their chances of seeing anything interesting happen tonight were getting slimmer by the second. Unfortunately, that meant he was left with his own thoughts to keep him entertained, and they went back to the same place they had since last night—the murdered woman and dead dogs that he and Lacey had stumbled over.

The homicide cops, crime scene techs, and medical examiner had arrived shortly after he'd called it in. The

detectives had taken his statement—multiple times—
then marginalized him. He understood—he really did.
He was the cop they called when it came time to kick
in a door, rescue a hostage, or tackle a drugged-up suspect. He wasn't the cop who combed a murder scene for
evidence. Of course, he couldn't tell them he'd already
discovered a huge piece of evidence. They probably
wouldn't have believed him if he could.

He'd picked up two human scents off the dogs in that
pile. The first one had only been on the five dogs who'd
had their throats slit, which meant he was the asshole
who'd killed them. The second scent had been on every
one of the dogs, meaning it almost certainly belonged
to the man who'd been responsible for dumping the
animals after they were dead. Beyond that, things got
strange. The second guy's scent had also been on the
woman's body. Even stranger, the woman and the dogs
had the scent of fireball on them too.

Alex couldn't figure how dogfighting, drugs, and a
murdered woman were all connected, but after the scent
training with Khaki, he was sure he was right. He'd
also used every trick Khaki had taught him so he could
remember those two scents, just in case he ever ran
across the dirtbags again. He knew that was unlikely,
since he'd never be involved in the investigation into
either the woman's death or the dumping of the dogs'
bodies, but still, he wanted to remember those scents.
Because if he ever ran into those two men out on the
street, he would make damn sure they paid for what
they'd done.

Lacey had been really torn up last night, of course,
and understandably so. She'd been forced to sit in his
truck at the crime scene for nearly two hours, telling the

cops over and over what she'd seen. He hated she'd had to go through that.

Even after they'd finally left and gone back to her place, her heart had been pounding in her chest half the night. She wasn't just upset by what she'd seen. She was furious. It was like she blamed herself for what had happened to the dogs and the woman. They had talked until nearly sunrise before Lacey had finally fallen asleep in his arms. He'd lain there in her bed, watching her twist and jerk in a fitful sleep that he would have given anything to make more restful.

At least she'd calmed down by the time they'd gotten out of bed around ten and had a late breakfast with Kelsey. He guessed she'd finally come to some sort of peace over what she'd seen.

"Everything going okay with Lacey?" Remy asked as if reading his mind. "You still think she's *The One* for you?"

Alex threw a quick glance at Remy, wondering why his teammate would bring that up in front of Vaughn. It wasn't like they could talk openly about it. But he could be honest about one part for sure.

"Yeah, she's *The One* all right." He grinned. "No doubt about it."

Vaughn smiled as she swiveled back and forth in her chair. "That's so cool that you've met someone who can put up with you not just being a cop, but in SWAT. I'm thinking it takes a certain kind of woman to handle a guy in your line of work. Make sure Corporal Brooks knows I'm that kind of woman."

Alex was assuring the outgoing narcotics officer that he'd pass along that particular piece of information when Remy interrupted him.

"Is Lacey a spur-of-the-moment, just-go-crazy kind of girl?"

Alex chuckled. "Hell no. If anything, she's the complete opposite. She thinks everything through to a fault."

Well, there was that sex-up-against-the-wall thing, but he sure as hell wasn't going to mention that to Remy.

"Then why did I just see her climb over the fence and go into the junkyard?" Remy asked.

Alex thought his friend was joking. It was the kind of dumbass thing Remy would say. But Remy looked completely serious.

"Holy shit," Alex muttered. "You're not kidding, are you?"

Remy hit a button on the console, backing up the tape from one of the perimeter cameras covering the south side of the property.

Alex prayed his pack mate was wrong, but sure as shit, there was Lacey, climbing over the fence, almost killing herself in the process, and dropping into the junkyard—almost killing herself again. Even in a black top with dark jeans and a knit cap on her blond hair, he would recognize her anywhere.

"That's your girlfriend?" Vaughn asked in confusion. "What the hell is she doing in there?"

Alex could have asked the exact same question.

"It looks like she's sneaking around Bensen's junkyard," Remy remarked. "Only she doesn't seem to be very good at it."

Just before Lacey moved out of the camera's view, Alex saw her bump into a rack of car parts, knocking something to the ground. It wasn't her fault—it was dark as hell in there. But the clatter of the metal part tumbling off the rack and hitting the ground could be heard all the way out to the surveillance van, and he didn't need his werewolf hearing to do it.

"Turn off the cameras and back them up," he ordered. "I'm going in there to get her."

Alex tore out of the van even as he heard Remy explaining to Vaughn that everything would be fine—and that no, they didn't need to call Rodriguez.

He rounded the corner of the building they'd parked the van behind and ran across the dark street separating him from the junkyard, already feeling his fangs and claws slipping out. He'd never been good at maintaining control in tense situations, and the idea of Lacey getting caught by Bensen's security people—especially Pendergraff—definitely qualified as a tense situation.

He hurdled the ten-foot-tall fence that surrounded the junkyard, barely touching it with his hand in passing. He tried—and failed—to keep from growling when he hit the ground a moment later, but he couldn't help it. He could already hear people coming out of the main building, no doubt checking to see what the racket Lacey had made was all about. She was in more danger then she could ever have realized.

Alex's eyes adjusted easily to the deep shadows filling the spaces in between the various car parts, equipment racks, and garage structures as he moved in the general direction Lacey had headed. His head was spinning at a hundred miles an hour the whole time he tried to navigate the bewildering maze of rows and aisles that made up the junkyard. What the hell was she doing in here? She was a fucking vet. How the hell did she even know about this place—or Bensen?

A moment later, he finally picked up Lacey's scent, mostly because he'd let himself shift so far. He angled a

little to the left, moving to intercept her as she continued
to head for the main building. Didn't she realize that the
noise she'd made earlier had drawn the guards outside?
Was she completely clueless about how dangerous these
people were?

The answer to that was obviously a resounding yes.
Even his semifunctional nose could tell she still hadn't
turned to go in another direction, even as several of
Bensen's guards moved her way.

He caught sight of one of the guards as he zipped
between two of the garage structures, and what he saw
freaked him out even more. The damn guy was carrying
an automatic weapon. If he needed any other evidence
that Bensen was involved in making and dealing drugs,
he had it now. Guys guarding junkyards didn't normally
carry assault rifles.

Alex instinctively reached for his .40 caliber SIG
Sauer but immediately moved his hand away. He
couldn't get into a shoot-out in here. There would be
no way to keep Lacey's name out of this, and he had no
idea how she would explain her presence here. Hell, he
wouldn't even be able to explain his presence here, not
without blowing this investigation wide open.

As he closed in on Lacey's position, he could hear
her heart pounding on the other side of the stack of crap
he was moving along, when he realized her luck had
run out. There was a guard heading straight for her, and
there was no way in hell Alex could get to him before
they crossed each other's path.

Alex let out a low growl and ran faster, letting himself shift as far as he dared, then pushed it a little more.
His leg muscles twitched and spasmed, bulking up and
lengthening in response to his call for more speed, and

he felt himself flat-out hauling ass along the ground, rocks and dirt flying behind him. But shifting to produce that kind of speed came at a price, and he felt his jawbone crack as more teeth came out than he had room for. If anyone saw him, he was fucked. He knew it was insane, but what the hell could he do? Those asshole guards would shoot Lacey on sight and worry about who she was later. He only prayed Remy had turned off all the cameras.

He was probably doing thirty miles an hour by the time he reached the end of the row. He was barely in control as he turned the corner and raced to close the distance between him and the guard he'd sensed earlier.

While Alex was moving fast, everything around him seem to slow down as both Lacey and the guard came into view at the same time. She was standing in the shadows fifteen feet away, completely immobilized by the sight of the armed man right in front of her, his weapon already turning toward her. Even in the darkness, the fear in her eyes was obvious.

Seeing Lacey terrified and in danger was too much for Alex. He cut loose a roar that echoed off every metal surface around them, sounding like a whole frigging pack of wolves had descended on the junkyard.

The guard snapped his head around in the direction of the sound, but it was too late for the man to see anything more than a snarling blur coming his way. The man tried to get his weapon up and around, but he was too late for that too.

Alex didn't slow down to punch the guy or even disarm him. He was too crazy mad to even think of anything that rational. He was just glad he was able to resist the urge to rake his claws across the man's throat. All he needed was for Lacey to see blood flying everywhere as he tore a man to shreds.

Instead, he lowered his shoulder and slammed into the guard's chest at full speed. The impact was horrendous. The guard flew backward so hard, he probably went ten feet before he hit anything. Unfortunately, the thing he hit was a pallet of hubcaps, and the racket it made was almost as bad as the wolf howl Alex had just let out.

The guard went through the pile of hubcaps, bounced off a heavy-duty support structure, and then bounced five times across the gravel-covered ground before coming to a stop with a thud against the rack of equipment a full row over. He didn't get up.

The pounding of feet converged on their location immediately. Alex didn't have time to screw around, not unless he wanted to face a whole lot more bad guys. If that happened, the possibility of getting them both out of here without being identified would be just about zero.

Alex spun around to face Lacey, intending to grab her hand and head for the perimeter fence. But when he saw her face, he knew that plan wasn't going to work.

He'd hoped that the shadows in between the aisle would hide his werewolf features—the claws, the canines that extended well over his lower lip, the glowing eyes. But obviously, that hadn't worked out. Lacey's eyes were locked on him, and they were as big around as saucers.

He tried to shift back, but he knew that was never going to happen. He was too freaked to manage that yet. When he was high on adrenaline like this, it tended to take a while for him to change back to normal. Usually the only thing that sped up the process was having a higher level alpha like Gage or Xander around who could snap him out of his werewolf haze.

Lacey opened her mouth, but whether she was planning to ask him what the hell was going on or start screaming her head off, he didn't know. Unfortunately, he didn't have time to wait to see what happened. There were more guards coming, and they'd be here any second.

"Sorry," he said. Then he charged straight at her.

Lacey's eyes widened even more, and when she opened her mouth again, he was pretty sure it was in preparation for a scream that would likely be heard over a good portion of North America. Alex clamped his hand over her mouth, sweeping her off her feet and into his arms.

She kicked and struggled to get free, but he ignored it as he ran through the junkyard as fast as his legs would carry them. Lacey was so light in his arms that he barely felt her weight at all. He sure as hell could feel her panic, though. He heard shouting behind him, but he didn't have time to risk a glance over his shoulder. He didn't have to look to know the other guards were coming fast.

A moment later, Alex reached the end of the row and the T-intersection there. Lacey still struggled in his arms, but he didn't bother to slow. He couldn't. The itching between his shoulder blades warned him that he was close to running out of time. A werewolf had to trust his instincts—that was the first thing Gage had taught him when he'd brought him into the Pack.

He didn't try to turn left or right at the intersection but instead jumped as high as he could. Lacey went completely stiff in his arms as his feet left the ground.

He hated scaring her like this, but what other choice did he have? Damn, he was using that excuse a lot tonight.

While his leap got them to the top of a heavy-duty metal rack, it made more noise than he would have liked, though not the spectacular crash he'd been worried about. The metal under him creaked a few times as he quickly moved along it, but it didn't collapse or fall over. When he finally got his balance, he crouched down and waited a few moments to see if anyone had heard him.

Twenty seconds later, a man came running down the aisle where Alex had been mere moments before. Even if Alex hadn't been able to see in the dark, he would have still been able to identify the man. The guy's pale skin glowed in the darkness, making him seem like a frigging ghost running through the stacks of car parts.

Bensen's personal security goon stopped just beneath the storage rack Alex was on, swinging his automatic back and forth and cocking his head to the side as if he sensed Alex and Lacey somewhere nearby. Lacey had been struggling since Alex scooped her up, but the moment she saw Pendergraff, she went completely still. She was terrified but smart enough to recognize an even greater threat when she saw it.

The albino man stood unmoving below them for nearly a minute. The whole time he stood there, lights started coming on all across the junkyard, and at least a dozen men began to sound off from all around them, announcing they hadn't found anything.

Alex was thinking he might have to jump down and make a run for it, even if that meant getting shot at all the way across the junkyard. He didn't like that idea, but if he kept Lacey tucked against his chest, he should be able to keep her from being hit. He, on the other hand, wouldn't get off so lightly.

But just as that was beginning to look like Alex's only option, Pendergraff turned and walked off.

Alex breathed a sigh of relief, then looked down at Lacey. Her eyes widened again from seeing his shifted features up close and personal, and he swore silently. He didn't bother taking his hand away from her mouth as he jumped down to the far side of the storage rack and ran for the perimeter fence. He jumped over it at a dead run, freaking Lacey out so badly that she ended up biting his hand. Crap, she was going to be so furious with him.

He kept running until he got back to the building the surveillance van was hidden behind, only to discover it wasn't there any longer. No surprise there. After the shitstorm he'd started in the junkyard, Remy and Vaughn would have known they had to pull out of the area. If not, the whole operation could have been compromised. They'd probably grabbed up all the cameras and moved the van to an alternate location a couple of blocks away. Alex would call and find them soon enough. Right now, he had a more pressing task to handle.

Lacey was so eager to get away from him that she stumbled and almost fell on her butt the moment he put her feet on the ground. She backed up until she was nearly ten feet away, and still she looked like she wanted to bolt.

The expression on her face—a combination of fear, confusion, and downright revulsion—twisted like a knife in Alex's gut. That, and knowing how badly he'd scared her, finally shook him out of his shift. He felt his claws retract and his canines slide back in. The way the night became a little darker let him know his eyes probably weren't glowing any longer, either. Not that it seemed to help. If anything, seeing him shift back had freaked Lacey out all over again.

"What are you?" she asked, taking another small step away from him.

The urge to follow after her was intense, but Alex forced himself to stay where he was. Moving toward her would only make it worse.

"I can explain everything." He held up his hands in a placating gesture, trying to make himself appear as nonthreatening as possible. Not that he expected it to work. He'd just sprouted claws and fangs and run around a junkyard with her like she was a rag doll. "I just need you to trust me. Whatever you think right now, I promise I'm not a monster."

He thought for a moment that she might listen to him, but then she backed up further. He couldn't keep from following this time.

She threw up her hands as if to ward him off. "Stop! Don't come near me. I don't know what the hell I just saw, but I know it wasn't normal. You…you had fangs, Alex!"

"I didn't have a choice. I had to do it to save you." He took a breath. "I can explain, if you'd just listen."

She shook her head, backing away even faster. "I don't want to listen. I don't want to talk. I just want to go home and process this. I need to think—alone."

Alex nodded. "Okay, I get that. Let me take you back to your car, at least. You shouldn't be out here alone, not with Bensen's men running around."

She shook her head again, tears starting to run down her face. "I can get to my own car. Don't come any closer. If you do, I'll scream, and I don't care who comes running."

With a sob, she spun around and took off down the street, heading away from the junkyard. Alex followed, hanging back far enough that he wouldn't panic her but staying close enough to keep an eye on her. Three blocks up, she turned into a used car parking lot and jumped into her car. Tires squealed as she sped away.

He stood there on the side of the road. A few minutes later, Remy came up to stand beside him. His teammate looked almost as bummed as Alex felt.

"That could have gone a whole hell of a lot better," Remy said.

Understatement there. "She saw everything."

"I know. I heard."

"What the hell am I going to do?"

Remy shrugged. "There's not much you can do. You just have to give her some time to get her head wrapped around everything she saw and trust that she'll do the right thing."

Alex swallowed hard. "You don't think she'll tell anyone, do you?"

God, he hoped not. They'd had to deal with that situation back when Gage and Mac had first gotten together, and it had almost ended up with all of them leaving the country. He really didn't want to leave Dallas. He liked it here. He liked Lacey.

"I don't think so," Remy said. "But if she does, we'll just have to deal with it."

Great. "Do you think we should tell Gage or Xander?"

Remy winced at that. Alex didn't blame him. He wasn't thrilled about telling either his team commander or his squad leader that he'd accidently exposed their secret.

"Maybe we should tell Cooper first," Remy suggested. "He's really good at fixing crap when one of us fucks up."

———

Lacey's head was spinning so fast, she wasn't even sure where she was going until she pulled into a visitor's space along the front of Wendy's apartment building. How the hell had she gotten here?

She should turn the car around and go home. It wasn't like she could tell Wendy what had happened tonight. She didn't even understand it herself. But that logic didn't keep her from getting out of the car and climbing the three flights of stairs to her best friend's apartment. Her feet continued to do their own thing until they reached Wendy's door, then she was ringing the bell before she could stop herself.

Lacey cringed as the noise echoed inside the one-bedroom apartment. She shouldn't be here. She should be home checking on Kelsey, then going straight to bed. Maybe she should stop at an all-night convenience store on the way and grab a bottle of wine—or two. That would certainly help.

She was still standing there when Wendy opened the door a few seconds later, wearing an oversized Texas Longhorns sleepshirt. Once again, Lacey told herself she shouldn't be here, but she knew it was too late to flee now.

Wendy blinked the sleep out of her eyes, then looked around the hall as if she expected someone else to be with her. Alex probably. "Lacey, what are you doing here so late?"

Lacey tried to answer, but all she could do was stand

there and sob like a baby, something she hadn't done since her dad left and her mom died. No matter how hard she tried to make the tears stop, they wouldn't. She wasn't even sure why she was crying. She should have been screaming in terror. She'd just learned that the guy she'd been falling for—the guy she'd slept with—was a monster.

Wendy grabbed her hand and tugged her inside, then shut the door and pulled her into a hug. That's when the waterworks really started.

"It's okay," Wendy soothed. "Tell me what happened. Is Kelsey okay?"

Lacey sniffed and shook her head, pulling back to look at her friend. "It's not Kelsey…it's…" She hesitated, then forced the words out. "It's Alex."

Wendy's eyes widened. "Oh God, what happened? Is he hurt?"

Lacey swallowed hard, not sure what to say. Finally, the words came spilling out just like her tears had earlier. "He's not hurt. He's a…a…monster!"

Wendy looked confused for a moment, then understanding dawned on her face, quickly replaced with fury. "Did that big, stupid son of a bitch try to force himself on you? If he did, I'll kill him!"

Lacey was taken aback at the anger in her friend's voice, and it took her a few seconds to catch up to what Wendy was talking about. She shook her head again. Why was this so hard to explain?

"No, he didn't try to force himself on me. We've been sleeping together for the past two days."

Wendy frowned in confusion. "Then what the heck are you talking about? If he didn't attack you, what do you mean he's a monster?"

Lacey groaned in frustration. This was why she hadn't wanted to say anything in the first place. It was making her sound like a lunatic. She was too frazzled to keep doing this.

"He's a monster," she snapped. "You know—with claws, fangs, and glowing yellow eyes. That kind of monster."

Wendy opened her mouth, then closed it again. Finally, she sighed and shook her head. "I don't understand a thing you're saying, and you're scaring the hell out of me. Maybe we could sit down so you could start from the beginning? What happened tonight?"

Lacey moved over to Wendy's big, overstuffed couch and flopped down. She hadn't realized how tired she was until just then. She guessed the adrenaline she'd been riding high on for the last hour was finally running out. Or maybe it wasn't adrenaline she'd been riding on. Maybe it was good, old-fashioned fear. After everything that had happened tonight, everything she'd seen, she had every right to be terrified.

"I went to Bensen's junkyard out on 20 again tonight," she said, eager to get the confession part out of the way and move on with the important stuff, namely the part where Alex had come running out of the darkness like some monster in a horror movie, but she didn't get a chance.

"Wait a minute," Wendy interrupted. "Why the hell would you go there again? I told you to stay away from that man. He's psychotic."

"You don't have to tell me he's psychotic—I already know that," Lacey said. "I'm the one who found all those dead dogs and that poor girl last night. The police can act like they don't know who the hell was involved, but I do. It was Bensen. I went there to get something I could use to convince everyone I'm right."

Wendy looked like she wanted to say something more about that but thankfully held her tongue. "I still think you're an idiot for sneaking into Bensen's junkyard, but let's forget about that for the moment and get to the important stuff. Where does Alex, this monster, and you standing on my doorstep crying fit into this?"

Lacey closed her eyes, thinking back to the moment Alex had first appeared in the junkyard, the moment everything she'd thought she knew about the man had changed. How had she missed something like that? She should have known he was too good to be true.

"When I got into the junkyard, I tripped over something and ended up knocking a bunch of stupid car parts," she said. "Guys with guns ran out of the main building like they were under attack. I thought for sure I was dead."

Wendy's eyes widened again. Lacey thought cops were supposed to be better at controlling their facial expressions than that.

"I was just about to get shot by one of them when Alex came out of the darkness, running faster than any human had the right to, and slammed into the guy, practically knocking him into next week."

"So he saved you?" Wendy shook her head. "Sorry, but I'm not seeing the monster part yet—or the problem."

"Yes, he saved me. Then he turned around. That's when I saw…everything."

"What do you mean, everything?"

"Wendy, Alex's face had changed. It was wider… and longer. And there were frigging fangs nearly two inches long sticking out of his mouth. His eyes were glowing so bright that I swore they were on fire. And he had claws, really long freaking claws."

Lacey didn't realize her voice had crept up a few octaves until she was done. She forced herself to stop and take a breath. Beside her, doubt was written all over Wendy's face.

"You said it was dark," her friend pointed out. "Maybe you just imagined that you saw all those things. Maybe it was just a trick of the light. Maybe you were in shock or something."

Lacey shook her head, not surprised her friend doubted her. Hell, Lacey had doubted what her eyes had been telling her too, and she'd been right there, ten feet away from Alex, when it happened.

"It wasn't a trick of the light, Wendy, and it wasn't shock. Alex had claws and fangs," she insisted. "But there's more. When the other guards started running our way, he picked me up like a toy and ran with me—faster than any human can run, with or without carrying anyone in his arms."

"Alex is really big," Wendy pointed out. "And muscular as hell."

"Wendy, he jumped to the top of one of those industrial storage racks Bensen has all over his junkyards. Those things are, like, fifteen feet tall, maybe higher. He jumped to the top with me in his arms. I don't care how big and strong he is. A normal person can't do that. And they couldn't jump over the big security fence around Bensen's junkyard either, but Alex did that too—with me still in his arms."

Wendy didn't say anything for a long time. Instead, she sat there regarding Lacey as if trying to decide whether to believe her. Finally, she sighed.

"What happened then?" she asked. "Did he say anything to you?"

Lacey shrugged. "He tried, but I have to admit I wasn't exactly in the right frame of mind to have a meaningful conversation. I was in the middle of a nightmare. I pretty much bailed after that and ran to my car. I just left him standing in the street."

Wendy nodded as if that had been the perfectly rational thing to do. Had it? Lacey had no clue if it was or not. She'd been operating on plain, old-fashioned, fear-induced panic. Driving away from Alex had made her feel like crap, but she'd been so scared. She didn't know what else she could have done. The guy she'd been sleeping with—the guy she'd let into the house with Kelsey—was a monster. Not the metaphoric kind of monster, but an honest-to-goodness claws, fangs, and violent rampage kind of monster. For all she knew, he'd killed that guard in the junkyard.

"I take it you believe me then?" Lacey asked, unable to take the silence anymore. "About Alex, you know... being a monster?"

"I don't know about the monster thing," Wendy admitted. "But I believe you saw what you say you saw—the claws and stuff. I mean, people have said for a while..." She stopped as if she thought she shouldn't say anything else, but then continued. "Cops talk amongst themselves, you know? A couple of people I know and trust have mentioned that the guys on the SWAT team are a little...different. They've done things that maybe they shouldn't have been able to do or probably should have gotten them killed. I even know a female cop in the narcotics division who was out with a couple of the SWAT guys a week ago, and she told me that one of them…well…tackled a car. He hit it so hard, he almost knocked the damn thing over."

Lacey waited for the punch line, for her friend to laugh and say she was joking, but Wendy was staring off into the distance, lost in thought.

"Wait a second." Lacey leaned forward. "What are you trying to say…that the whole Dallas SWAT team is a bunch of monsters?"

Wendy looked at her sharply. "I didn't see what you saw, Lacey, but even if I had, I'm not sure I'd call them monsters. I don't know why Alex was at that junkyard tonight, but he saved your ass. The SWAT team has saved a whole lot of asses in the past few years, including more cops than I can count. You can call Alex a monster if you want, but I think I'm going to hold off using that particular word until I have more information."

Lacey sat there, her face warm from being chastised so blatantly. Yeah, Alex had saved her, she knew that. But she'd slept with the man. Shouldn't he have told her that he was some kind of…whatever he was? Didn't sleeping with a man gain you that much trust at least?

"What are you going to do?" Wendy asked quietly.

Lacey thought about that for a while. "I don't know. What can I do? If I tell anyone besides you, there'd be a race to either put me in jail for breaking into Bensen's junkyard or fit me with one of those nice white jackets with wraparound sleeves. Even if neither of those things happened, I really don't want Bensen to know I was there. I honestly think he was involved in that woman's death, and I don't want him setting his sights on me."

"I don't blame you there," Wendy muttered, though whether her friend was referring to her ending up in jail, a psych ward, or on Bensen's hit list, Lacey wasn't sure.

"I guess it comes down to what you really think you saw," Wendy said. "Alex with claws and fangs...or a monster?"

Lacey knew what Wendy was trying to say, but right then, she wasn't sure if she was ready to make the distinction as easily as her friend seemed to be able to. Maybe it was simply because Wendy hadn't seen Alex change the way she had, but it was hard to think of him the same way now. Part of her insisted that was stupid, considering he'd saved her life. But another part pointed out that he was the first guy she'd ever started to believe in and trust. That belief and trust just didn't seem to be there anymore.

"You know you don't have to decide anything now, right?" Wendy said. "Why don't you go home and think about it for a while?"

"And then what?" Lacey asked morosely.

It wasn't like she could imagine ever being with Alex again. She wasn't sure she'd ever be able to look at him without seeing all those teeth and hearing that growl of rage that had shaken every building in the junkyard.

"Then you do what comes next," Wendy told her. "Whatever that might be."

Chapter 11

ALEX SAT ON THE COUCH IN HIS APARTMENT, THE GLOW of the morning sun streaming through the windows as he stared at his cell phone, not sure if he was doing it because he was hoping Lacey might call him back or because he was damn close to calling her again.

He desperately wanted to call her, just to hear her voice and convince himself that she was okay. But he knew he couldn't. She already thought he was a monster. He didn't want her thinking he was a stalker too. He almost laughed at how stupid that sounded.

By all means, go ahead and scare the crap out of the woman you love by sprouting fangs and claws in front of her, but don't offend her sensibilities by violating the three-calls-a-night rule.

He tossed the phone aside on the couch beside him with a curse. He'd already called and left two messages on her cell and one on her home answering machine. That would have to be enough. She would either call him back…or she wouldn't.

Alex let his head fall back onto his couch, replaying last night's events in his head for about the hundredth time as he tried to figure out if there was something he could have done differently. He couldn't come up with anything, of course. He hadn't been able to do so all night. Lacey had been in danger. He'd done the only thing he could think of at the time to save her. And he had saved her, probably at the cost of their relationship.

Alex had scared Lacey—really, really scared her. It probably wasn't a stretch to say she'd been far more terrified of him than she'd been of that man in the junkyard with the gun. The way she'd backed away from him in complete fear had torn at his insides like nothing he'd ever felt before. He'd rather be stabbed fifty times over with a dull knife than feel the kind of pain he was feeling right now.

The worst part had been watching her drive away. It had felt like something was being physically ripped out of him. In some ways, he supposed it was. He'd accepted a while ago that Lacey was truly *The One* for him. He supposed the horrible sensation he'd felt was that amazing link between them being torn apart. The legend of *The One* had been clear that the connection between a werewolf and his mate could never be denied. The fact that it could be destroyed had never come up in conversation.

Even though Remy had told him to give Lacey some space to come to grips with what she'd seen, his first instinct had been to chase after her. He hadn't done it, of course. He was smart enough to know that the harder he chased her, the faster she'd run. Besides, it had taken over two hours to get himself disentangled from the damn surveillance operation at the junkyard. Rodriguez had freaked out when they'd called him, thinking they'd done something stupid to blow their cover. That was only partially incorrect. They'd done something stupid, but it hadn't blown their cover, not completely anyway.

Luckily, he and Remy had been able to convince Rodriguez that they had nothing to do with the commotion at the junkyard and it had just been a wild dog running through the area. Thankfully, Vaughn had backed up their story—in return for them putting in a good word for her with Brooks. By the time they'd gotten the surveillance van back to the police equipment yard, it had been after three in the morning. That's when he'd called and left those messages for Lacey, saying he was sorry for scaring her and that they could talk any time she was ready.

He and Remy had stopped by Cooper and Everly's place after that, hoping he could do a little damage control. Cooper had taken one look at them and frowned.

"Since nothing good ever happens after midnight, this can't be good," the team's demolition expert said when he'd opened the door. "If you need money to help pay for some bar you and the guys busted up, you're going to have to count me out. I'm saving every penny I have for the honeymoon in Hawaii. You wouldn't believe how much the plane tickets alone cost."

"Dude, why are you guys paying all that money to go to Hawaii when you're probably never going to leave the hotel room anyway?" Remy asked. "We could put some fake palm trees and one of those ocean noise machines outside the window of the nearest motel, and you'd never know the difference. It would save you thousands."

Cooper gave Remy a wry look. "How is it that you actually get laid? Because it sure as hell isn't your romantic side."

Remy chuckled. "It's my mad skills in bed."

"Okay, Remy. TMI," Alex interrupted. "Can you try and remember why we came here in the first place?" He looked at Cooper. "It's Lacey. I sort of fucked up and was hoping you might know how to handle it."

He quickly filled Cooper in on the story, highlighting the part where Lacey ran off in complete terror.

"I tried calling her, but she's not answering," he added. "I'm worried she might tell someone."

Cooper was still considering that when Everly wandered into the living room, wearing an old Army Bomb Squad T-shirt of Cooper's that hung down to her knees and a worried expression.

"Did I hear Alex say that Lacey found out he's a werewolf?" she asked, pushing her long hair back.

"Yeah, the hard way," Alex said, then brought Everly up to speed.

"Do you guys think she'd go public with this?" Remy asked.

"No," Cooper and Everly said at the same time. They gave each other a quick look before Everly continued.

"I didn't talk to her that long the other night, but I get the feeling she's the kind of person who will think about what she saw, maybe even talk it over with someone she trusts. She's not going to run around screaming it from the rooftops or putting it on social media."

Alex relaxed a little at that. "Do you think I should tell Xander and Gage?"

Cooper shook his head. "I'll deal with them. You need to back off and give Lacey a little time. If she's *The One* for you, she'll come around."

Alex sighed. He didn't like it, but it was sound advice. "Remy pretty much said the same thing."

Cooper looked at Remy in surprise. "Really? I'll be damned. Maybe there's hope for you yet."

While Remy and Cooper were snarking at each over who gave better advice, Everly pulled Alex aside. "Maybe when Lacey calms down, I could go talk to her for you and give her another woman's perspective on the situation."

Alex would have hugged Everly right then if she hadn't been standing there in nothing but a T-shirt with her possessive alpha werewolf mate a few feet away. He settled for a heartfelt thanks instead. "I'd appreciate that."

Now in the clear light of day, he wasn't so sure Lacey would ever calm down enough to talk to anyone about what she'd seen last night.

Alex hadn't realized he'd drifted off until his phone beeped at him. He snatched it up, praying it was Lacey texting him back. But it was Remy checking to see if he had heard anything. He shot off a quick text to his friend, saying he hadn't.

Maybe tomorrow, Remy sent back.

He didn't bother to reply. Instead, he revisited the advice Cooper, Everly, and Remy had given him about backing off and giving Lacey some space. He knew it was the right thing to do, but there was a surprisingly self-ish part of him that wanted to go over to her apartment, bang on the door, and demand an explanation. Not about why she'd been scared—he got that part. What he wanted to know is how she could have driven away from him. Didn't she feel the connection between them as strongly as he did? Hadn't it ripped out her guts to walk away?

Alex knew Lacey had some baggage in her past and that she wasn't the most ardent believer in love, romance, or men, but he was having a hard time reconciling the whole concept of *The One* with the fact that Lacey had been able to walk away from him so easily. As far as he knew, it hadn't been like this for any of the other guys in the Pack when they'd found their soul mates. Alex got the feeling it wasn't like that with Lacey. If it had been, could she have ignored his calls and messages all night?

He was still contemplating that when the doorbell

rang, quickly followed by pounding. He wondered for half a second if it was Lacey but dismissed the idea. She wasn't the type to bang on any door, especially his. But as he crossed the room to answer it, he picked up an unmistakable scent.

Shit. It really was Lacey!

Alex covered the last several feet to the door in a sprint but then hesitated. What the hell was he going to say? He'd wanted to talk to her the whole night, and now he didn't have a clue where to start.

Taking a deep breath, he yanked open the door to find Lacey standing there. Her hair was disheveled, her eyes were red-rimmed from crying, her heart was beating a hundred miles an hour, and she looked exhausted as hell. The urge to pull her into his arms was overwhelming, but he controlled himself.

She's here. Don't screw it up.

Looking at Lacey, he couldn't help but think that maybe walking away from him *had* been as hard on her as it had been on him. Why did that make him feel good and bad at the same time? More important, did it make him an asshole?

"I'm glad you came," he said. "I wanted to explain… about what you saw."

She shook her head. "I'm not here to talk about that. I don't know what you are, and I don't care. All I want to know is whether you'll help me."

Alex felt like she'd kicked him in the balls. He thought she'd come here to talk about what she'd seen—about them. He thought she'd come because she'd missed him as much as he'd missed her.

"Of course, I'll help you any way I can, you know that," he said. "Come in and tell me what's wrong."

She walked into his apartment, her breath coming even faster, tears welling up in her eyes. "Kelsey is missing."

He frowned as he closed the door, his werewolf instincts kicking in and making him tense. "What do you mean, she's missing?"

"She never came home last night."

Alex let out the breath he'd been holding. "She probably just got tired and stayed at a friend's place. You told me she's done that before."

Lacey shook her head. "This is different. She always leaves me a message when she does that, but not this time. I tried to call her, but she's not returning my texts or calls. Her friends said they haven't seen her since last night when she left the restaurant they went to for dinner. They all thought she'd left with someone else. They hadn't even bothered to check with each other until I started looking for her."

Lacey's heart was beating so fast, Alex thought she was going to pass out. The more she talked, the paler she became.

"Calm down, okay?" he said. "There has to be a logical explanation for this. Maybe she just met someone…"

That earned him a sharp look, and he knew without asking that Lacey would never believe Kelsey was simply shacking up with a hot guy she'd met. In Lacey's world, Kelsey would never do that.

He was about to point out that they needed to at least consider that as a possibility when Lacey spoke.

"I called campus security just to see if they knew anything, and they told me that Kelsey sent the registrar's office an email this morning saying she was dropping out of school to go to California and become an actress."

Okay, that changed things. It sure as hell didn't sound

like Kelsey. That horrible feeling settled in the pit of his stomach again. He gestured for Lacey to sit on the couch, then joined her, asking her to go over everything from the beginning.

"I talked to her last night before I went to Bensen's place," she said.

Alex didn't say anything. He would have liked to follow up on that part of the conversation, but it wasn't important right now.

"She said she was exhausted from all the studying she'd been doing and had been planning to hit a local popular burger joint with her friends," Lacey continued. "She wasn't home when I got there and still wasn't in her bed this morning. That's when I started calling everyone."

"And what exactly did campus security say?"

She shrugged in the most heartbreaking gesture he'd ever seen. "They don't understand why I'm so freaked out. According to them, they have dozens of students who bail each semester without telling anyone. They took a report, but as far as they're concerned, I'm just making a fuss for no reason. They keep saying she's a college kid and that's what college kids do. But they don't know my sister like I do."

"Did you go to the police?" he asked.

Lacey nodded. "I went down to the police station and filed a missing person report, but the guy at the front desk didn't seem very hopeful. He told me he'd pass the report to the Missing Persons Squad but admitted he was concerned the email to the registrar's office would put Kelsey's case on the bottom of the stack."

Alex ached to wipe the tears from her cheeks, but he didn't dare.

"Something has happened to Kelsey," she said

brokenly. "I can feel it in my heart. I know I don't have any right to ask you this, and if I had any other option, I wouldn't be here now, but I need help. You're the only one I can turn to."

They weren't exactly the words Alex had been hoping to hear from Lacey when he'd first opened the door, but none of that mattered now. Whatever was going on between them—or wasn't—he couldn't turn his back on Lacey or her sister. His gut was saying the same thing Lacey's was. There was no way in hell Kelsey had run off to California.

"You don't even have to ask," he told her. "I know some people down at missing persons. Let's see what we can find out down there."

———

Lacey hadn't even realized the missing persons division was a special part of the DPD, kind of like SWAT. She thought that each police station had their own. But they had a separate office on Lamar Street, which was where Alex took her. Even though his SWAT uniform got them in to see a detective who took a second report, the man said they'd look into it but that there wasn't much they could do without some concrete evidence that Kelsey was missing. Ever since that poor girl Abigail Elliott had disappeared, they'd been swamped with missing person reports. Glancing around at the office packed with worried-looking people, Lacey didn't doubt it. That made her only more desperate to find her sister.

By the time she and Alex left, she was so exhausted, she could barely stand. She had no idea what to do or where to turn next.

"When was the last time you ate?" Alex asked as he opened the passenger door of his truck for her.

Lacey stared at him, trying to remember. She'd been a complete mess when she'd gotten home from Wendy's place last night. All she'd wanted was to fall into bed and forget the evening had ever happened. She was wrung out like she'd run a race, and there was an ache in her chest that was impossible to ignore—and just as impossible to explain. She'd lain awake for hours, staring at the dark ceiling, thinking about Alex and everything she'd seen.

She was having one hell of a time reconciling the amazingly gentle man she'd laughed with, kissed, and made love to with the violent monster she'd seen in that junkyard. There hadn't been a single gentle quality about that thing. It had been all power, carnage, and violence.

Yet through it all, a little voice whispered in the back of her mind that Alex had kept her safe. If not for him, she'd be dead. Even so, she never would have come to Alex for help, not if she had a better option. But for her sister, she'd swallow her pride and do whatever she had to do to find her.

While she was pretty sure she hadn't eaten since before going to Bensen's place last night, the thought of food made her stomach turn.

"I don't want to eat," she said, climbing in the seat. "I want to find my sister."

"So do I, but we can't do that if you pass out." He sighed. "Since missing persons was pretty much a bust, I'm going to ask some of my SWAT teammates to help us find Kelsey. We might as well grab something to eat while we wait for them to meet us."

Lacey was too tired to complain as Alex drove her to the nearest diner and led her to a booth way in the back. After they ordered, he pulled out his phone.

"Hey, Xander, it's me. Did Cooper talk to you this morning?" A pause. "Good, because I need some help."

She sipped her coffee, listening as Alex told him about Kelsey being missing.

"I could use Remy and Becker, since they have the most experience with finding people," he said. "But I'll take anyone else Gage is willing to let me have."

Alex gave Xander the address of the diner, then hung up.

"The guys will be here in fifteen minutes," he told her.

She mechanically spread jelly on the whole wheat toast the waitress had brought while Alex was on the phone, then took a small bite and chewed slowly. "You said Remy and Becker have experience finding people," she said after she swallowed. "What kind of experience?"

"Remy was a U.S. marshal before joining SWAT. He can track anyone, anywhere," Alex said, digging into his scrambled eggs. "Becker is good with computers and all things electronic. He's handy to have around if you need to see video footage or find someone's digital footprint."

That all made sense to her, but for some reason, she could only think of one particular question. "Are they... like you?"

Alex didn't say anything for a long time, but she could feel his disappointment—and anger—coming from the other side of the table. "Does it matter that much to you if they are?"

Lacey looked away. She had no right to be asking any questions, especially since she was the one who'd come begging for help. "I guess not. I just want my sister to be okay."

They both fell silent after that, concentrating on their food until they were done eating, then staring at their coffee. Anything to keep from having to look at each other. Lacey shifted in the booth, more uncomfortable than she'd ever been in her life. It was hard to believe that so much had changed so quickly. She supposed finding out your boyfriend was a monster could do that.

Lacey breathed a sigh of relief when Alex's teammates showed up. She'd met Remy, Becker, Max, and Brooks at the engagement party but hadn't given much thought to how big and muscular each of them was at the time. Now that she realized they were like Alex, it made sense. It was difficult not thinking about them having fangs and claws, though. She needed their help, so she'd just have to deal with it.

Since they wouldn't all fit in the booth where she and Alex were sitting, they moved to a nearby table. After the waitress poured coffee for each of them, Lacey told Alex's teammates the same thing she'd told him that morning about Kelsey's disappearance. They took turns asking her questions after that, mostly about Kelsey's friends.

"Can you call them and see if they'll meet with us?" Max asked.

She frowned. "Do you think they know something about what happened to Kelsey?"

Alex exchanged looks with his teammates. "They may know something and not even realize it."

Lacey sighed. She wasn't sure what they could possibly know that they hadn't already told her, but she dug in her purse for her cell phone and called them anyway.

—w—

Alex opened the door to Lacey's apartment, urging her inside with a gentle hand on the small of her back. The fact that she didn't flinch and pull away from him was just another indication of how tired she was, not to mention how shell-shocked from everything they'd learned about Kelsey today. He felt for Lacey. It couldn't be easy finding out she hadn't known Kelsey nearly as well as she'd thought.

Lacey walked straight to the couch and dropped down into it with an exhausted sigh. She was falling apart in front of his eyes, and it killed Alex to have to stand all the way on the far side of the room and watch it happen. But he knew she didn't want him beside her no matter how much he wanted to be there.

Giving him a sad look, Leo moved to sit on the floor beside her and rest his chin on her knee. Lacey ran her hand gently over his head.

"How could I have missed all that?" she asked softly, close to tears.

The urge to pull Lacey into his arms and tell her it was all going to be okay was hard to resist, but Alex managed.

"How could you have seen it?" he said. "Kelsey never gave you a reason to think she was lying to you, so you trusted her."

She let out a sound of frustration. "This is like our mom all over again."

"What do you mean?"

"Drinking. Clubbing. Guys." Lacey shook her head. "Kelsey is doing all of that and now she's going to end up just like our mother."

Alex frowned. "No, she isn't. Because we're going to find her."

Lacey didn't say anything.

"Kelsey isn't like your mom, Lacey. She's a normal college student doing what every other college student her age does."

Lacey didn't look convinced, but she didn't argue. "I didn't know about anything Kelsey was doing, but you and your teammates figured it out right away. How?"

He gave her a wry smile. "The job requires a certain level of cynicism."

Within minutes of sitting down with Kelsey's girl-friends at a coffee shop near the RTC campus, one of them had admitted that Kelsey had two drinks last night. When Lacey had flipped out, saying that Kelsey wasn't old enough to drink, the girl immediately tried to backtrack, but it was too late. That's when everything started to unravel, and Lacey learned that her sister was a lot more like a typical college sophomore than she'd ever guessed.

After dinner at the restaurant, Kelsey and her friends had gone to a big honky-tonk bar on Cedar Springs Road. Not only did Kelsey have a fake ID, but she kept clothes at her friends' places to change into when they went out partying. According to her friends, with the right makeup, she could appear five years older.

Lacey had looked like someone slapped her at that revelation. She'd sat there stunned while Alex and the other guys had peppered Kelsey's friends with questions. They admitted that Kelsey had left the bar before they had.

"We thought she'd just met a cute guy and gone home with him," a petite redhead with freckles explained. "She's done that before a few times, so we didn't think anything of it."

That overdose of reality about her little sister had been too much for Lacey. She'd spent the rest of the day in a daze. The only time she'd looked alive was when Brooks had picked up Kelsey's scent at the honky-tonk bar and followed it out a back exit. But when the trail disappeared, so had that tiny spark of hope.

"Could you and Brooks really track Kelsey's scent back in the bar?" Lacey asked now as if reading his mind. The tears that had been threatening to fall earlier were gone, replaced by an intensity that had been absent most of the day.

Alex hesitated. He wasn't sure how much he wanted to get into this, since he still didn't know what Lacey planned to do with the knowledge she already had about werewolves. But ultimately, she needed something to give her hope, just to give her a reason to keep going.

"Yeah," he finally admitted. "Brooks has a better nose than I do, but I'm more familiar with Kelsey's scent. Between the two of us, we were able to follow it outside."

"Do you think she got in a car?"

"Most likely. Unfortunately, there's no way to tell if she went willingly or not."

Lacey absently ran her hand over Leo's fur as she considered that. "I heard Brooks say that you could probably track her scent even if she was in a car if you did a full shift. What did he mean by that?"

Alex had to bite his tongue to keep from cursing out loud. He'd been so focused on Kelsey that he hadn't realized Lacey had overheard him talking to Brooks. If he'd known she was listening that closely, he would have chosen his words more carefully. Not because he was worried about spilling the Pack's secrets, but because he didn't want Lacey to get her hopes up.

In addition to tracking Kelsey's scent through the club, he'd been able to pick up traces of it here and there along the road even after she'd gotten in the car. It wasn't enough to follow, though. Brooks seemed to think that since Alex knew Kelsey's scent so well, he might be able to track the vehicle purely on trace remnants if he could shift into a full wolf.

"I might be able to," he admitted. "But unfortunately, I don't know how to do a full shift."

She stared at him in confusion. "What I saw in Bensen's junkyard wasn't a full shift?"

He snorted. "Not even close."

She opened her mouth to say something, but before she could, the doorbell rang. Hope flared in Lacey's eyes for a split second but then disappeared just as quickly when she realized her sister wouldn't need to ring the bell.

Alex walked over to answer it, knowing without looking through the peephole that it was Wendy. He would have recognized her by scent even if he hadn't called her when Lacey had disappeared off to the ladies' room.

"Hey. You didn't have to come over," Lacey said. "I would have called if we heard anything."

"I know," Wendy said. "But Alex asked if I could come over and hang out with you while he took off."

Lacey turned curious eyes on him. "Where are you going?"

"I need to go see if Becker and Max have found anything on the videos from the bar yet," he said. "I didn't want you to be by yourself."

Lacey jumped to her feet. "I'm going with you."

Alex cursed silently. Lacey was so tired, she could barely stay awake. She needed to take some time to recharge. He just wasn't sure how to say that without sounding like a heartless jerk.

Luckily, Wendy beat him to it. "Lacey, honey, you need to let Alex and his teammates do what they do best. He'll be able to move faster if he doesn't have to worry about you falling asleep on your feet."

Lacey chewed on her lower lip, looking doubtfully at him before finally nodding. "Okay. But you'll call me the second you learn anything, right?"

"I promise," he said.

Damn, it was hard to walk away from her when she needed him most. But he wasn't going to find her sister by sitting there holding her hand. He was going to have to leave that to Wendy. Lacey likely preferred it that way.

Chapter 12

LACEY STARED AT THE TURKEY SANDWICH WENDY SET down on the coffee table in front of her. The thought of eating anything made her feel ill. "Thanks, but I'm not hungry."

"You don't have to be hungry to eat," Wendy said as she sat down in the overstuffed chair that matched the couch. "If you don't, I'm going to badger you all night."

Lacey considered arguing, then changed her mind. Her friend was just trying to help. Besides, Leo was looking at her with that same worried look on his face as Wendy. If she didn't eat soon, the big baby would probably crawl into her lap and lick her face until she gave in.

Shaking her head, she picked up the sandwich and took a big bite. "Happy?"

"Hey, I slaved away in your kitchen for five minutes making that sandwich," Wendy said. "I expect you to appreciate it and eat at least half."

Lacey grudgingly took another bite. How was her friend supposed to know she was so sick with worry over Kelsey that it was hard not curling into a ball and just giving up?

The last twenty-four hours had been the worst day of her life—and she'd had a lot of bad ones. She'd woken up this morning to the knowledge that the guy she'd been falling for was some kind of monster, then she discovered Kelsey was missing. Those two things alone should have been enough for the world to dump on her. But no, she had to learn that she didn't know a damn thing about her baby sister as well. Finding out that Kelsey had a fake ID so she could get into bars was bad enough, but hearing that she slept with guys she barely knew was hard to wrap her head around. It was even more difficult knowing that the sister you thought shared everything with you had been lying to your face the entire time.

If Alex and Wendy hadn't been here for her, Lacey wasn't sure what she would have done.

That thought brought her back to problem number one—her ex-boyfriend. Lacey sipped the iced tea Wendy had brought in with the sandwich. She had no idea why the hell Alex was even helping her. She'd run screaming from him in terror only to come back because she needed something from him. He could have just as easily slammed the door in her face, but he hadn't. She didn't really understand that. No more than she understood why she felt better and more hopeful when he was around, like maybe this would all work out somehow.

That was beyond stupid. Any woman with a lick of sense in her head knew that depending on a man to walk in and solve your problems was a surefire way to end up disappointed and alone. She should know that.

Lacey reached for her sandwich again, keenly aware of Wendy and Leo watching her with worried expressions, when the doorbell rang. She put down the sandwich, praying it was Alex back with good news, but when Wendy opened the door, she saw it was Everly.

"Hey." Everly gave her a small smile as she walked over, her long, colorful boho skirt swishing around her ankles. "Hope you don't mind that I stopped by. I just wanted to see how you're holding up and if you've heard anything yet?"

Lacey felt a sharp reply bubble up, but she forced it down. She didn't know why she was suddenly so angry at Everly. Then it hit her. She was mad because Everly had almost certainly known what Alex was and hadn't told her. Not only was that stupid, but it was immature too. What did she expect, that Everly was going to come out and announce to a person she'd just met that her future husband and the rest of the SWAT team were monsters? Hell, maybe Everly didn't know. Come on, how could she not know? She was marrying one of them.

"No," Lacey said. "We haven't heard anything yet. But Alex left a little while ago to talk to Becker and Max. Something about videos."

Everly's smile faded to be replaced by concern as she sat down on the couch beside Lacey. "How are you holding up?"

Lacey shrugged. "I'd say I'm okay, but that would be a lie, so I won't bother."

"Stupid question, I guess," Everly admitted. "But here goes another one. Is there anything I can do to help?"

Lacey leveled her gaze at the woman. "It would be nice if you could tell me how long you've known what Alex and the rest of the SWAT team is."

She expected Everly to immediately go on the defensive or say she didn't know what Lacey was talking about. She didn't do either. Instead, she looked from Lacey to Wendy and back again.

"I'm not sure this is the best time to talk about this," she said quietly.

"You don't have to worry about Wendy," Lacey told

her. "She already knows about Alex. She's the first person I talked to after seeing…what I saw. She knows everything I know, which isn't very much. I'd appreciate it if you could help change that."

Everly considered that, then sighed. "I'll tell you what I can. There are some things I can't tell you because I don't know them and other things I can't tell you because they aren't my secrets to share." She looked from Lacey to Wendy. "But it's very important both of you understand that you can't reveal anything I tell you to anyone else. There are people out there right now who would kill people like Landry and Alex—and everyone else on the SWAT team—because of what they are. If you repeat what I tell you to anyone, it's as good as killing them yourselves."

Lacey didn't really understand what Everly was talking about, but she nodded all the same. It wasn't like she was ever going to breathe a word about it to anyone anyway. They'd think she was insane.

"I learned Landry's secret shortly after we met," Everly continued. "Like you, I was stunned. And like you, I didn't handle it very well."

Lacey wasn't sure if she'd agree with that assessment. She'd handled it like any normal, rational person—she'd run away.

"What about the others?" Wendy prompted. "When did you learn about Alex and the rest of the SWAT team?"

"Shortly after learning about Landry," Everly answered. "I'm sure you've seen how close the members of the team are. It's no coincidence. They were all brought together because of how unique and special they are."

Lacey exchanged looks with Wendy. Her friend had been right. The entire Dallas PD SWAT team was made up of monsters. That was scary enough, but one thing bothered her a whole lot more.

"There's something I don't understand," she said to Everly. "You've seen what Cooper turns into, and yet you still decided to marry him?"

Everly smiled. "I love him, more than I ever thought possible. Claws, fangs, and fur could never change that. Like I told you at the engagement party—when you meet *The One* for you, nothing else matters."

Lacey had expected that to be her answer. Everly seemed even more idealistic than Kelsey.

Her doubts must have shown on her face, because Everly took her hand. "The most important thing you need to understand is that Landry isn't a monster, and neither is Alex. There are lots of real monsters in the world out there, and few of them have fangs and claws."

Lacey wasn't so sure about that. "If they're not monsters, what are they?"

Everly hesitated. "What has Alex told you?"

"Nothing." Lacey shrugged. "Though to be truthful, I really haven't given him a chance. I ran away from him last night, and today I've been focused on Kelsey."

"Understandably," Everly said. "If it helps you to know exactly what they are, the answer is simple. They're werewolves."

Lacey blinked. Everly had to be joking. But when the other woman didn't even crack a smile, Lacey realized she was being serious.

"Werewolves aren't real, Everly. They're stuff made up in books and movies."

Lacey looked at Wendy, expecting some backup, but her friend was sitting there with a thoughtful expression on her face.

"Have you ever wondered where all the werewolf stories came from for those books and movies?" Everly asked softly.

Lacey thought about that for a moment. Taking into account the claws and fangs, she supposed she could understand how a person could see what she'd seen and make the leap to werewolf.

Crap. Was she seriously buying into this idea that Alex was a werewolf?

"How did Alex get this way? Was he bitten, like in the stories?" Then she remembered how many times Alex had nipped her neck—and other places—with his sharp teeth. "Will I turn into a werewolf if he bit me?"

Both Everly and Wendy raised their brows, but thankfully, neither asked for details. Lacey had no desire to get into what she and Alex had done in the heat of passion.

Everly shook her head. "That's the part the stories and legends all get wrong. Werewolves don't get turned with a bite. People who become werewolves are born with a gene that lies dormant for most of their lives. They won't change unless they go through some kind of horrible, life-threatening event."

"So...him biting me?" she prompted.

"Won't do anything to you," Everly promised with a smile.

Lacey was relieved she wouldn't get fangs and claws anytime soon, but she had so many questions whirling through her head that she couldn't focus on that quite yet.

"You said something horrible had to happen to turn a person into a werewolf," Lacey said. "What happened to Cooper?"

Everly looked down at the floor for a moment. When

she lifted her head, Lacey saw tears shimmering in her eyes. "He was caught in an IED blast over in Iraq. He almost died—he would have died—if he hadn't changed."

Suddenly, all Lacey could think about was what kind of traumatic event Alex had gone through to turn. She remembered running her hands over his muscular body and feeling several barely there scars along his left side. Had whatever happened to give them to him been the event that had changed him? She wasn't sure why she wanted to know, but she did.

"Do you know what made Alex change?"

Everly slowly shook her head. "I have a general idea, but that's one of those secrets I have no right to share. If you really want to know what happened to him, you'll need to ask him yourself."

Lacey nodded, though she could never imagine asking Alex, not after everything had changed between them. Some roads just couldn't be traveled again, not after you burned all the bridges along the way.

Everly answered as many of Lacey's other questions as she could, being honest about those she couldn't. For a while at least, Lacey could almost forget that her sister was missing—or worse. But when the questions ran dry, the concern for her sister came flooding back. Kelsey had been missing for more than twelve hours. Was she even still alive? Unbidden, images of the dead girl who she and Alex had found Saturday night popped into her head. Is that the way they would find Kelsey? Oh God, she hoped not.

"Alex is going to find your sister," Everly said. "You just have to trust him."

Lacey gave her a wry smile. "I'm not very good at trusting people—especially men."

"But Alex isn't like any other man you've ever met. You have no idea what he's capable of or how far he'd go for you."

After the way she'd bolted away from Alex, Lacey wasn't so sure of that, but part of her prayed Everly was right.

—⁓—

"Where's your pack?" Alex asked as Jayna led him into the living room of the five-bedroom loft apartment over near Baylor's Dallas campus that everyone had started calling the Beta House. The place was usually packed to the gills with Becker and Jayna, Zak and Megan, Moe, Chris, Joseph, and lately, Mia. Six werewolves and two humans were a lot of people to fit into a single apartment, even if there were five bedrooms. But that was just the way Jayna's beta pack preferred it.

"Zak took them over to Dave and Buster's," Jayna said over her shoulder. "He knew Eric needed to get some work done."

Becker, Max, and Remy were in the living room, studying the big screen TV as grainy video footage slowly scrolled by.

"What do you have so far?" Alex asked as he grabbed a seat on the end of the couch and tried to figure out what he was looking at. It seemed to be some kind of stationary footage, maybe from a commercial security camera, but it was so dark, it was nearly impossible to make out anything.

Becker paused the video and sat back on the couch. Remy and Max took the opportunity to sit back and rub their eyes, clearly tired from looking at tape.

"Right now, not much," Becker admitted. "I have a

facial recognition program running on all the video I got from the bar, but we're doing it manually too, just to make sure we don't miss anything. Fortunately—or unfortunately, depending on how you look at it—there were sixteen different cameras in there. You add those to the street cameras around the bar, and we're looking at maybe thirty or forty hours' worth of grainy crap to look through. Even if we limit it to the time period we think Kelsey went missing, it's going to take a while. I don't expect to have it done until tomorrow morning sometime."

Alex cursed. "Don't you have anything we can work with now?" Frustration made the words come out louder than he intended. The guys didn't seem to care. They were used to dealing with alpha werewolves who frequently lost their cool.

Becker grabbed up a notepad covered in his neat writing and started flipping pages. "Not much. Brooks went back to the bar. He's going to wait until they close, then shift and try to track Kelsey's scent when no one's around. Since Lacey's name is on the wireless bill and she gave us permission, we were able to pull Kelsey's cell phone records without a warrant—or hacking—which was nice."

Becker paused as he read his notes. "Like a lot of college kids Kelsey's age, there are way more texts than phone calls, with the exception of calls to and from Lacey. Bottom line—there's nothing there. A lot of chatting with her girlfriends about school, professors, hot guys, getting together to go out—stuff like that. Nothing to indicate she was seeing anyone regularly or that she was having trouble with anyone."

"What about last night?" Remy asked.

Becker shook his head. "There were only two texts after she got to the bar, both about how sucky the music was. Nothing since."

Alex cut loose a growl. He didn't have a good feeling about any of this. "Any reason to think someone was using the bar as a hunting ground or that Kelsey was being stalked?"

"I checked out the bar," Remy said. "Reports of fights, assaults, suspicious people hanging around—the usual stuff. Nothing to raise any red flags."

"I sniffed around the neighborhood near the club," Max added. "I talked to at least fifty people, asking if they'd heard about any girls getting messed with in the area, but no one heard a thing. They didn't see anything unusual last night, either."

"When I dug into Kelsey's social network accounts, I came up empty," Becker continued. "No enemies, no drunk pictures, no stalker boyfriends. Hell, no boy-friends at all. She's slept with some guys, but she seems to be smart about selecting men who aren't dirtbags. As a last resort, I even checked out her Find My Phone app. Nothing came up on that, either."

"What's a Find My Phone app?" Alex asked. God, he hated all this tech crap.

"It's an account you can set up with your phone," Jayna said, coming back into the living room. "If you lose your phone, you can log into the account, and it will use the phone's GPS to track its current location."

Alex frowned. "Okay, that's seems creepy."

"It's the twenty-first century." Becker chuckled. "You might want to hop on board the train, bro, because it left the station more than a decade ago. Regardless, it didn't give us anything. The app requires the phone to be turned on and in an area with cell phone, Wi-Fi, or Internet connection. Kelsey's phone isn't showing up anywhere. Either it's in an area with no wireless signal of any type, it's off—or worse, destroyed."

Alex rubbed his hand over the back of his neck. Damn, he hadn't been this tense in a really long time. Not since he'd gone through his change and moved to Dallas.

"So what do we think we're looking at here?" he asked. "A date-rape abduction, a random kidnapping, a serial killer?"

Max shrugged. "Since we've ruled out the obvious stuff—family, boyfriend, coworker, jealous girlfriend—then yeah, I think we could be looking at any of those worst-case scenarios you mentioned."

Alex's gut clenched. If this was one of those worst-case scenarios, the chance of Kelsey being found alive was slim. If Kelsey died, he wasn't sure Lacey would hold it together. Her sister was her whole life.

"You know, there is another way to look at this," Remy murmured almost to himself as he leaned back on the other couch. "Instead of focusing on Kelsey so much, we need to pull back a minute and consider the fact that Kelsey is the third girl from RTC to go missing, along with her friend Sara Collins and Abigail Elliott."

Becker frowned. "Alex already told us that Sara sent an email to the registrar's office saying she went to Mexico with some guy. Then Kelsey got a text from Sara a couple of days ago, saying she was having a wonderful time."

"Yeah, the registrar got an email from Sara just like they got from Kelsey, but we know for a fact that one's bullshit," Alex said. "If we believe someone faked Kelsey's email, it's not that big of a stretch to assume they did the same with Sara. And that supposed text from Mexico wouldn't be hard to pull off if whoever kidnapped Sara had her phone."

"Okay, assuming you're right," Becker said, "why would the person who grabbed the girls send something to the school to cover their tracks with Sara and Kelsey but not the first girl, Abigail Elliott?"

"I don't know," Remy admitted. "But there's another question I'm much more interested in getting an answer to."

"What's that?" Max asked.

"If there are three girls missing from RTC that we know of already, how many more are missing that we haven't heard about yet?" Remy said.

Alex glanced at Becker. "Any chance you can hack into the RTC computers and figure out if there are any other missing girls who meet our profile?"

"Yeah, I can do that," Becker said. "It might take a while, though. Colleges have really good firewalls, since students are always trying to break in to change grades. It would mean putting the video footage on the back burner, though."

Alex didn't have to think about it very long. "Do it."

Becker glanced at Remy, then at Jayna, who was still leaning against the kitchen counter, watching them.

"What?" Alex said impatiently.

"Nothing," Becker said. "It's just that... Isn't there something else you could be doing than hanging around here?"

Alex frowned. He wasn't so great with computers and technology, but he could still look at video footage with Remy and Max.

"Like maybe going to see Lacey and find out how she's holding up?" Jayna suggested.

Alex immediately felt bad for not thinking about doing that himself, but then again, why would he? It wasn't like Lacey would be very pleased to see him. "I don't think that's a good idea."

"That's the problem," Jayna said. "You're thinking too much. Look, Lacey might not believe it right now, but she needs you. When she figures it out, be there for her."

Alex looked around the room and saw that Becker, Remy, and Max were all looking at him like they thought the same thing. Maybe they were right. Lacey would probably want an update anyway. And with Wendy there as a buffer between them, maybe things wouldn't have to be awkward between them.

He stood and dug his keys out of his pocket. "Okay. Call me if you get anything."

Alex spent the twenty-minute drive to Lacey's apartment wishing he could tell her they had a lead on Kelsey. Hopefully, they would soon. The longer Kelsey was missing, the less chance they had of finding her alive.

He squashed that thought as he pulled into the parking lot of Lacey's apartment complex. Lacey didn't need to see the worry on his face when she opened the door.

Wendy was the one who opened it. She held her fingers to her lips as she motioned him inside. Lacey was sleeping on the couch, Leo curled up at her feet. She looked so fragile underneath the blanket.

"She fell asleep a little while ago," Wendy said softly. "She's exhausted."

Alex nodded. "I'll go, then. I just stopped by to make sure she was okay."

He turned for the door, but Wendy caught his arm. "I'm leaving. You're staying."

Alex opened his mouth to protest, but Wendy was already grabbing her purse. "Everly stopped by. She told us a lot about werewolves and about your pack. Lacey dealt with it better than I thought she would, but go easy on her, huh? This has all been a bit much for her."

Alex was glad Everly had decided to come over and talk to Lacey, though he was a little surprised that she'd been so forthcoming with the werewolf tutorial. No doubt that had been Cooper's idea. Having recently learned that keeping secrets can come back to bite you in the ass, he'd probably thought it was best to get out in front of all this.

"You seem to be doing okay with it," he observed.

"It's easy for me." Wendy shrugged. "I haven't had the guy I'm sleeping with change right in front of my eyes, and it's not my sister who's missing."

Alex couldn't argue with that.

At the door, Wendy turned back to look at him. "Don't let Lacey push you away, Alex."

Wendy left before Alex could respond, which was good, since he had no idea what to say. Wendy was the second woman that night to insist Lacey needed him. He wasn't so sure of that.

Alex locked the door, then walked into the living room. The blanket had slipped off Lacey's shoulders, and he leaned over to adjust it. She groaned in her sleep and tugged it up under her chin. He smiled despite himself.

Sighing, he dropped into the chair adjacent to the couch, then sat there watching Lacey sleep and praying this all worked out. Not getting back together with her—he was pretty sure that ship had already sailed. But he didn't want Lacey to lose her sister. The world had already been unfair to her, and he just hoped that God, or fate, or whatever power ran the universe let her have a pass on this. She'd already lost so much in her life. Losing Kelsey too would be beyond cruel.

Chapter 13

"NICOLE ISN'T IN TROUBLE, IS SHE?" THE DARK-HAIRED resident advisor asked with concern as she led Alex and Remy down the hallway to Nicole Arend's room. Nicole was one of two RTC female students whom Becker discovered were also mysteriously missing.

"No, it's nothing like that," Remy assured the girl. "We're just checking to see if she might have some outside involvement with another case we're looking into."

The girl eyed Remy dubiously but quickly forgot what she was going to say when he flashed one of his charming smiles her way. The flustered girl couldn't get her set of master keys out fast enough.

Becker had called Alex at Lacey's apartment that morning to tell him that buried among the forty students who'd dropped out of classes recently, only five of them—all young women—had left without coming in to talk to their advisors and fill out formal withdrawal paperwork in person. Four of those five had sent emails to explain their sudden disappearance.

"Guess who didn't?" Becker asked.

"Abigail Elliott," Alex said.

"Bingo. In addition to Kelsey and Sara, the other two girls who supposedly sent emails are Nicole Arend and Carla Jones. Nicole has a dorm on campus. Carla lives with three roommates at an apartment close to the school."

Alex had agreed to meet Remy at the RTC dorms

to check out Nicole's room while Becker, Max, and Brooks would see what they could dig up over at Carla's apartment.

Lacey had wanted to come with him, but he'd convinced her to stay home. He had no idea where the investigation was going to lead him after checking out Nicole's dorm, and he couldn't focus on Kelsey if he was worried about Lacey.

Thankfully, she seemed to understand, saying something about going into work for a while, then hanging out with Everly again. Alex was glad she had someone she could talk to, especially since she obviously couldn't talk to him.

"Nicole left about three weeks ago, but since she didn't have a roommate and we won't have anyone showing up needing a room until the fall semester, I still haven't packed up her stuff yet," the RA said as she unlocked the door. "I was hoping she might come back at some point. She was a really quiet girl and didn't have a lot of friends, but we got along well." She smiled at Remy. "I'll be downstairs if you need anything else."

Alex followed Remy into Nicole's room, taking in the motivational posters and school paraphernalia covering the walls.

"Would have been nice if Nicole had a roommate we could talk to," Remy remarked. "We can check with the other students on the floor, I guess, but I get the feeling Nicole didn't talk to many people."

"Might be why she was targeted in the first place," Alex murmured. "It doesn't seem like anyone even noticed she was missing except for the RA."

Remy went through the girl's desk while Alex searched her nightstand. He was flipping through a dream journal she kept in there when he picked up a familiar scent. He closed his eyes, using the scent recovery tricks Khaki had taught him. There were a lot of them, but the one he found most useful was to imagine himself digging through a bunch of old boxes stored up in an attic, with each box holding a different scent he'd picked up at some point in the past. The idea was to stimulate his memory by going through the mental process of searching for a scent. He had no idea why it worked, but sometimes it did. Like now.

Shit. He tossed the journal back in the drawer and closed it.

"We can stop worrying about finding Nicole," he said.

Remy looked up from the drawer he'd been searching. "Why's that?"

"Because I recognize her scent. She's the girl Lacey and I found dumped with the dogs."

"You sure?" At Alex's nod, the other werewolf swore. "Damn, that poor girl. Well, this is officially no longer just a kidnapping case, and it got real ugly fast. Lacey is going to freak out when she learns about this."

All Alex could do was nod as he reached for his phone and called Gage. His pack alpha answered on the first ring. "What do you have?"

Alex quickly filled him in, telling him about Becker tracking down two more suspected kidnapping victims and their subsequent search of Nicole's room. "She's the dead woman I found when I was out with Lacey the other night."

Gage muttered a curse. "Homicide's going to need to know about this, but we have to come up with some other way to explain how you identified this girl. We can't exactly tell people you ID'd her by scent."

"Maybe Mac can say someone dropped her an anonymous tip," Alex suggested.

"If we do that, homicide is going to hone in on the tipster, assuming that person knows something about the murders. We need another way. One that won't lead to more questions." Gage was silent for a moment. "Get down to the ME's office with a picture of the girl. Tell them that you were digging into the missing girls from the college and thought you recognized one of them as the dead woman you saw. That should get the ME close enough to confirm the identification."

"Roger that," Alex said.

As Alex hung up, he realized he was going to have to do some serious tap dancing with the ME's office to make this work. Nicole Arend's face had been unrecognizable. If he didn't handle this right, they were going to know he was full of crap.

———

Samantha Mills, one of the staff medical examiners at the county ME's office, regarded Alex and Remy with curious blue eyes. Tall and slender, she had on a white lab coat over a silk blouse and a pair of dark slacks. "I know you found the body, Officer Trevino, but I'm not sure I understand your continued involvement in this case beyond that."

Alex hesitated for a moment as he looked around the fancy crime lab. He'd never been to the place before, but the huge glass-and-brick facility known as the Southwestern Institute of Forensic Sciences didn't look anything like the dark, dank basement he'd envisioned as the home of the county's medical chop shop.

He was also surprised to run into the extremely

suspicious blond-haired doctor now regarding them
with her arms crossed over her chest in a blatant I-think-
you're-full-of-crap stance. Remy had tried to use his
patented Cajun charm on the doctor when they'd first
walked in, but she ignored him as if he wasn't even
there. Remy fell silent after that, apparently deciding to
let Alex try it his way while he attempted to repair his
damaged ego.

This wasn't their first run-in with Samantha Mills.
She was the ME who'd been out at Gage's in-laws'
ranch after it had been shot to hell by the Albanians
and Jayna's old pack alpha. She was also the woman
whom Senior Corporal Trey Duncan—the team's other
medic—had a thing for. Alex had been worried the
woman would find something conclusive concerning
the existence of werewolves among all the dead bodies
at the ranch, but the ME report had come back surprisingly generic.

Trey had sworn it was all because of him. The doctor
hadn't been able to focus on her work once she'd gotten
a look at the hunky Trey Duncan. In some ways, Trey
was nearly as delusional as Remy.

Fortunately, Alex had expected the ME to be suspicious, so he'd spent most of the ride over coming up
with a believable story to explain why he thought the
woman in their cooler was Nicole Arend. One close
enough to the truth that Dr. Mills wouldn't be able to
catch him up in a lie when it turned out he was right.

"To be honest, we're not officially involved in the
case at all," Alex admitted. "We were helping out a
friend whose sister disappeared a couple of days ago.
While we were looking into it, we stumbled on a picture
of another student who'd dropped out of classes at RTC

three weeks ago, named Nicole Arend. The moment I saw her picture, I recognized her as the dead girl I found over on Ridgecrest."

Dr. Mills lifted a brow. "That's hard to imagine, considering how badly damaged the girl's face was."

"Trust me, after finding her like that, I'm never going to forget her face. Ever."

The medical examiner sighed. "That I can believe. Come on. Let's go take a look."

Alex glanced at Remy, who just shrugged as they followed the woman out of her office, down a long hall, and through a door with a swipe-card security pad on it. Alex hadn't expected the ME to take them to see the body, but if it helped make the ID, that was fine with him.

"If this woman—Nicole Arend—disappeared, why hasn't her name shown up on the missing persons database?" Dr. Mills asked over her shoulder.

Since the ME seemed like the kind who could sniff out bullshit almost as fast as Gage, Alex decided he'd better be straight with her and explained their theory about the missing college girls and how they thought the crimes were being covered up.

The doctor stopped to swipe her card again at another door, then turned to look at them. "That's a pretty serious cover-up you're talking about and not something I'd expect SWAT to be involved in."

"It's not a cover-up yet, just a theory," Alex clarified. "And that's what it will stay if you can't confirm this girl is Nicole Arend."

They walked into a room with a lot of those morgue freezers you see in all the TV shows. Mills looked on a list attached to the wall, then walked over to one of the doors and opened it. Inside was a zippered white body bag with a clipboard resting on top. She reached for the zipper and started to tug it down, but then stopped to look at both of them.

"You two sure you want to do this?" she asked. "It's definitely not as gruesome as that mess of a body that blew himself up in June, but it's worse than the dead Albanians SWAT tangled with a few months before that. It's even worse than those organized-crime types that all had their throats ripped out after getting in a showdown with you guys at the airport last year."

Dr. Samantha Mills seemed to know an awful lot about SWAT, especially the stuff that involved a lot of people getting messed up. Realizing she was waiting for an answer, Alex nodded.

Mills pulled the bag's zipper down far enough to expose the girl's face. The blood had been cleaned off, but it was still as hard to look at as it had been before. There wasn't a single inch of her that wasn't covered with cuts, scrapes, and deep bruises. Damn, she'd really been worked over.

Alex pulled out the photo of Nicole that Becker had gotten from the RTC student records and held it up beside the body bag. He didn't need to match the face to the picture, because the body's scent matched the one he'd smelled in the dorm room, but he had to make it look good for the ME.

On the other side of the body, Mills nodded thoughtfully. "I can see why you might think this could be the same girl. The bone structure is identical. It's definitely close enough to justify getting her dental records. That should tell us for sure, even with all the postmortem damage."

"Postmortem?" Alex frowned. "Are you saying all this was done after she was dead?"

Mills nodded. "Yes. Small blessing, I guess. Nearly all the damage you saw when you found her was done well after her death. The chief ME is still in the process of doing the full examination, so nothing is final, but if you ask me, this looks like a ritual killing."

"What kind of ritual?" Remy asked.

"I have no idea," she admitted. "But what else do you call it when a girl's been tortured and has organs missing?"

"Missing?" Alex asked.

"Her heart and one of her kidneys are gone."

Alex felt queasy at the thought. He hoped Lacey never had to hear about any of this.

They left Nicole's picture with the doctor, along with as much personal information as they had on the girl. As Mills led them back up to the front of the building, she agreed to call Alex the moment she was able to confirm the ID.

Dr. Mills smoothed a stray tendril of long blond hair back into her bun, her face grim. "If you're right, and this girl is only the first of five college girls who have been kidnapped, we could definitely have a serial killer on our hands."

Chapter 14

LEO LIFTED HIS HEAD FROM HIS PAWS THE MOMENT LACEY and Alex walked in the door, an expression on his face that could only be described as hopeful. But when he saw that Kelsey wasn't with them, the look faded from his furry face, and he put his head down again. Lacey knew the feeling. She wished she could deal with it the same way he did. It certainly would have made her horrible day better if she could have gone to bed and acted like it had never happened.

Four hours ago, the dead woman she and Alex had found the other night was positively identified as Nicole Arend. An hour after that, missing persons connected all the dots with the information Alex and his SWAT teammates provided them and announced that Kelsey, Sara, and Carla had officially joined Abigail on the list as missing, like Kelsey hadn't been *missing* before, only *misplaced*.

Minutes later, the story hit social media and the TV news circuit. A little while after that, someone from Councilman McDonald's office asked Lacey and Alex to come downtown for an impromptu press conference.

Lacey didn't believe getting up in front of a camera would help find Kelsey, especially since pictures of Abigail Elliott had been on TV for two weeks, and it hadn't done them any good at all. But Alex had said that getting word of Kelsey's abduction out to the public was a good thing, that it might catch someone's attention and trigger a memory that could lead them to her.

In a word, the news conference had been awful. The entire event turned out to be nothing more than an orchestrated PR event. First, they'd dragged Alex up to the raised platform at the front of the room and positioned him between Councilman McDonald and an older man in a dress blue uniform who turned out to be Chief of Police Randy Curtis. The chief talked first, throwing some praise Alex's way for the work he'd done finding the link between the five missing girls, but mostly taking all the credit for himself and his department.

Then they pulled Lacey and Abigail Elliott's mother—Sheryl—up to the podium. They weren't asked to say anything as the councilman flashed pictures of Nicole Arend and the four missing girls up on the screen behind them. McDonald asked for help in finding them, but to Lacey, it all sounded horribly similar to the news flashes she'd heard before, except now there were more girls missing, one of whom was dead. She prayed with everything in her that Kelsey didn't end up the same way.

Just when Lacey thought it was over, a man in a suit stood up and introduced himself as a detective from the homicide division. He talked about taking over the case and about the task force he was putting together. While he made promises about finding the killer-slash-kidnapper and the girls, Lacey got the feeling the detective was far more interested in catching the killer than in rescuing the girls.

Things had gone downhill after the reporters left. Lacey had been talking to Sheryl while Alex had been up on the dais with McDonald, Curtis, and the detective. Whatever they were saying, it wasn't making him happy. She'd seen his eyes get that reflective flash she'd always thought was a trick of the light. Then she'd realized that both his hands were dripping blood. His claws had come out, and he was squeezing his hands into fists to hide them, which was making his palms bleed.

Mumbling an apology to Sheryl, Lacey had hurried onto the dais and taken his arm, saying she wasn't feeling very well and asking him to take her home. That had snapped Alex out of whatever haze he'd been in, and he led her out of the building. His claws had retracted back to normal by the time they got to his truck, though he had to use a rag from under the seat to wipe off the blood.

It didn't seem like Alex had wanted to talk on the drive to her place, so Lacey hadn't said anything, but now that they were back in her apartment, she couldn't contain her curiosity any longer. She glanced at him as she scooped some dry dog food into Leo's bowl. At the sound, Leo trotted into the kitchen.

"Are you going to tell me what got you so upset at the press conference?" she asked Alex as she opened the fridge.

She didn't feel like eating, but she'd figured out over the past few days that Alex needed food—frequently. She scanned the shelves, spotting the covered casserole that Wendy must have dropped off that morning while they were out. Lacey pulled off the foil and revealed beef and black bean burritos smothered in red sauce.

"You mean besides McDonald and the chief using the entire event to score political points with the television audience?" Alex asked caustically as he took the casserole out of her hands and slid it in the microwave.

Lacey couldn't help noticing that they still seemed to work well together in the kitchen, even though everything had changed between them. "Yeah, besides that."

Alex's eyes flashed gold for a moment, and he let out a little growl. By rights, it should have freaked her out, but for some crazy reason, it didn't. Was she really getting used to this whole werewolf thing?

"It was that prick from homicide. He told me that he was taking over the investigation, and that SWAT assistance was no longer required."

She frowned. "But they wouldn't have a case without you and the other guys from SWAT."

"Tell me about it."

Lacey chewed on her lower lip, remembering the sensation she'd gotten that he was more about finding the murderer than Kelsey and the other missing girls. "This guy knows what he's doing, right?"

Alex shrugged. "I don't know a lot about him... except for the fact that he's one of Chief Curtis's pet detectives. He runs around inserting himself into every case that might have high visibility. Curtis backed him up. He doesn't want SWAT to have anything to do with the investigation."

Her heart began to beat faster. "But we're still going to keep looking for Kelsey too, right?"

Alex put gentle hands on her shoulders. "We're going to keep looking for Kelsey until we find her. I won't let anyone get in our way."

Lacey gazed up at him. "Do you think Kelsey is still alive?"

"I do," he said.

She was surprised by how much comfort those words gave her, and she found herself leaning into him. She'd almost forgotten what it felt like to have his big, warm hands on her.

His hands.

Crap!

She reached up to grab them, then flipped his hands palm up, expecting to see four deep puncture wounds in each. Instead, there were only some light pink marks that couldn't even be called scratches.

"Your hands were bleeding when we left the press conference," she said. "How can they possibly be healed up already?"

He laughed and carefully pulled his hands away. Then he reached over her head and opened the upper cabinet beside the stove, taking out two plates. "I guess that's something Everly hasn't gotten around to telling you yet. Werewolves heal faster than regular people. Simple puncture wounds usually heal up in a couple of minutes."

The nonchalant way Alex said those insane words should have shocked Lacey, but she supposed she was past that. Maybe she was finally coming to terms with the bizarre world she suddenly found herself living in.

Over the past few days, she'd spent a lot of time with Everly and Wendy. They'd both tried to get her to accept that knowing werewolves were real didn't necessarily have to be such a big deal. She could understand why Everly was so invested in getting her on board, but she was a little shocked that Wendy had bought in so easily.

Still, she had to admit that she'd gotten to the point where she could truthfully say that Alex and his pack mates—God, she felt ridiculous saying that—weren't monsters. But it was still a lot to take in all at once. None of that had kept her from being curious, though.

"There are some things that Everly didn't want to tell me about. She said they should come from you instead. I guess this is one of those things."

Alex nodded and went back to getting the stuff out for dinner while she got them iced tea to drink. She carried their glasses out to the coffee table in the living room. She hadn't been able to eat at the kitchen table since Kelsey disappeared. It just didn't feel right eating there without her sister.

"Did it hurt when you dug your claws into your palms?" she asked as she walked back into the kitchen.

Alex shrugged. "Yeah, but that was the idea. I was hoping the pain would get me to focus on something other than what that jerk from homicide was saying so I wouldn't shift right there in front of them."

Her jaw dropped. "That could have happened?"

He leaned back against the kitchen counter, resting his hands on either side of him. "I hate to admit it, but yeah. That guy was being a jackass, and sometimes when I get mad, or fired up, or worried, my inner werewolf can come out on its own."

Lacey leaned back against the opposite counter as she considered that. "You mean like it did at Bensen's junkyard?"

"Yeah. Exactly like that," he said softly.

In the silence of the kitchen, the microwave dinged. Alex grabbed the potholders she kept on a hook near the stove and took it out. She took her time using a spatula to get the steaming food out of the casserole—one burrito for her and two for him. Alex reached over and took the spatula out of her hand, adding another burrito to her plate and two more to his. Then he carried both plates into the living room before she could complain.

"Were you mad at the junkyard?" She glanced at him beside her as she picked up her knife and fork. "Is that why you shifted?"

He cut into one of the burritos, not looking at her. "No, I wasn't mad."

She waited patiently for him to say more.

"We had Bensen's junkyard under surveillance. Supposedly, he's moving drugs through one of his properties," Alex said, still staring down at his plate. "When I saw you on that surveillance camera, stumbling around in the dark about to get yourself killed, I kind of lost my mind. I'd had uncontrolled shifts before, like you saw at the press conference, but that night at the junkyard, I shifted further than I ever had in my life."

A crappy feeling slid down her throat to settle uncomfortably in the pit of her stomach. But at the same time, she felt another sensation too, one she was sure she'd never felt before. "Because you were worried about me?"

"Because I was terrified." He turned his head to look at her. "You could have died in there. I wasn't going to let that happen."

"So you came and saved me, even though you knew I'd see you as a werewolf?"

He turned his attention back to his plate. "I didn't have a choice."

But I did.

They ate in silence for a while. The burrito was very good, hot and spicy, just the way she liked it. Wendy wasn't usually quite so adventurous in the kitchen.

While the food did a good job of distracting her for a bit, it wasn't long before that recriminating voice in her head stepped up and pointed out that Alex had been forced into shifting because she'd been stupid. And in return, she'd treated him like a monster.

Suddenly, she didn't really like herself very much.

Deciding she wasn't hungry anymore, she placed her plate on the coffee table and sat back on the couch.

As the quiet started to stretch out longer and longer, she felt the connection that had been developing between them start to fade, along with that funny sensation in her chest. She didn't want either of those things to go away.

"Can I ask you something?" she asked softly. "If you don't want to answer, I completely understand."

"Go ahead."

"How did you become a werewolf?"

Alex took a bite of the third burrito on his plate. "Everly didn't tell you?"

Lacey shook her head. "All she told me is that werewolves are born with a gene and that it takes a traumatic event to trigger the change. Usually something bad."

He took another bite of burrito, then set his plate down on the table and leaned back on the couch next to her. "It happened when I was a cop up in Rochester. I got a call for a noise disturbance in a residential area. Since it was right after the Fourth of July, I assumed it was some kids messing around."

His face took on a distant look, like he was replaying that night in his head.

"When I got to the address, the neighbor who reported the noise wasn't really sure what he'd heard or where the sound had come from. I wasted some time talking to him before I heard a noise coming from the home across the street, then pissed away another few minutes checking around the outside of the house like an idiot."

Lacey wasn't sure she wanted to hear the rest of this.

She had the feeling it was going to be even worse than she'd imagined.

"If you haven't figured it out yet, the house belonged to Jessica—the girl in the photo you saw at my place," he continued. "She and her parents were victims of a home invasion. An old guy and an eighteen-year-old kid broke in. We never really figured out why they'd done it or why they'd picked that particular house. The kid was a runaway and had been missing since he was eleven. We never ID'd the old guy. By the time I stopped screwing around and got into the house, Jessica's parents were already dead. I got upstairs just in time to stop the two psychopaths from killing Jessica and her dog, but in the process, I got shot twice. If I hadn't been a werewolf, I would have died." He let out a derisive snort. "Considering how badly I screwed up, I probably should have."

Lacey's head was swirling with emotions at the thought of Alex getting shot. She now realized that those barely discernable scars she'd seen along his rib cage when they'd made love really had been as terrible as she'd thought. The idea of him being hurt so badly twisted her insides up in knots so intensely she thought she might be ill. She was still trying to figure out why she was reacting this way when she finally comprehended what he'd said.

"What do you mean, how badly you screwed up?" she asked. "You saved that girl's life."

Alex gave her a wry smile. "I might have saved Jessica, but her mother most likely died while I was out on the street, wasting time."

"You couldn't have known that," Lacey protested.

"No, but that doesn't keep me from blaming myself

anyway." His jaw clenched. "If I'd driven a little faster, used my sirens, kicked in the front door right away—done something—Jessica wouldn't have lost both her parents. Jessica's life changed forever that night because I didn't get there in time."

Lacey hated seeing Alex in pain, and it was clear to her that he was. It was the kind of pain that came when you blamed yourself for not doing enough to save another person's life, even if there wasn't anything you could have done. She knew a little something about that kind of pain. It could be a heavy load to carry, making you doubt yourself in almost every way that mattered.

Lacey scooted closer to Alex. "You know that I'm speaking from experience when I tell you that guilt can really mess with your head, right? That it will make you doubt yourself at the worst possible time?"

"Yeah, I know. Maybe after we get your sister back, we can get a reduced rate on therapy sessions. Cooper knows this really great shrink."

She laughed, amazed she could even do that with everything going wrong in her life. But it felt nice to be this close to Alex again. "That could be fun."

His mouth quirked. "I don't think a shrink session is supposed to be fun."

"But it could be," she said.

Then she kissed him.

It was sudden, spontaneous, reckless, and probably stupid. But when their lips met, all the silly crap that had been going on between them disappeared.

The kiss deepened, and in a flash, Lacey was transported back to that first date, that first kiss, that first moment when she thought Alex was a guy worth

spending time with. Why, exactly, had she been so
stupid and let him go?

She was still trying to come up with an answer to that
when the phone rang.

—–∿∿∿—–

Alex disengaged himself from Lacey with a growl and
dug his cell phone out of his pocket before it went to
voice mail, even though he would have preferred kissing her to talking to whoever the hell had called him.
He wasn't exactly sure what had just happened, but it
seemed as if a small corner of the polar ice caps had
warmed up a few degrees.

Brooks's name showed up on his phone's screen, and
he thumbed the button. "What's up, Brooks?"

"Is Lacey with you?" The senior corporal's deep
voice vibrated through the phone. "If so, she's gonna
want to hear this."

Alex glanced at Lacey to see her sitting there with a
concerned look on her face. "I'm putting you on speaker
now, Brooks."

"Max and I stopped by Lacey's apartment earlier
to drop off some food and decided to search Kelsey's
room while we were there. We came across something
we thought you should know about."

Lacey's brows shot up. "Wait a minute. You searched
my apartment? Who let you in?"

Brooks hesitated. "No one. Max was on the wrong
side of the law before he became a cop. He picked the
lock."

Lacey did a double take. "And Leo didn't care?"

"Nah," Brooks said. "He met us last week at the
engagement party, so he was cool with it."

On the floor beside them, Leo opened one eye to look at them, then closed it again.

"What did you and Max find in Kelsey's room?" Alex asked.

"Birth control pills."

Lacey's jaw dropped. "*What?*"

"Before you get all upset and lose it over the fact that your baby sister had birth control pills, you might want to focus on the real reason I called," Brooks said. "Becker did some of that hacker crap he does and found out that two of the other missing girls—Nicole Arend and Abigail Elliott—had prescriptions for birth control pills from the same doctor Kelsey used."

"Shit," Alex muttered. The odds of three college-age girls being on the pill wasn't that high. But all three of them getting the pills from the same doctor in a city the size of Dallas couldn't be a coincidence. This was the break they'd been waiting for. "What do we know about this doctor?"

"His name's Pettine," Brooks said. "He's a surgery specialist, but he also volunteers at a clinic near the RTC campus. The clinic has an ongoing relationship with several of the local colleges, and they refer students there for immunizations, health and wellness exams, and general appointments. It's entirely possible that the other two missing girls had gone to the clinic as well, but there wasn't any indication they ever had a prescription for birth control pills."

"Tell me you have a location on this guy," Alex said.

"Max is on him now," Brooks said. "Pettine left Charles Hospital about an hour ago and went straight to some kind of research facility near there. Max says the place has been quiet since Pettine went inside. I'm heading over there now."

"Text me the address, and I'll meet you there," Alex said.

"Shouldn't we get this information to the councilman and the rest of the task force he's put together?" Lacey asked as he hung up.

Alex shook his head. "They'll only want to drag Pettine in for questioning. It's more important to them that they appear to be on top of the case by talking to people of interest than in accomplishing anything. They bring this doctor in, and he'll lawyer up in seconds. They'll never get anything out of him, and our lead will be meaningless. You have to trust me on this."

Lacey didn't look convinced, but she nodded. "Okay. Just bring Kelsey home. Please."

He leaned in and kissed her. "I will."

—∿∿—

The research facility wasn't what Alex expected. With the familiar snake and staff symbol of the medical industry attached to the front of it, the three-floor glass building looked like a cross between a high-tech computer firm and a hospital. It definitely didn't seem like the kind of place a psycho killer would take his victims.

Alex drove past it, pulling up behind Max's black Camaro a few blocks down the street. Max and Brooks were standing beside the car, waiting for him.

"What the hell kind of place is this?" Alex asked as he got out of his truck and closed the door.

"I don't know," Brooks said. "Becker is trying to find out who holds the lease right now. He said he'd call as soon as he has anything."

"About five minutes before you guys got here, Pettine and everyone else in the place bailed like it was

an evacuation drill," Max told them. "We have the doctor's license plate info, but the others took off before I
could get anything on them. I tried to follow, but they
scattered. Something's not right here, I can feel it."

Alex's gut clenched. Max was the youngest werewolf
on the team, but he was a good cop. If he thought something was wrong, then it was.

Alex reached down and pulled his off-duty SIG P224
out of its holster. "I have zero probable cause to go into
that building, but I'm going anyway. If you two want to
hang out here, I'm completely okay with that."

"Hell no," they both said in unison.

Brooks and Max followed his lead, pulling out their
weapons as they ran for the back side of the building and
what Alex hoped would be an easy way in.

They found a metal door along the side of the building
that wasn't facing any of the streets that ran past the facility and wasn't well lit. Max probably could have picked
the lock, but Alex didn't have the patience for that.
Instead, he ripped off the knob, then yanked open the
door. Pieces of metal fell to the concrete with a clatter,
but he ignored it as he led the way into the dark building.

They'd barely gone twenty feet before Alex picked
up Kelsey's scent coming from somewhere down the
hall. He glanced over his shoulder, motioning in that
direction. Brooks and Max nodded, spreading out along
the corridor and checking each room as they went past.

The air was heavy with antiseptic odors and industrial
cleansers, but underneath them, Alex picked up a myriad
of human scents in addition to Kelsey's. He ignored the
rest and focused on hers, following it to a stairwell and
down into a dark basement.

He was halfway down the stairs when he realized that

the basement was empty. Kelsey had been there but was gone now. They were too late.

Alex continued down the stairs anyway, Brooks and Max at his heels. The girls might be gone, but they needed to check to see if whoever had kidnapped them left any evidence behind. His stomach churned at the thought of what they might find. He didn't smell any dead bodies, but still... He'd seen what the killer had done to Nicole Arend. The basement was made up of a big main room with five smaller rooms off it. Each held a small cot and not much else. Alex could pick up Kelsey's scent in one of the rooms, along with that belonging to a man that was oddly familiar, even though he couldn't place it. Strangely enough, he also smelled fireball. What the hell would that crap be doing here?

Alex walked back into the main room and joined his teammates as they searched the utility cabinets. He'd just opened one and started looking through it when Brooks's phone vibrated. Brooks pulled it out of his pocket and glanced at the screen, then thumbed the green button.

"I have you on speaker," he said. "Go ahead, Becker."

"Things just got real weird," Becker said. "Councilman McDonald owns the building you followed Pettine to. It's one of his medical research facilities."

"Shit," Alex muttered.

No sooner was the word out of his mouth than footsteps echoed upstairs, first in the hallways, then in the stairwell. A moment later, the basement was lit up bright as day as fluorescent bulbs in the ceiling blinked to life. *Double shit*.

"Do we fight them?" Max growled, his eyes glowing in a partial shift.

He was seconds away from wolfing out. Alex couldn't

blame him. He was clenching his jaw so hard to keep his inner wolf from coming out that he thought his teeth might shatter.

Alex glanced at Brooks to see the other werewolf regarding him with a questioning look in his blue-gray eyes. Alex shook his head. Kelsey and the other girls weren't here, and without evidence of a crime, they couldn't very well justify attacking whoever was getting ready to storm in here. This wasn't something they could fight their way out of.

Giving him a nod, Brooks walked over to grab Max by the back of the neck and give him a rough shake. The gold immediately faded from Max's eyes, and they went back to their usual blue.

Just in time too. A split second later, the door to the basement burst open, and three private security guards ran down the steps. The way the idiots stormed into the room, they probably would have shot each other if they actually had to use their weapons.

"Westcott Security!" one of the men shouted. "Drop your weapons and raise your hands!"

"We're Dallas PD," Alex called out, but the security guards didn't seem to care.

"Drop the weapons!" they ordered.

Alex cursed silently. The idiots had probably been waiting their whole lives to say those words. Frig it all to hell. He could have wiped the floor with these guys by himself if he wanted to.

He slowly bent and placed his weapon on the floor and gently pushed it aside, then stood and held up his hands. He'd paid for his off-duty SIG out of his own pocket. He sure as hell wasn't kicking it anywhere. On either side of him, Brooks and Max did the same.

"If you give us a minute, we can show you our badges," Alex began, but two of the guards were already cuffing Brooks and Max. When they were done, the shorter of the two men quickly moved to do the same to Alex. He ground his jaw. The embarrassment he, Brooks, and Max were going to have to deal with when the rest of the Pack heard this would be horrible.

But not nearly as horrible as knowing he'd come within minutes of saving Kelsey.

———

"You expect me to fucking believe that the three of you were responding to an anonymous tip telling you that the missing girls were at this research facility, and you just happened to find a side door with a broken lock?"

Alex didn't answer Chief Curtis. He was too busy digging through the old boxes in his mental attic trying to remember where he'd smelled the other scent he'd picked up in the room where Kelsey had been held. It had been the same one he'd smelled on Nicole Arend and the dogs, which meant it belonged to the guy who'd probably dumped the bodies.

Gut instinct told Alex there was a good chance the asshole was also linked to fireball, since everywhere he'd smelled the guy, he'd also picked up the drugs as well.

"Are you even listening to me, Officer Trevino?"

Alex jerked out of his musings to see Chief Curtis standing in front of him, his face so red, Alex thought it might explode. Shit, he'd better answer before Curtis blew a gasket.

"I'm listening, sir."

Chief Curtis, Detective Asskisser from homicide, and

Gage—as well as Councilman McDonald—had shown up at the research facility ten minutes after the private security guards had taken Alex, Brooks, and Max into custody, which was a nice way of saying they'd cuffed them and put them in the back of their spiffy Toyota Camry security cruisers. Alex prayed no one had gotten a picture or video of them in the back of those cars. It wasn't something he ever wanted to be reminded of.

The security guards let them out of the cars and took off the cuffs the moment the DPD brass got there, then reluctantly left. Gage didn't look any more pleased than the chief, but he hadn't intervened as Curtis and Asskisser questioned Alex, Brooks, and Max about why they'd been at the facility. McDonald stood off to the side with a smug expression that Alex would have loved to rip off his face—from the inside.

Alex hadn't told them anything. He wasn't sure if he could trust Curtis, but he definitely knew he couldn't trust McDonald.

"I didn't expect any better out of you and Corporal Brooks, Officer Trevino, not with that crap you both pulled a couple of months ago with the FBI." Curtis sneered before turning disapproving eyes on Max. "But I expected much better from you, Officer Lowry. I had you pegged as an up-and-comer. What the hell were you doing out here with these two?"

Max grinned. "I volunteered to help."

Curtis's face darkened. "You think this is funny?"

Max tried to look abashed—and failed. "No, sir."

Curtis drew himself up to glower at each of them. "I know Deputy Chief Mason has always given you SWAT boys a lot of leeway, but I'm here to tell you—that's over. Starting right now, the three of you are suspended pending a full investigation by IA. If I hear you coming within a mile of this case again, you'll be out of a job. Is that understood?"

"Yes, sir." Alex nodded.

Curtis gave Gage a nod. "Commander."

Gage waited until Curtis and McDonald walked away before turning to them. Alex braced himself, sure his boss was going to tear him a new one, but Gage surprised him.

"I'm assuming you had a good reason for breaking in here?" his boss asked.

Alex did a double take. Mac must be a good influence on Gage. It wasn't too long ago that he would have picked Alex up by the throat first and asked questions later.

Figuring he'd better take advantage of Gage's good mood, Alex quickly explained why they'd broken into the research facility, saying that he'd not only picked up Kelsey's scent, but also that of the man who'd dumped the dead dogs and Nicole Arend's body.

"I got a whiff of fireball in there too," Alex added. "I don't think they were making it here, because the smell isn't strong enough for that, but they were definitely storing it."

Gage cursed and glanced at Curtis and McDonald, who were standing by the councilman's car, talking. "A city councilman involved with drugs, dogfighting, and kidnapping. What the hell is going on here?"

All Alex could do was shrug.

"If you're going to make a move on a man like McDonald, you'd better have some damn good evidence," Gage said. "He's as close to bulletproof as you're going to see in this town."

Alex couldn't argue with that. "Now that we know McDonald is involved, it gives us a whole new direction to investigate. I just wish I knew how the hell McDonald's people knew we were onto him. They bailed right before we got here, like they knew we were coming. No one knew about this lead but us."

Gage's mouth tightened. "That's not true. Lacey knew. I overheard McDonald tell Curtis that's how he found out you were here."

Alex frowned. "That can't be right. She'd never do something that would put her sister at risk."

His boss shrugged. "All I know is that she told him. If you want to know why she did it, you're going to have to ask her."

The only reason he could think she'd tell McDonald was because she simply didn't trust Alex to find her sister.

* * *

Lacey paced back and forth across the living room while Leo watched from the couch. She'd almost called Alex twice already but hadn't wanted to bother him. She was close to giving in and finally picking up the phone when he walked in the door—alone.

Her heart seized in her chest at the grim expression on his face. "Oh God. What happened? Is it Kelsey? Please tell me she's not…"

Alex shook his head. "She's fine—at least I hope so. We found the place where she and the other girls were being held, but whoever kidnapped them moved them right before we got there."

Tears stung Lacey's eyes. Being so close and missing her by minutes was almost worse than not knowing where Kelsey was in the first place. "Why would they move them?"

A muscle in Alex's jaw flexed. "Because they knew we were coming."

"What do you mean they knew you were coming? How is that possible?"

"Because you told Councilman McDonald."

She stared at him, even more confused now. "No, I didn't."

"According to him, you did." Alex muttered a curse. "Dammit, Lacey, I told you to trust me."

"I do trust you!" The disappointment in his eyes made her heart hurt. "McDonald's lying. I haven't talked to him since we saw him at the press conference. The only person I talked to after you left was Sheryl Elliott." She gasped. "Oh God. *She* must have told him."

Alex's eyes narrowed. "Sheryl Elliott?"

Lacey nodded. "She called right after you left. She was so upset and desperate for someone to give her hope, so I told her that you might have found a connection between the doctor at the clinic and the kidnappings. She swore she wouldn't tell anyone."

Alex snorted. "Well, she told McDonald."

Lacey felt like she was struggling in deep water. "I don't understand. Why would he warn the kidnappers?"

"Because he's involved," Alex snapped. He took a deep breath and ran his hand through his dark hair, making it stick up. "The doctor we followed led us straight to a medical research facility owned by McDonald. I picked up Kelsey's scent, so I know she was there."

Lacey's heart began to pound. "Was she…you know…"

"Alive?" He nodded. "She was when they took her

out of there. Look, we don't know what McDonald's involvement is with this doctor and the girls, but he's into it up to his neck. Unfortunately, the private security company the councilman pays to watch the place showed up a few minutes after we went in. They caught us, then McDonald walked in with the chief of police—and Gage. Brooks, Max, and I have been suspended."

It felt like the floor had suddenly fallen out from under Lacey. This was all her fault. If something happened to Kelsey, she would never forgive herself. She hugged herself, wishing it was Alex's arms around her.

She looked up at him. "I thought telling Sheryl was the right thing to do. You have to believe me."

Alex sighed, his expression softening. "I do, but getting suspended makes finding Kelsey a lot harder."

"You're going to keep looking even though you've been suspended?" she asked.

"Yeah. Like I told you before, we're going to keep looking for Kelsey until we find her," he said. "I won't let anyone get in our way."

Lacey didn't know what to say. She'd given Alex every reason to bail on her and Kelsey. She'd run away from him, treated him like a monster, refused to let her heart open up for him, and now she'd gotten him and the other members of his pack suspended.

Yet here he was, still sticking his neck out for her. That's when she remembered what Everly had said to her the other day—about Alex not being like any other man she'd ever met. That Lacey had no idea what Alex was capable of or how far he would go for her, if she would only trust him.

Lacey hadn't understood what Everly meant then. Now she did.

She closed the distance between then, wrapping her arms around him and hugging him tightly. "Thank you."

Alex's arms came around her, holding her close. She might not have given him a reason to trust her, but that was going to change. Starting at this moment.

She stepped back and gazed up at him. "What do we do now?"

"We figure out where McDonald has your sister and the other girls, then we go get them."

Chapter 15

WHEN ALEX ASKED LACEY IF SHE WANTED TO GO WITH him to see Becker the next morning, she'd jumped at the chance. She'd felt so helpless hanging around her apartment waiting for him last night and was grateful for the chance to take a more active role in finding her sister. It was either that or wear a hole in her carpet from pacing back and forth all day. Not that she'd probably be much help. Especially since Alex had made her promise to do whatever he told her.

She'd been okay with that deal. They'd talked a lot last night, about her sister and how worried she was about her, and also about what it was like to be a werewolf. While they weren't back to where they had been, she felt good about where they were. She knew she had a long way to go before he realized that things would be better between them, but going with him today was a good place to start.

Finding a parking space, Alex turned off the engine, then came around to open her door. While he looked handsome in his jeans and T-shirt, it was strange seeing him out of his uniform. Yet another reminder of what she'd done last night.

They took the steps to the top floor, then walked to the door at the end of the hallway. Alex knocked once, then opened it and stepped back to let her enter. A typical loft, the living area was one big open space made up of a living room and kitchen, with a modern-looking staircase leading to the second floor.

Brooks, Remy, and Max were in the living room along with half a dozen other people Lacey remembered seeing at Everly and Cooper's engagement party. Becker was on the couch, tapping on a wireless keyboard while text and documents popped on and off the big-screen TV. The coffee table in front of him was covered with notepads full of scribbles and a bunch of monster-sized coffee cups.

She gave Brooks and Max an apologetic look. "Sorry about getting you guys suspended."

"Don't worry about it," Brooks said. "If we get fired and can't pay our rent, we'll just come live with you and Kelsey."

Lacey laughed, pretty sure he was kidding. Kelsey and Leo would love it. Kelsey would drag all her girl-friends over to drool, and Leo would have someone to play with him all the time. It struck her then that Brooks had inserted Kelsey into his plan so smoothly that she hadn't even noticed him doing it. Clearly, Alex wasn't the only confident werewolf in this pack.

As she and Alex found a seat, she realized the four guys and a girl must be Jayna's beta pack. But that couldn't be right. The girl in the corner holding hands with the guy beside her was way too small to be a werewolf.

"Are all of these people werewolves?" she whispered to Alex after he made quick introductions.

"Yeah. Well, except for Zak," he said, gesturing to the bespectacled guy holding hands with the girl. "Oh, and don't bother whispering. Everyone but Zak just heard what you said."

Lacey winced at her faux pas. She'd forgotten he'd told her that werewolves have exceptional hearing. She looked around to see Jayna's pack regarding her with blatant interest. She supposed that to them, she was the different one.

She gave them an embarrassed smile. "Sorry about that. I'm still learning how this werewolf stuff works."

Beside her, Alex leaned forward on the couch. "What have you learned about Councilman McDonald, Becker?"

Chris—one of the beta werewolves in Jayna's pack— held up his hand. "Before he starts, I'd just like to point out that I have a serious issue with the fact that we've sat here all night watching Eric hack into a hundred different secure and confidential websites and databases— including some really scary federal places—yet he refuses to get us free cable TV."

"That'd be illegal," Becker said as he started paging through a notepad. "Don't you guys have to get to work?"

"I have to get going too," Zak said, helping his werewolf girlfriend, Megan, to her feet.

"Can you tell them I'm going to be late, Chris?" Jayna asked.

The blond guy gave her a nod and a wave as he and the rest of Jayna's pack left.

"Okay, back to McDonald," Becker said. "He's from a filthy rich family, but he seems to have made most of his fortune on his own. He's a board-certified surgical doctor and has made a name for himself in the field of organ transplant. He's played a major role in the creation of half a dozen new transplant techniques and drugs that have saved thousands of lives. He's on the board of a buttload of research firms, mostly related to transplant drugs and artificial organ development. He also mentors younger doctors, and he's on the committee for a bewildering number of transplant organ procurement organizations, both at the state and federal levels."

"Shit, the man sounds like a damn saint," Alex muttered. "How does he have the time to do all that and his job on the city council too? Why the hell would he bother?"

Becker couldn't answer that question, though he pointed out that the man almost certainly had political aspirations far beyond the local level. "He already has an organization in place to start planning for mayoral and gubernatorial offices."

"It's hard to believe a man like him is involved in kidnapping and murder," Remy commented. "Not to mention drugs."

"So, how the hell are all these things connected?" Brooks asked.

Everyone was quiet as they considered that. Finally, Max spoke.

"Do you think maybe they're using the girls as test subjects for new versions of fireball? Like human guinea pigs?"

"Dude," Remy said sharply.

He jerked his head in Lacey's direction, but it was too late. She already had the visual, and there was no way she could forget it now.

"Sorry, Lacey," Max mumbled, a flush creeping into his handsome face.

Lacey could only nod. She prayed he was wrong.

Alex reached out and gave her hand a squeeze. "Max was just thinking out loud. I'll call the ME in a little while to see if there was any heroin in Nicole Arend's blood workup. That should tell us if we're onto something."

Lacey listened with trembling hands as Alex and his SWAT teammates bounced from topic to topic, in some cases faster than she could follow. One second they were scouring the different properties McDonald owned, the next they were looking for a connection between the councilman and the doctor who'd written the birth-control prescriptions.

"Keep an eye out for the guy I smelled at the body dump and the research facility," Alex said. "A man with connections to both drugs and dogfighting can't be that hard to find in McDonald's world."

Lacey was just thinking she really didn't want to hear any more, when Jayna caught her eye and jerked her head toward the kitchen. She slipped out as the guys continued batting different ideas around. She wanted to help, but she had no idea what she could add to the discussion, and some of the stuff they were talking about—like using Kelsey and the other girls for drug testing—scared the hell out of her.

Telling Alex she'd be right back, Lacey followed Jayna into the kitchen. Jayna took two mugs out of the cabinet and filled them, then handed one to Lacey.

"Here. It looks like you could use this," Jayna said with a small smile.

Lacey took the mug and nodded. "Thanks."

Jayna opened the fridge and came out with a carton of creamer, then took the top off a plain white canister filled with yellow packets of sweetener.

"It's going to be okay," she told Lacey. "They'll find your sister."

Lacey didn't say anything as she added sweetener and creamer to her coffee.

"How's everything working out between you and Alex?" Jayna asked as she poured creamer into her own coffee.

Lacey winced. "Is there anyone associated with the

SWAT pack who doesn't know how badly I handled the situation with finding out Alex is a werewolf?"

Jayna gave her a small smile. "Not really. A pack is like a family—only closer. There aren't any secrets."

"Wonderful," she said with a groan. "I felt stupid before. Now I feel even worse."

"Don't worry about what any of us think. This is about you and Alex. You'll get it straightened out. It's just a matter of time." Jayna sipped her coffee. "Besides, it's not like either of you guys have a whole lot of say in the matter."

Lacey frowned over the rim of her mug. "What do you mean?"

"I thought Everly told you, but I guess not." Jayna sighed and set down her mug. "Have you had the crazy sensation since walking away from Alex that you were making the dumbest mistake of your life? Or felt sick when you think about not being with him?"

Lacey stared down at her coffee, letting the warmth seep in. "I was crying my eyes out before I got more than a mile away from him the night I saw him shift, and I haven't slept worth a crap since then." While she tried to tell herself it was because she was worried about Kelsey, she knew that wasn't all of it. "And sometimes when I think about him and how much I miss him, I feel like I'm dying inside. Which is crazy, since we barely started dating."

"It's not crazy," Jayna insisted. "And it's not just you. Alex feels the same way."

"Did he tell you that?"

"He didn't have to. That's what happens when two people who are supposed to be together try to fight it."

Lacey took a quick gulp of her coffee, not sure if she liked where this was going. "That's not possible. We just met."

"It's very possible, because I felt it when I tried to walk away from Eric." Jayna sighed. "This is really difficult to explain, but I'll try. There's a legend about *The One* that says there's one perfect soul mate out there for each werewolf, and that when they meet that perfect person, nothing can stop them from being together. Well, except for stupidity, of course. Unfortunately, to some degree or another, that's what happened to everyone in the Pack lucky enough to meet *The One*—Mac and Gage, Xander and Khaki, Everly and Cooper, and Eric and me. The only couple who didn't have to experience the pain of what it's like trying to walk away from *The One* is Megan and Zak, and that's simply because they were a lot smarter about it than the rest of us. They figured out they were in love from the beginning and stopped trying to slow down the train."

"Wait a minute," Lacey said. "First you're talking about legends, then soul mates. Now it's love?"

Jayna looked at her like she thought Lacey was an idiot. "Well, yeah. What the heck do you think is making you feel like this—acid reflux?"

Lacey shook her head. "I don't know about the legend of *The One*, but two people can't just fall in love the moment they meet. That's crazy."

Jayna snorted. "You mean like a six-foot-four, two-hundred-and-forty-pound guy growing fangs and claws and jumping over ten-foot-high fences with you in his arms—that kind of crazy?"

Lacey opened her mouth to tell Jayna that she was dead wrong, but the words wouldn't come out. Because

finally, it all made a bizarre kind of sense. The tug she'd
felt toward Alex from the second she'd met him, the
pain and confusion she'd felt every second of the day
since she'd run away from him, the incredible sense of
calm she felt when she was with him, like everything
was going to be okay as long as they were together. It
really did make sense.

"I'm in love with Alex?" she murmured softly.
"That's what this is all about?"

Jayna picked up her mug and sipped her coffee. "Yes,
that's what this is all about. You being in complete and
total, cosmically inspired, can't-live-without-it love."

Lacey stood there, letting that sink in for a while, her
gaze drifting to where Alex sat on the couch in the living
room. Then her eyes went wide.

"Did Alex and the other guys just overhear the entire
conversation we had?" she asked Jayna.

"No way," Jayna laughed. "When it comes to two
women having a private conversation, they tune it out. I
think they're terrified we might be talking about PMS.
They'd rather charge into a building full of gun-toting
psychopaths than overhear a woman discussing femi-
nine issues. So don't worry. Your secret is safe with me
until you decide it's time to let Alex in on it."

Lacey considered that. "If Alex is feeling the same
way, doesn't he already know we're in love? I mean,
he's a werewolf. He's supposed to know about this
legend already."

"Yeah, but he's a guy too," Jayna pointed out. "That
means he's probably clueless about what's really going
on. At some point, you're going to have to tell him."

Lacey's gaze went to Alex again. Exactly how did
she do that after the mess she'd made of everything?

"Bingo!" Becker said from the living room, jarring her out of her thoughts.

Alex looked up from the notebook he was flipping through. "You find something?"

Becker's gaze didn't waver from the big-screen TV. "Maybe."

Lacey walked into the living room, Jayna right behind her.

"Apparently, McDonald is a big proponent of giving people second and sometimes third chances," Becker continued, still fixed on his screen. "He employs a lot of people who have done some really stupid crap, including Dr. Pettine. According to multiple newspaper articles and court proceedings, Pettine screwed up a surgical procedure about five years ago and was on his way to being sued for everything he had. Losing his medical license seemed to be the least of his problems, but then McDonald stepped in, and *poof*, the lawsuit disappeared, and the medical board dropped their investigation. The next thing you know, Pettine is working directly for one of McDonald's research groups, like nothing ever happened."

Becker tapped the keyboard, and a photo of a guy in his midtwenties with brown hair and eyes and what could only be called a bored expression popped up on the TV.

"If you think that's interesting, look at this guy," he said. "This is another doctor named Peter DeYoung. He only recently graduated medical school but immediately found his way to one of McDonald's research companies. Nothing unique there, since the councilman hires a lot of doctors fresh out of college. The interesting part is that DeYoung decided to pay his way through med school by making and selling meth in the basement of his frat house."

Lacey snorted as she sat down beside Alex. "I thought I was ambitious just waiting tables. I'm guessing he got caught?"

Becker nodded. "You guessed right. And guess who helped him not only get out from under that arrest, but also get his record expunged?"

"McDonald?" Alex surmised.

"The one and only," Becker said.

"That has to be our link then," Alex said. "Lacey and I will track down DeYoung. Remy and Max, you follow Pettine. Brooks, you take McDonald. One of these guys has to lead us to wherever they're hiding the girls." He looked around the room, his gaze meeting each of his teammates. "Whoever finds something first, call the rest of us for backup. We get those girls out and deal with the fallout afterward."

Chapter 16

LACEY AND ALEX FOUND DEYOUNG A LOT MORE EASILY than she anticipated. They simply went to the research facility where he worked and waited in the parking lot until he came out and got into a lime-green Honda Accord. She practically bounced in her seat when they pulled onto the road and followed him, sure he was going to lead them straight to Kelsey and the other girls, but all he did was pick up paperwork from one research facility, then drive across town to deliver it to another.

As the adrenaline rush she'd gotten at the possibility of finding Kelsey began to fade, Lacey found herself thinking about the conversation she'd had with Jayna. If someone had told her a month ago that she'd meet a guy and fall in love with him in two weeks, she would have said they were off their meds. Then again, if someone had told her a month ago that guy and practically all his friends were werewolves, she would have said they were off their meds too.

So much for meds.

As crazy as it seemed, Jayna's words made sense. Alex made Lacey feel things she'd never felt with another man. Things she'd never imagined feeling with any man. But could she really be in love with him?

Lacey always thought she'd never fall in love because she was broken when it came to that most basic of human emotions. Part of her wanted to stop thinking and simply go with it, to believe in the fairy-tale magic and accept that she and Alex were meant to be together. But there was another part—a bigger, pragmatic part—that warned her to slow down, take a step back, and consider that what she probably felt for Alex was nothing more than extreme gratitude. After all, the guy was risking his career to help find her sister. This thing with Kelsey had her caught up in a storm that was threatening to tear her apart. It wasn't too much of a leap to think that maybe she was simply grabbing hold of the only stable thing she could find to keep her grounded. Kind of like wrapping your arms around an oak tree in the middle of a tornado.

She glanced at Alex as he drove, wishing she could simply talk to him about how she felt so she could get some idea of what he was thinking. But how the heck did you start a conversation like that?

Hey, Alex. It seems that I'm The One *for you and vice versa. Care to discuss your thoughts on the subject?*

But before she could say anything, his phone rang.

Alex pulled it out of his pocket and thumbed the green button. "You're on speaker, Becker. Go ahead."

"Hey, guys. I dug up some more stuff on DeYoung. Considering he was making meth, it's not surprising that he was a chemistry major before transferring over to premed. After getting involved with McDonald, he did his internship at a research center that specializes in drug addiction and recovery. And get this—his intern project focused on the addictive effects of newer synthetic opiates."

"He could definitely be the guy making fireball, then," Alex said.

"It gets better—or worse—depending on your POV," Becker said. "The guy also volunteers at the clinic where

Kelsey and the other missing girls got their birth control pills. He helps out Dr. Pettine."

Alex glanced at Lacey. "Now we have our link between the missing girls, Pettine, the drugs, and McDonald." He started to say something else, but his phone beeped. "Hold on a second, Becker. The ME is calling. Stand by." He thumbed a button. "This is Trevino."

"It's Samantha Mills at the medical examiner's. We got the toxicology report back. While there wasn't any heroin in Nicole Arend's system, there was a cocktail of other drugs, the most significant ones being propofol and hyoscyamine."

Alex asked the medical examiner what they were, but Lacey barely heard him. She was too busy hyperventilating. Propofol was a general anesthetic. There was only one reason to give those to a person.

"Despite what the killer did to try to disguise it, Nicole Arend's kidneys and heart were surgically removed," the ME was telling Alex, even though Lacey was doing everything short of slapping her hands over her ears to keep from hearing. "All the other damage was done postmortem to cover that up. This was an organ harvest, pure and simple. The only surprise is that you found the girl's body to begin with. Typically, bodies of victims like this are never seen again."

Alex cursed under his breath. "Thanks, Doc. I owe you one." Thumbing a button on the phone, he quickly brought Becker up to speed, then disconnected the call.

Lacey clenched her hands together in her lap in an effort to keep from going insane with panic. Kelsey and the other girls had been kidnapped to harvest their organs. It was like something out of a horror movie, only real. All Lacey could do was sit there and think about that mutilated girl. Was that going to be her baby sister too? Had it already happened?

Alex reached over and placed his big hand on both of hers. "We're going to find Kelsey, I promise. Just hold it together a little while longer."

—◦◦◦—

Alex was so furious that his claws dug into the steering wheel as they followed DeYoung off the I-20 belt loop and headed south on Interstate 45. He had no idea where the asshole was heading, but if he didn't get there soon, Alex was going to ram him from the road and start tearing off important body parts until the man told him what he wanted to know. He probably would have done it already if DeYoung hadn't abruptly changed his routine at the last small lab facility where he'd stopped, loading the backseat of his Honda with five big cardboard boxes instead of the normal folders he'd been ferrying back and forth all over the city.

Alex had no idea what was in those boxes, but the furtive look that came over DeYoung's face as the man loaded his car convinced him the son of a bitch was definitely up to something. As they drove farther away from the center of the city, Alex hoped that maybe they were going to the place the girls were being held.

"It's getting dark," Lacey said nervously. "Shouldn't you get closer so you don't lose him?"

Alex glanced at her. She was still pale, but at least she wasn't shaking as much as she'd been earlier. "I won't lose him. I can see in the dark."

Lacey nodded but didn't say anything.

A few minutes later, the Honda turned off the highway and onto a narrow two-lane road. Alex slowed down and let the other car get farther ahead of him. There weren't many people on this road, and he didn't want DeYoung figuring out he was being followed.

Up ahead, DeYoung pulled into a gravel driveway that led to a large metal building with tall roll-up doors — like the kind of place big trucks were taken for maintenance work. Alex continued past the driveway, then did a U-turn when he was out of sight. Flipping off his lights, he crept back the way he'd come until he could just make out the front of the building. Then he pulled into the trees at the side of the road. Besides DeYoung's Honda, there were three other cars and more than a dozen motorcycles. In the distance, Alex could hear dogs barking.

DeYoung had already gotten out of the car and was dragging the first box from the backseat as the door of the building opened and a man came out. It was impossible not to recognize the unusual white skin and pale blond hair.

Beside Alex, Lacey gasped. "Pendergraff!"

Alex threw her a surprised look. "You know him?"

She nodded, her gaze intent on the scene in front of them. "He's Bensen's head of security. Wendy and I found evidence of a dogfighting ring at one of Bensen's other properties, so when you and I found all those dead dogs and the girl, I was sure Pendergraff was the one who'd done it. That's why I snuck into that junkyard where you found me. I was hoping to find evidence I could turn over to Wendy so she could arrest Pendergraff and Bensen."

Alex stared. All this time, he'd been so focused on Kelsey and everything that was going wrong between him and Lacey, he'd never once thought to delve into exactly why she'd snuck into Bensen's place. More important, why the heck hadn't the drug task force known about Bensen's supposed involvement in dog-fighting? Didn't anybody in the DPD talk to each other?

He had about a million questions to ask Lacey, but he didn't get a chance to ask a single one, because just then, the cardboard box DeYoung held ripped open, spilling plastic baggies all over the ground. Pendergraff cursed and shouted at him to pick them up.

"What is that stuff?" Lacey asked in a whisper.

"Fireball—and a lot of it. I'm guessing DeYoung makes the junk at McDonald's research labs, then Bensen and his people distribute it."

"Why would McDonald be involved in drugs?" Lacey asked. "He's already rich."

Alex snorted. "Yeah, well, in my experience, people with money always want more of it. He damn sure isn't harvesting organs for free."

Lacey chewed on her bottom lip. "Do you think Kelsey and the other girls are in that building?"

Alex studied the place, taking in the greasy smears around the roll-up doors, the old truck tires stacked along the side of the building, and the large number of motorcycles. It didn't strike him as a good location to stash girls they were planning to harvest body parts from. They'd want to keep them someplace cleaner and closer to the city, not to mention near medical facilities like the kind McDonald owned. Still, it would be easy enough to find out.

"Stay here," he told Lacey. "I'm going to sniff around. Don't get out of the truck."

Lacey opened her mouth to protest, but he didn't give her a chance. He jumped out of the truck, then took off at a sprint, hitting the woods that encircled the big metal-sided building. He moved around the back, wanting to avoid running into DeYoung or Pendergraff.

It was dark as hell behind the building, but he didn't have any problem seeing as he maneuvered among the truck parts and chain-link dog runs. The pit bulls and Rottweilers there barked when they saw him, but once they got a good sniff, they quickly calmed down.

"I'll get you guys out of here too," he told them. "Just sit tight."

Alex worked his way over to a dirty window and peeked in. There were a few big trucks and a car inside, along with toolboxes, spare parts, and tables loaded with fireball and weapons. Twenty guys gathered around the tables, repackaging the drugs into smaller plastic bags.

There wasn't any sign of Lacey's sister or the other girls, and he definitely didn't pick up Kelsey's scent. He turned to head back to his truck when he heard Lacey calling out to him in a sound just above a whisper.

"Alex, if you can hear me, hurry up! DeYoung and Pendergraff are leaving."

Shit.

Alex ran back to the truck and yanked the door open so fast that Lacey let out a gasp. She recovered quickly, though.

"Pendergraff came outside to talk to someone on his cell phone," she said. "Whoever was on the line said something that got his attention, because he jumped in his car and took off. DeYoung was right behind him."

Alex pulled out onto the road and floored it, wishing for once he had Gage's Charger instead of a pickup truck. But he caught up with the green Honda just before it turned onto I-45 heading north. Alex tucked in a hundred yards behind him and slowed down.

"If DeYoung doesn't lead us to the girls this time, I'm grabbing DeYoung—and he will talk," Alex vowed.

———

Lacey's heart thudded in her chest as she listened in on Alex's phone call with Gage. He'd called his boss a few minutes after they got on I-45 to tell him about what they'd seen at the big metal building.

"They've got five huge boxes of fireball and probably some other drugs too, so tell narcotics to hurry up and get their asses over there before everything's gone," Alex said. "There are also about twenty men armed with automatic weapons, so make sure you guys watch your backs in there."

Lacey grabbed Alex's arm. "Tell him about the dogs."

Alex nodded. "Gage, there are also fifteen dogs locked up in back of the building, so watch your crossfire. Anything coming out the rear of the place is likely to hit those dogs."

After Alex hung up, they both sat there tensely as he followed both Pendergraff and DeYoung back into the city. Twenty minutes later, the men pulled into the parking lot of a research facility DeYoung had visited earlier. Alex pulled into the parking lot of an office building a few blocks down that gave them a good view of the research facility. He chuckled softly.

"What is it?" Lacey asked. Nothing about this was even remotely funny.

He gestured at the two vehicles parked in the darkest corner of the lot. "That's Remy's Mustang and Brooks's truck."

No sooner were the words out of his mouth than Remy and Max jogged over to meet them.

"What are you guys doing here?" Alex asked.

"We followed Pettine here about thirty minutes ago," Remy said. "McDonald showed up ten minutes ago with Brooks right behind him. Brooks is out sniffing around now."

Alex was in the middle of filling in Remy and Max on DeYoung and Pendergraff when his phone rang. It was Brooks.

"McDonald and Pettine just left," the man's deep voice said over the speakerphone. "I let them go, because I caught a whiff of Kelsey's scent. She's definitely in the building somewhere."

Lacey's heart beat faster.

"Where are you?" Alex asked Brooks.

"There are some azaleas along the front of the building. I'm right behind them."

"Best way in?" Alex wanted to know.

"The front doors," Brooks said. "There are some private security types in there, so we'll need to neutralize them."

The muscle in Alex's jaw flexed. "Standby. I'm calling Gage."

Lacey held her breath as Alex got his Pack alpha on the line and told him where they were and what they were up against.

"I can't get anyone there to back you up," Gage said, frustration clear in his voice. "Deputy Chief Mason had me empty the shop to support the raid on the drug location on I-45 that you told me about. Can you wait?"

Alex didn't hesitate. "No."

"Then the four of you are going to have to do this on your own," Gage said. "Hit them fast, and don't hold back. I'll get backup to you as soon as I can."

Alex thumbed the red button on his phone, then called Brooks back. "We're on our own. I'll be there in two minutes." He hung up, then looked over at Remy and Max. "If we go in there and Brooks is wrong, we're hitting the unemployment line."

Remy and Max only shrugged.

Alex looked at Lacey. "This is all going to be over soon. We'll get Kelsey out of there safely. I promise."

Lacey grabbed his arm as he started to get out of the truck. Then she leaned over and kissed him. It was just one quick touch of the lips, but she prayed it said everything she hadn't been able to say to him before.

"Be careful," she whispered.

Alex nodded, then was gone, racing with Remy and Max toward the building so fast, they were a blur.

Chapter 17

ALEX DIDN'T PAUSE TO HAVE A LONG, DRAWN-OUT conversation with Brooks when they met up with him in front of the building. He told his teammates what he intended to do, and that was it. Brooks eyed him thoughtfully for a moment, then nodded.

"It's Lacey's sister in there," he said. "I'll follow your lead."

Giving them a nod, Alex led the way to the front door of Central Texas Medical R&D. He jerked open the door so hard it partially tore the hinges away from the frame, but he didn't care. Kelsey was in here, and he wasn't leaving until he got her out. Her scent hit him the moment he stepped inside the building, making his claws and fangs extend on their own.

The security guard at the desk jumped to his feet and rushed around in front of it, one hand out in front of him in a step-back gesture, the other on his holstered weapon.

"This is private property," he said. "You can't come in here."

"Dallas SWAT," Alex announced. "And yes, we can."

Alex didn't give the security guard a chance to reply or pull his weapon but simply strode over and punched the guy in the face. Despite being fired up, Alex forced himself to hold back. If he hadn't, the guy would be dead, and since he didn't know how involved the security guards were in this scheme, he didn't want that on his conscience. As it was, the man still flew backward a good ten feet before hitting the floor and sliding another ten.

Alex glanced over his shoulder at his teammates. "Try not to kill anyone if you can help it, but don't let them slow you down."

He pulled his weapon and headed straight down the main corridor, following Kelsey's scent. Remy fell in beside him. They didn't get more than twenty feet when Alex picked up the smell of four men coming their way.

"We've got company," he whispered.

He and Remy stepped out into the crossing of two main corridors just in time to catch a pair of men in white lab coats coming toward them from the left. A third doctor, this one accompanied by another security guard, came from the right. Unlike the guard at the front door, this one wasn't in the mood to talk. Instead, he drew his weapon and started shooting. The doctor beside the security guard froze, but the other two immediately turned and hauled ass down the hallway.

The guy wasn't a great shot, so he didn't hit Alex or Remy, but soon enough, he'd get lucky. Alex hadn't wanted to harm any of the security guards until he knew exactly how they were involved, but it looked like he wasn't going to have a choice. He lifted his weapon, ready to put a bullet through a part of the guard that wouldn't kill the man, but just then, the remaining doctor turned and shoved his way through a door, giving Alex a quick glimpse of a set of stairs and a fresh burst of Kelsey's scent.

"She's upstairs," he growled at Remy.

"Go!" Remy ordered. "I'll back this guy out of your way."

Before Alex could tell his friend that wasn't necessary, Remy stepped around him and walked straight toward the guard. The guy got off another shot, this one burying itself somewhere in Remy's shoulder. Remy didn't slow down but simply lifted his gun and started popping shots into the cinder-block wall inches from the guard's head. The man ducked away from the exploding concrete, then began backpedaling down the hallway as Remy put round after round into the wall near his head.

Alex didn't hang around to see more. He hit the stairs at a run, just as more gunfire erupted throughout the building. It sounded like Brooks and Max had run into trouble too.

Kelsey's scent grew stronger with every step. Alex shoved open the metal door to the second floor just in time to see the doctor and another guard dragging a very woozy Carla Jones toward the elevator at the far end of the hallway. The guard turned, holding Carla in front of him while he drew his weapon and aimed it in Alex's direction.

Seeing the man with one of the kidnapped girls put an end to any uncertainty in Alex's mind about the guards' involvement in the situation. Alex's bullet went through the part of the man's shoulder that wasn't hidden behind the girl. The guard went down, taking Carla with him.

That left the doctor standing there alone. His eyes widened in fear as Alex advanced on him. The gun probably didn't scare him nearly as much as the sight of Alex's fangs and glowing gold eyes. Alex didn't give a damn. Closing the distance between them, he dug his claws into the man's lab coat and smashed him against the nearest wall before tossing him down the hallway.

Bending down, Alex gently picked up Carla from the

floor, moving her off to the side so he could sit her up against the wall. She was heavily drugged, so she was pretty much out of it, but her eyes still widened when she caught sight of his face.

"Shit," he muttered.

Alex closed his eyes and took deep, slow breaths, trying to get his shift back under control. He'd done it. He'd found the girls. He could calm down now.

He was almost there when he heard pounding coming from either side of him. He opened his eyes and saw two girls peering at him through the slim glass insert of the doors they were locked behind. Sara Collins was on his left, Abigail Elliott on the right.

Alex was up and moving, still fighting to get his fangs and claws to behave themselves. He reached the door on the right in two strides and slammed his shoulder into it. The minute it flew open, he had an armful of frightened girl trying to attach herself to him like an alien life form.

He put his hands on Abigail's shoulders, gently trying to get her to arm's length so he could check for injuries, but now that she'd latched on to him, she refused to let go. She didn't seem injured, but she was definitely in full-on panic mode, and the terror burning brightly in her eyes was heart-wrenching to see.

Murmuring something he hoped would calm her down, he wrapped his arm around her and led her across the corridor so he could rescue Sara. Fortunately, Max came running out of the stairwell just then and helped get the terrified girl off him.

"I got her," Max said softly.

Alex took advantage of the assistance, gently disengaging from Abigail so he could smash open the other door. Thankfully, Sara didn't latch on to him like

Abigail, but instead hurried down the hallway to check on Carla. Alex quickly moved to the next door down the corridor, knowing from the scent coming from underneath that it was Kelsey's room.

But when he burst inside, Kelsey wasn't there.

His heart beating faster, he ran out and kicked in the next door, then the next, even though he knew those rooms were empty too.

Alex raced back down the hallway. Carla was still out of it, and Abigail seemed too frazzled to help, but Sara looked reasonably calm.

"Where's Kelsey?" he asked urgently as he dropped to a knee beside her.

She shook her head. "I don't know. They came and took her out of here on a stretcher five minutes before you showed up. I don't know where they took her."

Alex growled, his fangs sliding out again. Fuck!

Getting to his feet, he turned toward the door to the stairwell before looking back at Max and the three girls. Sara might be able to walk out of here on her own, but the other two sure as hell couldn't.

"I'll get them out of here," Max said. "Go after Kelsey."

Alex nodded, then turned and sprinted for the stairwell, praying he wasn't too late.

Lacey was waiting as patiently as she could in Alex's truck, sure everything was going to be fine, that Alex and his SWAT teammates would get Kelsey and the other girls out, when an ambulance pulled into the parking lot and backed up to the loading dock along the rear of the building. Ten seconds later, a guy in a white lab coat came out the back door of the building, wheeling a gurney with someone on it. The driver, also dressed in a white lab coat, got out and helped the man shove the gurney into the back of the ambulance. Then both men turned and disappeared inside the building.

She thought her heart had been pumping hard before, but she'd been wrong. Right now it was thudding so wildly, she thought it might jump out of her chest. The person on that gurney was almost certainly one of the girls who'd been kidnapped—maybe even Kelsey. Lacey couldn't let these people drive away with whoever it was.

For half a second, she wondered if she should try to call Alex, but then chided herself for how dumb that was. He wasn't going to answer his cell phone in the middle of looking for the girls. If she wanted to tell him, she'd have to go into the building and find him, and she didn't have time for that. She had no idea where he and the other SWAT guys even were.

Opening the door, Lacey hopped out of the truck and ran for the loading dock before she lost her courage—or came to her senses.

She was gasping for air before she even got to the knee-high loading dock, for no other reason than she was so terrified, it felt like her throat was closing up. She slowed as she ducked her head to peek in the back of the ambulance, suddenly scared of what she would see. What if whoever was on the gurney was already dead?

Her breath hitched at the sight of the girl's blond hair. Heart in her throat, she climbed into the ambulance, sobbing out loud at the sight of her sister lying there so still. But Kelsey was breathing, albeit slowly. Knowing she'd never be able to carry her, Lacey jerked on the gurney, trying to back it out of the ambulance. She didn't have a lot of time before those men came back.

She nearly jumped out of her skin when the building behind her erupted with gunfire. The urge to run inside after Alex shocked her to the core. It was so strong that she almost gave in. Then she got a grip on herself. Alex was a werewolf. He could take care of himself. Kelsey couldn't. Lacey had to get her out of here—now.

She'd just figured out the wheels of the gurney were locked into the ambulance and that she was going to have to release the latch on the floor to get her out when a familiar voice right behind her froze her solid.

"Well, isn't this precious?" Pendergraff said.

Lacey snapped her head around just in time to see the butt of a pistol coming down straight at her temple. Stars exploded in her vision, and she found her knees giving out no matter how much she fought to stay upright.

"Drive!" Pendergraff snarled to someone in the front of the vehicle.

Lacey stumbled backward, falling to the floor as the ambulance sped away from the loading dock. Her head hit something on the way down, but while it made her vision swim even worse than it already was, oddly enough, it didn't hurt. A part of her realized that was probably a bad thing.

All those thoughts got pushed aside as a man in a white lab coat leaned over Kelsey. Lacey grit her teeth, trying to push herself upright so she could grab the man's leg. Pendergraff kicked her in the shoulder, knocking her down.

"The only reason I didn't shoot you on sight is because there might be a few parts in you that someone can use," he sneered, the scars on his face making the expression even more evil looking. "But if you piss me off, I'll shoot you in the head. No one will need that."

Lacey stopped trying to get up, but only because she realized they wouldn't do anything to Kelsey while they were in the ambulance. She needed to wait and pray that Alex would find them in time—or she lucked out and managed to rescue them both on her own.

Chapter 18

ALEX FOLLOWED KELSEY'S SCENT THROUGH THE FIRST floor and out the back of the building, ignoring the growls and shooting going on all around him. When he came out on a loading dock, he discovered that things were even worse than he'd feared. Kelsey's scent was definitely back here, but so was Lacey's, which meant she'd been on this dock mere seconds ago. He glanced hopefully at his truck, but she wasn't there. His head started to spin. What the hell had Lacey been doing back here?

She'd been trying to help her sister, because he'd completely fucked up that task himself.

Shit.

As much as Alex wanted to continue the mental ass kicking he was giving himself, he needed to focus. He sniffed the air, picking up the smell of burnt tires. A vehicle had just squealed away from the building, and his gut told him Lacey and Kelsey were inside it. Looking up, he saw a pair of taillights disappearing into the darkness in the distance. That had to be them.

Alex took off running, only to stop before he'd gone a hundred feet. He could run damn fast, but there was no way he could catch a vehicle, not with the head start this one had.

He stood in the middle of the road, weighing his options. Knowing Kelsey had been kidnapped so they could harvest her organs, he could make a few educated guesses about where that vehicle had been taking Lacey

and her sister. This part of town had a lot of hospitals
and surgical clinics, which was likely why so many of
McDonald's research facilities were located in this area.
If they were planning to cut into Kelsey, it would stand
to reason they were heading for a place that could handle
a major surgery. Even if he threw out all the hospitals—
they'd definitely notice something weird going on—it
still left a lot of places to search.

He reached for his phone, thinking Becker and his
damn computers could do something, but then stopped.
He couldn't just wait around and hope Becker might
figure out where Lacey and her sister were. He'd wasted
time once before up in Rochester, and innocent people
had paid the price.

Alex jogged back to the loading dock, going with the
only real link he had to Lacey and Kelsey—their scents.
While he could smell both of them, Lacey's scent was
much stronger. Maybe it was thanks to the connection
that had been developing between them before everything went wrong.

He closed his eyes, pushing his shift and trying to
lock onto her scent. Once he had it, he moved away from
the loading dock, praying he could stay on her scent
even though she was in a moving vehicle. But the scent
began to get lighter the farther he moved from the loading dock. Within fifty feet, it disappeared completely.

He doubled back and picked up the scent again, then
leaned down closer to the ground as he fought to force
his shift as far as he could take it. Both Khaki and Brooks
had said his inability to push his shift was holding back
his sense of smell. Now was the time to get past that.

He pushed so hard that his jaw ached as the bones
popped, making room for more teeth. Lacey's scent

immediately got stronger, and he broke into a run as he moved out onto the main road in front of the building. But once again, the trail began to fade the moment he got to the place where the vehicle he was trying to follow had picked up speed. Alex let out a growl of rage and frustration that reverberated off the nearby buildings. Spent, he dropped to his knees in the grass beside the road.

He closed his eyes and sat back on his heels, shoving against that wall inside himself that had always kept him from fully connecting with his inner wolf. Even though he'd spent years training with Gage and the other members of the Pack who could pull off a full shift, he'd never knocked a dent in that wall. He had no idea why he hadn't been able to do it, and right then, he didn't care. He needed to track Lacey's scent, or she was going to die. He was going to push his shift as far as he had to, because he flat-out refused to let another person—especially Lacey or Kelsey—die because he'd screwed up again. What had happened with that family in Rochester was never happening again. He didn't care what he had to do.

Gage always talked about relaxing and letting the shift roll through you, but Alex didn't have time to *relax and let* anything happen. He needed to shift—and he needed to do it now.

Eyes still closed, he visualized the wolf form he wanted to take, then reached out to that shape. He dug his fingers into the fur of the mental image of the beast in his head, dragging it toward him. He poured every ounce of rage, frustration, and fear he had into the effort, imagining himself becoming one with the wolf inside. He didn't have to try very hard to find the ragged and raw emotions necessary to do it. The thought of Lacey and Kelsey ending up like Nicole Arend was all it took.

He hadn't realized he'd fallen forward onto his hands until he felt his arms explode in pain. He ignored the sensation and kept reaching for the image of the wolf in his head.

He could feel the change coming, so fast it seemed like every part of his body was ripping apart at the same time. The pain of bones and muscles twisting into new shapes, ligaments and tendons popping like pieces of wet string, and fur shoving its way through his skin was so intense, all he could do was let out a sound that started as a shout and quickly became a howl so loud, it seemed to tear apart the night air.

A part of Alex realized he probably should have pulled off his clothes before trying to shift, but it was way too late for that. There was no way to stop it now. He wouldn't know how to stop this even if he'd wanted to.

His T-shirt shredded like tissue paper as his back elongated and shoulders twisted downward in a totally different shape. The jeans didn't hold up much longer, though the big leather belt started to hurt like hell as it constricted across his stomach. He instinctively reached down with his head and snapped through the thick leather with a mouthful of teeth he hadn't realized he'd grown. He was more worried about the boots, but they were the easiest part. When his feet changed into paws, he simply stepped out of them.

He felt powerful, ready to explode into motion as he stood there on all four paws instead of his hands and knees. He would have expected everything to feel strange and off-balance. But he felt as comfortable in his wolf form as he did in his human one.

He looked down, lingering on the broad expanse of his furry chest before moving to his huge paws sinking deep into the grass. He took a few quick steps and was relieved to discover that all four legs seemed to work together properly without him having to think about it. He glanced back at the remains of his clothes, wallet, cell phone, and weapon. There was nothing to be done. He would have to leave all of it here.

Alex moved forward, not sure if it would be as easy to run as it was to walk, but he didn't have time to worry about it. He had bigger concerns to focus on, namely Lacey. He took a deep breath through his nose, and a million different scents seemed to explode in his head. Within seconds, he filtered through them and tossed aside all of them but Lacey's.

If he wasn't so freaking worried about Lacey and her sister, Alex would have laughed at how easy it was to pick up Lacey's scent now—if a wolf could laugh. It was almost like there was a glowing line of fireflies flowing in the air above the road. But the line wasn't visible to his eyes, only to his nose.

He took another deep breath and locked on the direction of her scent, then tore after the vehicle. Fortunately, his paws and legs behaved, gathering more and more speed by the second.

Alex had no idea what the hell he was going to do when he found Lacey and Kelsey, since he was in wolf form and didn't have a gun, but it was something he'd deal with later. He would find Lacey and her sister in full wolf form—or his naked human one. He didn't care which. All that mattered was that he saved them.

The buildings began to blur around him as he leaned forward and pushed for more speed. He had no idea how fast he was running, but it was definitely in the hauling ass category. As he ran, he couldn't help but take in the world around him. He was surprised how different everything looked. He seemed to be missing some parts of the color palette, with most of the colors seeming to be toward the red end of the spectrum. He could see better and farther in the dark than he would ever have thought possible.

Alex abruptly realized that he'd veered onto a fairly busy road and was running right down the center of it. Drivers honked their horns and veered off the road to avoid him. He couldn't blame them. He was as big as a bull and probably ten times as scary looking. Alex winced when he accidently sideswiped a car that steered too close to him.

He wasn't sure how long he ran. Time didn't seem to feel the same to him in his wolf form. All he knew was that he covered fifteen miles in a ridiculously short period of time. He followed the unwavering scent trail to another fancy brick-and-glass facility called West Ridge Surgery Center. He ran straight past the main entrance and around to the rear of the building. The place looked nearly empty, with only a few of the windows lit on the upper floors and maybe a dozen cars scattered around the parking lot.

The nondescript ambulance parked by the automatic doors in the back told him he was at the right place. Lacey's and Kelsey's scents were all over the vehicle. He could smell them clearly, even though he was still two hundred feet away.

Three of those damn Westcott Security guards were standing outside the automatic glass doors, obviously stationed there to keep people out. Alex headed straight for them, letting out a long, deep growl and picking up speed as he closed the distance between them.

Three heads jerked up and looked in his direction, eyes widening in shock and amazement. One of the men threw himself to the side to escape Alex, while another froze, completely paralyzed by fear. The third man drew his weapon and started firing wildly in Alex's general direction. Bullets smacked into the pavement around him. One nicked his right foreleg, but just barely. The guy was too freaked out to shoot straight.

The man was still shooting when Alex leaped forward and rammed his shoulder into the guy's chest. The crush of the impact was loud, but not nearly as loud as the sound of shattering glass as the security guard flew backward and crashed through the automatic doors.

Alex spun around to face the other two guards before the glass had even stopped falling. One man was already running away, while the other finally reached for his weapon. Alex wasn't going to give him a chance to fire it.

He lunged forward and swiped his paws across the man's chest and arms, ripping through the fabric and skin underneath, sending the guard tumbling backward. The urge to rip into the fallen man was intense, but Alex ignored the animalistic instinct. This was taking too long already. He gave a low warning growl as the guard made a move to retrieve the pistol that had gone flying. The guy immediately scrambled to his feet and ran in the other direction.

Alex leaped over the fallen guard lying bloody and unconscious in a pile of broken glass, once more turning his attention to tracking Lacey's scent. It was so close, he felt like he could reach out and touch her.

Then a new scent hit his nose, a scent that had the hackles on the back of his neck standing straight up and a vicious growl rumbling from his throat. He'd never smelled that particular scent before, but he knew exactly what it was—Lacey's blood. It completely overrode every other scent in the building, making hers the only one that mattered.

Even though his wolf instincts screamed at him that there were other armed men in the building who would be coming for him any second, all he could think about was getting down the dimly lit main corridor of the surgical center to the heavy steel door at the end of the hall where his werewolf nose told him the scent of blood was strongest.

That single-minded focus almost cost him as two men stepped out of the stairwell doorway near the reception desk and started shooting the moment they laid eyes on him. There was another man in the stairwell too, but that one turned and headed back upstairs.

The two men who stayed seemed to be more determined than the security guards outside. Their hearts might be beating at a hundred miles an hour, but they didn't let it show as they took aim and did their best to kill him.

Alex ran right at them, closing the distance in the blink of an eye. He felt himself get hit, once in the chest, another in the left shoulder, and a third creasing a line down his right side. The bullets stung, but just barely. He wondered if that meant the wounds weren't serious or if his wolf form was just better at ignoring the pain.

He slammed hard into one of the men, knocking him backward into the reception desk. As the man rebounded, Alex raked his claws across his neck. Blood flowed freely, but he paid no attention to it as he spun and lunged at the second guard. That one went down just as fast.

Sidestepping the bloody mess he'd made, Alex turned and headed for the far metal door again, only to have to stop as the elevator doors about halfway down the corridor opened with a ding and a clank of metal.

Alex recognized the scent before the guy even stepped out of the elevator. It was the man who'd cut the throats of the dogs he and Lacey had found.

When the man finally stepped into view, pistol in hand, Alex wasn't shocked to see that it was Pendergraff. In all the times Alex had encountered the man, he had never caught his scent. Now that he had, it didn't surprise him in the least that the man was a dog-killing piece of shit.

As Alex moved toward Pendergraff, he realized the man had another scent on him besides his own—Lacey's blood.

Snarling in rage, Alex sprinted toward Pendergraff.

The man didn't run but instead started shooting at Alex. Bullets ripped through his body, but he was too mad to pay any attention to them. He lunged for Pendergraff's throat, not caring how many times he was hit.

Pendergraff threw his free arm up in front of his face to protect his throat, leaving Alex no choice but to clamp on that. He bit down until bones crunched, but Pendergraff didn't even make a sound. Instead, he moved his gun until it was pressed against Alex's chest, then squeezed the trigger. Alex howled in pain, releasing Pendergraff's arm.

The world started to go black, and for a moment, Alex was sure the man had just put a bullet through his heart. Werewolves could absorb a lot of damage, but a bullet through the heart would kill any of them, and it didn't have to be a silver one.

Pendergraff smiled up at him, as if he enjoyed hearing Alex's grunts of pain. Just thinking of what this sick, sadistic bastard might have done to Lacey—and what he would certainly do to her if Alex didn't finish this—was all the motivation Alex needed to drive back the wave of unconsciousness threatening to overwhelm him. Growling through the pain in his chest, he lunged for Pendergraff's throat while the man was busy gloating.

Eyes widening, Pendergraff cried out in terror, but that lasted for only a gurgling second as Alex closed his jaws over the man's throat and bit down, shaking from side to side to make sure the asshole never hurt another woman—or dog—again. Considering Pendergraff's crimes, the punishment seemed to fit.

Leaping over the man's still body, Alex charged for the steel door at the end of the hall. He slammed his shoulder into it at full speed, even though the impact almost made him black out again. The door completely tore off its hinges and slammed to the floor, sliding several feet with him on top of it.

The room was dark, but Alex had no problem seeing that it was some kind of a medical supply room with metal racks full of boxes and bottles. Lacey stood in the middle of the room, her eyes wide, a long metal rod from an IV stand held firmly in her hands.

Alex's heart almost seized up at the sight of her. Not just because she was alive and well, or even because she was so beautiful, it took his breath away, but because she was standing there holding a makeshift weapon, ready to beat the first person who walked in the door. She was amazing.

Then the heavy scent of her blood hit him, and he realized that there was a lot of it matting the hair on the right side of her head. So much that some had flowed down and soaked the shoulder of her shirt.

He took a step toward her, only to stop when her eyes widened to the size of teacups. That was when he remembered he was still a frigging wolf. He was freaking her out.

All he wanted to do right then was run over and hold her and never let go, but he couldn't.

"Alex?" she asked slowly, taking a tentative step forward.

He tried to make the most nonthreatening sound he could, but it came out as a guttural chuff.

She moved another step closer and reached out her hand. He found himself moving to meet her without thinking if he should.

Lacey threw her makeshift weapon to the floor with a clatter, running the last few feet between them to drop to her knees in front of him and wrap her arms around his shoulders, pressing her face into his neck. Then she started to cry, great wracking sobs that tore through him like another bullet to the chest.

Emotions surged through Alex, deeper and more powerful than anything he'd ever felt in his life. The realization of just how frigging much he loved her couldn't have been any more obvious to him if it had been spelled out in neon. He knew that Lacey probably wouldn't ever get to a place where she felt the same, but right then, all he wanted to do was wrap his arms around her and squeeze her tightly.

That was a little tough to do in his current form, but as he stood there leaning into her hug, imagining what it would feel like to wrap his arms around her again, he felt the shift come over him.

Lacey stumbled back and fell on her butt when the first spasm hit his muscles. Then she sat there wide-eyed as his bones cracked and twisted back into a human shape.

Maybe it was just his imagination, but it didn't seem like the shift was quite as traumatic going in this direction. It definitely didn't hurt as much.

The moment the shift was done and Alex was kneeling there on the floor, naked on his hands and knees, Lacey grabbed him again and threw her arms around his shoulders. She squeezed him tightly, and it felt even better now than it had before. He knew it was all about her being grateful he'd come to save her and her sister, but it still felt good anyway.

Almost immediately, she pulled back and started to say something. Then she stared at his chest in wide-eyed shock. "Oh God! You're bleeding!"

He looked down and realized Lacey was right. He had four holes in his chest—one damn near his heart, two in the left shoulder, and one along the right side of his rib cage. He was a bloody mess.

Fortunately, all but one of those shots had punched right through him. While none of them felt very good, a werewolf's body could heal almost any wound as long as the bullet wasn't still in there. The bullet stuck in his shoulder hurt the worst. He'd need to get in there and dig the thing out before it could clot up and stop bleeding. But for right now, he was content to just hold Lacey.

"I'll be fine," he whispered softly as he looked around for Kelsey. The sooner they got out of here, the better their chances were of not being caught by the police when they responded to all these shots being fired. He would have one hell of a time explaining what he was doing here all bloody—and naked—with a clinic full of ripped-up thugs and security guards.

But it was as he was looking around the shadows of the small storage room that he realized he couldn't pick up Kelsey's scent anywhere. He might not be in his wolf form now, but he should still be able to smell her.

"Where's Kelsey?" he asked urgently.

Panic filled Lacey's eyes. "Didn't you save her first? I thought the other members of your pack were with her."

Alex's heart started pounding, and he could feel his fangs sliding out again. "No. I'm here by myself. Did you see where they took her?"

She shook her head. "I don't know. They were wheeling her away on a gurney when Pendergraff shoved me in here. They've taken her off to surgery. Alex, we have to find her!"

Alex shook his head. Though every instinct in his body screamed for him to stay here and protect Lacey—or at least get her out of the building first—he knew he couldn't do that. He had to find Kelsey before he did anything else. Before it was too late.

"Correction," he said. "I'm going to find her. You're going to stay here."

"But—"

"Lacey, I can't focus on finding your sister if I have to watch out for you," he told her firmly. "Stay here. I'll be back as fast as I can."

"Hurry," she begged. "Please."

Alex ran out of the storeroom, scooping up Pendergraff's pistol before slamming open the door to the stairwell and racing up the steps. He didn't know which floor Kelsey was on, but his gut told him that if he followed the scent of the last man who'd gone up these steps, he'd find her.

—⁓—

Lacey tried her best to stay calm but failed. How could she be calm after everything that had happened in the last few minutes? She'd thought she couldn't get any more freaked out than when Pendergraff had tossed her in this storage room and wheeled her sister toward the elevator. She'd been trying to use a piece of metal she'd gotten from an IV stand to wedge open the heavy steel door when she heard shooting and growling coming from the hallway. She'd known instinctively it was Alex, though she didn't have a clue how he'd found her so fast.

When the door finally burst open, it was all she could do not to scream when she'd seen a wolf the size of a small horse standing there. She wasn't sure how she'd known it was Alex, but she did. There was just something about the way he looked at her that convinced her the huge gray wolf was the man she loved.

She'd gotten a little emotional then, overwhelmed by the realization that she had yet to fully grasp that there was nothing Alex wouldn't do for her, whether it was staying with her even when she stupidly tried to push him away or shifting into a wolf so he could smash through a steel door to save her.

Earlier today, she'd tried to find the right time and the right words to tell Alex how she felt about him, but then Pendergraff had grabbed her, and she realized she might never get a chance to say anything to him ever again. So, she'd dropped to her knees in front of him and wrapped her arms around that big, muscular, furry neck, intending to tell him everything. But then reality had intruded, first when Alex had changed back into his human form and she saw that he'd been shot multiple times, then when he'd asked where Kelsey was.

With those simple words, he proved that none of this was over yet.

Now Alex had run off to save her sister while she stood there terrified that she was about to lose the two most important people in the world to her.

Lacey jumped as gunfire suddenly echoed somewhere upstairs. *Crap*. She knew she'd promised Alex that she'd wait here, but that was before whoever was up there with him and Kelsey started shooting. She'd never forgive herself if anything happened to them.

Heart pounding, she ran out of the storage room, desperate to find the stairs. She could have taken the elevator, but that would mean stepping out of it into the middle of a gunfight—if she were lucky enough to guess which floor to get off on.

She hesitated when she came to Pendergraff's bloody body lying in the middle of the hallway. While she knew Alex had torn out the man's throat, she simply couldn't find it in her to care. Pendergraff had been a vicious killer, and Lacey couldn't help thinking he'd gotten exactly what he deserved.

Edging around Pendergraff, she continued down the hallway, finding two more bodies before seeing the door to the stairs. There were two pistols lying on the floor beside the dead men, and for a moment, she seriously considered picking up one of them. She immediately dismissed the notion. She had no idea how to use a pistol and wouldn't be able to hit anything she aimed at, even if she could get the thing to work.

No, the best thing she could do was sneak upstairs, find Kelsey, and get her out of the building. Then there wouldn't be any need for Alex to fight every single killer in the place.

Lacey had barely entered the stairwell when her plan went to hell as Peter DeYoung came running down the stairs toward her. Anger surged through her. After helping Pettine kidnap Kelsey and the other girls, making and selling drugs, disposing of animals killed in the dogfighting ring, this jerk thought he could simply walk out of here? Not if she had anything to say about it.

She was ready to kick him in the balls if she had to in order to stop him. But then she saw the fire extinguisher mounted on the wall just beside the door and decided that would work even better.

"Get out of here, lady!" he shouted at her. "There's some kind of monster up there."

Lacey yanked the fire extinguisher from its wall mount and jerked out the pin. At least this was one weapon she knew how to use.

"Yeah, I know," she said. "And you're it."

DeYoung's eyes widened as she pointed the nozzle straight at him, then squeezed the handle. The white powder spray hit him full in the face. He immediately threw up his hands to shield himself, but all he did was lose his balance and end up falling down the last few stairs in a tumble.

He cursed and jumped to his feet, then came at her. Getting a firm grip on the handle of the fire extinguisher, she swung it hard at DeYoung's head. The impact echoed in the chamber of the stairwell long after he fell on his worthless ass.

Lacey stood over DeYoung, ready to hit him again if he got up, but the doctor was slumped against the stairs, out cold. She started to drop the empty fire extinguisher, but then thought better of it. She wasn't going to be caught without a weapon again.

Stepping over DeYoung's unconscious body, she ran up the steps, ready to kill the next person who tried to hurt the people she loved.

———◆———

Alex heard the councilman shouting long before he reached the fourth-floor stairwell.

"I'm telling you, there's no fucking wolf in this building, you moron," McDonald insisted. "It's probably one of those damn SWAT cops with a dog from the K-9 unit. Get down there, finish off both of them, then get this place cleaned up before the rest of the DPD shows up from all this damn shooting. The surgery needs to go off without a hitch, or I'm out five million dollars."

Alex's blood went cold at the word *surgery*, his fangs and claws slipping out even further. *Please God, don't let me be too late*.

His bones and muscles started to twist and crack again as his body responded to the anxiety by trying to shift again, but he clamped down on the urge. He didn't know what he would have to do to save Kelsey. His capacity for violence as a wolf was useful but not nearly as useful as having opposable thumbs.

His nose—which seemed to be working a whole hell of a lot better since he'd gone through a full shift—told him there were at least four men in the hallway before he even yanked open the door and charged into the hallway.

McDonald and the other men were standing in front of a set of swinging doors with a sign over them that read *Operating Rooms 1 and 2*. Kelsey was in one of them. Getting to her was the only thing that mattered now.

All three men stared at him like they'd seen a monster. Alex supposed he couldn't blame them. It wasn't every day they came face-to-face with a six-foot-four, armed and naked man, sporting fangs and claws, not to mention covered in blood. He probably looked like something out of a nightmare.

Unfortunately, their surprise only lasted a few seconds. McDonald cursed and reached into his suit jacket to pull out a small pistol. The security guards quickly followed his lead, drawing their own weapons and pointing them. Alex charged, letting out a growl that echoed off the walls and drowned out even the sounds of their gunshots. Their aim wasn't very good, so except for one shot that got him in the chest, the other bullets barely grazed him. It didn't even slow him down.

Alex waited until he was ten feet from the men before lifting the weapon he'd taken from Pendergraff. He aimed for the security guards first, since they were both armed with .45 caliber weapons that could do more damage than McDonald's little .32. The only thing he thought about as he put them both down was how these men had almost certainly been part of Nicole Arend's horrific death, whether by doing nothing to stop it or helping to cover it up.

He'd just turned his weapon on McDonald when he ran out of ammo. McDonald smirked, probably assuming this was over and that he'd won. His expression soon turned to shock as Alex closed the distance separating him from the crooked councilman and smacked the pistol out of his hand to send it flying across the room. In the same fluid move, Alex reached up and grabbed McDonald by the throat, yanking him up on his tiptoes and walking him backward down the hall to the OR doors.

McDonald ripped at Alex's hand, trying to get free while also lifting himself up at the same time in an attempt to relieve the pressure that was slowly choking him.

"It doesn't have to go like this," McDonald gasped. "Bensen is dying of kidney failure, and he's paying me millions to get him two perfect new ones. I can make us both rich. A million dollars cash in your pocket right now. All you have to do is look the other way."

Alex wasn't sure what pissed him off more, the fact that the pig thought he could buy him off or that he was trying to swindle him right off the bat.

He pulled McDonald closer, making sure the man got a good look at his fangs. "I was in the stairwell when you told those idiots who worked for you that that you're getting five million dollars from the man in surgery. Makes me think you were planning to cheat me on our very first deal. Is that any way to develop a lasting business relationship?"

McDonald's eyes widened. He struggled twice as hard against Alex's grip, but whether to get free or renegotiate was anyone's guess. Regardless, Alex didn't care. He was done talking.

Alex used the councilman's head to slam open the doors at the end of the hallway, then tossed his unconscious form to the floor. The impact was extremely loud—and extremely satisfying.

He was surprised at how easy it was to let his fangs and claws retract as he stepped into the first operating room. Maybe going through his first complete shift had improved more than just his sense of smell.

Bensen was on his stomach on one operating table, red lines drawn on his back. Kelsey was on the other, the same marks on her back. Two women in hospitable scrubs were standing beside trays loaded with a bewildering amount of surgical equipment, while a man dressed the same stood at the head of the operating table Kelsey was on. Pettine stood beside her, a sharp scalpel glinting in his hand.

Suddenly, everything clicked into place. The questions had always been why Bensen would get involved in drugs and dogfighting and why McDonald would get into the black market trade for transplant organs. It had been money, pure and simple. While the automotive king was definitely well-off, he sure as hell didn't have five million lying around in his petty cash drawer. He would have needed to sell everything he owned to raise that kind of money quickly, and he still wouldn't have gotten a new kidney the traditional way.

As for McDonald, the councilman had the connection to doctors like Pettine and the technical know-how to put together a black-market organ-harvesting ring. Not to mention a desire for even more money than he already had.

Two scumbags like them finding each other was only a matter of time. But none of it mattered now, because this operation was closed for good.

Pettine regarded Alex haughtily over his cloth face mask. "I don't know what you think you're doing, but you need to leave immediately. I'm trying to save both of these people's lives."

Ignoring the three other people in the room, Alex walked around the table Kelsey was on. He didn't say a word as he walked up to Pettine and wrapped one hand around the man's neck, then lifted him off the floor. Pettine plunged the scalpel into Alex's chest, but Alex immediately yanked it out and tossed it across the room. Then he tightened his grip around Pettine's throat, watching as the bastard turned an unhealthy shade of purple.

Alex glanced at the man standing petrified near Kelsey's head. "You can bring her out of this anesthesia on your own, right? Before you answer, make sure you're completely honest. Because if you hurt that girl in any way, I'm going to damage you beyond all possible repair. Do you understand?"

The guy gulped and nodded.

Satisfied he wouldn't need Pettine for anything, Alex threw him across the room where he bounced off a wall, joining McDonald on the floor.

"Bring her out now," Alex ordered. "And if anything happens to her, I'm going to start harvesting organs myself—without anesthesia or a knife."

The man gestured to one of the women, who hurried over to help him bring Lacey's sister out from the anesthesia she was under. The other woman stared at Alex, watching with wide eyes as he picked up a pair of forceps from one of the trays and calmly started to dig the bullet out of his chest.

Chapter 19

BY THE TIME LACEY REACHED THE FOURTH FLOOR AND found Alex in the operating room, one of the doctors had already given the proper drugs to Kelsey and Bensen to bring them out of the general anesthesia. Lacey was stunned to discover that Bensen was the transplant patient but ignored him as she checked Kelsey's vitals to make sure she was okay. Her sister would be out for a while yet, but she was going to be fine.

Lacey helped Alex lock up all the doctors and McDonald in a supply closet just off the operating room, where he also found himself some medical scrubs to wear so he wasn't standing there completely naked as he continued to try digging the bullet out of his chest. He said he wanted it out before the cops showed up, which should be soon.

"Here, let me do that," Lacey finally said after watching him root around like a man trying to make the buzzer on that electronic game Operation go off as many times as he could.

Standing there with her sister and Bensen only a few feet away, Lacey took the forceps and gently slipped them into the wound, working both by feel and guided by the soft direction Alex made every once in a while. Apparently, he could actually *feel* the bullet in his chest, so he was able to help her navigate the forceps in the right direction. She was shocked that what she was doing didn't seem to hurt him. She was even more stunned that the wounds where the bullets had passed straight through him were already closed up and had stopped bleeding. As a veterinarian who'd seen a lot of gunshot wounds, that was pretty hard to accept. But she supposed when it came to Alex, she was going to have to learn to accept a lot of things on faith if nothing else.

They didn't talk much as she worked, and for a while, that was okay. Even if she was digging in him with a medical instrument, at least she was getting a chance to be close to him, touching his warm skin with her hands. It wasn't what they'd had before, but it was something.

Finally, though, the weight of all the words that weren't being said began to pile up, threatening to crush the air out of her lungs.

"Sorry about freaking out over the whole werewolf thing," she finally said, not sure how else to start the conversation.

He shrugged, taking her hand and gently nudging the forceps in a slightly different direction. Lacey felt the tips of the metal instrument bump into something hard, and she prayed it wasn't something important.

"It's okay," he said. "It's not every day a woman finds out that her boyfriend has claws and fangs. You got a little overwhelmed there at Bensen's junkyard. It's understandable."

She winced, wishing this could be as simple as just saying she was sorry. "Yeah, well, I wasn't just talking about how I reacted that night. I was kind of apologizing more for how I've been behaving since then."

"O-kay," he said slowly, clearly not really under-standing what she was talking about.

Lacey knew she had to keep going, because there was so much more she needed to tell him, and she didn't know if she would ever get the chance again. Jayna might think Lacey and Alex were *The One* for each other—and maybe they were—but there was also a good chance that Alex had only been hanging around after the way she treated him because he felt he had an obligation to help her find Kelsey. Now that he'd done it, there might not be anything keeping him in her life anymore. After the cops showed up and everything was straightened out, she might never see him again.

"This is really hard to say, so I'm just going to start talking and hope this comes out right, okay?" she said, glancing up at him.

He nodded, but then she was forced to wait as the forceps clamped down on something solid. Tightening her grip on the handle, she carefully pulled out the bullet. Not that it looked much like a bullet anymore. It was nothing but a smashed-up, bloody bit of jagged metal. She dropped it on one of the surgery trays, glad the task was done.

She picked up a piece of gauze from the tray and held it against the wound to stop the bleeding even though she didn't need to. As she did, she gathered her thoughts on how she really felt about him. The answer was simple. Saying it out loud wasn't.

"When I first saw you…shift…I was sure you were a monster," she admitted, quickly hurrying on when she saw Alex's eyes harden. "But after I talked to Wendy that night and thought about it some, I knew you weren't. Yes, you have claws and fangs, and sometimes you can be scary as hell, but you're not a monster."

Alex didn't say anything, so she kept going. "I should have told you all this before, and that's the part I'm really sorry about. I'd like to say it was because I was worried about Kelsey, but that would be a cop-out. The real reason I didn't say anything is because I was scared. As lame as it sounds, I found it easier to let you keep thinking I thought of you as a monster than tell you how I really felt."

"Why was it easier?" he prompted when the silence had begun to stretch out again. "What were you so scared of, if it wasn't the fangs and the claws?"

She took a deep breath and jumped in the deep end of the pool. "I thought that if I told you how I really felt, you'd end up bailing on me at some point anyway."

Alex didn't say anything for so long that she thought she'd spoken too softly for him to hear, even with his werewolf senses. She prayed she didn't have to say the words out loud again. Once was enough.

"You mean like the way your father and those other men bailed on your mom?" he finally asked.

She opened her mouth to tell him that wasn't it, that she wasn't her mom, but stopped herself. Maybe that was it. As wonderful as everything had been between her and Alex in the beginning of their relationship, there'd been a part of her waiting for the other shoe to drop and for Alex to turn into the asshole her dad had been, the same assholes her mom had gone out with all those other times.

"Yeah, just like that, I guess," she murmured. "Stupid, huh?"

"It's not stupid at all," he said. "I'm a product of the dysfunctional family situation I was raised in. Why should you be any different? Every guy you've ever been around has disappointed you, so it's not shocking that you assumed I would at some point too. When you saw me shift, you figured the big bad you'd been waiting for had just happened, and you bailed on me before I could do the same."

She looked up at him, trying to figure out how any man could be so rational about something like this. "You're not mad at me?"

"Why?" he asked with a smile. "For protecting yourself?"

"But I wasn't protecting myself," she admitted. "I was being a coward. I've known for a while that you're the best thing that has ever happened to me. I think I knew from the very beginning, but I didn't want to get hurt, so instead of taking a chance and going for it, I turned and ran the moment things got tough."

"You're not running now," he pointed out. "What changed?"

It was her turn to shrug. "What changed is that I talked to Jayna this morning. She told me about what it means to find *The One*. A lot of things started making sense after that. Like how terrible I felt after I ran away from you, and how depressed I was when I thought we were over."

Alex seemed surprised by that confession.

"Don't be mad at Jayna for telling me about the legend," she said. "She helped me understand all these feelings that were churning around inside me and figure out what they meant."

He shook his head. "I'm not mad at her. It's just that I hadn't realized it was like that for you."

"You thought you were the only one feeling these things?"

Even though Jayna insisted that he did, Lacey wasn't too proud to admit that she wanted to hear him say he felt the same.

"Yeah," he said. "I fell in love with you the first day I met you in the vet clinic. Then I felt all this pain when you walked away, and to tell the truth, I couldn't understand how you could do it if we were really meant to be together. I convinced myself that it must be a one-way thing, or that you'd somehow severed the connection on your side."

Learning that he'd been in love with her all along was painful to hear, and Lacey felt tears well in her eyes as she thought about how stupid she'd been. She was so scared of being hurt that she'd ended up hurting not just herself but Alex as well.

"It definitely wasn't a one-way thing, and the connection between us was never broken either," she said. "I've been in love with you the whole time too. It just took me a lot longer to see it. I wish I could have been brave enough to tell you sooner."

He smiled, and it took her a second to realize she'd just admitted to loving him.

She blushed. "Um, I'd hadn't really planned for those words to slip out quite that way."

He did a double take. "What, you didn't mean it?"

"Of course I meant it!" she said. "I just thought that… you know…there should be some kind of big, dramatic moment when you say those words."

"I agree we didn't say the words the way you'd hear them in the movies, but we both said them, and for us, that's what matters," he said softly. "And as far as needing a big, dramatic moment, you've been standing here digging a bullet fragment out of my chest with the medical equivalent of a pair of needle-nose pliers, while your heavily sedated sister lies only a couple of feet away and the people who tried to kill her are locked in a supply closet." He grinned down at her. "I don't think you could come up with a bigger moment than this."

She laughed, feeling like a weight had been lifted from her shoulders. They were three simple words, and yet it felt like she could suddenly breathe easier.

"Let's make sure the bleeding has stopped, so I can kiss you," she said.

Lacey started to turn her attention back to what she'd been doing, but before she could get started, Alex slipped his finger under her chin and tilted her face up.

"Leave it for right now. It can wait," he murmured. "Kissing you can't."

As his lips came down on hers, Lacey could almost forget where she was and what kind of day this had been. She melted against him, thanking God that everything had worked out okay, despite doing her best to screw it up the whole time.

───

Alex had heard the convoy of patrol cars arrive. The squawk and static of their radios was impossible to miss, even from the fourth floor. But the uniformed officers who'd entered the facility must not have liked the look of the three mangled bodies on the first floor. Alex heard a gruff order to pull back and establish a perimeter until SWAT arrived. Alex didn't blame them. What those cops saw down there wasn't anything they were trained to deal with. Without having a better idea what they were up against—and not seeing any innocents in immediate danger—it made sense for them to pull back and wait for backup.

A little while later, Gage, Xander, Khaki, and Cooper

showed up to find Alex and Lacey standing watch over Kelsey. Lacey's sister was still out of it, but her quickening heart rate told Alex that she was slowly coming out from the anesthesia.

Xander and Khaki headed straight for the supply closet and the people Alex had locked inside. A few moments later, they led the doctors and nurses out in cuffs while calling for an ambulance for McDonald.

"You got here fast," Alex said to Gage. "How'd you know where to find me?"

Gage didn't answer. Instead, he glared at Alex, his teeth grinding together so hard that Alex thought they might shatter.

Cooper chuckled and held out his cell phone. "Dude, you're all over YouTube."

Alex did a double take at the blurry video clip of a huge gray wolf running down the middle of the street and slamming into a car.

Shit.

"Over ten thousand downloads in the last thirty minutes." Cooper's grin broadened. "First full shift, and you're trending. It's freaking epic!"

Something told Alex that *freaking epic* were not the words his alpha would choose to use to describe the current situation.

Gage shook his head at Alex, then glanced at Lacey, his expression softening. "Is your sister going to be okay?"

Lacey nodded. "Yes. Alex got to her just in time. Another few minutes, and we would have been too late."

"Good." Gage smiled at her. "I'm glad to hear it." He turned back to Alex. "I don't need to ask what the hell happened here, since it seems obvious, but I'm going to do it anyway, just so you have a chance to get your story straight before the heavy hitters show up."

Alex gave his boss a rundown of everything that had happened since that morning, highlighting how they'd followed DeYoung and Pendergraff from the building where he'd dropped off the drugs to the facility where the girls were being held, then how Lacey had been grabbed and what happened after he'd shifted and tracked Lacey and Kelsey here.

"You ran up here and fought these guys totally naked?" Cooper asked with a laugh. "Now that is frigging badass."

Gage growled at Cooper. "Don't you have something you could be doing?"

Cooper grinned. "Nope. Xander and Khaki have it all under control out there. Besides, hearing all this is much more fun."

Gage scowled. "Hearing doesn't require you to open your mouth, does it?"

Cooper pantomimed zipping his lips. Alex doubted that would last very long.

"Okay, I'm tracking you so far," Gage said to Alex. "So, what about the unconscious guy in the stairwell?"

Alex frowned. "What guy in the stairwell?"

His boss lifted a brow. "The one covered in fire extinguisher powder with the big bump on his brain bucket."

From the corner of his eye, Alex saw Lacey lift her hand tentatively. "That was me. DeYoung was trying to leave. I sprayed him with the fire extinguisher, then hit him with it."

Alex gaped at Lacey. Well, damn.

She gave them a tiny smile. "Maybe we should downplay that part of the story?"

Gage probably would have commented, but just then, the paramedics showed up, along with Chief Curtis.

The chief looked like he was about to explode as he took in the scene. Between the paramedics loading McDonald, Bensen, and Kelsey onto gurneys, then tending to Lacey's minor head wound, and Alex standing there wearing hospital scrubs and no shoes, there was a lot to piss him off.

Surprisingly, Curtis waited until the paramedics had left with their patients before he turned to glower at Alex.

"I have no idea what the hell happened here, but you're done in this department. Attempting to function as a law enforcement officer while under suspension, assaulting a city councilman, and interrupting a medical procedure in process. Do you have any idea what you've done?"

Alex was this close to punching the silly SOB in the face. He probably would have done it if Gage hadn't put a firm hand on his shoulder.

"He saved your political ass, that's what he's done," Deputy Chief Mason said as he walked into the room. "I just came from one of McDonald's other medical research facilities," Mason continued. "It turns out that the councilman kidnapped those four missing college girls and was holding them captive. Three of the girls were still there, but Kelsey Barton had already been transferred here to have her kidneys removed by a doctor on McDonald's payroll."

Curtis paled beneath his fake tan, but Mason cut him off before he could say anything.

"McDonald—who is one of your major political supporters, if I remember correctly—was running a black-market organ-transplant ring. Bensen—another of your supporters, if I'm not mistaken—was to be the recipient of Ms. Barton's kidneys. Even though he was under suspension and investigation, Officer Trevino still took it upon himself to track down the girls, then come here when it became obvious that Ms. Barton was in immediate danger."

Curtis pinned Alex with a hard look. "Is that true?"

Alex flexed his fingers, fighting the urge to wrap them around the chief's throat. Gage squeezed his shoulder, as if sensing his dilemma.

"Yes, sir," Alex said.

Chief Curtis eyed him suspiciously. "What about those men downstairs? They looked like they were attacked with a chainsaw."

Gage squeezed again, nearly crushing the bones in Alex's shoulder.

"I'm not sure, sir," he told Curtis politely. "That's the way I found them when I arrived. Perhaps they fell through the automatic doors. There was an awful lot of glass lying around."

Curtis didn't look like he was buying it. "And McDonald. What happened to him?"

"He tripped and fell in the process of attempting to keep me from reaching this surgical suite. He hit his head on the swinging doors outside."

Curtis was still considering that when Mason cleared his throat.

"Chief, if I were you, I'd get on board with Officer Trevino's story. The press was already setting up as I came inside. You might want to talk to them before they start making their own connections between you, McDonald, and Bensen."

Curtis's mouth tightened, and for a moment, Alex thought the man was going to buck at Mason's blatant manipulation. But then the chief's political instincts kicked in, and the man turned to look at his deputy.

"Suggestions?" Curtis asked.

"For one thing, you might want to drop a hint that you personally placed Officer Trevino and his fellow SWAT team members under a fictitious suspension to allow them to carry out their investigation of McDonald's allegedly illegal activities without drawing unwanted attention," Mason said.

Curtis thought about that for a moment, then nodded. "Fine. That's the line I'll take for the press conference." He glowered at Gage. "But I want formal statements and paperwork from everyone involved in this clusterfuck, and I want it neat, tidy, and clean as a whistle. Is that clear, Commander?"

Gage nodded. "Yes, sir."

Giving them one more scathing look, Curtis turned on his heel and headed out of the room. Alex was just about to let out a breath when the chief stopped and spun around.

"And why the hell are you wearing hospital scrubs?" he demanded.

Alex hesitated, trying to figure out the best way to bullshit his way through this one. Coming up with a cover story about what happened tonight had been a piece of cake in comparison.

"I was technically under suspension and couldn't wear my uniform, so I put these on, figuring I'd blend in," he said, then added, "They're very comfortable."

The chief looked at him like he was full of shit. "And the blood stains?"

Alex looked down at his chest, noticing for the first time that the blood from the wounds on his chest and side had seeped through the green material.

He shrugged. "They were like this when I found them."

Curtis stared at him, then shook his head. "Whatever. Just don't let the press see you when you leave."

It took Alex forever to disengage himself from a determined paramedic who refused to believe that the blood on his scrubs wasn't his. He barely made it downstairs in time to catch Lacey climbing into the back of an ambulance with Kelsey. Her sister was groggy as hell, but she seemed to know where she was and that she was safe.

"Are Sara and the other girls okay?" Kelsey asked when she saw him.

"They're fine," Alex assured her.

Kelsey nodded and lay back on the gurney, relief in her eyes.

"The paramedics want me to go to the hospital and get checked out too." Lacey grimaced. "I told them I was fine, but they insisted."

"They're right," Alex said. "Concussions are nothing to fool around with."

Lacey didn't seem to agree with him but nodded. "Can you come with us?"

"I wish. Unfortunately, I'm going to be doing paperwork for a while. Then I have to go find my wallet, cell phone, and weapon. I left them on the side of the road across town. I'll come to the hospital as soon as I can."

Lacey smiled. "Good. The sooner the better. Do I need to worry about anyone asking me what I saw?"

Alex shook his head. "I doubt it. But if they do, say that you're in shock from everything that happened and don't remember anything."

"I can do that." She took his hand. "Be as quick as you can. We have a lot to talk about."

"We're ready to go," the paramedic announced, giving Alex a look that said he was in the way. Alex couldn't care less.

"Yes, we do," he told Lacey.

Bending his head, he kissed her right there in front of everyone. It was shocking how turned on he could get from a simple touch of the lips, especially after everything that had happened tonight. Unfortunately, scrubs did a lousy job of hiding boners.

Lacey laughed as she broke the kiss and pushed him out of the ambulance. "See you later."

Alex heard Kelsey giggle as the paramedic closed the door. "Does that mean you two will be making out at the apartment on a regular basis now? Instead of running off to the bedroom like you did the last time I nearly caught you, I mean."

"We'll talk about how often Alex will be hanging out at the apartment later," Lacey said, clearly back in big-sister mode. "After we talk about underage drinking and when you started having sex with random strangers."

"They weren't strangers by the time I was done with them," Kelsey pointed out as the paramedic closed the doors of the ambulance.

Alex cringed. Maybe he'd give it a couple of hours before he showed up at the hospital. Something told him that Lacey and her sister were going to be in for a long discussion.

Chapter 20

LACEY SAT AT ONE OF THE PICNIC TABLES IN BACK OF THE SWAT compound, watching the volleyball game. It was hot as sin out today, but you'd never know it from the way everyone was running around the sand-filled pit. While she was totally in love with Alex, she had to admit it was fun ogling his teammates, especially since they were playing with their shirts off. Every single one of the SWAT guys was seriously built and outrageously attractive. Being in love didn't mean she couldn't appreciate a good-looking man when she saw one.

It wasn't just all the muscles that caught her attention, either. The wolf-head tattoo that each of them sported on the left side of their chest was extremely eye-catching, as well. Of course, the tattoo meant a lot more to her now than it had the first time she saw it on Alex. Back then, she'd thought it was nothing more than cool art. Now she realized the ink was an inside joke for the Pack. Just another way for them to hide in plain sight.

Part of her was still stunned by the reality that werewolves existed and that she was in a committed relationship with one. But overall, she was handling the big secret rather well. Surprisingly, seeing Alex shift from man to wolf the first night they'd spent together since rescuing Kelsey made everything easier for her. Okay, the transformation part was kind of scary, but the end result—a great big, lovable-looking wolf—made it hard to think of him as anything but adorable after that.

She heard a familiar laugh by the volleyball net and looked up to see Kelsey on her butt in the sand. It was hard to believe, but her sister seemed even more unco-ordinated than she was. Alex had tried to drag her out there to play with them, but Lacey had firmly refused. She was smart enough to keep her butt over here on the sideline and avoid the embarrassment of proving to the world that she couldn't play volleyball to save her life. Kelsey clearly didn't have that hang-up.

Then again, there was a good chance the only reason her sister was out there was because that's where all the hot guys were, especially one particular dark-skinned hunk by the name of Moe. Lacey smiled as Moe took Kelsey's hand and helped her to her feet, then gently wiped a bit of sand from her face. Not that long ago, Lacey would have been worried that her sister was too young to get involved with a guy, or that she should focus on school, or that the guy was just out to get her in bed—or any of a dozen different concerns. But over the past two weeks—and after a lot of long talks with Alex, Everly, Jayna, Wendy, and even Kelsey—Lacey had finally come to the realization that she was going to have to take a step back from her overprotective big sister role and accept that Kelsey was old enough to make her own decisions about men and about life.

Besides, if Kelsey were going to get involved with a guy, Moe was a good choice. Not only was he the same age as Kelsey and enrolling in RTC in the fall, he was also as polite, gentle, and thoughtful as any big sister could ever hope for. Then there was the whole beta thing. Lacey was still trying to get a handle on the differ-ence between alpha and beta werewolves, but she knew one thing for sure. She never had to worry about Moe dragging her sister off to Mexico on a whim. According to Jayna, Moe would never stray more than a couple of miles from his pack—ever.

It was probably manipulative—and completely against Lacey's promise to let her sister make her own decisions—but she liked knowing that if Moe and Kelsey got involved, they wouldn't be backpacking through Europe or anything crazy like that as soon as she finished college.

Alex had warned her not to get her hopes up, of course. The chances that Moe and Kelsey were *The Ones* for each other were slim to none. Apparently, it was exceedingly difficult for a werewolf to find their soul mate. Still, a big sister could dream, couldn't she?

She was still thinking about that when Remy called out from over by the grill that the food was ready. Everyone went running, grabbing up paper plates and piling them high with chicken, steak, and burgers, all seasoned with some kind of Cajun spice. Even Leo and Tuffie got into the food fest, each getting a bowl of steak pieces—minus the spices, of course.

"Hey, Brooks. Where's Vaughn?" Remy asked as he came around the tables with a big pot of sausage gumbo and started ladling it out to everyone. "I thought she was coming today."

The big SWAT cop grimaced. "She was, until I showed up wearing my graduation ring. Once she realized I went to school at LSU, it was over. She said there was no use being with a man she could never take home to meet her parents."

Lacey stared at him, a spoonful of gumbo halfway to her mouth. "She dumped you because you went to LSU? Why?"

He shrugged. "Because she's an Alabama fan, born and bred. Can't really blame her. Once I realized she was a Crimson Tide girl, I probably would have had to dump her if she hadn't dumped me first."

Lacey frowned. "But what if she was…you know… *The One*?"

Brooks shook his head. "She couldn't be, not if she pulls for 'Bama. Fate would never be that cruel."

Lacey shook her head. "That's insane."

Remy laughed and leaned over her shoulder to place a piece of corn bread on her plate. "That's not insane. That's SEC football. It's not something you can understand, just something you have to accept."

Around the table, everyone nodded in agreement, so Lacey dropped it. But she still thought it was stupid. Who the heck would put football before a chance at love?

She snuggled up closer to Alex and finally tried the gumbo on her spoon. Dang, Remy could cook his butt off.

As it usually did whenever Alex and the other SWAT guys got together, the conversation quickly turned to bad guys and crime, in this case what the DA was going to do with McDonald, his black-market transplant ring, and drug operation.

"Technically, McDonald wasn't involved in the drug part," Alex clarified. "That was mostly DeYoung. The little weasel never told McDonald that he was using his research lab facilities to make fireball. Apparently, he didn't tell Bensen either, even though Bensen supplied the start-up capital for the drug operation and took all the risk distributing the drugs through his junkyard connections."

"So, what's going to happen to those three?" Brooks

asked. "There has to be enough on DeYoung, Bensen, and McDonald to put them all away for a long time."

Beside her, Alex bit back a growl. Lacey knew this was a sore subject with him. Nothing was quite working out the way they'd expected, considering how many people had died as a result of this whole nightmare, and it pissed him off.

"DeYoung flipped immediately," Alex said. "The charges related to Nicole Arend's death, as well as the drug-related deaths due to fireball, were dropped in return for an agreement to testify for the prosecution. That piece of crap will probably see less than ten years for various drug charges, maybe as little as five."

Lacey reached under the table and squeezed his leg to calm him down. She'd quickly learned that it didn't take much more than a touch from her to back him down from a partial shift.

"What about McDonald and Bensen?" Brooks prompted.

Alex shrugged. "McDonald is still in a coma at some cushy private hospital, and the doctors aren't sure when he's coming out. The DA has prepared the charge sheet against him, naming him as the person responsible for Nicole Arend's death, along with Pettine. There have to be about a hundred other charges related to the black-market transplant ring—kidnapping, assault, false imprisonment, even violations for using the information in the girls' medical records at the clinic to screen them for organ matches. Right now, the DA is waiting to file those charges until he sees whether McDonald wakes up."

"That sucks," Remy said. "But Bensen's going to jail, right?"

"Yeah, he's in a jail hospital ward, but he probably

won't live long enough to go to trial for everything he did. His kidneys are totally shot, and he won't be around long enough for the DA to bother pushing for an early trial."

"So, DeYoung gets off almost scot-free, McDonald is sleeping it off in a cushy private hospital, and Bensen is getting free medical on the state." Cooper frowned. "Did anybody get any time out of all this?"

"You mean beyond Pettine and the other doctors and nurses involved in the transplant surgeries going to jail?" Gage answered from across the table. "Not really. And if you think that's hard to swallow, you want to know who really came out of this smelling like a rose? Chief Curtis."

Cooper did a double take. "Seriously?"

Gage snorted. "Thanks to Deputy Chief Mason, Curtis has everyone thinking he created this elaborate suspension ruse so he could send a team of SWAT guys after McDonald, even though everyone knew the two men were tight. The press is eating it up, and now there's talk of Curtis being a viable candidate for mayor."

Alex looked ill at that, and Lacey didn't blame him. Curtis had showed up at the hospital only hours after she and Kelsey had been admitted, dragging a TV crew with him as he checked "to make sure they were being taken care of."

At the other end of the table beside Xander, Khaki looked up from her gumbo. "There's one thing I never understood in all this. Where did the dogfighting stuff fit in? It never made any sense that Bensen would involve himself in a high-risk activity like that at the same time he was trying to sell drugs."

"That's how he was raising the money to fund

DeYoung's drug lab," Alex explained. "He knew the
cops were watching all his legitimate accounts, so he
needed outside funds to allow DeYoung to buy the raw
material to make fireball. Apparently, Pendergraff was
a big player in the dogfighting community, so it wasn't
difficult for him to get started."

Lacey couldn't help but think of all the dogs the
SWAT team had saved by raiding that place out on I-45.
There had been a lot of dogs there, and most of them
had been in bad shape. Every vet clinic in the city had
taken a hand in caring for the animals and getting them
new homes.

"I suppose in the end, while things didn't exactly
work out as well as we could have hoped, at least we
stopped McDonald's black-market transplant ring,
Bensen and DeYoung's drug lab, and Pendergraff's
dogfighting operation," Alex said. "I guess we can count
it as a win of sorts."

"Except for one thing," Gage said softly. "There's
still the issue of a half dozen YouTube videos we have
to worry about."

Alex frowned. "You don't really think anyone is
buying those blurry videos, do you? I mean, the media
is already calling it a hoax."

Gage scowled, those steely eyes of his making Lacey
squirm—and she didn't even work for the guy. To say
that the Pack alpha had been unhappy with Alex running
down the middle of a busy highway in full wolf form
was an understatement. While the media had put dozens
of witnesses on camera, it turned out to be the best thing
that could have happened for Alex and his teammates.
Hearing some guy rant about seeing a wolf as big as a
bull, only to have a passenger in the same car insist that

the animal hadn't been a wolf at all but had instead been a chupacabra, pretty much convinced most people that Texas needed to work harder on tightening up their open container laws.

"I don't care what the average Joe looking at YouTube thinks," Gage said. "I'm more concerned with attracting the attention of the hunters, who *will* buy those blurry videos."

A little shiver ran up Lacey's spine. She had thought that werewolves were indestructible, but then Alex told her there were people out in the world who hunted down and killed werewolves for a living. The thought scared the hell out of her.

"What are we going to do about them, boss?" Xander asked.

Gage swung his dark gaze on his senior squad leader. "Not much we can do. We collect information from the newcomers to the area, like those new betas that Alex met, we watch out for each other, and we make sure we see them before they see us."

Silence reigned for a while after that until Alex cleared his throat. "And what are we going to do about Samantha Mills?"

This subject had stumped Lacey when Alex first mentioned it a few days ago. Before leaving the crime scene at McDonald's surgical center, Alex had slipped back into the operating room to clean up a little hard-to-explain werewolf evidence, namely the bullet fragments and the scalpel Pettine had used to stab him. But Alex hadn't found either of those things. Instead, the medical examiner was in the room, taking blood samples from every corner of the place and looking mighty uneasy when Alex had asked her about the bullet and scalpel.

She'd claimed she hadn't found anything like that in the room, but Alex was sure she'd been lying.

"You think we need to check her out, Gage?" Xander asked softly.

"I can do a little sniffing around and see what she knows," Trey offered from beside Lacey.

Tall and good-looking with brown hair and blue eyes, Trey was kind of quiet, and beyond the fact that he was the team's other medic, she didn't know much about him.

"I know what you're trying to do, dude," Remy said with a laugh. "But you can forget it, because it's not going to work out."

Trey frowned. "Why not?"

"I don't think Dr. Mills is into guys."

Trey's frown deepened. "What makes you say that?"

"I laid a double helping of Cajun charm on her, and she didn't even notice me. There's only one reason for that."

"Yeah. Because she has good taste." Trey snickered. "Don't think I'm doubting your prowess with the females of the species, but I think I'm going to sniff around the doc a little anyway. Just in case you're wrong."

Remy's hurt expression made Lacey laugh, along with everyone else. That was all it took for them to forget about criminals not getting their just punishment, hunters running around out there, and MEs who swiped bullets and scalpels. Instead, the conversation moved to lighter topics, like Cooper and Everly's upcoming wedding and why Remy hadn't brought any of his dozens of girlfriends to the barbecue.

After everyone was finished eating, most of the tables cleared out as they ran back to play more volleyball. Lacey wasn't sure that was a very good idea on a full stomach, but she didn't complain, since it left her alone with Alex.

She slid a little closer to him, smiling as he draped his arm around her. They both knew they had some issues in the past to deal with, but they were taking it slowly.

Something told her that things were going to be changing a lot in the near future, and she was surprised at how much she was looking forward to it. There was a good chance that Kelsey would be moving into the RTC dorms next semester. Lacey still planned to keep Kelsey's room set up, but at some point, they might turn it into a home office, maybe even a nursery. Either way, Alex was going to move in with her full-time next week. He was over there nearly every night anyway, so it just made sense.

As she sat there beside him, watching the game, Lacey couldn't help but smile at how different the world looked now. Brighter and more hopeful. It was hard to believe the difference one man could make in your life.

"I love you," Alex whispered in her ear.

Lacey smiled and kissed him. After all these years of telling herself that she would never believe a man who said those words to her, she believed them with all her heart.

WOLF HUNT

REMY DIDN'T REALIZE HOW MUCH HE'D MISSED NEW Orleans, but as he walked down Bourbon Street, basking in the ambience of the city he called home, he remembered why he loved it so much. To make it even better, he was getting the chance to show it off to the most important people in his life—his pack mates. SWAT officers-slash-werewolves Max Lowry, Jayden Brooks, and Zane Kendrick took in the bright lights, crowds of partying people, various music coming from nightclubs on either side of the street, and the unique combination of scents hanging in the air with a mix of curiosity and excitement.

His mouth twitched. Yeah, New Orleans had that kind of effect on people.

Gage Dixon, their boss, pack alpha, and commander of the Dallas SWAT team, had sent the four of them to New Orleans to cross-train with the city's SWAT teams. At the same time, four officers from NOPD SWAT would take part in a week-long exercise in Dallas. Cross-training with cops who weren't werewolves meant hiding their abilities, so Gage had made his expectations extremely clear.

"Don't run too fast, lift anything you shouldn't be able to, let your tempers get away from you, and whatever you do, no claws, fangs, or frigging glowing eyes," Gage reminded them before they'd left.

Remy let Zane and Max lead the way as the four of them headed down Bourbon Street.

"Is it always this wild here?" Zane asked as a group of attractive women passing by gave them long, lingering looks and dazzling smiles.

"Yeah, it's always like this," Remy confirmed. "New Orleans is a city that takes the concept of having a good time to a whole different level."

Remy whipped his head around when an unusual but extremely tantalizing scent caught his attention, sniffing the air. His nose was okay, certainly nothing special. It made him wonder why he was picking up this particular smell so clearly.

There were a lot of scents on Bourbon Street. Sweat, booze, perfume, cigarette and cigar smoke, moldy wood, drugs, sex—you name it. This particular scent stuck out like a rose in the middle of all that other stuff, demanding his attention.

"Hey, you okay?" Brooks asked.

Brooks was one of his pack mates blessed with a good nose. Remy turned to the big guy.

"Do you smell that?" he asked.

Brooks sniffed. "I smell a lot of things. Which one are you talking about?"

"That flowery, spicy scent."

Brooks sniffed again. Beside him, Max did the same. They both looked at him and shook their heads.

"I don't smell anything like that," Brooks said.

Remy breathed deeply through his nose and almost

got weak-kneed. What was more, he actually started getting a boner. *What the hell?*

He glanced at Brooks and Max. "You guys are screwing with me, aren't you? You seriously can't smell that?"

He didn't have a clue what he was smelling, but he damn well knew he needed to figure out what it was. He'd go nuts if he didn't.

"I'm going for a walk," he said.

Zane and the other guys followed as he moved down the street.

He realized he was following a woman. He tried to tell himself that was insane. He'd smelled thousands of women since becoming a werewolf. None of them had ever possessed a spicy, flowery scent this delectable. Not even close.

Remy walked faster. The curiosity was killing him. What kind of woman could generate a scent so powerful it gave him a hard-on the moment he caught a whiff?

Remy wasn't sure how long he followed the scent, but the next thing he knew, he was walking into a nightclub with a throbbing dance beat. In bloodhound mode, he headed straight to the second floor, moving like an arrow through the crowded, noisy room until he was standing in the middle of the dance floor full of gyrating bodies.

Right there, dancing with her back to him in a group of four other women, was the source of the scent that had dragged him across the French Quarter. This close, the scent was damn near overwhelming. If he wasn't such a gentleman, he probably would have leaned forward and licked the small portion of her neck that was exposed every time her long black hair swung aside. If she smelled this good, he could only imagine how she tasted.

He was trying to figure out the best way to initiate a

conversation—tapping her on the shoulder and saying he'd been tracking her scent for blocks might come off as a bit stalkerish—when the woman turned to face him.

Maybe she'd sensed him behind her, or perhaps it was because her friends had stopped dancing to stare over her shoulder at him. Either way, when she spun around, Remy swore his heart stopped beating for a second. No shit, it actually hiccupped like a drunk on a bender.

It was dark on the dance floor and the flashing strobes were bright enough to practically blind him, but it didn't matter. The light brown–skinned beauty would have stood out in any light. Hell, she would have stood out in complete darkness, too.

He was still taking in the smoking-hot curves, perfect skin, and exotic amber eyes when a realization struck him so hard he almost stumbled backward.

He *knew* her. Not in the biblical sense, though that was obviously one hell of a shame. He'd known her back in high school when she'd been a skinny, awkward teenager who never seemed to look anywhere but at the ground.

She was a lot different now—understatement there—and easily the most beautiful woman he'd ever seen. Now she possessed a confidence that made it hard to look at anything but her. Even with all the changes, he would have known her anywhere. He hadn't talked to her since high school graduation, but they'd been friends, and probably would have been more if he hadn't been such a chickenshit back then.

"Triana?"

COMING JUNE 2017

Acknowledgments

I hope you had as much fun reading Alex and Lacey's story as I had writing it! Hope you also enjoyed reading more about the SWAT team's adorable dog, Tuffie, as well as meeting Leo and Ralph. My hubby and I are huge animal lovers and are so thrilled to be able to include them in this series. Because of that, it was difficult including something as horrific as dogfighting in the book. While the city of Dallas has animal control officers, they don't have an animal cruelty squad as of yet. But hopefully someday soon, Dallas—as well as every other town and city in the US—will have a unit of brave men and women dedicated to keeping animals safe. Even if your town or city doesn't have an animal cruelty squad yet, if you see evidence of animal cruelty, please notify the authorities.

While our books and the characters in them are fiction, it's difficult not to think about what happened on July 7 of this year when real-life Dallas police officers lost their lives. Our thoughts and prayers go out to the families and friends of the slain officers. This book is dedicated to them.

I also want to give a big shout-out to the real Season and Allen, our friends from the band The Wide Open. They're as unique and cool as their characters in the book, and totally thrilled to be werewolves, so you'll definitely be seeing them again in future SWAT books!

This whole series wouldn't be possible without some

very incredible people. In addition to another big thank-you to my hubby for all his help with the action scenes and military and tactical jargon, thanks to my agent, Bob Mecoy, for believing in us and encouraging us and being there when we need to talk; my editor and go-to-person at Sourcebooks, Cat Clyne (who loves this series as much as I do and is always a phone call, text, or email away whenever I need something); and all the other amazing people at Sourcebooks, including my fantastic publicist Amelia, and their crazy-talented art department. The covers they make for me are seriously droolworthy!

Because I could never leave out my readers, a huge thank-you to everyone who has read my books and Snoopy Danced right along with me with every new release. That includes the fantastic people on my amazing Street Team, as well my assistant, Janet. You rock!

I also want to give a big thank-you to the men, women, and working dogs who protect and serve in police departments everywhere, as well as their families.

And a very special shout-out to our favorite restaurant, P.F. Chang's, where hubby and I bat story lines back and forth and come up with all of our best ideas, as well as a thank-you to our fantastic waiter, Andrew, who takes our order to the kitchen the moment we walk in the door!

Hope you enjoy the sixth book in the SWAT series coming soon from Sourcebooks, and look forward to reading the rest of the series as much as I look forward to sharing it with you.

If you love a man in uniform as much as I do, make sure you check out X-Ops, my other action-packed paranormal/romantic-suspense series from Sourcebooks.

Happy Reading!

About the Author

Paige Tyler is a *New York Times* and *USA Today* best-selling author of sexy, romantic suspense and paranormal romance. She and her very own military hero (also known as her husband) live on the beautiful Florida coast with their adorable fur baby (also known as their dog). Paige graduated with a degree in education but decided to pursue her passion and write books about hunky alpha males and the kick-butt heroines who fall in love with them.

Visit Paige at her website at www.paigetylertheauthor .com.

She's also on Facebook, Twitter, Tumblr, Instagram, tsu, Wattpad, Google+, and Pinterest.